HIDDEN
PATH

ALSO BY THE AUTHOR

Fiction by Rebecca Carey Lyles

PRISONERS OF HOPE SERIES

Shattered Dream (Book One)

Tangled Truth (Book Two)

Hidden Path (Book Three)

KATE NEILSON SERIES

Winds of Hope (Prequel)

Winds of Wyoming (Book One)

Winds of Freedom (Book Two)

Winds of Change (Book Three)

Short Stories by Rebecca Carey Lyles & Friends

Passageways: A Short Story Collection

Nonfiction by Becky Lyles & Friends

It's a God Thing! Inspiring Stories of Life-Changing Friendships

On a Wing and a Prayer: Stories from Freedom Fellowship, a Prison Ministry

PRISONERS OF HOPE SERIES
BOOK THREE

HIDDEN PATH

REBECCA CAREY LYLES

Perpedit✓Publishing, Ink

COPYRIGHT © 2020

DEDICATION

This third novel in the PRISONERS OF HOPE SERIES is dedicated to the sweet ladies in my Bible study group who graciously prayed me through the two-year writing process. I am grateful for their faithful friendship and support and for our faithful Savior who hears and answers prayer. Many thanks to Amy, Barb, Becky, Bonnie, Fariba, Jan, Jane, Janis, Jill, Kaci, Kathy, Mai, Melinda, Nancy and Pam!

Hidden Path is also dedicated to Cole Community Church, a wonderful group of believers who seek and teach truth from God's Word, who worship and pray together, and who serve one another as well as the community. Unlike the church members described in this series, Cole Community congregants are equals with their leaders. They're honored rather than humiliated, nurtured rather than castigated, appreciated rather than abused, and loved rather than exploited. Personal integrity is expected for leaders and adherents alike, and management of the church's finances is transparent and open for review. I am truly blessed to be a part of a church body that strives to follow biblical guidelines.

The Lord is my light and my salvation—whom shall I fear? The Lord is the stronghold of my life—of whom shall I be afraid? When the wicked advance against me to devour me, it is my enemies and my foes who will stumble and fall. (Psalm 27:1-3a NIV)

The light shines in the darkness, and the darkness can never extinguish it. (John 1:5 NLT)

Grace and truth came through Jesus Christ. Your Word is truth. You will know the truth, and the truth will set free you.
John 1:17b; 17:17b; 8:32 (BLB)

CHAPTER ONE

My excitement grows with each step I take along the busy terminal. I can't wait to see my parents and my brother again. But, oh, how I wish Grandma Hunt's impending death wasn't the reason for our gathering—and that I'd been able to visit her earlier.

I'm not sure how many years have passed since I last saw my nanna. Life blurred after my husband died. Thanks to grief and alcoholism, I lost track of everything important.

Pain stabs my heart. Eric, my sweet Eric. If he were here, we'd have so much fun with Mom and Dad and Kip—and Grandma Hunt, even in her semiconscious condition. She and Eric loved to tease each other. His goodbye surely would have brought a smile to her lips. However, he died young, and she had to say goodbye to him first. *I* had to say goodbye to him first.

A courtesy cart approaches, and I step aside to let it pass. The driver lifts his hand. I smile and nod, but my thoughts remain with Eric. Saying a final farewell to my husband was the worst moment of my life. I begged him to hang on, but he couldn't do it. Sometimes, I resent that he didn't try harder. Other times, I focus my anger on the doctors who failed us. More often than not, I regret I didn't do more to keep Eric alive.

But anger and regret can't bring him back. I take a long breath, blow it out, and for the millionth time, pull myself from the self-pity brink.

The woman walking next to me gives me a funny look.

I turn my head so the floppy borrowed hat I'm wearing hides my face. She doesn't know I don't dare stop at the bar up ahead, that I can't risk being sucked into alcoholism again, which is what self-pity does to me. I want to enjoy my family during the short time I have with them and celebrate the wonderful woman I call "Nanna."

Though I'm anxious to see my family, my excitement is tinged with apprehension. Not only do I dread saying goodbye to my sweet grandmother, I dread running into Noreen Nystrom, the woman who conned me into joining Faithful Followers of the Way. She knew I was desperate to leave jail and willing to do whatever she asked to get into the church's rehab program.

Noreen and Bruce Nystrom's unwelcome presence on the airplane and in the airport has tarnished my homecoming, to say the least. They were seated in first class during the flight from Bozeman, Montana, to Portland, Oregon. I was at the very back of the plane and much slower to disembark. But still, they can't be too far ahead of me.

Spotting the women's restroom, I adjust my sunglasses and check for Bruce, who could be waiting for Noreen, but I don't see him outside the entrance. I pull my hat over my eyes and step inside, where hand soap and hairspray aromas compete with the underlying urine odor common to public bathrooms. Head down, I hurry into a stall, determined to maintain my disguise until I'm safely out of the airport and on my way to my parents' home in Salem.

In theory, Noreen can't stop me from seeing my family. A Bozeman judge gave me permission for this trip. But I wouldn't put it past her to make a scene in the middle of the airport and have me arrested on a trumped-up charge the way Ruby Jade, the church's lead pastor, did.

No doubt, Noreen would stomp her stilettos and scream the name Ruby Jade forced on me, the name I'm known by at church. "Cassandra Turner! What are you doing here? Ruby Jade didn't say you could leave Montana!"

I don't want to risk a clash with the nasty woman, if for no other reason than the fact she'd steal precious minutes, maybe hours, from my court-allocated time with loved ones. Too many years have passed since we were all together. I'm hoping and praying this bathroom stop is the only delay before I see my family again.

Mom and Kip are waiting for me at an airport coffee shop. They'll hug me and welcome me home. And call me by my real name, Cassie True.

I hang my pink purse, the black hat and the flower-covered tote I borrowed from my friend Myrtle Mae on the stall hooks and take a brush from the bag. Running it through my hair, I think about the last time I saw Mom and Dad. They'd traveled all the way from Salem to Bozeman to visit me in the Gallatin County Detention Center where I was a skinny, stringy-haired resident dressed in orange. The sight of me must have broken their hearts.

Just like in the jail bathroom, restroom noises resound. Toilets flush. Stall doors open and close. Water splashes. Hand dryers roar. I'm grateful I'm no longer confined behind bars, yet some days I wonder if I stepped from the frying pan into the fire when I entered the Transformation Way rehab program.

Finished, I drop the brush in the bag and twist my hair on top of my head. I'd rather wear it down, but for now, I add the hat and angle it over my eyes. My purse on one shoulder and the tote on the other, I cautiously open the door to survey my surroundings via the mirror across from the stall. Women and girls come and go, their suitcase wheels clattering against the tile floor.

Not seeing Noreen, I hurry to the mirror to check my disguise. I'll be shocked if my family recognizes me, and it's not just because of the hat. Though I hate to admit the church has made even one positive contribution to my life, my appearance is less scary, more human than when my parents last saw me. My hair is styled and highlighted, and my teeth are fixed. I've even put on a little weight since I joined FFOW. Mom and Dad should be pleased.

"Love your hat." The woman at the next sink is smiling at me in the mirror.

I return her smile. "Thank you."

"It's very cute on you. You must be one of those women born to wear a hat."

"You think so?"

She winks and turns to go.

Before I follow her out of the restroom, I remove my FFOW-issued watch. One less identifier to catch Noreen's attention. I think about my true self, the personality I was born with, not just how I look in a hat. Does my individuality shine through the cookie-cutter façade the church forces on us? Corban Dahlstrom seems to see and appreciate the real me.

But do I know the *real* Corban? He's a longtime Follower, yet I believe his core personality shines through now and then. When we work together away from the church, he's relaxed and fun. He seems genuine. At the church, he's polite but guarded—and distant. The easy-going side of him is definitely my favorite.

I look both ways before I step from the restroom into the ever-moving throng that traverses the terminal. Hat pulled low, I weave between travelers to access the moving walkway. Once I'm on it, I hurry ahead at a pace slightly under a jog. Noreen and Bruce are probably down at baggage claim by now. Thank God I didn't check any luggage.

I'm meeting my family at Mom's favorite pre-security coffee shop, Portland Roasting Company. But like Corban,

I can't let my guard down, at least not yet. The Nystroms might decide they need coffee before they go wherever they're headed or—

I stop. Or they may not have bags to claim. I could run into them anywhere along the way. My heart begins to pound, and I start walking again. *Please, God... If they see me, please don't let them recognize me.*

Gentle words penetrate my agitation, and I hear a man named Harmon's voice. He prayed for me on the airplane and assured me God "had" the flight just like he "has" what happens in Oregon. Thanks to Harmon, and thanks to God, I slept all the way here. I eye the terminal ceiling. *You gave me a kindhearted seatmate, Lord, and wonderful rest. Now, I give you my worries.*

As promised, Mom and Kip are standing near the Portland Roasting Company counter. My beautiful Jamaican mom's chocolate skin glows beneath the overhead lights. The wonderful aroma of roasted coffee beans greets me, but not my mother or my brother. Neither of them shows any sign of recognition. I pull off the hat, shake out my highlighted hair and walk over to them.

I'm two steps away when Mom exclaims, "Cassie, it's you! I didn't recognize you under that hat."

"Sis!" Kip says. "What's with the movie-star disguise?"

I take off my sunglasses and we share a long three-way embrace. The warm tang of my mother's favorite Jamaican body oil, which I happen to know is a mango, papaya, lemon-lime blend, mingles with Kip's soapy cedar scent. Being enveloped by my loved ones and hearing their laughter feels even better than I anticipated. "Is Dad at work?"

"He's with your grandmother," Mom says. "Doesn't want her to live her last days on earth without at least one of us by her side."

"That's so sweet." Tears mist my eyes. "But sad."

"I'm pretty sure she knew me," Kip says. "Gave my hand a squeeze." He takes my bag from me. "I know she'll be glad you came."

Back at the Bozeman airport, Corban jokingly said real men carry women's luggage, no matter how humiliating. I tell my brother, "Kip, it's kinda girly. Might ruin your masculine reputation."

"Real men don't let a few flowers stop them from helping a little ole lady across the street."

"Hey, I'm not—"

"I love your hair, Cassie," Mom says. "Cute cut and great highlights, but…" My fashion-writer mother eyes my long-sleeved blouse and polyester pants. "You don't look like the daughter I remember in that outfit. And where in the world did you find a pink purse?"

"Don't go there, Mom." I put the hat and the sunglasses back on, in case the Nystroms are nearby. But I leave my hair down. "As long as I'm in the program, I have to do as the Romans do."

"Or dress as my grandmother dressed." She shudders. "What happened to the clothes I sent you?"

"Long story. I'll tell you later. Right now, I'm anxious to see Grandma and catch up with you guys."

"We would have talked more," she says, "if your phone calls hadn't been so—"

"Something else to discuss another time." My family's focus should be on my grandmother, a dear, dear woman who deeply loves us all. I need to honor her, not disrupt a sacred gathering or muddy everyone's minds with Ruby Jade horror stories.

"You seem tired, Mom." I hug her waist. "Have you been putting in long days with Grandma?"

"Yes." She wraps her arm around my shoulders. "If I didn't sit with her a few hours every day, your dad would be there twenty-four-seven. He needs to get away, sleep, catch

HIDDEN PATH | 7

up at work, take a walk or whatever. Your Uncle Gabe has come a couple times, but he can't stay long."

She sighs. "When I'm not with your grandmother, I try to keep your dad fed, help him with final arrangements, make phone calls, send out texts and emails to the family. Those sorts of things."

A barista calls Kip's name and we walk over to claim our coffees. "Don't know how you're drinking your coffee these days," Kip says. "I ordered you a regular. You can doctor it however you want."

I stir in a tablespoon of the shop's superfood creamer. I've never had it before, but it sounds interesting. And then, with Mom on one side and Kip on the other, I savor the simple act of walking to the parking garage with two of my favorite people. This is the safest and happiest I've felt in a long, long time.

"I can't wait to see Dad and Grandma," I tell them. "Seems like an eternity since I've been with you. Except you, big brother." I nudge Kip. "Your Bozeman visit was way too short, but seeing you was a huge bright spot in my crazy life."

He waggles his eyebrows. "That's what all the girls say."

"Yeah, sure. As if you take time out for girls between climbs."

"What's the point?"

"One of these days, Kip." Mom shakes a forefinger at him. "You'll be smitten so hard the mountains will melt into prairies for you."

"I hope not." He looks alarmed.

I give him a sideways glance. "I take it no sister-in-law is in my immediate future."

"Not if I can help it."

"Bummer. I always wanted a sister."

We haven't traveled far on the road to Salem, when Mom rests her head against the passenger window and goes to sleep. Kip, who's driving, glances over at her and then at me in the mirror. "About meeting you for lunch, have you had any more trouble with that guy?" He peeks at Mom again. Her breath comes in soft whispers.

I bend as close as the seatbelt allows and keep my voice low. "No, other than the fact he told the church leaders he saw me there. He also said you and I are having an affair."

Kip's eyes blaze. "Ludicrous."

"There's more, so keep your eyes on the road." I don't want us to have an accident because of a weird church controlled by weird people.

"If I ever get my hands on the numbskull, I'll—" He clutches the steering wheel like he's about to rip it off.

I smirk. "Numbskull" is one of our dad's favorite words for bad drivers.

Three motorcyclists pass us, their long hair flapping behind their helmets. I wait until their noisy machines are in front of our car before continuing. "I was lambasted before the entire congregation for patronizing a bar that plays…" I finger quote. "'Carnal country music' and serves alcoholic beverages. I supposedly not only drank alcohol there, I drank it with a *Gentile*, which I think means anyone who isn't in their church. And not any Gentile, mind you, but a despicable *male* Gentile, the one with whom I'm having an affair."

"Argh." Kip shakes his fists in the air. "That's, that's so—"

"Tell me about it." I'm glad he finished his coffee, or it would be splashed it all over the car by now.

Scowling, he grabs the wheel. "You told them the truth, right?"

"Yes, but it wasn't what they wanted to hear. They wanted me to confess my horrific sin right then and there."

He grimaces. "What did you do?"

"Vance's mother is the leader—I think I told you that already. She interrupted the inquisition because she wanted time to speak. But she said she'd deal with me later. Knowing her, it's a promise she'll keep."

"Any idea what she might do to you?"

"No, but it won't be pleasant."

"You have to get out of there."

"I wish." I drink the last of my coffee and place the empty cup in a cup holder. "Thanks for the coffee, Kip. It was really good."

My brother drives us straight to the memory center where Grandma Hunt has lived for several years. As we cross the parking lot, Mom tells me she and Dad considered taking Grandma to their home for her final days. But because of her dementia, they decided not to remove her from familiar surroundings.

Mom greets the receptionist and signs us in. We're barely in the hallway when she whispers, "If this place used real floral arrangements rather than silk, they might be able to mask the unpleasant aroma."

I forgot I always need a few minutes to adjust to the stuffy smell in nursing homes. A nurse friend once told me the source is aging bodies, not poor hygiene. Random bouquets of fresh flowers couldn't compete.

Dad stands when we walk in and greets me with one of his wonderful bear hugs. "Good to see you, Girl."

"I'm so happy to be here with you." I sink into his loving embrace. "And Mom and Kip and..." I turn to Grandma. Tears spring to my eyes. Always an active, fun-loving woman, now her eyes are closed, and her face is pale, with only a hint of color. Her beautiful white hair is crumpled against the pillow.

"Take my seat," Dad says, rolling his shoulders. "I need to move a bit and stretch my back."

I slip into the chair he was sitting in. It's still warm. Clasping Grandma's soft hand, I murmur, "Hey, Nanna. It's me, Cassie."

She presses my fingers, ever so slightly.

The tears I've been trying to contain spill over my eyelids. "I've been praying I'd get to say goodbye to you in person." I sniff and swipe at my wet cheeks. "But I'd rather be strolling through your garden with you, like we used to do. You were always so patient with my questions about plants and bugs and life."

Her eyelids flutter. I swear she's trying to say something.

CHAPTER TWO

I lean closer to my grandma. Despite the antiseptic environment, she smells the same as always—grassy and musty with a hint of Dove soap.

The softest of whispers escapes her lips. "Kit-ten."

My heart hiccups. "Oh, Nanna, you remember." I stroke her hand. "I'll always be your Kitten."

Right after Eric christened me "Cat," she started calling me "Kitten." And I'd tell her, "You're the one with the fur coat."

She had a fake fur cape she loved to wear, mostly to annoy the PETA crowd, who'd invariably shout insults at her. Their creativity amused her, especially the slurs comparing her to a snake. That's when she'd throw open her cape to show off her snakeskin belt.

"Be...a...tiger." Her words are so faint, I wonder if I heard right.

"Mom." Dad drops into the chair on the other side of the bed. "It's good to hear your voice."

Her only response is a tiny smile.

Kip brings over two more chairs, and the four of us sit around Grandma's bed, telling our favorite family stories. We remember the twinkle in her eye, the funny things she said and did, how she taught me to ice skate and make a perfect pie crust. But she taught Kip the fine arts of mashed-potato sculpting and knife-throwing.

"You know, Nanna…" I rub her arm. "I have to admit I was jealous of Kip because I needed knife-throwing lessons, too. Every time I threw his knife at the hay-bale target out by the barn, it landed in the dirt."

Kip snorts. "She didn't give you lessons because you were so hopeless at it."

"Not true."

Mom rolls her eyes. "Hush, you two."

We sing Grandma's favorite worship songs, including one I wrote about heaven and seeing Jesus face to face. Again, I'm convinced a smile touches her lips. I caress her velvety skin. She's soft as a kitten, inside and out.

After a while—I have no idea how much time has passed—her breathing slows and the color seeps from her face.

I rest my cheek on her pillow and whisper in her ear, "I love you, Nanna. I don't want you to leave, but Jesus is calling you home. He's ready to give you a new body. You can be your ornery self again." I giggle. "Well, maybe ornery in a good way. And you'll be with Grandpa. What a wonderful reunion you two will have."

My tears drip onto her pillow. "Be sure to watch for us. We won't be far behind. One of these days, we'll all be together in heaven."

Dad lifts her hand and kisses it. "Gabe said to tell you he couldn't have asked for a better mom. I agree." He swallows. "Bye, Mom. I look forward to joining you and Dad in heaven one of these days."

Kip lays his hand on her shoulder. "You are the best grandma ever. I will never forget you."

"I can say the same about having you for a mother-in-law." Mom swipes at the tears coursing down her brown cheeks. "Even when I was a clueless bumbling bride from a different culture, you were kind and patient with me." She chokes out the words. "I grew to love you as much as I loved my own mother."

Dad gently lowers Grandma's hand to the bed.

She whispers, "Oh…" and lifts both hands like she's reaching for something—or Someone. A golden glow lights her face.

As quickly as it came, the ethereal radiance fades. Lowering her arms, she exhales a long, quiet sigh. The only trace of her joyful yet peaceful departure is the smile that lingers on her lips.

"Goodbye, Nanna," I whisper. "Say hello to Jesus for us."

Dad calls Uncle Gabe and they talk softly for several minutes. A half hour later, we're still sitting beside the bed, sharing memories. For some silly reason, we're whispering.

At the sound of a rap on the door, Dad says, "Come in," and Rev. Tucker, my parents' pastor, steps into the room. He's portlier than I remember—too many potluck dinners, perhaps—and his gray hair curls on his collar. First time I've seen him in a polo shirt.

"Sorry," he says. "I didn't mean to—" His eyes brighten. "Cassie. Good to see you. What a pleasant surprise."

I stand and hug him. "I was able to get away from the rehab program for a short while."

"Wonderful." He turns to my brother, who's also now standing, and embraces him. "Good to see you, too, Kip."

Motioning to my parents, he says, "I don't want to disturb your family gathering, so I won't stay." He looks at Grandma. "How is she—?" He shifts a questioning gaze Dad's direction.

"She left us." Dad smiles. "Hasn't been long."

"I'm so sorry. She was a dear woman." Pastor Tucker moves to the end of the bed and regards her still form with obvious fondness. "A true saint. I will miss her." He extends his hand to my parents. "You have my condolences, and when you're ready, we can finalize the arrangements we discussed earlier. Until then…" He turns to go. "You'll be in my prayers."

"Wait." I grab his arm. "Don't go."

He stops, eyebrows raised.

"Could we have a private service right here, right now?" I plead with him through a veil of tears. "I missed Grandpa's service and I really want to be here for Grandma's…if you don't mind."

I face my parents. "And if it's okay with you. I know you said you'll have the service soon, but the rest of the family isn't here yet, and I can only stay a couple days."

"Yes." Dad looks thoughtful. "I believe a private service would be good for all of us, if you have the time, Pastor."

Mom wipes tears from her cheeks, tears I know are for me and my grief. "We could use a little TLC, but this is spur of the moment."

"I'd be happy to. Some farewell services are difficult because I didn't know the person." Pastor Tucker smiles. "Or I did, and they were such cantankerous so-and-sos, I couldn't come up with anything good to say about them.

"But Dory Hunt?" He chuckles. "We might be here for hours, recalling what a spunky, gracious woman she was." After a pause, he says, "Before we begin, I have a request. As you know, Dory and my wife team-taught Sunday school for many years. They were the best of friends." He glances at each of us. "With your permission, I'd like to ask Isabelle to join us and bring my Bible with her."

Mom smiles. "Of course."

"We'd love to have her come," Dad says, "providing Cassie and Kip are comfortable with the idea."

Kip shrugs and I nod. Isabelle is a super-nice lady. When I was in high school, she asked about school and told me how much she enjoyed my music almost every Sunday.

Saying an official goodbye to Grandma Hunt is somehow more painful than watching her pass from this life into the next. Yet, Pastor Tucker's words and the Scriptures he reads are comforting. And the memories he and Isabelle share have us vacillating between amazement and laughter at my nanna's crazy sense of humor.

She could do anything she set her mind to—and she always added a measure of fun. More often than not, she'd forget the motions to Sunday school songs. According to Isabelle, her improvised actions tended to be more energetic than the original ones.

"She'd have the kids jumping off chairs, pounding the walls and conga-dancing around the room." Isabelle's eyes sparkle. "I sometimes wondered if she purposely forgot, so she'd have an excuse to enliven things a bit."

"I'll never forget the time she treated us to a roast beef dinner," Pastor Tucker says, "then fixed bananas flambé for dessert. She was adding the rum and—"

"Caught the potholder on fire!" Isabelle giggles. "It wasn't funny, but it was. She bounced all over the kitchen, flapping the potholder in the air."

"And," Pastor Tucker adds, "shouting the most creative swear words you ever heard."

"Like what?" Kip asks. Of course, my brother would want to know. He has his own list of unique words he probably learned from Grandma.

"Offhand, the only two I remember are 'great Caesar's ghost' and 'son of a skunk.'" The pastor's face is alive with humor.

We all laugh, but Dad and Kip eye each other. I get the impression they've heard those words before.

"Finally," Isabelle says, "Harold waved his hands to get her attention and shouted, 'Goodnight in the morning, Dory! Toss the blasted thing in the sink before you burn down the house!' Which she did, or we might not be here today."

Tears stream down our faces, and I laugh so hard my stomach hurts.

"Too bad you don't have a video of Grandma dancing around the kitchen," Kip says. "It'd go viral."

"Funny how Mom and Dad never told us that story." My father shakes his head. "But I don't need a video to picture those two in action."

And neither do I. I smile, delighted to have another Grandma story to add to my memory bank and grateful I can laugh with my family again.

That evening, Mom and Dad crash early. They haven't gotten much sleep in the last couple weeks. Kip and I sit on the front porch, drinking lemonade, listening to crickets sing and talking about whatever comes to mind. The blossoms on the big apple tree in the front yard infuse the night air with their sweetness. The only light comes from a streetlamp two houses away.

During high school, the two of us often stayed up late to share the happenings in our lives, especially on weekends. Our conversations were shorter after Eric and I married, but we still talked often. While I was in jail, I missed my long chats with my brother more than anything else.

"When you finish the rehab program," Kip says, "you can move in with me, if you want. Spokane would be a good place to resume your music career. The city has a growing music scene."

"Thanks, Kip. What a generous offer." I trace the wicker weave on my chair arm. "I hadn't thought of leaving Bozeman, but it might be good for me to go where people don't know my history. I'll definitely think about it."

I don't tell him Corban and I are hoping to spend more time together when I'm done with Transformation Way. We've got nearly a year to sort out our relationship, and I need to take one day at a time. The way life happens at FFOW, I see no sense in planning too far ahead.

Kip leans back in the wooden rocking chair. The porch's floorboards creak a protest. "I get why you stay in the so-called church. A judge sent you there. But what about the others? Why don't they fire the Ruby Jade twit? At the very least, why don't people leave?"

"I've asked several people that question." I set my glass on the top rail beside Myrtle Mae's phone and push my rocker into motion. "As you might imagine, I'm cautious with my, uh, research. Questioning anything about the church has to be done discreetly."

"No surprise, from what you've told me."

"The first response is always, 'If I leave, I'll either die from cancer or in a car accident and go to hell.'"

He flips forward, elbows landing on his knees. "You're joking."

"Nope. That's what keeps them there, the belief they're the only ones going to heaven. Anyone outside Faith Followers of the Way is supposedly destined for hell."

"That's…it's not in the Bible. How can they—?"

"All I know is their leader has them convinced." I rest my head on the chairback, breathing in the cool night air. "When I dig a little deeper, the answers tend to revolve around two things. Family and money.

"According to Ruby Jade, someone who leaves the church's hallowed halls is a…" I make air quotes. "'Reprehensible person' to be avoided at all times. I'm told much planning and preparation is needed because the person knows they'll no longer be able to communicate openly with church members, whether relatives or friends."

"Even if they live in the same town?"

"Even if they live in the same town."

"I can't imagine that kinda life."

"Have you noticed how little contact I've had with you and Mom and Dad since I joined? Family members who aren't in the group are considered evil hell-bound Gentiles. Those who question FFOW's legitimacy, like you're doing right now, are called liars."

Kip sits upright. "Makes me want to knock a few heads together."

"Want to know why a permanent separation is imposed?"

"I hate to think."

"Ruby Jade says it's because Jesus came to divide the righteous from the unrighteous and to divide families."

"Argh!" He pounds his chair arm. "She twists Scripture." His scowl is replaced by a questioning gaze. "So, what's the deal with money? Are people forced to give most of their income to the church?"

A bicycle passes on the street, its red taillight winking on and off and its tires whirring against the pavement.

"Wouldn't put it past them," I respond. "But I don't have an income, so they haven't bugged me about contributing to the church coffers."

He squints at me. "You have a job, but you don't get paid?"

"I work for the leader, which evidently means I'm on volunteer status."

Seeing he's about to erupt, I lift my palm. "In addition to passing the offering plate several times in a service, Ruby Jade has a way of indebting people to herself. When she puts a couple together, I'm told she buys the rings—expensive rings—and hosts the kiss-less engagement in her office. She also organizes and officiates the wedding."

He snorts. "I suppose she goes with them on their honeymoon."

"Honeymoons aren't allowed because the couple would be alone and away from the group's oversight. They might do something evil, like have sex."

"That's insane!" Kip runs his fingers through his hair. Backlit by the streetlight, his spiked strands remind me of a porcupine.

"Nice hairdo, Kip." I smirk. "The couples and/or their families are charged for the wedding expenses. But she rarely lets them pay in full. Instead, she gives them a multi-year loan with a high interest rate. Could be for a wedding, a car, a house—any big-ticket item. From what I've heard, her contracts forbid people to prepay the balance. Actually, I guess they can repay loans before they come due, but then huge fees are added."

"Can't be legal." He begins rocking again, faster.

"I know some people who borrowed from Ruby Jade to remodel their home. Their loan agreement is similar to what I mentioned, but a Bozeman lawyer recently told them he can get them out of the contract."

"I'm amazed they even dared talk to a local attorney. Sounds as though the woman runs the town."

"These members have been around a while, so they know the ropes. They're gradually working themselves out of the group, but it's hard because all their friends are there, friends they've known for years and years. The good news is the whole family is on board with the exit plan, so they won't be leaving any relatives behind."

As if on cue, Myrtle Mae's phone buzzes against the porch rail. Since the first time he saw the phone, Kip has teased me about it. "My, my, Grandma, what big buttons you have. Can you see to dial, or do I need to help you?" I respond with, "My, my, big brother, what a big mouth you have. Do I need to help you close it?" He takes my threats as seriously as he did my attempts to wrestle him to the living room floor when we were younger. All he does is laugh at me.

I reach for the phone, tap the screen and smile. Corban is responding to a text I sent earlier to tell him Grandma Hunt died shortly after I arrived in Salem.

I'm sorry. Even if you expected her to go, losing your grandma is hard. Did you get to say goodbye?

Yes, I type. *She whispered my nickname.*

A moment later, he responds. *Sweet. I'd like to know that nickname. Can you talk now?*

Maybe later. Will you still be awake in an hour?

Only if it doesn't take away from your family time.

Let's do it.

I set the phone on the railing and grab my lemonade.

Kip is watching me, his eyebrows scrunched and a strange expression on his face.

"What?" I take a sip.

"I thought you couldn't text, at least not often."

"True. But remember, this isn't my phone. Church leaders don't have any idea it exists or that I'm using it. Actually, other than the woman who owns it, only two people know I have a cell phone with me—Sebastian, my supervisor you met, and the guy who's picking me up when I return."

"A guy, huh?"

"Uh-huh."

"Did he send all those texts just now?"

"What is this, Kip, an interrogation?"

My brother's countenance doesn't change. "Is he in the church?"

"Well, yes, but—"

"I saw the way you smiled." He points a forefinger at me. "You get seriously involved with him, Cassie, we'll never see you again."

"I understand your concern." I stop rocking. "The family I mentioned with the remodel loan? He's part of that family.

Not only do they plan to leave, they've already been helping people escape and get their kids back and—"

"What?"

"Leadership takes kids away from their parents and has other couples raise them."

"You've got to be kidding me." He grips the chair arms.

"Wish I was." I rock forward. "Between you and me, Kip..." I beckon him closer and whisper, "I helped reunite a little guy with his mom."

"Why, you rebel, you." He high-fives me. "Way to go, Sis."

"Shh." I put my finger on my lips. "I haven't told another soul. Please, *please*, don't mention it, not even to Mom and Dad. It's a huge secret I share with a certain deputy. If Leadership learned I was responsible, they'd find a way to discharge me from the program. I'm certain of it."

CHAPTER THREE

Having a phone conversation with Corban feels as natural as sitting beside him in his car. I'm not sure where our relationship is headed, but I'm enjoying the ride.

Guilt stabs my heart. How can I think such a thought when Corban is not Eric? I force my brain to switch from my emotions to my intellect. I see my husband lying on the couch in our little apartment and hear the awful words he whispered shortly before he died. *I'm happy for your future, Cassie. I release you to live and to love.*

Oh, how I rebelled at those words. But he was right. I need to move on. I'm free to move on. It's *time* to move on.

"Must have been good to be with your family," Corban is saying, "yet a sad time for everyone."

"Today's been bittersweet, for sure." A pillow behind my back, I lean against the headboard of my bed, the one Mom and Dad bought for me the summer before I entered high school. It still smells like the citrus scent I wore back then.

I tell him how Grandma Hunt seemed to see heaven or maybe Jesus before she died, how she left with a smile. I also tell him about the private service Pastor Tucker officiated for us and some of the memories we shared, humorous as well as inspiring.

He's quiet when I finish, and I realize I've talked nonstop. "Sorry, Corban. You haven't been able to get a word in edgewise, as my grandma would say."

"I've loved every word, Cassie, not just because I enjoy hearing your voice, but because having grandparent memories is a foreign concept for me."

"You and Logan don't have grandparents?"

"We do, but I barely remember them." He releases a long sigh into the phone. "Both sets lived in other states. We saw them occasionally when Logan and I were small and the church was a regular church. But eventually, our parents were forced to cut off communication with their families, something both Mom and Dad deeply regret. Once they started talking with their siblings again, they learned one of my uncles and all of our grandparents are deceased."

"How sad."

"I'm ashamed to say that for most of my life, I had negative feelings about our relatives because they refused to move to Bozeman to join the church. If I had run into them on the street, I wouldn't have acknowledged them—not that I had any idea what they looked like."

"You were just believing what you were taught." My heart hurts for him.

"Yeah, but I'm over it and I can get a feel for what we might have had through your stories." He pauses. "Your grandmother sounds like a wonderful woman, but you haven't said much about your grandfather."

"Grandpa was an amazing guy. I'll tell you all about him one of these days. How about you? How'd your day go?"

He chuckles.

"That good, huh?"

"Even better."

"Okay, you hooked me." I twist a strand of hair around my finger. "I'm dying of curiosity."

"Two words. Wait for it…" He taps a drumroll on his phone. "Twin. Trunks."

Biting my lip, I try to grasp why he's implying. *Twin trunks?* And then it hits me—he's talking about my missing boxes. That was the name Myrtle Mae gave their box-retrieval "operation."

"You didn't."

"We did. Ground Zero."

Oh, so my guitar *was* in the Pritchards' basement, like I suspected. "And?"

"Mission. Accomplished."

He sounds so proud, I wish I could shake his hand and pin a medal on his chest. And kiss him—on the cheek, of course. "Congratulations. First chance I get, I'm going to give you both a big hug. But I wish I had something more to offer. You took a huge risk for me."

"Truth is, we enjoy the adrenalin rush. You've probably noticed a dearth of fun-and-games in the FFOW world."

"How did—?"

"The less you know, the better."

"When did—?"

"Two more words. Work. Project."

"Oh." Was everyone in the household gone on a work project?

"As I said, the less you know, the better off you'll be when the dragons swoop in. Trust me."

"I do trust you, Corban." Thank God he's a musician who knows how to care for instruments. Someday, he'll be able to tell me the full "Operation Twin Trunks" story, and I'll be able to tell him my part in Zachary's rescue from the same basement.

"Make that six words," Corban says. "Twin trunks. Work project. Two boots."

"Two boots?"

"Right on top."

I grin. He's talking about the hiking boots Eric gave me. I may not be able to wear them for a year, but now I know they're safe. "You remembered. Thank you. Thank you so much, Corban. Knowing they're out of harm's way gives me great comfort. Did you happen to see a bag of cookies on top?"

"So that's what was in the empty plastic bag stuffed between the boots. It sure smelled good."

Olivia. I bet she's the one who ate Mom's chocolate oatmeal nut cookies.

The next morning, Kip and I fix breakfast for Mom and Dad while they sit at the kitchen table, drinking coffee and talking with us. I love being surrounded by all the aromas and foods and contentment of an unhurried breakfast with my family. Because I'm tempted to regret our eventual separation before it happens, I relish the moment and thank God for this lull in the storm I call life.

Actually, it's more than a lull. It's a breath of fresh air, a shot in the arm, a reestablishment of who I am, where I've been and where I hope to go. And a whole lot of love. From my growing bond with Corban to my family reconnection and my sweet nanna waiting for me to say goodbye—what more could a girl want? Despite all I've put my family through, they still love me. Their patience and forgiveness are amazing.

Now that I think about it, my detention center "time out" not only got me off the streets and away from alcohol, it enabled me to think rationally. Long conversations with my parents when they visited also helped. Talking with them enabled me to see how much I'd hurt them and gave me an opportunity to apologize.

I'm lifting bacon from the pan when the house phone rings in the living room. Dad gets up from the table. "Probably your aunt or uncle, or one of your cousins." I notice he's not moving fast this morning and his phone greeting is more subdued than usual. Poor Dad. He's been through a lot lately.

After his "hello," he pauses and then says, "Sorry, there's no Cassandra Turner here. You must have a—"

I drop the bacon slice onto a plate and dart past Kip and Mom into the living room, tongs in hand.

"Yes." He gives me a funny look. "My daughter is Cassie True. Who's calling?"

Standing in front of him, I watch his face.

"Very thoughtful of you to check on her, Evelyn." He sounds pleasant enough, but he's frowning, and his voice is firm. "But she's not available. Please tell your pastor we're grieving the loss of a loved one and cannot be disturbed."

I wince. *That'll go over like a lead balloon.*

"Goodbye." He drops the phone on the receiver then studies me for a moment. His mussed gray hair pokes from his scalp. "I got the impression the caller was demanding to speak with you rather than asking. If you want to talk with your pastor, you can call back—after breakfast, if you don't mind. This is family time for us, something we've not had for several years."

"I don't care to speak with her, Dad, and even if I did, being with you guys is far more important to me than the church."

The phone rings again.

We eye each other.

Finally, he picks up the handset. "Hello." His eyes are hard, and his voice is flat.

The caller's voice is so loud I can hear it. Ruby Jade. Leave it to her to ruin a perfect morning.

"Your daughter," she says, "who is under my jurisdiction, left the Transformation Way program without my permission. I demand to speak with her immediately."

Dad covers the microphone hole, lowers the phone to his side and whispers, "Is that true?"

"No." I shake my head and talk over her ranting. "I have a judge's permission, the program director's permission, and my boss's permission to be here. I don't need hers."

He raises the phone to his ear.

Ruby Jade is still talking. "...authorities at your door before you can snap your fingers. She'll be arrested. Is this what you want for your daughter, Mr. Hunt?"

"As I told the previous caller..." His eyes flash. "We are not to be disturbed. If you call again, I'll file a harassment claim." This time, he slams the phone onto the base and shakes his head like he's trying to clear it of her angry voice. "She's a pastor?"

"Yeah." I sigh. "But I would never call her *my* pastor. She—" Before my mouth gets ahead of my brain and I say something I'll later regret, I turn toward the kitchen. "We'd better eat. The food's getting cold."

After we're all seated, Kip thanks God for the food and prays for the relatives traveling to the funeral. He's barely said "Amen," when Mom asks about the phone calls.

We need to discuss those calls," Dad says. "But first, I'd like to go over funeral plans and which relatives are coming in at what time."

"Okay." Mom doesn't look happy. "But this may be our only time to find out what in the world is going on at that rehab program."

I pass the eggs to her. "I'll update you before I go, I promise." I don't want to talk about the program or the church, but my family has a right to know the sordid details of my life.

Our breakfast is like old times, except for the added sorrow and tension I wish we didn't have. I'm pouring another round of coffee, when Dad says, "Let's relocate to the patio. Should be warm enough out there by now." The patio is heavily shaded and extra cool in the mornings.

He pushes his chair away and stands. "I want to take advantage of this short time we have when it's just the four of us."

"I'm all for family time, Dad," Kip says. "No mountains to climb today."

Dad arches an eyebrow.

"Kidding," Kip says. "Just kidding."

"You can take your cousins out for a hike tomorrow," Mom says. "I'm sure they'd enjoy getting away from the old folks."

"I'd like it, too." I glance at my parents. "The hike, that is, and spending time with my cousins. I haven't hiked since Eric got sick, and I need to get in shape. When I graduate from the program, I want to celebrate by climbing a certain trail. You're all welcome to join me and my friends."

"Count me in." Kip gives me a thumbs-up. "My kind of party."

We settle on the patio, and I inhale the backyard's earthy yet flowery fragrance. Though some foliage and flowers are still in the bud stage, the tulips, daffodils and fruit trees are in bloom. "I love your pansies, Mom. They're everywhere."

"Thank you. I got a bit carried away when I saw all those colors in the garden center and decided I needed ten of each."

Dad laughs. "You get carried away every spring, Veronica. I have the charge card bills to prove it."

"Oh, stop your grousing. You helped me buy all those pansies." Turning to me, Mom says, "Speaking of Eric, I hope watching another loved one pass from this life to the next hasn't been too painful for you, Cassie."

"I hadn't connected the two deaths, which is good, I guess." I lift my chin. "But now that you mention it…"

She puts her hand on my forearm. "Cassie, I'm so sorry—"

I laugh. "I'm teasing, Mom. I'm okay, really."

"Are you *really* okay?" Dad asks. "I'm not talking about family members we've lost. I'm talking about your general wellbeing. Our contact with you since you got into the new program has been infrequent and, for lack of a better word, odd. To be honest, we haven't known what to think."

Staring into my coffee, I contemplate what to say, what not to say. If I tell them everything, they'll be worried sick. However, picking and choosing from the craziness is hard. Nothing about FFOW is normal. The longer I'm on the outside, the more obvious it is.

"How about you begin with your birthday?" he suggests.

"Okay." I appreciate a starting point.

"Your supervisor indicated our presence—"

"Wait." Mom jumps to her feet. "I'll be right back."

Dad blinks. "I was—"

"Hang onto your thought, Edward." She hurries into the house. A moment later, she calls from the kitchen window, "Kip, could you come help me, please?"

He gets up, and I turn to Dad. "I'm sorry my calls have been so erratic. When I finally got my own phone, I assumed I'd be able to talk more often, but the leaders discourage family contact, especially for those in the rehab program, and we're always working."

"Working at what?"

"In addition to their regular jobs, members are expected to do volunteer work. They mow, trim and landscape yards, rake leaves in the fall and shovel snow in the winter. They paint and clean houses, offices and warehouses—and, of course, clean the church. Sometimes they organize warehouse shelves. The church charges the homeowners and businesses but never pays the workers, as far as I know.

"I do yardwork every afternoon, but I've also prepped a house for painting and handed out flyers at a flea market. I don't know everything the others do, but I imagine it's whatever the leaders can dream up that will promote the church or provide a profit."

Kip slides the patio door open and begins singing, "Happy birthday to you, happy birthday..." He's carrying a small chocolate torte. A candle flickers in the middle.

Dad joins in, singing bass, and Mom follows Kip, adding her lovely alto. She has a beautifully wrapped gift in her hands.

When they finish, I clap. "What a wonderful trio you are. Thank you. The church people don't harmonize, so you are a treat to my ears."

Kip bows. "Keep us in mind to sing backup when you go on tour."

"I'd love to tour with you guys."

"I know we just ate," Mom says, "but the torte is small, and we can't let you return without celebrating your birthday. We didn't even get to talk with you on your special day."

"Mom, you're the best." I stand and hug her. "I knew you and Dad were thinking of me."

"Sit down." Kip places the torte on the table. "And blow out the candle before it ruins the frosting."

I do as he asked, extinguishing the candle with one puff. My silly family claps as if I'm a one-year-old who's conquered my first candle. Mom gets plates and silverware, and I cut four slender chocolate slices and pass them around.

They wait for me to take the first bite. I let the morsel melt on my taste buds. "Amazing." I smile and take a sip of coffee. "Nothing better than chocolate and coffee."

"You can say that again," Kip says. "Give me a minute and I'll be ready for a second piece."

"You planning to eat most of this," I tease, "like you ate most of my birthday cake at the restaurant?"

"Let her open her present first," Mom says. "It's been to Montana and back, and I don't want to miss this opportunity to give it to her."

"Sorry about the mix-up, Mom." Instead of delivering the package to me, like a kind, thoughtful person would do, Olivia refused it and had it returned to my parents. I pull off the silver ribbon and teal paper and lift the lid. Beneath the tissue paper is a blue dress and matching sandals. I stand and hold the knee-length sleeveless dress in front of me. "This is so cute. Thank you, Mom and Dad."

Dad nods. "You're welcome."

"Model it for us," Mom says.

"Okay." I drop the dress into the box and carry it to my bedroom to try on. It's a perfect fit. I check the mirror on the back of the door. The dress looks great, but my legs are as white as winter. Oh, well.

The sandals have a cute blue flower on the toe strap. I slip them on and remember the kiwi necklace is still in my purse. I forgot to find a hiding place for it, but I'm glad I didn't because now I can wear it for Kip and show it to my parents.

I won't tell them I have to leave everything here. If I return to Montana with their gifts, they'll be taken from me. I'll hide everything in the closet corner, where I stashed my stuffed toys, dolls and yearbooks from long ago.

Twirling before my family, I describe my new outfit. First, I dangle the kiwi bird. "A dainty silver keepsake from a land down under." Next, I swish my hand up and down the dress. "And a delightful summer dress in periwinkle blue with a slightly flared skirt."

Lifting the sides of the skirt, I do a little curtsy before I indicate my shoes with a flourish of my fingers. "Charming coordinated sandals complete the altogether look." I extend first one foot, then the other, pleased with my audacious use of Noreen's pet phrase.

"That's my girl." Dad has a proud grin on his face.

"Yes, it's not only the altogether look." Mom smiles. "It's the Cassie look. The necklace is perfect, Kip. Adorable."

He smiles but doesn't say anything.

"Thank you, all of you." I give them each a hug. "Your thoughtfulness means a lot to me." Clasping my hands behind my back, I take a breath, determined to be honest with my family.

"Being with you reminds me who I am and where I came from. I slipped into a dark hole after Eric died, and I was just climbing out when I got into the rehab program. I hoped it would be a good thing, better than the other programs I tried. However, the church leaders seem determined to steal members' individuality and shame them into becoming spineless zombies who do their every bidding."

My father frowns. "Then leave."

"I wish it were so simple, Dad, but the judge ordered me to attend the church as well as the program."

"What about separation of church and state?" Mom asks.

"Yeah," Kip says. "A good lawyer could get the ruling overturned in a heartbeat."

"That's the problem." I slip into my chair. "A good lawyer costs money, which I don't have. You've already paid a fortune in attorney fees, Mom and Dad. Enough is enough." I cut another torte slice for Kip. "Anyone else for a second piece?"

My parents shake their heads.

I set the knife on the plate. "To finish what I was saying, these reminders of how much you love and care for me bring me back to reality and restore my sense of identity."

I glance from my parents to my brother. "Spending time with you has done something for my soul. I'm surrounded by people every day, some of them friends, yet I often feel all alone in the world. Now, I'm filled with your love, and the lonely feeling is gone." I pause. "I don't know if I'm making sense, but thank you for being you."

Mom places her hand over mine. "All of us together in this house again has been healing for me too."

"Yes," Dad says, "a gift from our Creator and Sustainer." He leans his forearms on the table. "I'd like to talk about this church of yours, Cassie. Sounds like something is way off kilter."

CHAPTER FOUR

"We can talk about Faithful Followers of the Way, or F-F-O-W, which the members pronounce as *fow*," I tell Dad. "But just so you know, I don't claim it as *my* church."

"Gotcha." He nods. "I understand."

I gaze at the patio ceiling, wondering where to begin. "A while back, I was super upset about an incident at the church and I saw my life as a choice between two mountains. One involved begging the judge to send me to a different program and the other was to grit my teeth and stick it out."

"That bad?"

"Worse. The church—"

"Call it what it is, Cassie," Kip says. "Like I told you, it's a cult."

Mom frowns. "Where did you get such an idea, Kip?"

"What I saw and heard in Bozeman, in addition to what I read on the internet, all add up to *cult* with a capital C. Three women—one of them ruling from the top of the triangle—control every aspect of the members' lives. An unholy trinity, for sure."

"Cassie?" She peers at me. "Is it true?"

"Yes, unfortunately." I fold my arms. "Ruby Jade, the woman who called earlier, is the top dog. She labels herself the group's pastor, prophetess and psalmist and expects everyone to grovel at her feet. She's a hefty woman who knows how to throw her weight around the church—or cult, that is—and around the town. She's formidable, to put it mildly, and feared by many."

"Why?" Dad asks.

"I'm not sure, but people seem to adore her as well as fear her. Hard to explain. Her sidekicks, Noreen and Inez, are feared but not adored, as far as I can tell."

"From the research I did online," Kip says, "I'm convinced the leader is a narcissist."

"Oh, yeah?" I find it hard to believe Ruby Jade could be so easily classified.

"The Mayo Clinic says it's a personality disorder."

"Interesting..."

"Here, I'll look it up." He pulls his phone from his back pocket and after a bit begins to read. "Narcissism is a mental condition in which people have an inflated sense of their own importance, a deep need for excessive attention and admiration, troubled relationships, and a lack of empathy for others. But behind this mask of extreme confidence lies a fragile self-esteem that's vulnerable to the slightest criticism."

"Wow." Everything he read fits Ruby Jade, except fragile self-esteem. I find it hard to believe such an iron-fisted leader has fragile, vulnerable self-esteem.

"People with those personalities need admiration and control," Kip says. "They crave attention and power. Life is all about them—and no one else. They want all the attention, and to obtain it, they become experts at manipulating people."

"How?" Mom's brow furrows.

"Get this." He leans toward us, warming to his topic. "You might be as surprised as I was to learn narcissistic leaders are charming, maybe even charismatic individuals.

They love-bomb people and make them feel special and welcome, that they're an integral part of a caring, loving community, one like none they've ever experienced. But once they suck people into their supposedly elite group, they use guilt, shame and peer pressure to dominate their followers. Right, Cassie?"

I run my fingers through my hair, considering what he just told us. "I hadn't thought about the process before, yet it's like you said, Kip. My experience started out positive and quickly went downhill. Ruby Jade is all about control. She uses all the tactics you mentioned and more to maintain control. Guilt, shame, fear, peer pressure, ostracism, punishment, threats. I've seen it all, including unpredictability. She can switch from nice to nasty in a nanosecond."

Dad grunts. "I got a taste of nasty earlier."

"Sorry about that, Dad."

"Don't be sorry. You're not responsible for her actions."

"I figured out something," Kip says. "Cults take..." He finger quotes. "'You are enough' out of culture. Get it?"

Mom and I shake our heads. Dad says, "Run it by us again."

"As you all know, culture is spelled c-u-l-t-u-r-e."

"Okay." Dad nods.

"Delete the ending." Kip slows his speech, like he's talking to children. "The U and the R and the E. Then add 'nough' and you get what cults are all about, telling people 'you–are–*not*–enough.'"

Mom groans. "Bit of a stretch, Kip."

I sit taller, grateful for a label for Ruby Jade as well as an explanation for her behavior. "You described the leader to a T, Kip. I don't know if her sidekicks are also narcissists or merely evil women out for the money she filters their way."

"The pastor controls the money?" Dad frowns. "It's not ethical."

"Nothing is ethical about that place."

"How so?" Mom asks.

A wasp lands on Kip's plate, and he flicks it away.

"It's, it's overwhelming." I clasp my hands in my lap. "I don't know where to begin, except to apologize for lying to you."

My parents pull back, foreheads creased.

"One lie led to another." I look down. "I didn't want to admit I hadn't started the program, didn't want to admit the program had folded, didn't want to tell you I only lasted a week at my first job." Raising my gaze to meet theirs, I add, "I was too ashamed."

"The program folded?" Mom looks confused. "Why did a judge—?"

"Maybe he didn't know. Maybe he did." I cross my legs and fold my arms. "But from what I hear, he does whatever Ruby Jade asks of him."

I start by telling them I was given a new name. But I don't mention that, according to Ruby Jade, my parents were ignorant when naming me and my name was "ill-chosen." From there, I give them an overview of life at FFOW, omitting the personal attacks, like being told my skin color is corrupted by Mom's Jamaican blood. And Inez saying Kip is too good-looking to be my brother, so he and I must be having an affair. I also don't mention my injured feet, the Vance incidents or Zachary's rescue. I want to give them an idea of my current world, but we don't have time for *all* the craziness.

What I do tell them is that after only working a week as a teacher's aide, I was moved to Ruby Jade's yard crew because I interrupted a child's cleanse, which was actually a false accusation followed by a beating. Before my family can ask the questions I see in their eyes, I summarize the cleanses I've experienced, Zachary's and mine. Mom, Dad and Kip are, of course, appalled, not only by the abusive practice, but by the notion anyone can accuse another person of an alleged sin or sins. And that confession is expected, even when evidence is absent.

Before we can dive too deeply into a humiliating subject I don't want to think about right now, I offer my most confident smile. "What was supposed to be a demotion has been a wonderful opportunity to work outdoors with a great boss and kind, supportive coworkers. Another huge plus happened when the rehab program reopened, and I was moved from the Pritchards' house to the dorm."

I thank Mom for sending my guitar and the box of clothing. "They were taken from me by Olivia Pritchard," I tell her, "but some friends just found them and put them in a safe place for me."

She frowns, and I'm quick to enlighten them on the evils of worldly clothing and guitars.

"So much more I could say." I spread my arms. "But I'll just add that the leaders do everything in their power to separate families. I doubt they'll return our cell phones anytime soon. I may be able to borrow a phone now and then, but don't be surprised if you don't hear from me for weeks or months at a time."

"This is a free country." Mom's eyes spark. "We should be able to see you and talk with you anytime we wish."

Dad and Kip grunt their agreement.

"It is what it is." I shrug and lift my palms. "I'm sorry to burden you with all this garbage when we so recently lost Grandma. Her passing is far more important than my troubles." Resting my hands on the chair arms, I add, "Mom and Dad, you're exhausted. I can see it in your faces. I'm afraid knowing all this about the Followers will make you worry more about me."

"I'm glad you told us," Mom says. "Guessing at what was going on with you was almost as difficult as not hearing from you when you were homeless. We were going nuts in our attempt to make sense of your phone calls—or lack thereof."

"Hey," Dad says, "speak for yourself."

Mom gives him a side glance. "Edward…"

He leans over to put his arm around her. "Well, yeah, I might have gotten a little perturbed."

"Whatever." She rolls her eyes. "But seriously, Cassie, we need to get you out of there. And report them to the authorities—"

I lift my chin. "Ruby Jade *owns* the authorities."

"So, how do you fight that?" she asks.

"I don't. My plan is to lay low and graduate in a year, which will complete my sentence. Then I'll leave the place. I don't plan to remain there a single minute after they hand me my certificate."

"We'll hire an attorney," Dad says, "a good attorney who can request a different judge."

"Thanks, Dad, but—"

Through the open patio door comes the sound of the doorbell.

Mom stands. "Women from church were supposed to bring food. It's probably them."

Dad glances at his watch. "Afternoon already. I had no idea." He rubs his jaw. "Before things heat up around here, Cassie, I'd like to share some thoughts about religious groups."

"Okay." I give him an encouraging smile.

"I'd like to hear what you have to say," Kip says, "unless you want me to greet the ladies with Mom and show my appreciation for the food."

"Yeah, Kip." I snicker. "I'm sure you'd kindly sample first and then declare your appreciation."

"Stick around." Dad chuckles. "You can sample later."

My brother plops his feet on the table, ankles crossed. "Shoot."

"A church can walk a straight path for years," Dad says, "teaching and following the Bible, loving God and loving people. And then a pastor or teacher comes along who leads the congregation onto a rabbit trail. Usually, it's a case of…" He finger quotes. "'Faith plus.' Faith plus good works, faith plus church attendance, faith plus rituals, faith plus putting money in the offering plate, faith plus keeping the Ten Commandments and conforming to all the dos and don'ts people dream up."

I think of Ruby Jade's endless list.

"Something in our self-centered psyches suggests we can earn brownie points with God," Dad says. "We think obeying rules or being so-called 'good people' will convince him to do what we want, whether it's granting us our desires here on earth or welcoming us into heaven. The problem with faith-plus is that it rejects the incredible gift Jesus gave mankind when he paid the penalty for our sins by dying on the cross in our place. Instead of accepting his amazing gift as is, we tack on other things to try to prove we're good enough, that we've done enough to please him and gain his favor."

"Okay." I nod. "Makes sense."

"Some groups practice faith plus prayers to saints," he continues. "Or faith plus door-to-door visitation, even faith plus euphoric experiences, dreams and visions. And then there's faith plus idolatry."

"Idolatry?" I ask.

"I'm not talking about bowing to a statue. I'm talking about worshipping ourselves based on the belief we can have it all, that we *deserve* to have abundance in our finances, our work, our relationships and our health. All we have to do to gain abundance is give more money, spend more time serving the ministry or organization, attend more seminars, study more of the group's teachings, confess more sins, pray more, meditate more, speak more affirmations, have more faith." He runs out of breath.

"Like in the New Testament," Kip says, "when Gentiles first became believers and Jewish Christians wanted them to be circumcised and follow Old Testament laws. That was faith-plus, not salvation by grace alone."

"Right." Dad nods his agreement. "On occasion, a belief system will devolve to the point that faith in Jesus is no longer a priority. The emphasis becomes good works, rules, money, rituals, positive thoughts, emotional highs, pleasing the leader. We start checking off boxes, conforming to a manmade standard, not living in God's grace. In essence, we transfer the glory that rightfully belongs to God to ourselves by striving to be exemplary individuals, even though we can never measure up to his holy perfection."

"In other words," I say, thinking of the Followers, "we might look good on the outside, but by focusing on ourselves, we miss the point of salvation, which is to change us on the inside."

"From what I've read," Kip says, "checking off boxes and blindly submitting to the head honcho can also happen in secular settings. Could be a neo-Nazi or other terrorist organization, a political movement, a self-help group, a multi-level marketing company, or even a corporation or a union. Underlings work hard and do whatever is asked of them, good or bad, to gain favor with those in charge."

I can hear women chatting in the kitchen. Grandma died less than twenty-four hours ago, but the church ladies have already prepared and delivered food for us and our guests. I'm glad Mom and Dad are in a loving church that takes good care of them.

"This isn't anything new," Dad continues. "Over the centuries, thousands of false spiritual movements have sprung up around the world. You've heard of several, I'm sure." He puts his hands behind his head and stretches. "Here in America, there's David Koresh and the Branch Davidians, Jim Jones and the People's Temple in Guyana, David Miscavige with the Church of Scientology. And we can't forget that guru who founded a town not far from here."

"You mean the guy with the Rolls Royce collection?" Kip asks.

"Yeah. A total of ninety-three, I heard." Dad sighs and shakes his head. "Some leaders forget they're shepherds whose purpose is to love, nurture and lead the sheep. Instead, they enlist the dogs of fear to drive the sheep where they want them to go, so they can, as the saying goes, fleece the flock. Whether for power, money or sex, or all three."

"What about your group?" Kip asks me.

I frown at him. "Like I said, Kip, it's not *my* group."

"I know, I know." He raises his palms. "I'm only wondering if any of what Dad said sounds familiar."

"All of it." I sigh. "I've been told that in the early days before Ruby Jade came along, it was a good church, a great church. But now..." I shrug. "You basically described the Faithful Followers of the Way, Dad."

"I'm sorry to hear that."

"Even the sex part?" Kip asks.

"All I know is the leader has some kind of sex hang-up or obsession." I tell them about the "keep your hands outside the covers" rule and how Followers are never to touch private parts, even while showering or bathing.

Kip grimaces. "Weird, really weird."

"Yeah," Dad says. "Someone has a loose screw."

"Worse yet," I tell them, "the leader separated my roommate from her husband for months because they were caught—on video camera—being intimate."

"What?" Dad, who'd been leaning back in his chair, flips forward, elbows out, hands on his thighs. "On camera? A married couple?"

"My bedroom in the Pritchards' house had a video camera in the ceiling corner."

He scowls. "That's invasion of privacy."

"Yeah, it's a strange feeling to know someone, probably a man, is watching your every move. My roommate and I had to be very discreet with what we said in our room, what we wore, where we dressed—that kind of thing."

"Why would anyone in their right mind—?" Dad shakes his head. "I thought I'd heard it all. Those people need to be reported to the authorities."

Kip slides his feet from the table to the cement. "You're right, Dad. "They should be reported."

"Like I said…" I start gathering the plates and forks. "When it comes to that particular church, the local authorities are deaf and blind. About cameras in bedrooms, I was told the purpose is to prevent kinkiness within the membership. But I have a feeling the overriding objective is to prevent closeness, to keep us from talking freely. We might unite and dethrone the FT."

"FT?" Kip raises an eyebrow.

"Fearsome Threesome."

"Ah, yes. I get it."

After the church ladies leave, Mom tells me she'd like to take me shopping. "Not because you or I need anything, but because we haven't shopped together in ages."

"When I first got out of jail," I tell her, "one of the church leaders took me on a whirlwind shopping trip to buy me shoes and clothes because I had none. The whole time, I kept thinking I'd rather be with you, Mom."

"That's so sweet." She hugs me.

"I'd love to shop with you, but you should rest before you get inundated with company."

She grins. "We'll call it shopping therapy and I'll be fine."

I doubt she'll be fine, but who am I to tell my mother she can't go shopping? "I'll get my purse."

Upstairs, I'm reaching for my purse on the window seat, when through the bedroom window I see a white car parked in front of my parents' house. I do a doubletake. The vehicle looks familiar, but I don't know why. Must be someone bringing more food.

The doorbell rings.

I grab the pink purse and am tripping down the stairs in my new outfit, when Dad opens the door.

"Hi," a perky voice says. "My name is Noreen Nystrom, and this is my husband—"

Noreen? I backstep up the stairs and out of sight. How did she know where to find me? My heart thumps. No wonder the car looks familiar. They rented a Lexus identical to the one she drives.

"We were in Portland for a pastors' conference." Noreen's voice drips honey. "And heard one of our church members was in the area. We decided to stop by for a little chat and to offer her a ride home."

I roll my eyes. *Little chat, my foot. Big harangue is more your style.* I doubt they were attending a pastors' conference. But if they were, what would be the topic? How pastors can fleece their flocks, as Dad described, so they can have all-expense-paid getaways from the gullible sheep?

"Don't know what you're talking about," Dad says, "but you have the wrong house."

Mom echoes, "Definitely the wrong house."

You tell 'em, Mom.

From my vantage point, I can see Kip position himself behind our parents, shoulders back, hands on his waist. I appreciate his not-so-subtle hint. When they mess with his parents—and his sister—they mess with him too.

"Cassandra Turner." Noreen is sounding a little less sure of herself. "She's here, right?"

"No." Mom is even more forceful. "There's no one here by that name."

"She has another name," Bruce says.

"Oh, right." Noreen's voice is bright. "It's, uh, it's not coming to me right now. Starts with a C. Ca…"

"Please," I whisper, "just go away."

Dad bellows, "You people are ridiculous. Get off our porch!"

I jerk and take another step back. I don't remember my mild-mannered father ever shifting from pleasant to angry so fast.

"I don't understand," Noreen says. "We only—"

"I'm calling the police." Dad slams the door so hard the house shakes.

Noreen's muffled shout comes to me in stereo, from downstairs and through the open window. "We'll see you heathens in court. You'll be sorry!"

I scurry to my bedroom window. Trailed by her husband, Noreen is marching toward the white car, high heels clomping. Her head is high and her shoulders rigid.

Did they think they could force me onto an airplane with them? I'll hear about this later. For now, I'm grateful they're leaving.

"Cassie," Dad calls. "You upstairs?"

"Be right there."

I dart from my room to the stairs and am halfway down when he says, "You hear that?" He has a phone in his hand.

"Yes."

"Do you know those people?"

"Yes. She's a member of the unholy trinity Kip talked about."

Kip and Mom are peering through the living room window. "They're in the car," Mom says. Her voice shakes.

"Two phone calls this morning from the so-called church." Dad's face is red and he's breathing hard. "And now this. What's going on, Cassie?"

"They're pulling away," Kip says. At the sound of squealing tires, he adds, "Didn't know such a big car could make such a fast U-turn. Hope she didn't clip a sprinkler head on the neighbor's lawn."

Mom steps away from the window. "Thank God, they're gone." Her face is pale.

I continue down the stairs. "To answer your question, Dad, I've heard the leader sends people to find those who exit the church and—"

"Cult." Kip scowls. "Call it a cult."

"Okay." My knees wobble and I grab the handrail. "They supposedly harass members who dare to leave. In my case, maybe they're afraid I won't go back, which is crazy. They know one judge ordered me to be in the TW program and another judge gave me limited time in Oregon."

Dad returns the phone to its base and drops into a recliner, looking more tired than ever. I hope he doesn't have a heart attack or a stroke. The enormity of what just happened hits me. I've put my family through so much. Will I ever get it right? I sit on a step, my forehead in my hands.

Staring at the carpeted steps below me, I apologize for burdening them with my problems when they have plenty of challenges of their own. "I should be helping you, Mom and Dad. Instead, I've disrupted your lives and desecrated Grandma's memory by dragging my weird world here."

"Not true," Dad says. "Those people came of their own accord, with their own agenda."

"Your father is right," Mom says.

I look up.

She's smiling. "This helps us understand your weird world a bit better, Cassie. But it's a temporary world. One of these days, you'll be back on your own two feet and freed from the weirdness." She comes over and grasps my shoulders. "After that rude intrusion, I need shopping therapy more than ever. How about you?"

We're sitting outside a coffee shop beneath a wide umbrella, enjoying the shade and sipping iced tea. I tell Mom I like her redecorated living room. "So much color." I search my brain for words to describe the effect. "It's vibrant and warm, cozy yet cool."

"Thank you. I had a lot of fun pulling it together." She stirs her tea with her straw. "Good word choices, by the way. I should hire you to help me write the magazine articles."

"I'd run out of words so fast." I wrinkle my nose. "I'll stick with songwriting."

"I won't argue with that. I love your songs." She tilts her head. "I noticed the Bible you bought at the bookstore was a King James Version. The one I sent to you is a more contemporary translation, which you once said you preferred. Did the church leader disapprove of it?"

"Beside the fact my Bible is still in the box you sent, the leaders are adamant the KJV is the *only* version to read. It's not my first choice, but I'm excited to have a Bible again."

She studies me for a moment. "Mind if I ask you a personal question?"

"Go for it. This is evidently my day to bare my soul."

CHAPTER FIVE

I wait for Mom's next question.

The skin between her eyebrows creases and she says, "Your teeth—"

I blink. Discussing my teeth is a big change of subject from talking about Bibles.

"They don't look the same as when we last visited you at the detention center. Have you had dental work done?"

Instantly, I'm in Noreen's car. Her snooty laughter rings in my ears along with her promise to make sure I remain a spinster forever. I quickly push the vile memory to the recesses of my mind and tell Mom the group is heavy into appearance.

"Noreen, the woman who came to the door earlier, drove me to a beauty shop for a cut and highlights right after she picked me up from jail. She's the one who took me clothes shopping and later to a dentist. He whitened my teeth and fixed the chipped ones."

"Was that included in the program?" she asks.

"I thought so until recently, when I learned I may have to pay everything back."

"How will you know the amount they charge you is accurate?"

"I won't."

A grape-soda scent wafts from a nearby purple iris cluster, infusing the patio with the flowers' fragrant charm. I've missed these sweet times with my beautiful mother at our favorite coffee shop.

Myrtle Mae's phone chimes, and I remove it from the pink purse. *Corban*. I smile and open the text.

Hope I'm not interrupting anything. I'm praying for you and your family. Just want you to know we saw the missing item this morning. The owner understands. Fed us strong coffee, still warm, and powerful brownies. See you soon.

I type a reply. *Glad to know the cook's efforts aren't going to waste.*

"Everything okay?" Mom asks.

"My friend says the car I borrowed to drive here was returned to the owner this morning. I knew the authorities didn't have a good reason to keep it, but because it wasn't my car, I felt responsible."

"I'm proud of you." Mom's eyes shine. "You've always been a responsible person."

"Well, except—"

"Except when you were blindsided by grief, and alcohol got a grip on you. But I can tell those days are over. You know how?"

I shake my head. Does my mother know something I don't know?

"Your eyes and skin are clear, like before Eric died. And your hair has regained its shine. The Bozeman group sounds terrible, yet you're your beautiful self again."

I hear Inez telling me I'm homely and quickly shove her irritating voice from my head. "Thanks, Mom. God, counseling and Celebrate Recovery's twelve-step program have all been a big help—and the fact I haven't had access to alcohol."

Elbows on the metal table, glass in her hands, Mom asks, "Do any of the strange aspects of the church—or cult, as Kip says—trigger a desire to drink?"

"Yes, all the time. Thank God I don't have money or a car, or I would have driven to the nearest bar by now." I move my glass to a shaded spot on the table. "Something cool happened when Kip surprised me on my birthday. We met at a restaurant that serves alcohol. I could smell it, but I didn't get the urge. Not once. I was so happy to see my brother, nothing else mattered."

"Wonderful, sweetie. We asked him to go, not only because your supervisor discouraged your dad and me from going, but because I had a feeling you needed to connect with family."

"Kip being his down-to-earth ornery self helped me so much. My mind was a whirlwind."

My phone dings again. This time, a picture of Myrtle Mae standing between Corban and Logan appears. All three are wearing sombreros, curly black mustaches and ponchos. The caption reads, *The Three Amigos Miss You*. Does Myrtle Mae have more costumes in her closet, or did the brothers come up with the idea?

Laughing, I show the photo to Mom, who says, "Very cute, but the woman is older than I would expect for one of your friends."

"Her name is Myrtle Mae. She lives in the yellow house in the background and owns the car in the carport. It's the car I borrowed to drive here. She also owns this phone. It has big buttons because she has macular degeneration."

"That's too bad, but how kind of her to lend you her phone when she might need it." She touches the screen. "Who are these good-looking young men?"

"They're the brothers who do the mowing where I work. Myrtle Mae's daughter is the church leader. She lives in a huge house at the front of the property and Myrtle Mae lives at the back. She's a gracious lady who likes to bake goodies for us and serve us tea."

"She sounds wonderful." Mom smiles. "I'd love to meet her."

"You would adore Myrtle Mae," I tell her. "You can't imagine how she and Sebastian and these two guys keep me grounded."

"Wait a minute. Her daughter is the leader, but she helps you?"

"She doesn't agree with what Ruby Jade is doing and only goes to the church to visit with her friends. And it was Ruby Jade who sent the highway patrol after me, not Myrtle Mae."

"What about these brothers? Are they in the group too?"

"Yes, but…" I lower my voice. "You might call them the resistance movement."

Mom lifts her eyebrows.

"You can't tell anyone but Dad and Kip."

"I understand."

Another text comes on the phone. I glance at it and grin. This time, the picture is of Corban by himself. His lip pooches, his shoulders and mustache droop. Beneath the photo is the caption *Lonesome Buckaroo.*

I'm still smiling when Mom says, "Can I see?"

I hesitate. My friendship with Corban has turned a corner, one so surprising I'm not sure I'm ready to face it myself, let alone tell my mother. However, what better person to talk with about our clandestine relationship?

I show her the picture.

Her forehead crinkles. "Lonesome for you?"

Flipping to the picture I took in the airport, like I've done so many times since I boarded the airplane, I revel in Corban's handsome features and broad smile. I'm amazed I was able to be alone with him for more than a few minutes. And I can still feel the warmth of his arms around me, my head on his solid shoulder, his strong fingers intertwined with mine. His kiss on my cheek.

I hand the phone to my mother. "Never in all my wildest dreams did I expect it to happen, Mom."

She glances from the picture to me.

"I think I'm falling for a guy again." I look into her dark eyes. "His name is Corban." Saying his name aloud triggers a grin I can't contain.

"Corban, huh." She frowns. "And he's in the church."

"Right.'

A moment ago, she was smiling at Corban's photo. I thought she'd hug me and tell me how excited she is to learn I've come to the point I can allow a new man into my life. After all, she's the one who told me God might not agree with my vow to never remarry.

She returns her attention to the picture. My guess is she's trying to come to terms with my unplanned confession.

Birds sing in the tree branches that overhang the coffee shop patio. A motorcycle rolls into the parking lot and rumbles to a stop. The smell of roasting coffee beans drifts across the patio.

"You said you met him at work." She studies me, her eyes wary and her eyebrows tight. "Which I assume means he goes to the church you attend—the cult. Am I correct, Cassie?"

"Yes, but as I said, he's not really one of them. Not in spirit, anyway. He's part of the resistance movement. Actually, as far as I know, he and his brother and parents *are* the resistance movement. They're planning to leave the group and want to take as many people as they can with them when they go."

She sets the phone on the table. "From what you've said, it's a miserable place to be. Yet, you seem happier than you've been in a long time. Is Corban the reason?"

I sip my tea and ponder how to best answer her question. "Right now, I'm happy to be here with you and Dad and Kip, out of jail and away from the Followers. And maybe I'm a little giddy due to this whatever it is with Corban. I thought something might be growing between the two of us. However, we didn't express our mutual feelings until yesterday.

"This relationship change is brand new, Mom, so new I hardly know what to think." I push my hair behind my ears. "I mean, yesterday was the first time we were alone, just us, something church leaders would frown on. Yet, it felt natural. We talked on the phone last night and we've been texting, though private communication among members is forbidden, especially for singles."

"Why wouldn't the leaders condone your friendship?" She appears mystified. "You haven't done anything wrong."

"Oh, yes, we have."

"What?"

I laugh at her shocked expression. "We were alone in a car and a restaurant without permission, unchaperoned for hours. Worse than that, our friendship was not authorized."

My mother's eyebrows rise.

"Ruby Jade is the one who puts couples together and decides when they marry, where they live, when they have kids, where they work, and on and on. Even—get this, Mom—how they fold their laundry and secure their garbage can lids."

"That's appalling." She makes a face.

"Yeah, I know." I fold my arms. "Just so you know, Corban and I cannot have an open relationship until I graduate from the rehab program and we both leave the church."

Mom frowns. "How old is he?"

"Thirty-one."

"And you're now twenty-nine. You're both of age and then some, yet your pastor thinks she has the power to decide your futures?"

"Not just us, but a couple thousand other people."

"That's some kind of power." She hands me the phone. "This Ruby Jade person sounds like a sadistic puppeteer. But you're not a puppet, Cassie. Never have been. And I'm sure others in the group aren't easily manipulated. How does she do it?"

I silently vow to remember Mom's words. *You're not a puppet, Cassie. Never have been.* The truth is, I've already let Leadership tug my strings and push my buttons more than I care to admit. "Ruby Jade's key control mechanism is to tell people they'll get cancer or die in a fiery accident and go to hell if they don't follow her rules."

"Do the members not read their Bibles? It would quickly clear up their confusion."

"Bible reading is discouraged."

"By a pastor?"

"By a pastor. The household leaders read two or three assigned verses to their households at breakfast, but that's the extent of Bible reading. No study or discussion is involved." I watch a hummingbird flit between an iris and the feeder that hangs from the coffee shop eave. "She also uses guilt and shame, as Kip said, plus public humiliation and false accusations."

I think of Arnold, the church founder who tried to rise from his wheelchair at Ruby Jade's command. When he collapsed, she kicked him out of the church. I picture her with her arms around my friend Marcela and her husband, Rodrigo, saying she loved them right after she trashed them and punished them for being intimate. And then there was Logan who could barely stand after an accident on a riding lawn mower. Instead of being offered sympathy by the leaders, he was chastised and told he had to pay for the repairs.

But I don't tell my mother about those incidents, which still make me cringe. They're revolting. I hate to honor the evil by speaking of it. Besides, Mom would come uncorked.

"If you stay—"

"I have to stay."

"Hear me out." She raises her palm. "If you stay with those people, this thing with Corban is doomed from the get-go, which was only yesterday. Logic says, if you can't be with him or communicate with him, what's the point? Why not keep your relationship at the friendship level?"

"You're right, Mom. This is like crushing on a guy, but you don't dare tell anybody, not even your best friend, 'cause your pie-in-the-sky dream is focused on the high school football captain. It's an impossible fantasy."

"Yet..." She studies my face. "No matter how impossible the fantasy, you believe Corban is worth the potential pitfalls."

"It's, uh..." I blush because she knows as well as I do my heart is already in too deep to backpedal. "It's not like I'll never see him or be around him. We'll still work together, at least until winter, and I'll see him at church—on the other side of the sanctuary. Single men and women sit on opposite sides."

"Oh, good grief."

A barista with beaded blonde dreads and a scraggly goatee walks out the coffee shop door and begins clearing empty tables.

Her gaze on the skinny twenty-something guy, Mom asks, "Does Corban know you were once married?"

"Yes."

"Good." She studies my face. "Has he ever been married?"

"Several years ago, he was engaged to someone who died suddenly. Pneumonia took her in less than a week. Her name was Shelby."

"How sad. It's one thing for your elderly grandparents to die, but young people like Eric and Shelby…" Mom shakes her head. "Losing a loved one is a common bond for you two. Have you had a chance to talk about it?"

"Briefly. I wanted him to know I understand."

"Do you have any idea how he reacted to his fiancée's death?"

I suspect what she's really asking is, *Did he go over the edge the way you did?*

"He told me he OD'd, but not on booze. I guess he about killed himself doing volunteer work for the church day and night, in addition to his day job."

"Exhausts me to think about it." Mom brushes hair from her face. "Is he past that now?"

"Yes, thanks to his mom, who said, 'Enough is enough' and sent him to counseling."

"Yay for moms." She grins. "Sometimes we have to tell it like it is."

"Yay for you, Mom." I squeeze her hand. "You're the best mom in the entire world. I'm so grateful for you and your patience with me through my ups and downs."

"My greatest gift and privilege in life has been to be your and Kip's mother. And because I'm your mother—"

She waits until a noisy truck passes before continuing. "Because I'm your mother, I have to say I am very concerned. Very concerned. Even if I wasn't the one who birthed you, Cassie, I'd be worried about you returning to what appears to be the devil's lair."

"Pray I can stay focused on the program this next year and fly under Leadership's radar. Pray I keep my mouth shut. As you know, that can be a challenge for me."

She chuckles. "I remember your junior high years. You didn't hesitate to share your opinions in class. Or in Sunday school."

"Sorry about all those times you had to meet me in the principal's office. But if I remember right, you usually agreed with what I said."

"I tried to hide it, but you'd pester me for an opinion until I had to confess." She laughs again. "Back to my concerns. I'm also nervous about your budding romance. Corban sounds like a nice guy, but as you said, it's an impossible situation. If the leader got wind of it, would she kick you out of the program and return you to jail? She sounds nasty enough to retaliate in some way."

"I wouldn't put it past her. However, if she kicked me out, she'd lose power over my life as well as program income from the state. I think she'd do what she did to my roommate and her husband. They can't be in the same room, not even during services."

Mom squints at me. "She separated a married couple?"

"I told Dad and Kip about them when you were with the church ladies. Marcela and Rodrigo were caught being intimate without permission."

Mom opens her mouth and then closes it. "I, I'm speechless."

"Yeah, I know. Hard to believe."

"With so many people in the church, how does she keep your friends apart? I mean, how does she micromanage such nonsense? I assume she doesn't want anyone to miss a service."

"Ruby Jade micromanages through her two sidekicks. You met Noreen. Inez is the other woman. They also have security people who keep tabs on everyone. As for church services, the sanctuary has a side room where those in the doghouse, so to speak, watch the proceedings on a screen. My roommate sits in the sanctuary, and the guy sits in the side room with all the other members who've broken rules or somehow offended Leadership."

"Oh, so they don't target one or two people now and then?"

"From what I've heard, the side room is always full."

"So disturbing." Mom rubs her temples. "My brain is on overload."

"Sorry."

"Don't be. I appreciate what you've told us, Cassie. Gives me a much better idea of the issues you're dealing with and how to pray for you."

"Just so you know, Corban and I have already talked about potential potholes in our relationship."

"Good."

"He brought it up yesterday, so it's not like we're walking into the swamp blindfolded."

Then, again, maybe we are.

CHAPTER SIX

The rest of the afternoon and early evening are spent greeting relatives at the Portland airport and driving them to Salem, directing people to and from hotels and feeding them the wonderful food the church ladies brought over. I'm glad Mom doesn't have to cook for everyone. Of course, she'd have plenty of help. Even so, we're quite a crowd.

After we eat, we squeeze into the few available cars and drive out to my grandparents' farm. The moment their two-story farmhouse comes into view, tears spring to my eyes. My cousin Natalie, who's seated beside me in the backseat, sniffs and dabs at her cheeks. "Since I got pregnant," she says, "I cry about everything, like seeing their house for the first time in ages."

Her husband, John, is on her other side. He puts his arm around her shoulders.

I don't have an excuse for my tears, other than the sad fact my grandparents won't be waiting for us at the front door. And that I let alcohol keep me from them these last few years.

Breaking into clusters of three or four, we wander through the musty-smelling house and then the yard as the

sun sets behind the hills. We share memories and laughter—
and pass around a tissue box. The corrals and the barn,
cleaned out long ago, are as empty as the house.

The guys round up weathered lumber from dismantled
sheds and fences and start a fire in the firepit Grandpa Hunt
built when I was small. Darkness descends. One by one, we
settle onto the benches that circle the pit.

Dad stands and shoves his hands into his back pockets.
"Thank you for coming all the way here to honor a very
special lady." Firelight flickers on his tired face.

Uncle Gabe adds, "A very unique lady."

"Unique, for sure," my youngest cousin, Tim, says. "I
used to tell my friends no one had a grandma like mine.
Anyone who met her always agreed."

"I didn't have to tell people my sister was cut from a
different cloth." Great-Aunt Sally adjusts her skirt over her
knee-high nylons. "It was obvious."

Everyone laughs.

Flames rise and fall. Old wood crackles and pops. Sparks
fly, flickering into a night sky salted with stars. The smell of
smoke brings memories of happy summer evenings hanging
out with my grandparents and other family members in this
very spot.

"I wanted to take a moment," Dad continues, "to say
how good it is to see each of you. We all live busy lives, but
let's make a point to gather once or twice a year. Just because
this farm is no longer occupied by people we loved and who
loved us doesn't mean we're no longer a family."

"A great family," Uncle Gabe adds.

John asks, "What's going to happen to the farm?"

Dad looks at Gabe, who says, "Neither Ed nor I have
the time or the means to care for a farm, but we hate to sell
it. What we'd really like is for someone in the family to bring
this place to life again. If you have any interest in living here
and putting in some crops, or other ideas, let us know."

His grandson, who's seated beside him, says, "I know what we can do, Grandpa."

Uncle Gabe looks down. "What's that, Tyler?"

"We can make a go-cart track and buy some go-carts. People would pay to race them. Except for us. We wouldn't pay, 'cause they'd belong to us."

"Hmm. Interesting idea." My uncle appears to be stifling laughter.

Slumped on a bench, Tyler's bored teen brother comes alive. "Yeah, and a paintball field." He sits tall. "It would bring in lots of money."

"And a climbing wall." Kip, of course, can't pass up the opportunity. "We could build it inside the barn and——"

Natalie grabs my arm. "Let's get out of here," she whispers. "The guys are gonna go nuts thinking of ways to make this a fun place for themselves."

I let her pull me into the kitchen, where she switches on the light and says, "Dad said the gas and water are still on, and the cupboards have some canned goods in them. Let's see if we can find stuff to make coffee and hot chocolate for everyone."

"Good idea. Hot drinks will go great with the goodies the church ladies made for us. I'm glad Mom thought to bring them with us." Several foil-covered pans sit side-by-side on the counter.

Something about being in Grandma's kitchen with its shiny white cupboards and yellow-and-white striped wallpaper soothes my soul. She may have left us, but her essence lingers, triggering sweet recollections of when Nat and I were young and carefree—and spoiled by our grandparents. I may be imagining it, but I smell fried chicken, warm bread straight out of the big gas oven and fresh-brewed coffee.

"I love doing this with you." Nat opens a cupboard door. "It's like old times when we'd spend the night with Grandma and Grandpa and help make breakfast in the morning. I can almost hear bacon sizzling. Makes me feel as if Grandma stepped out the door to feed the chickens and will walk back inside any minute now."

"Funny, I was thinking the same thing." I pull a box of powdered milk from the top cabinet. "Powdered milk will have to do for the hot chocolate because we don't have fresh milk."

"Nobody'll know the difference." Natalie finds a red Folgers can, peels back the plastic lid and sniffs. "Smells okay to me. Looks like enough for tonight."

Grandma's big pots are in a lower cupboard. I lift the three-gallon one to the sink and fill it with water. Nat helps me haul it to the stove, though I try to discourage her.

In typical Natalie style, she insists, "Just 'cause I'm pregnant doesn't mean I'm an invalid."

I light the double burner beneath the pot.

Nat says, "About what my brother said when everyone was in the barn, when he asked if this rehab program is working for you, I hope you weren't offended. I mean, he put you on the spot."

"No." I turn the burners high, straighten and blow out the match. "You're my family. You've prayed for me for years, and you know I'm in yet another program. Tim had a right to ask how it's going."

"Yeah, but he could have done it in private."

I laugh. "Definitely not Tim's style."

"You said it. We never have to wonder where he stands on an issue."

"It's a good trait, right?"

"Most of the time."

We read the backs of the boxes to get an idea of how much powdered milk, sugar and chocolate to use. Nat measures and I stir with a long wooden spoon. She sets the measuring cup on the counter. "How are you doing, really?

Is the program hard? Do you have lots of classes and counseling sessions?"

"No." I shake my head. "Not hard, just…" What can I say that won't trigger another round of questions? "Different."

She cocks her chin. "Different in what way? Strange rules? Weird people?"

Oops. Wrong word. I shrug and continue to stir the chocolate. "Different from the other programs I've tried, though they have their similarities."

Our grandparents' big blue enamelware coffeepot sits at the back of the stove. Nat takes it to the sink to rinse it and add water. Then she spoons grounds into the percolator basket and sets the coffeepot on a burner.

I jiggle the glass knob. "Remember how Grandpa claimed the *proper* method for making coffee was to percolate it?"

"He wouldn't drink it made any other way." She lights the burner. "I wonder how long we should—"

"Seems they perked their coffee for six or seven minutes, once it got going. They never let it boil."

"Oh, right. Boiling makes it bitter." Natalie glances at the rooster clock on the wall. A white cord runs from the clock down to an outlet.

I check my watch. The clock is right. Someone must have set it to daylight saving time. Probably Dad. I don't remember him ever missing a time change.

Soon, the percolator's mellow rhythm seeps into the kitchen. Natalie lowers the heat. Coffee and chocolate aromas swirl about our heads.

"Oh, Nat, isn't this wonderful?" I breathe deeply, doing my best to capture the perfect moment. "If I could, I'd bottle the sounds and smells and memories in this house to take with me the rest of my life."

"We're lucky to have this quiet time together. Just the two of us in Grandma's kitchen." Natalie spread her arms. "Almost feels sacred because once someone else moves in, it'll never smell or sound or look the same again."

"But we'll always have the memories."

"Hey!" Tyler barges into the kitchen. The screen door slams behind him. "Anything to eat in here?" He stops, eyes wide. "Do I smell what I think I smell?"

Right behind Tyler comes my dad. "Cassie," he says. "I need to talk with you. Let's step into the other room."

I hand the spoon to Natalie and follow him into the living room. "Everything okay, Dad?"

He leads me to the farthest corner beside the stone fireplace. "That church secretary called again while you were shopping with your mom."

"I'm sorry they keep hassling you, Dad. What do they want now?"

"She said the pastor needs to know what time your plane is scheduled to arrive in Bozeman, so she can pick you up."

"Pick me up? The woman who tried to stop me from coming here? The one who didn't offer to drive me to the airport when the judge gave me permission to travel? Now, she wants to give me a ride?" I shake my head. "I don't think so."

"I had a feeling that's how you'd react." Dad folds his arms. "Raised my dander too."

"What'd you tell Evelyn?"

"I told her it was not her concern."

"Uh-oh. Did she—?"

"She very kindly said, 'Our pastor wants to make sure Cassandra arrives home safely.'"

I roll my eyes. "Ruby Jade wouldn't give a plugged nickel for me, unless she could somehow benefit. Truth is, she can't stand to lose control of anyone or anything, especially money. All I am to her is income from the state of Montana—and free labor."

Blowing out a long breath, I brush hair from my face. "Sorry, Dad. After what they've put me through the last several days, I'm a tad bitter. Did Evelyn hang up?"

"Not until I told her your name is Cassie, not Cassandra, and you're quite capable of arranging your own transportation. She said, 'I'm sorry to hear you say that,' which was a strange response, and hung up."

"Poor Evelyn." I picture the cowed woman with her fearful eyes. Serving as the secretary and receptionist for the church *and* the school *and* the rehab program must be the worst job in the country. "Ruby Jade decides who works where, which means Evelyn can't quit. I wouldn't be surprised if one of these days she jumps off a cliff to escape her awful life."

He grimaces.

In the kitchen, Tyler is telling Natalie all about his go-cart idea, which is exactly what she was trying to avoid by leaving the firepit. Yet, I'm glad she's not listening to my conversation with Dad, which would generate endless questions. I'd rather not attempt to explain my off-kilter world to her.

"Cassie." Dad grasps my shoulders. "You're grown and able to handle your own affairs. However, as your father, I'm concerned about this so-called church and its so-called pastor and her sidekicks. Even if I wasn't your father, I'd be concerned. I don't think you should return to Montana. It's not a healthy place for—"

"I wish I could stay here, but if I don't go back, I'll be defying two judges' orders."

"I understand you have to stay with the program." He works his jaw from side to side, a sign he's thinking hard. "But once the dust settles here, your mother and I will hire an attorney to get you into a different rehab center."

I extricate myself from his grip and give him a quick hug. "You're too good to me. But please don't. Your money would be wasted. Judge Snow does whatever Ruby Jade wants. On the plus side, the Transformation Way director and addiction counselor are not Followers, which gives me hope for the program. Along with my boss, they have my back. I'll be fine."

He doesn't appear convinced.

"If I reach a point where life becomes intolerable, I'll find a way to let you know. Okay?"

"Is that a promise, Cassie?"

"It's a promise, Dad."

I'm excited to be in the hills again, enjoying a beautiful day with my brother and our cousins and their families. Before we left, Kip told me he'd try to stay in step with the group and not get ahead of us. I'm grateful because this is my first outing since the foot injuries, and Natalie is eight-months pregnant. She and I tend to talk a lot faster than we walk. When the trail narrows, we fall to the rear of the line.

"You don't have to go slow for me," she says. "I'll spoil your fun." She's using hiking poles, which she says help with her "belly-centric" equilibrium.

Tall and slender, she's been active in sports since junior high. When Aunt Sally told Nat she looks like she's six-months pregnant, not eight, Nat said, "The doctor says I'm at thirty-three weeks and the baby already weighs over four pounds."

And then she told her what I've heard her tell several people. "Our little one is the size of a butternut squash. Isn't that sweet?"

The women get it, but the guys' dubious expressions suggest they're wondering what's so sweet about squash. I giggle every time.

"I'm not like you and Kip," I tell her. "I'm out of shape and need to take it easy." I don't see any reason to explain my foot issues. If I told her I injured them, she'd ask how I hurt them, which would lead to more questions I don't care to answer.

"Besides, I always have fun with you, Nat. This gives us a chance to visit some more. And don't forget, I have your snacks." I'm wearing her waist pack because she no longer has a waist. The pack holds two water bottles and is stuffed with nuts, dried fruit and God only knows what else.

"Oh, right." She laughs. "You'd better stay close."

I fall in behind her. "What are your plans, once the baby is born? Will you continue to teach?"

"John and I are streamlining our finances so I can stay home with our little one. I adore my first-graders, but I plan to breastfeed and hate to disrupt it by returning to work." She's beginning to sound a little out of breath. "I want to be with our children while they're young. Everyone tells me they grow up fast."

I think of Candice, my housemate at the Pritchards' place, and wonder how many months or years have passed since she and Scott last saw their daughter. "You'll be a great mom, Nat. I know you will."

Three crows perched on the uppermost branches of a dead ponderosa pine stare down at us. They caw at the top of their lungs, apparently annoyed we've invaded their territory. Or, maybe they're saying, "Welcome, wingless creatures." Who knows?

"I'm a little nervous, but mostly, I'm excited," Natalie says. "You can be sure I'll bombard you with pictures." She glances at me over her shoulder. "Reminds me—now that you're in rehab, do you have an email address?"

"Not yet."

"I could send pictures in a text."

"I'd love to get pictures, but I don't have a phone."

"Oh, I thought I saw you with one last night."

"I borrowed one for the trip. But as long as I'm in the program, I won't have a computer or a phone." Knowing the Fearsome Threesome, they'll keep our phones the entire year.

"Really? Seems a bit stringent."

"Actually, I'm serving the last year of my sentence there. If you look at it as a step up from jail, it's not so bad. But still, I'll be glad to get it over with."

"I bet you will."

We hike in silence for a while. Ahead of us, the others are chatting and laughing. Dad is right. Our family needs to get together more often. We enjoy each other's company. I breathe deeply, inhaling the invigorating mountain air with its random hints of pine, mint and mushrooms.

After a bit, Nat says, "I've said it before, but I'm so sorry you lost Eric. He was a great guy. Smart, kind, talented, fun—everything a woman would want in a husband. If you don't mind me asking, are you doing better? Has your grief lessened?"

I think about her questions before I answer. "I'm still sad, very sad. Eric was all you said and more. I loved being married to him. About grief, I can't tell you whether or not it's any less. What I do know is it doesn't overwhelm me the way it did the first few years. Missing him no longer incapacitates me."

"That's good to hear." She stops. "I'd better rest."

We step into the shade and drink from the water bottles. A tapping sound reverberates above us. I peer up into the tree and spot a brown woodpecker hopping about the trunk, driving its long beak into the wood in its endless quest for bugs. "Look, Nat, a flicker."

Necks craned, we're ogling the industrious bird when John comes bouncing down the trail. "You and Snookums doing okay, Natalie?"

"We're both fine." By now, she's caught her breath. "Thanks for checking on us."

"The trail gets steeper after those big rocks." He points to a boulder stack. "Maybe we should turn back. I don't want you to overexert."

"So far, I'm feeling great. I'd like to see how far I can go." Natalie has always taken fitness seriously. Her consistent exercise is the only reason Kip let her come with us, along with the fact she promised to stop if the hike becomes too much for her.

"Don't worry, John." I give Nat's husband what I hope is a reassuring grin. "I'll stay with her. You can catch up with the others."

"Okay, but yell if you need me." He gives her a quick kiss on the lips and then kisses her belly. "Daddy'll see you soon, Snookums." Sending a wink my direction, he hurries away.

"You've got a winner there," I tell her. "Sorry I didn't make it to your wedding."

"He's a great guy and he'll be a good dad. I just hope he doesn't keep calling our baby Snookums."

I laugh. "Snookums is better than some of the names women I met in jail gave their kids." I almost say, *Children, that is.* But this isn't Follower territory. "Names like Phelony, spelled with a ph not an f."

"You've got to be kidding."

"The mom was totally serious. Said it was similar to 'symphony,' only different."

"Yeah, different, for sure."

We work our way onto the path again. Pushing aside a branch, I tell her to go ahead. "Another woman named her baby boy Jester."

"Like Chester?"

"Yes, but with a J. Then there was Moxie and Jammy and Atomic. The worst was Lucifer."

"How awful. What were they thinking?"

"The woman said she and her boyfriend wanted their kid to have a different name than other boys."

Natalie groans. "They could have made up something, anything. To give a boy such an evil name is branding him from birth."

"Maybe they'll use a nickname."

"Like what? Luci?"

"You're right." I laugh. "Nickname options are limited. When he's older, maybe he'll try for a positive spin and call himself Lucky."

She raises her fist in a thumbs-up. "Nice. And if he's smart, he'll have his name legally changed the instant he turns eighteen."

At the big boulders John pointed out, Natalie stops for a breath. "Not only does hiking with this extra weight take my breath away, Snookums bounces my bladder with every step." She sets her poles against the boulder. "Be right back. Gotta find a bush."

Stepping around a boulder twice my height, I check to see what awaits us on the trail ahead. When Nat returns, I tell her, "John wasn't exaggerating. We've got some climbing to do. Are you up to it?"

"Give me another minute."

CHAPTER SEVEN

Leaning with my back against the rough rock surface, I close my eyes and breathe in the satisfying scent of warm pine needles. "Sunshine on my face and my favorite cousin at my side. What could be better?"

"Only one thing," Nat says.

"What's that?"

"If our baby were here, I could share him or her with you."

"Sweet of you to think of me."

"It'll be at least a year before I see you again, Cassie."

"I'll come visit your little family as soon as I'm free to travel." I look over at her. "I'm surprised you don't know your baby's gender yet."

"The doctor offered to tell us, based on the ultrasounds, but we said we'd rather not know until the big day. My mother, on the other hand…" She snickers. "She's anxious to shop for baby clothes and blankets, and she wants to help me decorate the nursery. I told her primary colors will work for the nursery, no matter the gender."

"Gonna be a long few weeks for her." I laugh and push away from the rock. "Ready? We shouldn't get too far behind."

When we're moving again, I ask if they've chosen names.

"We've tried, but it's hard. I run across a lot of cute names at school, and I love them all. John, on the other hand, is more practical than I am. The silly man insists we narrow the list to five possibilities for first names, male and female, and five for middle names. When Snookums makes his or her grand appearance, we're trusting the perfect combination will be obvious."

Within minutes, we're both huffing and puffing. But Natalie plows ahead. From behind, I can tell she's slowing, which is a good thing. My feet are beginning to object. I spy an outcropping up ahead and call, "Nat, stop at those big rocks. Don't know about you, but I could use a sit-down break."

"Sit down, nothin'. I'd go for a lay-down break."

When we near the granite stack, both of us are breathing hard, so I'm astounded when she says, "We'll be able to look out over the valley if we climb on top the rocks."

"Are you sure you should do that?" She's always been an intrepid daredevil, but now she's eight-months pregnant. And now, I'm responsible for her well-being.

She hands me her poles. "It'll be an easy climb and a great place to enjoy the view while we have a snack. I'm always hungry these days, so I packed lots of goodies."

Pregnancy has not dampened her enthusiasm for adventure or for food. "Okay." I place the poles at the base of the boulder she's about to tackle. "But you can be sure I'll tell John this was your idea, not mine."

By the time I straighten, she's already found a foothold in the rock and is about to clamor on top. I'm raising my arms to steady her, when she screams and falls backward, slamming me to the ground. Instinctively, I wrap my arms around her, and together we bounce and slide down the hill, faster and faster until we stop with a whump that knocks the air from my lungs.

Darkness envelopes me. When I come to a short time later—at least it feels like a short time—something prickly is stabbing my back and something heavy is on my chest and my arm. I can't see anything.

Fighting for a breath, I hear a ragged intake of air and realize Natalie is on top of me. No wonder I can barely breathe. "Nat, are you..." My words come in a hoarse whisper. "All right?"

"Yes." She draws another uneven breath. "You?"

"I think so. Can you tell if the baby is—?"

"Natalie!" John's voice.

Thank God. He'll pull her off me and get her to a hospital to make sure the baby wasn't injured. We bumped over several hard objects. Whether they were rocks or branches, I don't know.

"Over here, John."

"What in the world, Nat? I heard you scream."

A muffled scrabbling is followed by heavy breathing. "Where's Cassie?"

"Underneath me."

"I see her legs." He's closer now. "You two okay? Anything broken?"

"I don't know." She sucks in air. "Give me your hand. I need something to grab onto."

With my cheek against the ground, I feel more than hear pounding footsteps. Familiar voices call, "Natalie! What happened?"

"Where's Cassie?"

"John, is she okay?"

Someone skids to a stop near our heads, pummeling us with gravel. I squeeze my eyes closed.

"Hey, everyone!" Sounds like Tyler. "Aunt Natty is hurt!"

"Get back, Tyler," his mother says. "Stay out of the way."

"Lift Nat by her left arm." Kip's voice. "I'll grab the other. Make sure your footing is good."

My brother is here, thank God. He'll know what to do.

The pressure on my chest and arm eases, and I can breathe. My first deep breath draws in dust spiced with a cinnamon-like scent. I cough and look above me. We're in a buckbrush bush. I recognize the aromatic leaves, though the undersides aren't as shiny as the tops. I've always loved the smell, but right now, I can't wait to get out of this hollow.

Extricating pregnant Natalie from beneath the bush takes a team effort. With the help of the other guys, John and Kip hoist her out and set her on a log shaded by a big pine tree.

I'm trying to crawl from the depression and others are reaching to help, when my brother hurries back to me. His hand is the one I take. After a bit of floundering in the dirt, I'm finally upright and on my feet again.

Kip walks me to the log, helps me sit and then kneels in front of me. "Let's check out the damage, Sis." He looks me over, front and back. "Cough."

"Why?" I ask.

"Just do it."

I cough.

"Did that hurt?"

"No."

"Good. You probably didn't crack any ribs." He has me move my arms and hands and legs. "Can you wiggle your toes?"

"Yes. Forget about me, Kip. We need to get Natalie to a hospital to make sure the baby is okay."

He turns to her.

"I'm fine." Natalie says. "Just a bit shaken." Her mouth drops open. "Your arms, Cassie, they're all bloody. And your face…" Tears well in her eyes. "I'm so sorry. It's my fault."

"No, I should have stopped you." Her bare arms are scratched and bleeding, the same as mine.

"What happened?" Kip glances from me to Nat.

"I wanted to climb those boulders," Natalie says, "so we could enjoy the view while we ate a snack."

"What?" John's wide-eyed expression is a mixture of anger and horror. "You fell off those rocks?" He reaches for his phone. "I'm calling 911."

"I said I wanted to climb them. But I didn't because when I started up the first boulder, I came face to face with—" She shudders. "Eyes. Black beady eyes. Less than a foot away. An animal was staring at me from a crevice in the rocks."

"Eww," someone says.

"Exactly."

"So that's why you yelled." I'd already forgotten about her scream.

"I'm glad you hollered," John says. "Otherwise, we wouldn't have known anything was wrong and we might never have found you."

"What was it?" Kip, ever the curious one, asks.

"I have no idea." She frowns. "All I know is it scared me, and I lost my balance and fell on top of poor Cassie. And then down the mountain we rolled."

By now, Nat's brothers, Dave and Tim, and their families have surrounded our log.

"Hey, take a look at this." Tim walks over to examine the wide swath of displaced dirt and pine needles. "Looks like you two skidded all the way into the bush down there. Must be thirty, forty feet."

"Nat." I touch her back. "Notice the rocks and bumps along the way? We hit every one of them. You should go to a hospital to make sure you and the baby are okay."

"I agree." John pats Nat's tummy. "Snookums and I agree."

I avoid eye contact with the others but can't miss Kip's eyebrow twitch. He doesn't laugh, an amazing feat of self-control. Any other time, he would have given John a hard time.

"You both need to go to the ER," Kip says. "Or a doc-in-the-box. You have dirt in your scrapes and God only knows what else. Leaves, pebbles, mouse droppings, snake feces—"

"Kip, stop it." I glare at him. "Not funny."

"It's true. Medical professionals should clean your wounds, so they don't get infected."

I groan. After what the Bozeman ER staff did to my feet when I trashed them running barefoot to get help for an abused child, I dread enduring such torture again. And I'm struck by the fact this will be my fourth "cleanse" in recent days. First, the hospital foot scrub and then the two Follower scream-spit sessions—hard to say which is worse—and now this.

"I don't have health insurance, Kip. I'll wash at home." Something drips onto my cheek. I blink and look up. "What was that?"

"You're bleeding." Kip pulls a bandana from his back pocket, folds it small and carefully places it on my forehead. "Hold this."

I press my hand against the cloth.

"Ohh…" Natalie moans and grabs her abdomen.

"Natalie?" John wraps an arm around her shoulders.

Eyes closed, head lowered, she's breathing hard and doesn't respond.

"Kip." I poke my brother. "Call 911. Now." During my street days, I saw a girl go into early labor in an abandoned garage where we were spending the night. The baby didn't survive. Early labor may not be what's happening to Snookums, but we shouldn't chance it.

Kip yanks his phone from the clip on his belt, swipes at the screen and studies it for a second. "Got a signal, thank God." With quick taps, he punches in the number and turns to the others. "This would be a good time to pray."

I nod, grateful to be part of a praying family.

Phone at his ear, he says, "Yes, this is an emergency, a medical emergency. We're hiking and have a pregnant woman with us. Along with another woman, she fell off a boulder and rolled downhill." He pauses. "Yes, they're both conscious and sitting upright. No obvious serious injuries, but the pregnant one is groaning and hugging her belly."

He listens for a moment and then looks at John, who's focused on Nat. "How many months pregnant is Natalie?"

When John doesn't respond, I answer for him. "Eight months."

Kip repeats the information into the phone and glances at me. "First baby, right?"

"Yes."

Head down, Nat groans, whimpers and then groans some more.

Nat's sisters-in-law, Lori and Paula, tell the others to move out of the way. Lori kneels in front of Nat, and Paula crouches behind her, rubbing her back.

Natalie raises her head. Her face is pale, but she doesn't appear quite as white as she did. "It's better. Doesn't hurt as much. I'm okay, really." Her half-smile is not convincing.

I whisper to Kip, "Don't listen to her."

"She says she's okay now," Kip says into the phone. "But she was in a lot of pain a moment ago."

"Tell us about the pain," Lori says. "Can you describe what you were feeling?"

Kip steps away. He's telling the 911 dispatcher what trail we're on and our approximate location. I'm glad he knows where we are and isn't too rattled to communicate clearly.

"My back started hurting, the worst backache ever." Natalie squints, reliving the experience, and places her hands on her back. "And then it was like the pain went to the front and grabbed my stomach."

She slides her hands around her belly. "It got really hard, rock hard. I felt something pushing on my—" She stops, hands resting on her abdomen. "Was it a contraction? It's too early."

Lori takes her hands. "We can't be sure what's happening, Nat. But it's possible you experienced a contraction."

Behind Natalie, Paula nods. Apparently, it was more than a "possible" contraction.

"What should we do?" John asks. "We can't just sit here and—"

"We should stay calm." Lori's voice is firm. "The paramedics will—"

Kip turns around. "They're on the way, lifting off now. Be here in less than twenty minutes."

I can tell the others are as relieved as I am. Although she's regained some color, Nat doesn't look good. Something is off. Her hands are on her stomach again. I don't know if she feels pain or if she's unconsciously protecting the baby.

John pulls her close and whispers in her ear.

She responds with a weak smile.

"If they can't land on the ledge up there," Kip says, "they'll try for somewhere nearby. Pray they find a good spot." He pulls a portable charger from his pocket and plugs it into his phone. "Guys, let's climb onto those rocks, so they can see us."

I watch my brother walk up the hill with Dave and Tim, remembering how I used to call him bossy. Today, I'm more than grateful for my brother's unruffled take-charge demeanor. Hearing unfamiliar voices, I glance around. Several more hikers have joined my nieces and nephews in the shade on the other side of the trail.

"Ohh, ouch." Natalie bends over her abdomen. Her face reddens.

Paula and Lori eye each other. Lori turns to John, who's now as white as Nat was, and calls his name.

He's watching his wife and doesn't respond.

"John," she repeats, her voice more forceful. "We need your help."

Blinking, he gawks at her.

"You have a watch."

He extends his arm, a surprised expression on his face, like he forgot he has a watch.

"We need to time the contractions. The instant this one subsides, start counting minutes. Got it?"

Natalie's moans are beginning to sound more like sobs.

John shakes his head.

"You can do both," Lori says. "You can support Nat and monitor her contractions."

"Maybe…"

"Have you two attended birthing classes yet?"

"Had the first one last week."

"Did you learn about breathing?"

"Yes."

"Good."

She puts her palms on Nat's cheeks. "Nat, honey, breathe with me and John." She draws in a long, slow breath. John does the same.

Eyes half open, Nat tries to follow, but she doesn't breathe deeply.

Lori takes Nat's hands. "Blow it out and let's do it again."

This time, they're more in sync and Nat seems less frantic.

Kip comes running down the hill, phone at his ear. "Dispatch switched us over to the Life Flight paramedics. They're asking if she's had any more contractions."

"Yes," I tell him. "She's in the middle of one right now."

Nat's ear-piercing scream shatters the hushed whispers around us. Even the birds stop singing. "I need to push," she cries. "I have to push. I can't stop!" Her eyes are wide and beads of sweat appear on her forehead.

"Breathe through it," Lori whispers. "Breathe through it."

Paula murmurs, "Hold tight," and rubs her back.

Nat clutches John's arm. "I can't do it, John. I can't."

"Yes, you can. Focus on your breathing, sweetheart. That's your job right now."

"John." Lori touches his arm. "Good help with the breathing. Don't forget to time the contractions. The paramedics will want to know how far apart they are." She turns to Nat. "Breathe in, slowly now."

Kip settles beside me on the log. I can hear a female voice on his phone asking if we have a blanket or a towel or even a jacket Nat can lie on. Kip says he has a solar blanket in his backpack. The person on the other end tells him to put it on the flattest ground he can find and place Nat on it.

"Hang on," Kip says. "Gotta get it out." He hands me the phone with the charger, stands and pulls a small silver packet from a side pouch on his backpack. Unfurling the foil, he spreads the paper-thin sheet on the other side of the log.

Nat releases a long breath and drops her head. She looks exhausted. I have a feeling the ordeal has only just begun.

But maybe the medics can give her something to stop the contractions.

"Now, John." Lori taps his watch. "Count the minutes before the next contraction."

He lifts his wrist, his gaze on his watch as if Nat's life depends on his timekeeping. And maybe it does.

"You there?" The question comes from Kip's phone. Despite the helicopter noise, the woman's voice is distinct.

CHAPTER EIGHT

I place the phone against my ear. "This is Cassie. I'm sitting near Natalie. She's the pregnant one."

"This is Flight Nurse Shirley. Is she on the blanket?"

"Not yet. She just now finished a contraction."

"Get her on the blanket immediately and remove her pants and underwear."

"I'll pass the word." I turn to the others. "Put Nat on the blanket, fast, and remove her pants and underwear."

Kip's eyes pop wide. "I'm outa here." He aims his thumb at the ledge. "I'll be on the rocks if you need me." Jogging up the hill, he waves his hands at the onlookers. "Move away. Give her some privacy. And keep praying."

John and the sisters-in-law help Nat to her feet and guide her to the other side of the log. She looks dazed.

"Prop her head on a backpack or a log, or even a rock," the nurse says. "With some padding, if you have it."

"What about covering her?" I ask.

"Drape the pants across her legs. If the baby comes, we'll need to be able to get to him or her without anything in the way."

"Got it." I tell the others what we're supposed to do. They settle Nat on the foil and Lori helps her take off her shoes and pants. Paula rolls a short, fat branch over, unties a sweat jacket from around her own waist, folds it and places it on the branch.

Oh, God, I pray, *please keep the baby inside Nat, where it's safe. This isn't a good time or place for it to be born. I know you know that, but...*

Almost as soon as Nat lays her head on the branch, she jerks upright, yelling, "It's coming, it's coming!" She grabs her thighs. "I know it is."

"Two-and-a-half minutes," John says. His brow furrows. "Not very long."

We all stare at each other.

"Help me, God!" Nat yells.

"John, sit behind her," Lori says, "and support her, so she doesn't injure herself."

John plops onto the jacket and steadies Nat with his hands and knees. Sweat stains his shirt. We're all hot and sweaty from the hike—and now the stress.

Hearing a voice on the phone, I stand, wobble while my head clears, and step away. "Sorry, I couldn't hear you."

"I heard her yell." Shirley's voice is calm. Could be she deals with agitated moms and early deliveries every day. "We're still nine minutes out, Cassie. Have someone position themselves to catch the baby. If delivery occurs before we touch down, we'll provide guidance."

I relay her words, talking above Nat's moans. She's still bent over her belly, knees high, feet planted on the solar blanket.

Lori and Paula eye each other. "We'll do it together," Lori says.

Paula grimaces. "I hope we don't—"

"How about rubbing her feet?" John suggests. "It might calm her." He murmurs into Natalie's hair. "You love it when I rub your feet, don't you, hon?"

"Is it safe, considering trigger points and all?" Paula asks.

"I'll check." I ask Shirley about rubbing Nat's feet, and she says, "Is your phone on speaker?"

"No."

"Put it on speaker, so you don't have to relay information. Things may start moving fast."

I touch the speaker icon and tell her to go ahead. "Ladies," she says, "experts disagree on whether or not foot-rubbing can induce or affect labor. To be on the safe side, let's not do it. Is she in the shade or the sun?"

"We have plenty of shade," I say. "No sun on her."

Nat falls against John, panting.

I tell Shirley the contraction is over.

"I'd like to talk with Natalie."

"Just a minute." I hear the helicopter in the distance. They're almost here, thank God. I walk around the log. Nat is breathing hard. "Can you talk, Nat?"

"No!" She lurches upright. "The baby. It's moving. I, I gotta push! Oh, God, help me."

"Breathe," Lori orders. "Breathe."

"I can't stop the baby. It's coming."

We all pant with her.

Shirley tells me to move in front of Nat's legs, so whoever is catching the baby is sure to hear her voice. She asks for the others' names and then says, "Gently spread Natalie's legs, Lori—doesn't have to be far—and tell me what you see."

"I see..." Lori leans in. "Oh, her water just broke." Liquid puddles on the foil and around Lori's denim-covered knees.

"We need to get the baby out of there," Shirley says. "Pushing is okay. As soon as he or she is born, lift the mom's shirt and place the infant on her bare skin, head to the side. Cover the child with an additional shirt or jacket, if one is available. The baby must be kept warm."

The only extra piece of clothing I spy is the jacket John's sitting on. "Hand me that jacket beneath you, John." I toss the bloody bandana aside and extend my hand.

He raises as much as he is able with Nat's weight on him, slips the jacket off the branch and gives it to me.

I shake it, dislodging pine needles and bark chunks.

"Now, it's coming now!" Nat cries. "I feel it. Oh, God."

"Is the baby crowning?" Shirley asks.

"Yes," Lori says. "I see the head."

The helicopter is close enough I feel the whump-whump of its rotors and look up the hill. Just when it appears about to land, it pulls away.

I stare in horror. *Come back. Please come back.*

"Our pilot sees what he hopes is a better touchdown location a short distance up the mountain," Shirley says. "It's near the trail. We'll disembark soon and be right there."

Kip calls to me, "Any idea why they left?"

I put the phone behind my back and shout, "They have a better landing spot higher on the mountain."

He gives me a thumbs-up, and I move the phone in front again.

What's the baby's status now?" Shirley asks.

"The head is coming." Lori positions her hands at Nat's hips, palms up. "Almost out."

"Face up, down or to the side?"

The entire head emerges, and I tell Shirley, "To the side." I don't know much about babies, but this one's head seems super small.

"Perfect. Can you see the neck?"

"It's so tiny—"

"How about the cord? Is it free of the baby's neck?"

"Yes," Lori breathes. "Thank God." She cradles the head with her hands.

Paula squeezes Nat's arm. "How you doin', sweetie?"

"Tired, I'm really tired." Her eyelids are barely open.

John massages her shoulders.

"What did she say?" Shirley asks.

"She's really tired."

"Give her a sip of water and have her push again."

I pull a water bottle from the pack still attached to my waist and hand it to John. He opens it and helps Nat sip from it.

"Nat, you can't stop now," Lori says. "A couple more pushes, this baby will pop right out. Take a big breath with me, and let's do it another time."

Nat groans and bears down with all she has. And just like that, the baby is in Lori's hands, a human being so small its torso fits in her palms.

"The baby's here," Lori cries. She seems astonished, as if she has no idea how it happened. "I forget. What do we do next?"

The sound of rotors comes through the phone, muffling Shirley's voice. "Mother's belly, fast, face to the side. Cover immediately." And then she apparently speaks to someone with her. "Thank God, it's a warm day."

"Is…?" Nat doesn't finish her question.

I know what she's asking, and I assure her the baby is fine. It's skinny, but I can tell it's alive, unlike the one born in the garage.

Paula raises Nat's shirt, and Lori places the baby on her stomach. The cord trails behind. I carefully lay the sweat jacket over the miniature child, leaving the tiny head and one flailing forearm exposed. The baby could fit into one of the sleeves with plenty of room to spare.

"Quick. Is the child breathing?" Shirley asks.

Paula holds a knuckle in front of the baby's impossibly small nostrils and rests her free hand on the newborn's back. "I feel air and rib movement."

"Wonderful!" Shirley sounds relieved. "The face is to the side, right, so fluids can drain from the mouth?"

I answer this time. "Yes."

She asks, "How does the baby look?"

Not being a baby expert, all I can say is, "Tiny, wrinkled, messy."

"Coloring?"

"Hard to say, maybe grayish-beige or kind of a bluish-pink."

"Movement?"

"Yes, at least one arm is moving."

"Excellent."

John squeezes Nat's shoulders. "Snookums is doing good, honey."

Shirley murmurs something about hemorrhage to someone and then comes on again. "Ladies, we're about to land. Do a quick test for us. I need you to poke or pinch the baby or slap the feet and tell me what happens."

Paula pulls away. "I can't."

Lori, who's still stationed between Nat's legs, lifts the coat and flicks a tiny foot.

The baby jerks, grimaces and lets out a cry that sounds more like a baby crow than a baby human.

"Hey, little one." Nat pats Snookum's cloth-covered back with careful, cautious taps. "Don't cry. Mommy's right here."

The baby opens an eye and looks up at her, obviously recognizing her voice.

Tears drip down her cheeks. "You're going to be okay, Snookums."

I hope so. Snookums is so scrawny.

"We want to hear good hearty cries," Shirley says. "Pat the skin dry with the cloth, maybe even jostle the baby a little bit. But leave the umbilical cord intact. It's still providing nourishment. We'll suction the mouth and deal with the cord and placenta when we get there."

"Uh-oh." Lori stares at Paula. "I forgot about the placenta."

"We landed and are on our way," Shirley yells over the rotor noises. "Be there in a jiffy." Her breath puffs into the phone. "Drying the child is very important."

Rotor sounds recede and all I hear is Shirley's breathing. I'm grateful they're hurrying.

Nat turns her head. "Set me up, John, so I can dry our little one."

He helps her sit a little higher and then tilts toward the baby. "Hey, Snookums, welcome to the world."

The baby's incredibly small hand flutters—and so does my heart. Snookums is either responding to John's voice or to the crazy nickname.

"Did anyone check whether this pint-size person is a boy or a girl?" John asks.

We look at each other and laugh for the first time in what feels like hours. "Whoops." Lori grins. "Minor detail."

Hearing the sound of pounding feet, I glance at the trail. Two paramedics with all their paraphernalia are bounding down the slope. A man and a woman. I don't believe I've ever been so relieved to see total strangers. Actually, by now, I feel like Flight Nurse Shirley is a good friend.

The moment I end the phone connection, my knees give out. I plop onto the log, head swimming and ears ringing. A headache I hadn't noticed before is pounding behind my eyes. And every scrape and bruise on my body is on fire.

Kip jumps from the overlook to meet the emergency crew. "Over there, in the trees." But he doesn't come any closer. And neither do the other bystanders.

The paramedics slow to a trot. They appear to be assessing the situation as they approach.

I wave them over. "Thank you for coming."

John nods. "Yes, thank you." He's been encouraging Nat all along, yet he has a terrified expression in his eyes.

Lori stands, wipes her hands on her stained jeans and steps away.

The newcomers set their gear down, drop to their knees and slip on exam gloves. The guy introduces himself as Nicholas. The first thing Shirley does is swaddle the baby in the jacket and place the tiny bundle in Nat's arms.

"Oh, baby," Nat smiles at the newborn. "You're so beautiful."

John looks over her shoulder. He frowns. "And small."

Paula, Lori and I move to the other side of the log. Lori whispers, "Keep praying. They're not out of the woods yet."

I kneel on the ground beside the log, not to pray, although I am praying, but because I'm not sure I can stand. I open a water bottle, swallow a long drink and feel a bit better.

Shirley and Nicholas check vitals, both Nat's and the baby's, reassuring and comforting the little family with soft gentle voices. Shirley attaches an IV tube to the back of Nat's hand, while Nicholas slips a small needle beneath the baby's scalp and hooks tubing to it.

I cringe. But when Snookum's tiny arms wave, the medics say it's a good sign. Even so, I hate for the baby to suffer. Once our rescuers are satisfied with their work, they check the drips and hand the IV bags to John to hold.

"Nice job, ladies." Shirley glances at us. "You helped this dear family through an unexpected delivery."

"We couldn't have done it without you," Paula says.

When Lori doesn't respond, I peek up at her. Tears are streaming down her face. This has been an emotional experience for all of us, but I know she's worried about both Nat and the baby.

Shirley pulls out a tiny white knit hat and gently slips it onto the baby's head, over the forehead tubing and then over the ears. Next, she takes a blue rubber bulb syringe from her kit and suctions the baby's mouth. When it lets out a little peep of a cry, she says, "Hey, little girl, you can do better than that." She taps the feet bottoms, and the baby cries louder.

"Little girl?" Nat leans her head against John's chest. "We have a little girl, Johnny. Did you hear her sweet cry?"

"Wow." He grins. "I, I don't have words—"

"No one told you?" Shirley smiles at them but goes right back to tending the baby.

"We didn't check," Lori says. She sniffs and wipes her cheeks with the backs of her hands. "We were too focused on following your instructions."

"Because you did as Shirley directed," Nicholas says, "this child has a fighting chance at life."

John's smile fades. "Fighting chance?"

"We can't put on the party hats quite yet. Aftercare is extremely important for both your baby and your wife. The sooner we transport them to the hospital, the better."

Nat's abdomen puckers. "That felt like a contraction." She grabs Shirley's arm. "Does it mean another baby?"

John's mouth drops and his eyes grow big.

Nicholas touches Natalie's leg. "You're about to deliver the placenta."

"Oh." She releases her grip on Shirley. "Do I just let it happen?"

"Nope." He chuckles. "You have more work to do. Won't take long."

Shirley lifts the jacket-wrapped baby from Nat's abdomen and sits back. The cord is still attached.

Positioning himself at Nat's feet, Nicholas has Nat massage her abdomen for maybe half a minute. Then he tells her to bear down. "Massage and pushing help speed the delivery time, which is crucial right now."

The ringing in my ears has grown louder, and my headache is now so bad and all-encompassing I have a hard time seeing. Come to think of it, I don't have to see. Nat doesn't need me any longer. The coppery smell of blood fills my senses along with an earthy aroma I remember from the garage birth.

I unclip the snack-filled pack from my waist and place it on the log. Blowing out a long breath, I close my eyes and lay my head on the bumpy pack. Shutting out the sunshine is as satisfying as sliding between silk sheets. The last thing I hear is Nicholas saying, "Blood loss appears normal."

And Lori whispering, "Thank God."

Almost as soon as I close my eyes, or so it seems, someone is shaking me. "Cassie! Wake up! You can't sleep now."

"Why not?" I mumble.

"Open your eyes." The voice belongs to Nicholas, the paramedic. "I need to check for a possible concussion."

I squint at him. "I can't. It's too bright."

"Can someone please come shade this woman while I examine her?"

A shadow comes over us. I feel its coolness and the glare on the other side of my eyelids diminishes.

"I'm her brother, Kip."

Hearing my brother's voice assures me all is well. I can go back to sleep.

But a tap on my shoulder rouses me. "Cassie, can you open your eyes now?"

Why doesn't Nicholas leave me alone?

He slaps at my cheek. "Come on, Cassie. Nap's over."

I blink.

"Good." He spreads one eyelid wide, then the other.

I don't follow much of what happens from then on, except to ask about my cousin and her baby. Kip tells me they're on the way to the hospital. Shirley and John are with them, but the chopper will return for me immediately.

"Don't let them." I tug Nicholas's sleeve. "Please cancel the flight. I don't have insurance. I can take care of my injuries at home." I hope Mom and Dad have something strong to dull the head throb.

Nicholas grunts. "I wouldn't advise—"

"Neither would I," Kip says. "If you walk in the door looking the way you do right now, Mom will have a fit and Dad will drive you straight to the emergency room. One way or another, you're going to the hospital."

CHAPTER NINE

Though I don't open my eyes when Shirley returns, the sound of her voice is as comforting as Kip's shadow. On the other hand, nothing is comfortable about the stretcher trip on the mountain trail. With my body strapped to the board and my head immobilized, I feel like I'm on an uphill luge ride, if that were possible. I squeeze my eyes against the sunlight and the nauseating sensation of bouncing from one side of the path to the other.

Shirley and Nicholas shove the gurney into the back end of the helicopter and crawl in beside me. I wish I could enjoy the view after takeoff, but the windows let in too much light and all I want to do is sleep. Every once in a while, one of them asks me a question. I think I answer. But I'm not entirely sure if I do or if I make sense.

When they wheel me into the hospital, I try to thank them. The words come out funny, yet I think they understand because Nicholas says, "Our pleasure." Shirley squeezes my arm. They transfer me onto a bed and talk briefly with a doctor.

Nicholas pats my arm. "You're in good hands, Cassie. Take care."

"Nice work with the baby," Shirley says. "Now it's your turn for some TLC." She leans close and whispers, "I'll be praying for you."

Tears well in my eyes. "Thank you, Shirley, and thank you...Nat...baby."

She brushes hair from my face and is gone.

Later, whether it's minutes or hours, I don't know, someone grabs my toe. I frown and open my eyes. Mom, Dad and Kip are standing at the end of the bed.

"Hey, Girl," Dad says, "what're you doin' in bed this time of day?"

"Edward, stop it." Mom moves to one side of the bed and Dad to the other. Kip comes alongside Mom.

"Oh, Cassie." My mother gives me a sad smile before she kisses my cheek. "Kip warned us your injuries were more extensive than skinned knees, but I didn't realize..." Her voice trails off.

"That bad?" I ask. "I haven't looked in a mirror yet. All I know is my face feels stiff, like I'm wearing one of those peel-off beauty masks."

"Sorry, Sis." Kip snorts. "No one in their right mind is going to call your mug a beauty mask. You must have slid all that way on your face."

Mom smacks him in the chest. "Kip..."

Dad laughs. "Just like old times."

A familiar-looking nearly bald man walks in with a nurse who's pushing a computer cart. I'm trying to place him, when he says, "I'm Dr. Price." He indicates the nurse. "And this is Freida. Are you Cassie's family?"

After introductions all around, he turns to me. "You're looking much better than when you came in. How are you feeling?"

"I just awakened and haven't moved around much." I pause to assess my current condition. "The headache and the ringing are mostly gone. I can see better, too, and I think I'm talking better. I had trouble with words earlier."

Kip opens his mouth, ready to make another snide comment, no doubt. Mom elbows him and he clamps his jaw.

Now, it's my turn to snort, but I refrain.

"Good, good," the doctor says. "That's progress. Ready to sit up?"

"I'll try."

"We'll take it slow." He pushes the button on the bed. "Breathe deeply. You may be lightheaded at first."

While I'm adjusting to the change of positions, Dr. Price turns to my family. "I'm going to examine Cassie, so if you'll excuse us, we'll draw the curtain. This won't take long."

They step aside and Freida pulls the thick drape around the bed, sticks a digital thermometer in my ear for all of one second and types into the computer. After donning exam gloves, she peels the gauze from my arms.

The first word that comes to mind is ugly. I'm glad Mom is on the other side of the curtain. She'd freak out. The sight and smell of my raw arms brings back the memory of my feet after the Bozeman doctors got done with them. I'd say, "déjà vu," but no one in the room would understand what I'm talking about.

The doctor slips on gloves and pulls a penlight from his pocket. He checks my eyes and makes a comment I don't understand. Freida starts typing again and continues to do so as he examines me from head to toe.

All the while, he's telling her what to input. Because I was wearing jeans when Nat and I tumbled down the mountain, my legs suffered only bruises, not scrapes. Even so, the bruises are tender to the touch.

When he finishes, he pulls the covers over my legs. I'm thinking, thank God, that's over, when the nurse hands him a tube and he begins to coat my arm with an antiseptic-smelling ointment that stings like crazy. He glances at my face and once again tells me to breathe. I stare at the curtain, inhaling and exhaling.

Freida adds a fresh layer of gauze, securing it with medical tape. They dispose of their gloves, and the doctor pushes the curtain aside. "Cassie is making excellent progress," he tells my family. "Right on target."

"Wonderful!" Mom gives me an encouraging smile.

Dr. Price turns to me. "Any questions?"

"Yes. Can you tell me in lay terms what you said? I didn't understand any of it."

"Sorry." He grins. "Med-school profs not only neglect to teach us how to write legibly, they forget to teach us how to speak plain English." He studies my face. "As we told you earlier, you didn't break any bones, but you do have a mild concussion. The good news is your symptoms are lessening. However, dirt was deeply imbedded in several places, so we'll have to keep an eye on those areas. Your arms took a beating and you have a couple cuts." He stops. "Have you examined yourself?"

I hold out my arms. "Just my arms when the gauze was off."

"You sustained a cut on your forehead and one on your upper back. They were small enough we could use Steri-Strips. You also came away from your accident with significant bruising. In a day or two, you'll look like a world map."

Kip snickers. "Nice."

Mom elbows him again.

The doctor smiles. "My concern right now is your elevated temperature." He motions to Freida on the other side of the bed. "What was it?"

She touches the screen. "One hundred and three point three."

"A fever indicates your body is fighting the infection," he says, "which is good. However, I won't release you until it drops closer to normal."

"But…"

His forehead furrows. "Is that a problem?"

"I'm supposed to return to Montana by midnight tomorrow night. My flight is scheduled for—"

"Even if I allowed it, the airlines frown on folks flying with concussions and fresh wounds. Can you delay your return?"

I glance at my parents and then back to him. "Judge's orders."

"I see. Hmm."

"What if I drove her?" Kip asks.

I shake my head. "You'd miss Grandma's funeral."

"We already had our private service." He turns to our parents. "Unless you'd rather I stay."

"Your grandmother is gone," Dad says. "Your sister needs you now."

I bite my lip to keep from crying. My family is so good to me.

"Tomorrow would be better." The doctor pauses. "Let's do this. The staff will monitor you overnight, and I'll check you first thing in the morning, no later than eight. If the fever has subsided, you can travel—by car. You'll need to stay hydrated, take the antibiotic I'll prescribe, tend your wounds and get plenty of rest. Deal?"

Dr. Price holds out his hand and I carefully shake it. "Deal." The backs of my hands are trashed, but my palms are unscathed, for some mysterious reason.

He and Freida are about to leave when John pushes Natalie into the room in a wheelchair. "Ah," says the doctor, "the woman who wrestled you down a mountainside."

Dad laughs. "Hard to tell who won."

"You're both winners." Mom always finds the positive spin.

"You look awful," Nat says.

"So do you." I laugh. "But better than the last time I saw you. How is Snookums? I haven't heard an update."

"She's doing great." Natalie touches John's hand on her shoulder. "She's surprisingly alert, considering she's a preemie."

"We came to tell you Snookums has a name." John has a proud grin on his face.

"Glad to hear it." I lift my hand. "Not that Snookums was bad."

Kip snickers. "She'd be teased every day of her life."

John shrugs. "It'd make her tough."

"Huh-uh." Natalie shakes her head. "She's a tiny, delicate, beautiful little girl. Anyway, we thought you'd want to know we named her Cassie Anne because you saved her life."

"Very sweet," Mom exclaims. "An adorable name for an adorable little girl."

"Nat." I stare at her. "I'm touched you want to name Snookums after me, but I did not save her life."

"Oh, yes, you did. Right, Dr. Price?"

The doctor nods. "Appears you took the majority of the lumps and bumps, Cassie. You must have had quite the grip on your cousin."

Natalie laughs. "I have the bruises to prove it."

"I have no memory of—"

"Doesn't matter." She wheels close and gently takes my hand with her gauze-swathed hands. "You saved little Cassie Anne's life, and maybe even mine. Thank you, from the bottom of my heart."

I squeeze her fingers with barely more pressure than my grandma managed two days ago. "You're welcome." I start to tear up. "I'm truly honored you want to give your little one my name." I know better than to argue with Nat when she's made up her mind.

Before Kip and I leave the house the next morning, I apologize to my parents for making a difficult time even more difficult for them and for leaving before the funeral.

Dad frowns and Mom shakes her finger at me. "Cassie Anita True, you are not at fault. You and Natalie had an accident. Things happen in life that change our plans."

Kip pretends to be boxing. "Yeah, you gotta roll with the punches, Sis."

I ignore him and reach for Mom. "I know you're afraid to touch me 'cause of the bruises, and I'm afraid to be touched. But I can't leave without hugs from you and Dad." I've missed them both so much and don't know when I'll see them again.

"Take good care of yourself." Mom's touch is tender. "And stay in touch as best you can. We'll come running anytime you need us. Just let us know."

"Remember, you can call Sebastian's phone or Myrtle Mae's and they'll get a message to me. I left their numbers by your house phone."

After we finish our cautious embrace, Mom hugs Kip and steps back, tears in her eyes. "I hate for you two to go so soon."

Dad's hug is also tender. He whispers, "Remember, call anytime, day or night, and we'll get you out of the lions' den."

"Thanks, Dad. I won't forget."

He gives Kip a bear hug, pats him on the back, and hands him a wad of cash. "For food and gas."

Mom reaches into the laundry basket at her feet and loads my brother's arms with pillows and blankets. He spreads them on his Honda's backseat. The snacks and water he purchased are on the floor.

I opt to sit in the front as long as I'm able—with the sack from the pharmacy we stopped at on the way to our parents' house. In addition to the ointment and antibiotic prescriptions, the doctor prescribed a painkiller, after we discussed my alcohol dependency. He had Kip promise to dole out the pills per the instructions on the bottle and instructed him to not let me behind the wheel while taking the drug.

But I didn't fill the painkiller prescription, partly due to my issues. Mostly, I'm uneasy about returning to a dorm where the residents struggle with drug addiction. Kip won't be there to guard the pills in my unlocked room. Instead of the drug, I purchased a bottle of ibuprofen. I may be sorry, but the over-the-counter med should keep the pain at a tolerable level.

I blow kisses to my parents and wave a stiff goodbye as Kip backs the car down the driveway and maneuvers onto the street.

"Kip," I whisper, "they look so sad."

"Yeah," he says, "and the funeral hasn't even started."

"I wish..."

"Remember what Grandma used to say. 'If wishes were horses, we'd all take a ride.'"

"I can hear her now. And see her emphasizing her words with her big wooden spoon."

He chuckles. "Yeah."

I pull Myrtle Mae's cell phone from my purse and power it on. Several texts come one after another, sounding their arrival.

Kip grunts. "Lover boy checking on you?"

I peer at him over my sunglasses. "You really don't trust Corban, do you?"

"I don't trust anyone in that so-called church, not after what they've put you through."

You don't know the half of it, brother dear.

Before I read the texts, I call Dr. Hoffman to let him know I'm on my way to Bozeman. He doesn't answer, so I leave a message and call Sebastian, who answers after one ring. "Hey, Cat True, how's it going?"

"Okay. How are you?"

"Guess you could say I'm feeling a bit lost. My brother passed yesterday. Knew it was comin', but my head can't quite lasso the notion."

"I totally get it. Grandma Hunt died the day before yesterday, shortly after I arrived. I got to say goodbye, yet I feel as if she's still out on the farm, waiting for me to let her know I made it safely back to Montana."

"Ah, so maybe she and Quentin did ride the glory train together."

I smile. "Maybe."

"Give my condolences to your family. I hate to cut this call short, but I'm headed for a meeting with Quentin's attorney. Should be there in a jiffy. Can I call you later?"

"Quick question. I'm on my way to Bozeman, but I won't get to the dorm before the doors lock, so I need Eunice's number, if you still have it on your phone."

"I'll check when I get to the parking garage. If I find it, I'll send it."

I thank him and tell him I'm sorry he lost his brother. After we end the call, I scan the texts. Seems like forever since I talked with Corban. He has to be wondering what happened to me.

In two of the texts, he says he misses me, and in one, he includes a cute picture of Myrtle Mae holding Citrus. What a guy. He wants to know if I'll be on the eight-thirty flight. He and a friend have figured out a way to pick me up and deliver me to the FFOW campus without causing suspicion. *Just call Dahlstrom Delivers when you're ready for pickup.*

I send a single text back, thanking him for the picture and telling him I had an accident and can't fly. *My brother is driving me to Bozeman. The goal is to be there before Judge Bock's midnight deadline.* I finish with, *Miss you, too! OK if I send family pics to store on your computer? I took a bunch.*

Like heavy wet sand, exhaustion seeps from my head to my toes. Staring at the phone screen, even while wearing sunglasses, hurts my eyes, and a headache simmers at the back of my skull. I power off the phone and drop it into my purse. Head against the window, I fall asleep before we pass the outskirts of town.

When my groans awaken me, I push upright, mumbling, "Sorry."

Kip steers the car to the side of the road. "Time for you to move to the backseat. You'll sleep better there, after you down ibuprofen and drink some water."

He's right. I don't come to life until he stops for gas and a quick lunch. As soon as I'm back in the car, I fall asleep again. I hate missing one-on-one time with my brother. Yet, the doctor said rest will aid healing. I might not have much opportunity for sleep later.

The next stop is at a rest area. "I need to move." Kip unbuckles his seatbelt. "And get some fresh air. Long-distance driving makes me sleepy."

"I'm sorry I can't help with the driving."

"The way you're snoozing, you wouldn't last long behind the wheel, and I wouldn't be able to sleep, knowing you could conk out at any moment."

We walk the path around the treed rest area twice. It's out in the middle of nowhere, and a warm grass-scented wind is blowing across the hills and through the trees. The combination of breeze and shade feels good. Kip swings his arms. I hobble like a creaky old lady. Hard to believe I was hiking a mountain trail yesterday.

After a bathroom visit, I return to the Honda and sit in the front seat. Kip says he's going to do some stretches and buy us coffee at the vending machine. "Unless you plan to sleep some more."

"I want to stay awake for a while. Coffee might help."

I dig out the phone. Mom, Dad, Sebastian and Corban have all sent texts. My parents both want to know how I'm feeling. Mom reports Nat and little Cassie Anne are doing good. I am fully aware how blessed I am to have family and friends who care about each other's welfare. I've met dozens of people on the streets and behind bars who aren't so fortunate.

I reply, telling my parents the pain is tolerable, I've slept most of the trip, and I'm going to try to keep Kip company for a couple hours. I also thank them for the update on Nat and the baby and add, *I'm praying the funeral service is a sweet time for everyone.*

Sebastian says he can't find Eunice's phone number. Not good news. I chew at my lip. *Plan B. Please, God, give me a Plan B.*

Corban is disappointed he can't pick me up at the airport and asks, *Can we meet before you get into town?* His next text reads, *If you have time.*

I respond, *I'd love to meet. Will let you know when we're closer.*

Chapter Ten

Back on the highway, I tell Kip that Corban wants to connect with us.

He glances at the console clock. "Don't know if we can socialize and keep your deadline."

"I told him I'll let him know when we're closer. I hope we can meet because this is an opportunity for you to get to know him."

Kip shrugs and sets his coffee in the cupholder.

I sigh. "I realize you're not thrilled about my relationship with him, but you could at least try to open your mind to the possibility he's an okay guy."

"Eric was more than okay. He was a great guy."

"That's not how I meant it, Kip. Don't compare Corban to Eric based on one word."

"I don't want you to get hurt and end up on the street again, like after Eric died." He scowls at me. "You didn't have to be homeless, you know. You could have lived with me or Mom and Dad."

"I knew that." I take a sip of coffee. "But I also knew you'd want me to stop drinking, which I wasn't ready to do.

Besides, I was ashamed of what I'd become. I didn't want to embarrass my family any more than I already had."

"Yeah, whatever. You weren't thinking right back then. And now, after you got your head screwed on straight, some judge stuck you in with a bunch of loonies." Steering with his knees, he shakes peanuts into his palm and hands the bag to me.

"Actually, I'm the one responsible for being there." I place my coffee in the cupholder between us and pour out a handful of peanuts. "I didn't check them out, didn't ask questions of them or anyone else. Didn't pray about it. I just glommed onto the chance to get out of jail a year early."

Kip pops the nuts in his mouth, wipes his hands on his jeans and grabs the wheel again. "So, they took advantage of the fact you'd jump at a chance for early release. Who wouldn't? And now you're sober, yet from what you've said and from what I've read online, your life has become a minefield. From day to day, moment to moment, you don't know what's going to happen next, what button you might accidently push that'll trigger a detonation of some sort."

"True."

The smell of peanut-flavored coffee fills the car. Not the most pleasant smell, but the taste is okay.

He asks, "Why are you so sure you can trust this guy?"

"Well, other than the fact he's a genuinely nice guy, like Eric was, I've encountered him in a variety of situations and observed him to be a consistently considerate, independent-thinking person. When he has the freedom to speak his mind about FFOW, he doesn't hesitate to voice his disapproval.

"Plus, I know his brother, who's equally transparent." Picturing Logan, I can't help but grin. "And maybe a tad ornerier. The four of us who work in Ruby Jade's yard—that includes Sebastian—openly mistrust the leader and her cohorts. We speak our minds when we're around each other and Ruby Jade's mom, who lives at the back of the property. She serves us tea and muffins almost every day."

"She's her mother, yet you believe she's trustworthy?" He gives me a look, like, *Yeah, sure.*

"Myrtle Mae is a sweet, kind woman who's heartbroken about the way her daughter turned out."

"That Sebastian guy seems okay, but if he's one of them..." He swerves to avoid a big tumbleweed in the middle of the deserted highway.

"If he were one of them, he wouldn't have taken me to meet you at the restaurant, especially one with a bar in it."

"What's the deal? I don't get why he works for the leader."

"Ruby Jade is his ex-sister-in-law."

"What?" Kips eyes blink wide. "That doesn't compute."

"I know. Some people are convinced those two have something on each other. Others say Sebastian is biding his time, waiting for who knows what. He told me he was keeping an eye on his nephew for his brother, but now that Quentin has passed away, I'm not sure what his plans are."

I stare out the window. Sebastian is probably more than ready to move on, which would be good for him but terrible for me. I don't want to lose him as a boss or as a shield against Vance.

"You're telling me the four of you plus the leader's mother are in agreement about the cult. Is that right?"

"Yes. As I told you earlier, Corban and Logan and their parents help people escape."

"You know that for sure? Or did they *tell* you they help people?"

"Both. They helped my roommate." Actually, I can't be positive about them helping Marcela because I haven't talked with her since she moved out of the Pritchards' house. And I haven't seen my guitar, so I don't have proof they rescued it. Even so, my gut instinct—validated by observation—is to trust Corban and Logan.

"You helped someone escape, right?"

"Yeah, a little boy."

"Were your friends in on it?"

"No. In fact, they don't know about him. As I said, you're the only person I've told."

He's quiet for so long, I finally ask, "Run out of questions?"

"Sorry about the inquisition, Sis. Fact is, I hate for you to wade into more quicksand." He reaches for his cup. "But I'll be glad to meet this Corban guy, if we have time."

When we near Spokane, where Kip lives, I suggest he put me on a bus. "If you drive all the way to Bozeman and back tonight, you'll be exhausted."

"First off," he says, "we have no idea of the bus schedule."

"I can look it up on my phone."

"Secondly, remember how you're on a deadline and how buses stop at every little town?"

"Yes, but—"

"I don't want you to land in jail again, and neither do Mom and Dad. Believe me, I'll find great satisfaction in delivering you to your doorstep. It'll be worth having to listen to you snore half the trip."

"I do not snore."

"Yes, you do."

"It's the drugs in my system."

"Just keep telling yourself that."

Kip stops to top off the gas tank. He points to a bluff across the interstate. "My new apartment is just over the ridge."

"Take me there. I'd love to see it."

"We don't have time."

"It's close."

"Nah."

"Ah, I get it. Your apartment's a mess."

"I didn't say that."

"You didn't have to."

Three hours later, we come to the mountain pass outside Missoula where I was arrested. The awful moment when I realized the patrolmen were after me floods my memory. My heart hammers my sore ribs, and my breath comes in shallow gasps.

"Cassie!" Kip glances at me. "You okay?"

I gulp as deep a breath as I can manage, blow it out and then do it again. "The other side of the summit is where..." I wince.

"Oh, right, the idiotic arrest."

"It's still fresh. All the panic and frustration."

"I bet it is."

We stop for gas at the station where I called Kip before my trip from Bozeman to Salem was aborted. I use Myrtle Mae's money to buy a bag of trail mix—we've eaten most of the other snacks—and an energy drink for Kip. I also refill my water bottle and swallow more ibuprofen. So far, the over-the-counter painkiller has kept the aches and pains to a dull roar. I'm still moving slow as a slug, but I'm moving.

Back in the car, I turn on the phone. It dings twice. Kip gives me a look but doesn't say anything.

Mom had a good idea, Corban says in the first text. *For family night tonight, she suggested we deliver sandwiches to needy folks. We just won't say which folks.*

Uh-oh, I'm missing family night in the dorm. I wonder what the girls are doing. I hope they get a break from work.

The next one reads, *We have a meet-up location about a hundred miles northwest of Bozeman. Can you make it?*

I respond, *I'll check.*

Corban comes right back. *I'd like to meet your brother and for you to meet my parents.*

I read the texts to Kip. "What do you think?"

"We should be able to make it. What's this about family night?"

"Thursday nights are when the FFOW households do something together."

"Like play games or go to the park?"

"No, nothing like that." I choke on the thought. "Can't be something fun. The Followers don't play. Has to be spiritual, something to do with the church—"

Kip interrupts. "You mean 'cult'?"

"Whatever. Anyway, we can do work, preferably for the church. Anything out of the ordinary, like going to the park to distribute invitations, has to be preapproved."

"What non-fun things have you done so far?"

"Watched a video of the church's winter program."

"Sounds like entertainment to me."

"No, Kip. Believe me, I was appalled, not entertained. You would have reacted the same way. However, the video gave me a better picture of the group's cookie-cutter customs."

I put the phone on the dash and pop the energy drink top, pleased I still have strength in my fingers. "By the way…" I offer him the can. "I appreciated how you summarized the leader's personality when we were out on the patio."

"Anytime you need to access my vast storehouse of wisdom, let me know." He smirks and takes the drink. "What else happens during family night?"

"The women in my dorm did a prayer walk around the rehab center, which consists of three buildings. I was working and missed it."

"At least they got out of the dorm."

"Yeah. The campus is situated beside a nice cemetery. Maybe they walked in there, but I doubt it because it would require permission from Leadership." I lift the phone. "I'd better ask Corban for directions." I tap out my response, which includes informing him I told Kip about the resistance movement.

I'm watching for a return text from him, when he calls. I answer, "Hey, Corban, I'm surprised we have cell service out here on the highway."

"Yeah, this is great. I enjoy hearing your voice."

"Same here. Likewise." I giggle at my clumsy response. "Back at you?"

"I think I get the message." He laughs. "I'd better keep this short, in case we lose reception. Our meeting location is easy to get to. When you reach mile marker—"

"Hang on. I need to find paper and pen to write on."

"I'd rather you didn't. If it would help you feel more at ease, you can repeat the directions to your brother. Between the two of you, you won't have any trouble finding the place."

Corban is right. Our rendezvous site is easy to find. The small vintage "motor lodge," according to the sign, sits just off the highway beside an equally dated but still-open restaurant and gas station. Corban is waiting for us in the restaurant parking lot. He smiles and waves.

I do the same. Seems like months have passed since I last saw him, not days. On the other hand, I feel as though I left FFOW this morning and am an idiot for returning so soon. For returning, period.

We follow his car around the motel, past an aspen grove to a little bungalow set way back in the trees. A van with a Montana license plate is parked near the door. The license plate has a wheelchair symbol on it. Corban parks beside the van and Kip pulls in next to his car.

My brother glances around. Is he worried we've driven into a trap?

We've barely stopped, when Corban hops out and opens my door. He reaches for me, but then his eyes get big and he stops, hand outstretched. "You said you had an accident, but—"

"Hi, Corban." I raise my palms. "I'd love to have your help, but please don't touch me. I'm bruised, scraped and sore, but not broken. At least that's what the doctor says."

"Glad to hear it, I think." He steps back.

I work my way out of the car, trying not to groan.

Corban shuts the door for me.

Kip walks around the front of the vehicle to meet us. He extends his hand to Corban. "Hi, I'm Kip Hunt."

"Nice to meet you. I'm Corban Dahlstrom." They look each other in the eye and shake hands.

The bungalow door opens, and Logan comes out, followed by a smiling older man. A woman in a wheelchair remains in the doorway. Her dark hair is streaked with gray. They're the couple I noticed at church.

"Cat True," Logan says, "what in the world? You tangle with a cement mixer?"

I laugh. "I bounced down a mountainside, which I suppose is similar to being inside a cement mixer."

"Oh, my stars, honey," the woman says, "you must ache all over." She motions to us. "Come in, come in."

Handing my purse to Kip, I ask him and Corban to help me ascend the three steps onto the tiny porch.

"Want us to take your arms or your hands?" Kip asks.

"My palms are the least beat-up."

The process is painful. My legs are as stiff and sore as my arms, but I make it into the house.

The Dahlstrom family's welcome is warm. Following introductions, Corban and Logan's parents, Denise and Phil, offer us cold lemonade and invite us to sit in the living room. They're quick to inform us those are their real names. They were already members before Ruby Jade came along and before she started changing names. Kip and I share the loveseat and the Dahlstrom guys sit across from us on a couch.

Denise parks her wheelchair next to where Phil is seated. "Cassie," she says, "You can lie down on one of the beds, if you'd like."

"Thank you. I'm okay for the moment. Kip's the one who could use a nap. He's had to do all the driving."

"Yes, of course," she says. "Naps are permitted."

Kip shakes his head. "Thanks, but we can't stop for long." He studies his watch. "An hour at the most." His shoulders have lost the rigid tension that came on him after we committed to the get-together.

"I love the décor." I glance from the living room to the kitchen. "Comfortable and homey." The overstuffed off-white furniture, muslin-and-burlap throw pillows and wooden wall art suggest shabby chic. Mom would love it. A huge painted butterfly hangs beside a rustic *Today is the First Day of the Rest of Your Life* plaque. Above the kitchen table, another plaque with a scrawling font reads *Today is a Good Day for a Good Day*.

"My lovely wife gets all the credit," Phil says. "The men in this family don't know the first thing about decorating. We just put the stuff where she tells us to put it."

"Is this like a getaway cabin?" I ask. I thought Followers weren't allowed to spend time away from the group.

"This was originally rented along with the motel rooms," Denise says. "When the owner, an ex-Follower, offered it as a safe house, it was very plain and dated, as you'd expect. We knew we had to make it cozy and welcoming, a place of security and rest. I had a lot of fun converting it to a sanctuary for traumatized individuals."

"It's a well-used place," Corban says, "the first stop for many who leave the Followers."

"In fact..." Logan looks at his parents and then at Corban. "Okay if I tell them about the latest couple?"

Corban grins. "Cassie was the one who got the ball rolling."

CHAPTER ELEVEN

I eye one brother then the other. "Are you talking about my ex-roommate?"

"Yep," Logan says, "Marcela and Rodrigo had a second honeymoon here. Actually, a first one—"

"Hang on to your thought." I turn to Kip. "This is the married couple I told you and Dad about, the couple the leader separated."

He nods.

"The first separation," Denise says, "was for six months. At around three months, Ruby Jade tacked on six more months for a fabricated offense. Not to say the first so-called offense was valid."

"Marcela was my roommate at the time," I tell Kip. "She was devastated."

He narrows his eyes. "Why am I returning you to that place?"

"Like I said, I've been ordered to fulfill my sentence there. Anyway, we should let Logan finish his story."

"Not much more to say." Logan clasps his hands behind his head. "Other than they had a few days alone here, everything provided, and then they headed off this morning on a mini tour to check out colleges."

"You all are the best!" I clap, as best I can. "I know Marcela wants to be a teacher."

Corban adds, "Rodrigo is interested in electrical engineering."

"I'm so excited for them. They must be beyond happy." I hold my lemonade with both hands. The cool glass feels good. "Have you heard how Leadership is reacting? Are they frothing at the mouth?"

Logan snorts. "Does a rooster crow, does a coyote howl at the moon, does—"

"I think we get the point." Phil chuckles. "When neither Marcela or Rodrigo showed up at work, the other employees were questioned, at length. But I'm pretty sure we're the only ones who knew they planned to defect. My guess is three women are grinding their teeth, wondering how two more people managed to escape their evil clutches. They'll either say nothing about them or say they let go of Jesus and declare them reprehensibles."

I turn to Kip. "Might explain why Ruby Jade kept calling Mom and Dad's house and why Noreen and her husband came looking for me."

He shakes his head. "Paranoid bunch."

"I'm sorry they harassed you." Denise sets her lemonade in the cupholder attached to her chair. "They've been known to follow people all the way to the East Coast, Mexico and Canada, and on occasion, overseas."

"What about Marcela and Rodrigo's cars and his passport?" I ask.

"They left the cars," Phil says. "Ruby Jade's name was on both titles, of course, along with theirs. We've got an attorney working on the passport situation. Could have far-reaching consequences for others in similar straits."

"How did he get a green card to work at the restaurant? Or does he have a green card?"

"That's murky territory, something for the attorney to figure out. Rodrigo's card may have been forged. He says he was so overwhelmed when he came and understood so little English that he doesn't remember how he got it."

I tilt my head. "If they don't have cars, what are Marcela and Rodrigo driving?"

"They're using a vehicle from Marcela's dad's business," Corban says. "Until they can get on their feet."

"Cat stays in the group because a judge sent her there." Kip rubs his jaw. "I don't mean to be rude, but why are you still there, when you could walk away?"

"Good question, Kip." Denise sighs. "The short answer is once upon a time, FFOW was a wonderful church."

Phil nods. "A great church."

"We loved it," she continues. "When Ruby Jade came along, we were encouraged to give our all to Jesus, to let go of anything that held us back. Offering our lives and our possessions to God showed how much we loved him. We didn't hesitate to put more money in the offering plate, to spend more and more time at church, to volunteer for more work projects. Corban and Logan grew up watching us work and helping us when they were able."

"I remember the sleeping bags you got us," Logan says, "so we could nap in the corner. Mine was blue with red rockets on it."

"Wow, you've got a great memory, Logan." I smile at Corban. "Do you remember your sleeping bag?"

"I remember the spider at the bottom that bit my foot." He laughs. "Must have been traumatic because it's my only memory of the bag."

Denise grimaces. "It was a nasty bite."

"Our entire existence focused on Ruby Jade and FFOW." Phil takes Denise's hand. "Red flags popped up here and there. We could never give enough time or money, attend enough church events, or sacrifice enough family time. Leadership became increasingly cruel and demanding.

Those red flags fluttered in our peripheral vision like annoying gnats. But I was convinced I was too intelligent and had too much Bible knowledge to be deceived. Plus, we soon learned Leadership was not to be questioned."

"I wanted the lies to be true," Denise says, "so I believed them, if that makes sense."

"At what point did you admit to yourselves the lies were lies?" Kip asks.

Phil and Denise look at each other and then at their sons.

"Logan and I were both engaged to be married." Corban folds his arms. "Shortly before our wedding date, my fiancée, Shelby, became seriously ill, and her parents took her to the emergency room. But the doctors couldn't save her, and she died a few days later. Because her parents didn't call Ruby Jade for a healing ceremony, they weren't allowed to have the service at FFOW or bury her in the church cemetery."

"The worst of it," Denise says, "other than Shelby's death, was that no Followers were allowed to attend her funeral, except her immediate family. As you might imagine, Ruby Jade's heartless reaction to Shelby's death opened her parents' eyes. They never returned to the church. Of course, Ruby Jade claimed she kicked them out."

"Sorry to hear that," Kip says. "Must have been a really rough time." Shaking his head, he turns to Logan. "What happened to your fiancée?"

"Kalina didn't die, which is good, but Ruby Jade decided she should marry her son, Vance, instead of me."

I nudge Kip. "You met Vance at the restaurant."

"Oh, yeah, the jerk. But…" He squints at Logan. "Did the girl not have a choice in the matter?"

"She acted like she didn't have a choice. Gave me a big sob story about how she'd love me forever, but she had to do what she had to do. When I discovered they were buying her cooperation with clothes, jewelry and whatever, I decided maybe I was better off without her."

"I'm sorry you had to go through that, Logan. Someone, maybe Corban, told me the marriage to Vance didn't last. What happened?"

"She disappeared," Logan says, "like his other wife. No one knows what happened to either woman."

Kip frowns. "Sounds suspicious."

"And then Denise was involved in the accident that put her in this wheelchair." Phil squeezes her hand. "Ruby Jade has treated her like chopped liver ever since. She thinks anyone in a wheelchair is a useless weakling because they can no longer work their tails off for her."

I remember how mean Ruby Jade was to Arnold, the crippled guy she kicked out of the church.

"You could say it was the straw that broke the camel's back," Phil says. "Shouldn't have taken all of those incidents to remove the blinders, but we'd been sucked in deep for a lot of years. I finally called a family meeting in the most private location we could imagine, the top of Mount Killjoy."

"Oh, how cool!" I clap again, painful as it is. "Sorry to interrupt, but I plan to climb Mount Killjoy when I graduate from—" I stop. "Denise, how did—?"

She laughs. "A road on the backside goes almost all the way to the top."

"Good to know." I turn to Phil. "So, you called a family meeting."

"We took turns airing our doubts and concerns. When we allowed ourselves to stop and think, the red flags were endless, it seemed."

"That's when we decided to buck the system," Corban says, "and help others escape. We started by forming an organization called Triple F. It stands for Freedom from FFOW."

Logan grins. "Rolls right off the tongue."

"Freedom from FFOW." I give them a thumbs-up. "Perfect."

"In case Cassie hasn't told you, Kip..." Phil leans his elbows on his knees. "When we say 'fow,' we mean the acronym for Faithful Followers of the Way, F-F-O-W."

Kip nods. "I get it."

"We'd better eat." Denise steers her wheelchair toward the kitchen. "So we can get back on the road. Can't stay out too late on a household night."

Logan snorts. "We could say we got so busy spreading goodwill, food and FFOW pamphlets, we lost track of the time."

"The fewer fibs we tell, the better," Phil says. "Makes life easier."

Evidently, I'm not the only one who struggles to tell the truth.

We relocate to the dining area, taking our drinks with us. After Phil thanks God for the meal, he turns to Kip. "Corban tells us you're from Spokane. You're welcome to spend the night here before you return home."

"Thanks, I'm not sure how—"

"Kip," Denise says, "take a sandwich." She offers him the platter. "We also have potato salad and coleslaw."

"Mom's salads are the best," Logan says.

I spoon coleslaw on my plate and pass it to Kip. "Smells delicious."

"Hey..." Corban perks up. "You don't have to drive Cassie all the way to Bozeman, Kip. We can take her there, and you can either stay here for the night or head home."

I'd love for my brother to get some rest before he returns to Spokane, but I have to refuse Corban's offer. "If you drive me to the dorm, we'll all be in hot water."

"Meaning?" Kip asks.

"Meaning I spotted a camera over the doorway to the women's dorm. If any of the Dahlstroms were seen dropping me off, our unauthorized friendship would trigger all kinds of questions. I'd never be allowed in the same room with any of them again."

I turn to Corban. "Right?"

"Yeah." His shoulders sag, but then he brightens again. "I'll disguise my car to look like a taxi, like I was planning to do earlier."

"I vowed to return Cassie safely to Bozeman," Kip says. "I'll go the distance."

"Then spend the night with us in Bozeman," Phil suggests.

Kip gives him a weary smile. "I might take you up on your offer. But what about cameras and all your secrecy issues?"

"We live in town rather than in a Follower neighborhood and have ways to avoid oversight." He motions to Logan. "Pass Kip the potato salad."

"Cassie," Corban says, "tell us about your accident, if you don't mind."

"She saved a baby's life yesterday." Kip scoops a healthy helping from the bowl and hands it to me.

"Cool," Logan says. "Did you catch it when it fell off a cliff?"

"I inadvertently saved a baby's life by cushioning the mom, according to the doctor. Kip was leading us on a hike, and our cousin Natalie, who was eight-months pregnant, fell backward off a boulder, basically into my arms. We bumped and slid downhill until we slammed into the base of a bush."

Denise murmurs, "Ouch."

I take a breath, reliving the moment the impact knocked the air from my chest. "Shortly after the guys pulled us from the bush, Nat went into labor. The crazy part is we'd been talking about how I wouldn't be able to see her baby for a year. I wouldn't even get to see pictures.

"In case you haven't heard." I lift my eyebrows. "Noreen took our phones away."

Logan frowns. "I thought you and Corban were texting."

"Myrtle Mae loaned me her phone for the trip."

"It's all about control." Phil grunts. "All about control."

"What an experience," Denise says. "Did you deliver the baby?"

"I mostly relayed instructions from the Life Flight nurse to my cousins' wives who did the actual delivery."

"Life Flight." Logan's eyes grow big. "Did you get to ride in the helicopter?"

"Yes, but I don't remember much of it."

"Bummer."

"She spent the night in the hospital," Kip says. "The doctor released her this morning after he was certain her temperature had dropped to normal."

"Good." Corban nods. "Are your cousin and her baby okay?"

"According to our mom, they're both doing great. Kip and I saw the baby before we left the hospital. I have a picture." I take the phone from my purse, find the photo and pass it around.

The men don't comment, but Denise says, "Such a teeny thing. Boy or girl?" She sets the phone beside my plate.

"Girl." I tell them how we were so intent on a safe delivery we forgot to check the baby's gender.

Kip elbows me. "Tell them the baby's name."

I smile. "Cassie Anne."

"Nice." Corban winks. "I like it."

Somehow, the conversation turns to college football and the upcoming season. Kip chimes in as if he's known the Dahlstroms his entire life. I enjoy their easy banter.

Denise touches my arm. "Once they get going on football, there'll be no end to it. You look like you should be in bed. What can I do for you before you go?"

"I appreciate your offer, but I don't..." I hesitate. "Come to think of it, I could use help changing the bandages, if you have a strong stomach. The doctor said to reapply ointment before bed."

"Remember..." She laughs. "I had two active boys."

"Kip…" I nudge my brother. "Would you please bring in my bag? Denise is going to help me with the bandages."

He peers out the window, where the sunlight is dimming, and then at his watch. "Okay, but we need to leave soon."

I hand the phone to Corban. "Please thank Myrtle Mae for me and tell her this was, as you know, a huge help."

He pockets the cell phone. "I'll make sure it's clean before I give it to her."

"Can you wait until I show her the pictures I took of my family and explain who everyone is? Afterward, I'll delete the photos and you can doublecheck my work."

His brow furrows. "Okay, but don't forget."

"I won't." I give him a sad smile. I'll miss the brief bond we had. Will we ever connect again?

The bathroom is small, yet Denise manages to roll her chair inside and close the door. I sit onto the toilet lid, and she maneuvers as close as she can. One by one, I extricate the supplies from the satchel, hand them to her, and she places them on the counter.

As she washes and dries her hands, I tell her, "I hope you don't mind, but I'll have to take off my blouse so you can reach my shoulders." After using jail showers, I'm not self-conscious about disrobing, although stripping in front of Corban's mom is not something I ever expected to do. I fumble with the buttons.

"I don't mind. Here, let me help you with those buttons."

After the blouse is off, she removes the dressing from my forearms and shoulders and draws in a breath. "Oh, sweetie, that mountain sure did a number on you."

"Appears I left some skin behind."

One glance in the mirror tells me the bruises have spread since I checked my injuries in the hospital bathroom. Blue, green, yellow, red, purple. I should be quite a sight by the time I return to class tomorrow.

After Denise has removed the gauze, she dabs at the scrapes with a sterile pad soaked with an antiseptic the nurse sent home with me. "You have bruises on top of bruises," she says.

"The doctor predicted I'll soon look like a world map." I focus on my breathing to keep from jerking every time she touches me.

"I hope you plan to visit a Bozeman doctor soon."

"The Oregon doc set up an appointment for me. He was concerned about infection setting in."

"I can see why." She screws the lid on the antiseptic bottle. "What next?"

"The ointment."

As she gently applies the ointment, she says, "I owe you and Kip an apology for not mentioning your grandmother's death. From what Corban said, she must have played a very special part in your lives while you were growing up. And into adulthood."

The ointment's burn isn't as intense as it was in the hospital, thank God. "Grandma Hunt was amazing." Tears spring to my eyes. "Her funeral was this afternoon. Neither Kip nor I could attend due to my TW obligation." I sigh. "My problem, not Kip's."

She smiles. "Boys Town, the famous Nebraska children's home, used to have the motto, *He ain't heavy, he's my brother.* A long time ago, fifty years or so, several well-known singers sang a song based on those words."

I adjust my position on the toilet seat, so she can reach my other shoulder.

"Your brother loves you very much, Cassie. I read it in his eyes. He'd do anything for you."

"He's a great guy. This trip is a good example of how he goes the extra mile for me." I straighten. "You may be surprised to learn I know the song you're talking about. Before my husband died, I sang it at the coffee shop on—" I stop. "You probably weren't allowed to go to coffee shops."

"Right. I'm sure there's something devilish about them. I just can't remember what at the moment, which reminds me..." Her eyes flash. "Ruby Jade having you arrested while you were driving to visit your dying grandmother was despicable, hitting below the belt, as Phil said. I am so done with that woman."

I look her in the eyes. "If you're done, why do you stay? You could help Followers leave without being at the church."

"Cassie." Kip taps the bathroom door. "Don't mean to rush you, but we'd better hit the road."

Denise calls, "Almost finished, Kip." To me, she says, "We're on our way out, working with a lawyer on some legalities and with ex-members to make sure our pipeline is secure and without holes. Think Harriet Tubman and the Underground Railroad. It won't be as elaborate, but you get the idea."

She finishes and helps me with my blouse. "We also want to establish a website, social media and other means to let members know a safe route to freedom and counseling are available when they're ready to exit. We want to take as many friends with us as possible, including you, if you want to join us."

I'm pleased Corban's mom considers me a friend. "Escape is definitely my desire. However, I've got over eleven months left in the program."

"We'll work on it," she says.

I can't imagine what they could do to change a judge's decree. But, whatever. I'm game.

Kip drives us through the FFOW gate shortly after eleven.

I check the time. "Pray I can get into my dorm at this late hour."

He frowns. "You don't have a key?"

"I don't have the access code for the keypad." He must not have understood my conversation with Sebastian.

"What do they expect you to do?"

"Be in before ten or join a work crew transported by a driver—a male driver—who has the code."

In the dim dashboard light, I watch my brother open his mouth, close it, grimace and shake his head. "I guess I should expect something stupid to be the norm around this place."

"I have a feeling neither of us knows the half of it."

We wind through the dark deserted grounds. Near the church campus, tall streetlamps appear along the road and in the parking lots. Spotlights shine on the buildings. The parking spaces are empty, and no cars travel Paradise Path as we skirt the campus.

Nothing about the well-kept surroundings suggests the sinister evil that simmers here. Yet, I swear I can feel my blood pressure rising. Or maybe its adrenalin.

The entrance to the dorm is well lit. Kip walks me to the double glass doors and jiggles them. When they don't open, as I expected, we step back and survey the area. "If you weren't so beat up," Kip says, his voice low, "I'd find an open ground-floor window and boost you through it."

"That would trigger a visit from the Sheriff's Department, for sure."

"You live here, Cassie." His voice grows louder. "You oughta be able to get into your own home. We drive all this way for you to arrive before midnight and you're locked out. You can't even prove you're here on time."

"Shh. See that video camera over the door? It probably has audio, too. And a timestamp that'll show when we arrived."

He lowers his voice. "My guess is they use surveillance against people, not to help anyone make their case."

"You're right, but I'm not going to worry about it now. You need to get going. You're exhausted and the, uh, your hosts are waiting for you."

"You're injured and oughta be in bed. I can't leave you out here alone."

CHAPTER TWELVE

"D on't worry about me." I turn away from the video camera. "I'll be fine."

"We'll sleep in my car," Kip insists.

"Wait! I have an idea. Let's tap on the dorm mom's window. She can open the door from the inside. I hate to wake her, but I know she'd let me in."

I set my purse and bag on the cement and walk over to what I assume is Eunice's living room window. The next window is probably her bedroom window, but a big hedge makes reaching either window impossible.

"Do you have something in your car we could use?" I ask Kip.

"I'll check." He starts for the Honda but stops when a white van comes around the corner and screeches to a halt several feet beyond the car. The side door opens and Joleen steps out.

"Thank you, Jesus," I whisper. "Perfect timing."

Joleen looks at Kip and then at me. "Cassandra, you're back."

I walk over to meet her. My other dormmates exit the van and gather around. "What happened to your face?" "Are you okay?" "Did you see your grandmother?"

"Hey, everyone," I smile, as much as my stiff face allows. "I'd like you to meet my brother before he takes off." I step to the curb, where Kip is waiting. "This is Kip, the most wonderful big brother in the world. He drove me all the way from Salem, Oregon, today."

"Hi, Kip." The ladies wave. "Nice to meet you."

"Nice to meet you, too." He lifts a palm. "I'm glad to help Cassie, which is her real name, any time she needs me."

I cringe, hoping the powers-that-be don't hear his rebellious comment.

Hank climbs out of the van. My heart sinks. Just the person to report my brother's words. Because Leadership can't chastise Kip, they'll make me pay for his infraction.

"Hank!" I wave him over. "Come meet my brother."

He shuffles our direction, shaking his head. "You again." His wandering eye resets and focuses on me.

I ignore his comment. "This is my brother, Kip. He lives in Spokane and likes to climb mountains."

"Mountain climber, huh?" Hank looks him over.

They shake hands.

"Hank burns the candle at both ends, Kip. He's a campus security guard, plus he drives the work crew van." I lower my voice. "You're tired, Hank. I can see it in your eyes. Maybe you should cut back."

"Wish I could." He rubs his eyes and walks toward the doors.

I sigh. My heart goes out to the guy. He's as much a prisoner of this crazy place as I am. I turn to my brother. "I'd better not miss my chance to get inside. Thank you for all you've done for me. You're the best."

"I'd hug you goodbye, but I don't want to hurt you."

"Hug me anyway. Yours will be the last hug I get for a long time."

"Not even from Corban?"

"Not even." I wrap my arms around him.

Holding me like I'm made of glass and about to shatter, he murmurs in my ear, "Corban is an okay guy with a great family. If things get rough, have Sebastian or one of them call me. I gave them my number."

I fight back tears. "Enjoy your stay at their house. They're really nice." I try to smile. "Wish I could be with you."

"Next time."

He gets in his car and I watch him drive off. How long before I see my brother again? Tears trickle down my cheeks. I swipe at my face with a sleeve. The only upside to this heartrending moment is knowing he'll spend the night with the Dahlstroms rather than drive back to Spokane.

Hank holds the door open while I hobble to the entry and slowly bend to gather my things. "I should report you," he says, "for hugging a man."

"He's my brother." I straighten. "You know that."

"And for coming in late and sneaking in with the work crew."

"A judge told me to be here by midnight. I'm here on time." I look at the camera. "No sneaking involved. The camera sees all."

He heaves a weary sigh.

"Go home and get some rest, Hank. You need it." I step inside.

He closes the door and gives it a tug to ensure the latch caught.

The others are waiting for me in the foyer. They stare at me like I'm an alien lifeform.

Liliana says, "I don't mean this as an insult, but you look terrible. What happened?"

"I fell down a mountain with my cousin."

My dormmates breathe a unison gasp.

Before they can ask questions, I raise a bandaged hand. "I promise to give you the whole scoop at breakfast."

Eunice's door opens. She leans around it, squinting at us. "What's going on out here?" I wonder how much she can see without her glasses.

"Sorry to wake you," Merikay says. "We just walked in from the work project."

"Cassandra is here," Joleen announces.

"She is?" Eunice peers at us.

I step closer and catch a menthol-camphor whiff. "I arrived shortly after eleven, but the door was locked. Good thing these ladies came along, or my brother and I were going to throw rocks at your window. I really didn't want to wake you."

"Glad you're here on time. I have to, uh, report."

"Right." The reason why I mentioned the time.

"Goodnight, ladies," she says. "See you in the morning." She closes the door.

Anxious for bed, I turn toward the stairs—and groan. "Stairs. I forgot I have to climb stairs."

Merikay says, "We can help."

"If someone carries my things, I can use the handrail. I'll also need a hand for balance." I feel like a wimp, but I appreciate their support.

She takes my purse and bag, and Dana Marie takes my hand. I tell the others they can go ahead. I know they're exhausted. But they remain close. The railing is cool and smooth, unlike Dana Marie's warm hand.

"Dr. Hoffman told us your grandma was failing," Merikay says. "Is she, did she...?"

I lift a foot onto the first step, and then the second. "She passed away shortly after I arrived in Salem."

"I'm so sorry."

The others murmur their sympathy.

"Did you get to talk with her?" Liliana asks.

"I made it to her bedside shortly before she died, no thanks to our fearsome leader. Grandma never opened her eyes, but she squeezed my hand and whispered my name. A short time later, she slipped away. I believe she actually waited for me to say goodbye to her."

"Aw, so sweet yet so sad."

"What about our fearsome leader?" Dana Marie lowers her voice. "You mean Ruby Jade?"

"Yeah." I should probably be careful what I say, but it's the truth. "You didn't hear I spent two nights in jail?"

"What?!"

They all gasp, and Dana Marie says, "In Oregon?"

We reach the landing. I pause for a breath of rosewater-tinted air. "The short version is Ruby Jade's mother loaned me her car to drive to Salem. I know her because she lives at the back of Ruby Jade's property, where I work. I see her almost every day.

I'd just passed Missoula when patrolmen stopped me and brought me back to GCDC because Ruby Jade told them I stole her mother's car. Actually, she said it was her car. Her name is on the title."

"What a nightmare!" Dana Marie shakes her head. "How did you get out of jail?"

"A compassionate judge." I take another step.

Joleen snorts. "I didn't know there was such a thing."

"We have a new judge in town."

"Oh?"

Her surprise is echoed by the others. Those of us with experience on the wrong side of the law are always interested to learn a new judge is on the bench. We're rarely pleased with our "old" judges and hope a new one will go easier on us.

"He dropped the charges and gave me three days to visit my grandmother, including travel time."

"Wow, that's impressive," Liliana says. "He actually understood your situation. Must have been a huge relief."

"Yes and no."

Joleen, who's ahead of me, turns. "No?"

"Ruby Jade was in the courtroom with her attorney. You can imagine how furious she was when the judge dropped the charges and said I could leave town."

"One way or another..." Joleen sighs. "She'll have the last word."

"She tried. Called my parents' house several times and even sent Noreen and her husband to get me."

"Ha." Shakyra grunts. "The old 'we care so much about our members' ploy."

Everyone groans.

The next morning in the damp shower room infused with fresh shampoo smells, Dana Marie removes my bandages, adjusts the shower water and helps me into the stall. My reason for requesting her assistance was precautionary. If we're questioned about her seeing me naked, I'll say she massages Ruby Jade, so she's accustomed to bare skin. Such logic may or may not work for Leadership, but with any luck, they'll never know.

After the shower, which was painful, but not so bad I had to sit, Dana Marie helps me towel dry. "Oh, Cassandra, you're a beat-up mess. You should stay home from class."

"I've already missed too many days. I don't want to delay my graduation any more than I already have."

"I understand." She helps me slip on my underwear and pants and then squeezes ointment onto my shoulder. "But—"

"I'll take lots of painkiller." The ointment's sting is intense, despite the ibuprofen I downed thirty minutes ago.

After the ointment comes the gauze and then my blouse. Dana Marie deals with the buttons, I brush my teeth, and she runs a brush through my hair. Then we go to my room to deposit my things and put on my socks and shoes.

Joleen knocks on the open door. "What can I do to help you, Cassandra?"

"Good morning, Joleen. Dana Marie has graciously dressed me head to toe. Once she ties my shoes, my next challenge will be to negotiate the stairs. If you'll help me, she can get ready for breakfast."

"Be glad to."

Walking down the stairs is harder than last night's slow trek upward. My legs object to every stairstep, but the smell of coffee and toast keeps me going. Finally, I make it into the breakfast room, breathing hard. Most of the others are already there. Joleen pulls out a chair and I slowly bend into it, crouching like an arthritic old man.

"You should go back to bed," Liliana says.

Eunice, who's seated in her spot at the end of the table says, "I don't know what happened to you, but bedrest is an excellent suggestion. I'd be glad to validate your absence."

"Thanks, Eunice. I'll see how I do today."

"Don't thank me yet." The corner of her mouth twitches into a half smile. "I have to write you up for missing the household meeting."

I shrug. "Do what you have to do."

Shakyra brings me juice and coffee. "You drink it black, right?"

"Yes, thank you."

Joleen sets a toasted, buttered English muffin in front of me and sits on the other side. "You sure have a good-looking brother. Is he taken?"

"I'm afraid so."

"Ah, too bad."

"He's taken by mountains—the higher the better."

"Oh, yeah?" She beams. "Then there's hope."

"You can try."

"Ladies," Eunice says, "we'd better read our verses and have our prayer."

Dana Marie hurries in the door and over to the food counter.

"Before you start, Eunice." I rest my sore hands on the table. "I want to thank everyone for your help, including Nurse Dana Marie, who tended my wounds this morning and helped me dress. Without you sweet ladies, I'd be a disaster."

Dana Marie looks over her shoulder. "My pleasure."

The others chime in their willingness to do whatever I need.

Eunice, who'd been turning pages in her Bible, lifts her head. "You are a wonderful group of ladies," she says. "I'm proud of you for caring for Cassandra." She smiles at me. "Please let me know what I can do to help."

"Thank you. I will."

After she reads the verses and prays her prescribed prayer, she says, "I owe you ladies an apology."

Everyone stares at her, eyebrows bunched, shoulders tight. She's done nothing that warrants an apology, as far as I know. Is Leadership forcing her to do something nasty to us? I wouldn't put it past them.

"You ladies are amazing." She settles her hands on the Bible. "Not what I expected when I took this job."

I feel more than see those around me begin to relax. This place keeps us on edge.

"I thought you'd be dirty, stringy-haired, bitter lowlifes similar to some of the individuals I ran into when I lived in subsidized housing." Her morning voice is raspy and nasal. "Sorry for the derogatory term."

Behind her big lenses, she blinks her mismatched eyes. "You're respectful and kind to me and to each other. You keep things neat and tidy, which makes finding something to report to Leadership a challenge." She chuckles. "I appreciate the tissues and broken combs and used toothpaste tubes you leave out now and then.

"You are delightful women." A smile flits across her mouth. "Each one of you. I apologize for my snootiness."

"Thank you, Eunice," Liliana reaches over to squeeze her hand. "You're a sweetheart."

I add, "We love having you for our dorm mom."

The others nod their agreement.

"But about your expectations," I say, "if you and I had crossed paths on a Bozeman street not too long ago, that's exactly what you would have seen. A stinky, stringy-haired, bitter woman who'd do almost anything for a drink."

"Yep, been there, done that," Merikay says. "Glad those days are over."

"Tell us about your fall." Joleen stirs her coffee. "Did you say you were climbing a mountain?"

"My brother led me and my cousins and their kids on a hike in the mountains." I take a sip of the watery orange juice before I continue my story. "A crazy turn of events resulted in a baby being named after me."

"What?" All chewing, drinking and jelly-spreading stops.

"I'll tell you the condensed version so we can get to class on time."

Finished with breakfast, the others head upstairs to brush their teeth, but I forego another trip up and down the stairs and walk out the front doors. It'll take a while to get to the rehab center, so I might as well start early. I stop for a moment to breathe in the beautiful morning spiced with fresh air and sunshine—and to remember my brother and his final hug.

No, not a final hug, I tell myself. Someday, I'll be able to see him anytime I want. I just need to be patient.

Did Kip and the Dahlstroms have a chance to talk before he returned to Spokane? Knowing my brother now knows more about Corban's family life than I do, including where their home is located and how they avoid FFOW oversight, is a weird sensation. I have to admit I feel left out. Yet, Kip's acceptance of them and their acceptance of him is comforting and adds a sense of security to my rattled psyche. Could be false security, but for now, I'll take it.

I'm nearing the Transformation Way center when Ruby Jade's black Lincoln screeches into a parking space right in front. I groan. So much for false security. *Not this morning, Lord. Please, not this morning.*

Like a military contingent, all three members of the leadership team step out, heads high, shoulders back, eyes focused on me. Decked out in their usual finery, their attempt to appear militant in stilettos strikes me as ludicrous. Yet, my less-than-dependable legs begin to shake. I force a smile and keep walking.

Noreen and Ruby Jade fold their arms, and Inez steps forward, high heels striking the concrete. "I waited for you at the airport all day yesterday." Her face is red and contorted. You'd think I committed the most heinous sin possible. "How ungrateful of you to sneak out of the airport when I donated my valuable, precious time to transport you."

I stop ten feet from her, hands clenched at my sides. "I did not sneak out of the airport. My brother drove me here from Oregon." I indicate the dorm behind me. "I'm sure you saw him on the video."

"You harlot," she huffs, "you didn't have Ruby Jade's permission to ride with a man."

"Judge Bock did not indicate which mode of transportation I was to use or who to travel with. Also, as he requested, I kept the program director informed of my travels."

"That's irrelevant. You should have called us."

I know I'm pressing Leadership limits, but I say it anyway. "You took my phone, yet you expected me to call you?"

Inez rears back, eyes wide. She apparently has no idea how to respond.

Ruby Jade stomps two steps ahead of Inez. "I have told you before, Cassandra Turner, yours is not to question our authority. Such audacity will not go unpunished."

Of course not.

Behind the Leadership bullies, Samuel and Marco are walking toward the center. Maybe their presence will end the interrogation and I can go to class. I know it's silly wishful thinking, but I can hope. The men hesitate, murmuring to each other. If a way to avoid the three women miraculously appeared, I'm sure they'd take it.

"We cannot allow you to have further contact with your wicked father or your other deceitful family members," Ruby Jade continues. "He scorned me, your esteemed pastor, and mistreated Noreen and her husband."

Noreen's eyes flash. "The nerve of the man to slam the door in my face."

"Your father is the devil's tool." Ruby Jade glowers at me. "An evil influence on your pathetic life. No wonder you fell into alcoholism and ended up behind bars."

CHAPTER THIRTEEN

I clasp my hands behind my back, ignoring the pain, and clamp my teeth. Everything within me longs to defend my father and tell Ruby Jade where she can shove her so-called esteem.

From the trees behind the women, a flock of dark birds rises, screeching like a horde of demons. They circle and swoop, a shrieking, roiling thundercloud. Is God hinting at the forces that fuel the Fearsome Threesome?

Two more cars park in front of the center. My assailants pivot their direction. Jenica, the dark-haired rehab program counselor, gets out of one car, and Doctor, the director, steps from the other. They glance at the noisy birds and give the women curious looks. Their greetings are circumspect but polite.

Doctor motions to the oncoming men and to me. "Come on in, folks. Let's get started." He pushes a faded reddish-white strand from his forehead and adjusts his big aviator-style glasses.

Ruby Jade, obviously trying to regain control of the situation, lifts her chin. "Inez, Noreen. We have important matters to attend to. We cannot waste any more time here."

Yeah, important matters like finding someone else to harass. God help the person.

With parting glares my direction, they clomp to the car. I'm glad they're leaving, but I know better than to think this is the end of their retaliation. Ruby Jade reverses the Town Car into the street. All three occupants stare straight ahead, jaws clenched, lips pressed.

Tires squealing, the vehicle shoots along Transformation Way much faster than the posted fifteen-miles-per-hour limit. Whatever. The sooner they're out of here, the better. The birds quiet and settle into the trees.

My dormmates cluster around me. I didn't know they were close. They must have exited the dorm when the Fearsome Threesome were raking me over the coals.

"What was that about?" Joleen asks.

"The usual insanity." My vision darkens, my ears begin to ring, and my legs buckle. I grab the arms of the closest women.

Joleen says, "She needs to sit. Quick, get her inside."

They half carry, half drag my sore body into the classroom and seat me at a table. I lay my head on it, angled to protect my injured cheek and forehead. I smell the ointment on my gauze-covered hand, which is only a couple inches from my nose.

"Should I call an ambulance?" Dr. Hoffman's voice. He's nearby.

I whisper, "I'll be fine. Give me a minute."

Eventually, my vision clears and the ringing stops. I sit up and drink the entire glass of water someone brought for me. "Sorry." With a shaky hand, I set the glass on the table. "I didn't mean to cause a scene. Guess I wasn't ready for a confrontation with Leadership so early in the morning."

He lifts an eyebrow but doesn't comment. Instead, he looks at the clock above the door. "Please find a seat, folks."

Still trembling, I grasp the edge of the table to steady myself.

Doctor walks to the door and closes it.

Jenica leans over the table. "Welcome back, Cassandra. Your face…did you fall?"

I manage a small smile. "Down a mountain."

"Oh, dear." Her expression is tender, the opposite of the church leaders who couldn't be bothered to acknowledge my injuries.

"If you need to return to your room to rest," she says, "I'll be glad to walk you to the dorm." Her touch on my arm is soft. "I'm so sorry about your grandmother. Let me know if you'd like an appointment to talk about your loss. I can meet with you as often as you want."

I murmur my thanks. What a kind, thoughtful lady.

She joins Doctor at the front of the room. He arranges two chairs side-by-side, and the two staff members sit. Crossing one leg over the other, he clasps his hands around his knee. "Jenica and I met before class to—"

The door bursts open and slams against the wall. I jolt to attention, heart racing. Leadership again? But, no, not them. Someone just as evil. Vance. He struts into the room as if he owns the place, which is probably not far from the truth. Participants freeze and stare straight ahead.

Doctor indicates the clock above Vance's head. "Mr. Longpre, you are seven minutes late."

Vance shrugs.

What? Is he…? Oh, God, no. He can't be.

"Class," Doctor says, "this is our newest program participant, Vance Longpre. You may know him as Ruby Jade Paradise's son."

No one says anything. An air-conditioned draft blows his aftershave our direction. I am sickened by the smell and the knowledge I'll have to be in the same room with the lecherous creep five days a week. Why is he here? I thought his mother had sway in the courts.

"Please take a seat," Doctor says.

Vance plops into the nearest chair, which happens to be beside Dana Marie, who's seated in front of me. She scoots away.

"Mr. Longpre—"

Vance cuts in, "Call me Vance."

"Mr. Longpre," Doctor says, "because you're new to the program, we'll let this infraction pass."

"What infraction?"

"Your tardiness."

"I'm here, aren't I?" He lifts his chin.

"You're late."

"My mother, the leader of the church that owns this place, says all I have to do is show up."

Dr. Hoffman's eyes narrow. "The state of Montana says you'll show up on time or you'll be removed from the program." He stands. "Change of plans. After a quick break, we'll reconvene in two locations. Ladies, you'll meet in this room with Jenica. Gentlemen, please take a chair and go to the office at the front of the building."

Vance shakes his head. "You can't kick me—"

"Oh, but I can." Doctor strides out of the room. Eyes averted from Vance, the men follow, each carrying a chair. The women graciously wait for me as I slowly force my body into a standing position. I could stay here, but I need to move my muscles every chance I get.

Vance ogles me from my head to my feet. "Cas-*san*-dra... Did that guy I caught you with drag you here on your face?"

Ignoring him, I hobble toward the door. I can't believe we're trapped with the arrogant tattletale for months on end. Heaven help us.

Doctor peers around the doorjamb. "Mr. Longpre, on your feet. Bring a chair with you."

I shuffle out of the classroom and into the hallway without toppling over, pleased my legs have regained strength.

Vance sidles alongside, noisily pushing a chair. "Because of you," he mutters, "I'm stuck with these losers."

I roll my eyes but keep my thoughts to myself and continue toward the restroom. We've had this conversation before.

"I'm a winner because I get paid to come." He snickers. "You and these other deadbeats don't get a penny."

Joleen pushes the restroom door open and I follow her inside, even though I don't need a bathroom stop. When the door closes, she says, "What a creep. I'm shocked he didn't follow you in."

"Yeah." Dana Marie is checking her hair in the mirror. "He thinks he owns the place. I'm sure that includes the women's restroom too."

Paid to come... Is his mother bribing him to attend? Doesn't make sense. If she's paying him, Dr. Hoffman wouldn't be so sure of his power to kick Vance out of the program. But maybe he doesn't know how things work around here.

Following our dismissal for the day, I ask the director if he has time to drive me to work.

"I'd be glad to." Doctor glances at his watch. "My plane doesn't leave until later this afternoon. Would give me a chance to hear about your recent, uh, I hate to use the word 'adventures.' I'll just say 'travels.'"

The others straggle past, but Joleen stops on her way out. "I'll walk you to the lunchroom. I want to make sure you get there okay."

"Thank you, but I'm going to work."

She looks me up and down. "Sure you should do that?"

"My supervisor and I have both been away. I need to check the property. Before you go to lunch, could you run to the dorm and grab my purse for me? It's hanging in my closet."

"Glad to."

I don't feel like climbing the stairs to get the purse or change into work clothes. What I'm wearing will have to do.

Joleen brings my purse, and I hobble behind Doctor toward his car.

"You should stay home and rest," he says. "You've been through a lot lately, physically and emotionally."

"When you see the jobsite, you'll understand."

He sets his briefcase on the backseat and helps me into the passenger seat. The vehicle is a rental car, yet it has a familiar smell, reminding me of the pipe my grandpa used to smoke. In his tan corduroy jacket with its leather elbow patches, Doctor seems to be the kind of guy who might smoke a pipe. Maybe I've seen too many movies with aging men in easy chairs, smoke curling mysteriously above their heads.

He settles behind the wheel, switches on the AC and backs out of the parking slot. Before he has a chance to ask me about my fall, I tell him I have a couple things I'd like to say regarding Vance. "That is, if you don't mind me discussing another program participant. You can take or leave what I say, but I feel it should be said."

"Go ahead."

We pass the men's dorm.

"First, a question. Does Vance have to live in the dorm with the other guys?"

"Good question." He turns onto Paradise Path and follows it around the expansive campus. "If I remember the guidelines, all participants are required to live on campus. I'll check Mr. Longpre's status."

"I'm asking because during the break today, he made a point to tell me he's being paid to participate in the program. Makes me wonder several things. Is he a bona fide participant? Or is this another of his mother's money-making schemes?"

Doctor peers at me, one wooly eyebrow up, the other down.

"Sorry." I shrug, hoping I haven't crossed a boundary line between director and participant. But what's done is done. I surge ahead. "If you haven't figured it out by now, she's all about money. And power. And her son. Is it true he's being paid to attend? If so, why and by whom?"

His attention back on the road, he says, "Like most of the participants, Vance was sentenced to the program, so I don't understand why he'd be paid—"

"Could be Vance was lying about the money to make me jealous. Wouldn't put it past him. Do you know which judge sentenced him to TW?"

"Judge Snow."

I snort. "Now I know something is screwy."

"According to the court records, he had good reason to sentence him to a rehab program."

"I've heard Ruby Jade has pulled strings over and over to keep Vance out of the courts and out of jail. She has Judge Snow wrapped around her little finger, so it doesn't make sense that he'd sentence him to... Oh." Understanding hits me like a dust devil spinning across a Montana prairie.

"Oh?"

"She's paying him to spy on us, on you. And the state is her bank account."

"Whoa, hold on." Doctor's brow furrows. "You're jumping to conclusions, outrageous conclusions."

"This is an outrageous place." I'm not going to let him talk me out of my epiphany. "You won't let the leaders sit in on group sessions, which lessens their control over us. But now they have Vance to report everything we say. And believe me, he'll do it, but he'll distort the truth. I know from experience."

We approach the gate. As always, it opens automatically.

"First gated church complex I've come across," Doctor says.

"Another hint at the craziness and control."

He scratches at his faded scraggly beard but says nothing.

"I'm pointing out Vance's privileged, possibly paid, position." I tap the armrest. "Not advocating for him to live on campus. He'd be a pain in the you-know-what, tattling on everyone and stalking the women. He's a lecher and an alcoholic. When he's with us in the classroom, I promise you none of us will open up regarding our lives, past, present or future. He'll tell his mother everything we say, and that 'we' includes you and Jenica. We'll all suffer consequences. In short, he'll ruin Transformation Way."

Doctor purses his lips. "I noticed the men were more reticent to speak today than usual."

A dam has broken inside me. I probably shouldn't trust a man whose paycheck comes from FFOW, but he needs to know Vance is not a safe person. "Did you know the women residents don't have the code to get into our dorm, yet some men have it? If Vance ever learns the code, no female will be safe. I'm going to beg our dorm mom to let us make keys for our rooms from her set."

"You don't have keys?"

"No code. No keys."

"But some of the men have the code? I don't understand."

"They're the men who drive the women to and from work projects every night, volunteer work projects. Because the drivers often return the women after the ten o'clock curfew when the doors lock automatically, they need the code to get in."

He frowns but doesn't respond.

I want to tell him more, so much more, but I know I've given him a lot to digest.

Doctor doesn't say anything until I direct him to turn at the Fellowship Neighborhood sign a quarter mile ahead. "Is it a church-members-only neighborhood?" he asks.

"As far as I can tell."

"Interesting." He slows for the turn.

Farther along the street, we come upon the Pritchards' place, and I tell him, "I lived in that house before the program restarted." I swallow bitter memories. "Like Ruby Jade controls FFOW, a woman named Olivia reigns over that *household*, which is a group of people assigned to live together. Neither woman is a benevolent leader. They're both tyrants, as are Ruby Jade's cohorts, Noreen Nystrom and Inez Curtis."

Again, he's quiet.

"I'm sorry to be hitting you with all this at once." I hold out my palms. "But this may be my only opportunity to give you an idea of what actually goes on at the church. Everything you and Jenica do to help us is undermined by accusations, insults and threats, which is what was happening when you arrived at the center this morning. On top of that, participants go to class and then to jobs and then to volunteer work projects without ever getting a break, even on weekends. They're too exhausted to fully engage and comprehend what you say."

"I have noticed a lot of yawns and dark circles under participants' eyes."

We're coming up on Ruby Jade's house. "The house up ahead, the one with the purple shutters is Ruby Jade's house. I do yardwork for her—volunteer yardwork, *forced* volunteer yardwork."

Newspapers are crammed into the tube below the mailbox and several are on the ground. Funny how Ruby Jade can watch television, listen to the radio and read newspapers, but Followers can't. Seems the persnickety woman would send Vance or the maid to get the papers while Sebastian is away. I wonder if they bother to retrieve their mail.

He eyes the house and its parklike setting. "Does her son live with her?"

"Yes." I pause to let him mull the implications. *Why would Vance give up a mansion for a dorm room?* "Do you mind driving me to the back of the property, so I don't have to walk? I want you to meet someone."

"You do?" His leery expression matches his voice.

"This someone is nice." I smile, thinking how much he'll enjoy Myrtle Mae.

He negotiates the turn onto the long driveway and then the narrow road that passes the garage and leads to Myrtle Mae's little yellow house. All the while, he's silently surveying the surroundings.

Tempted to ask what he's thinking, I bite my tongue. Better to let him formulate his own thoughts and open himself to learning more about Ruby Jade's topsy-turvy kingdom. If he has questions, he'll ask them. I almost laugh out loud. Who am I to play psychologist to the psychologist?

Myrtle Mae is delighted to see us. "I was hoping someone would drop by to share lunch with me." She reaches to hug me but then steps back, her head angled. "Good heavens, sweetie. The Dahlstrom boys told me you had a run-in with a mountain. Looks like the mountain got the best of you."

I take her hands, so she doesn't embrace me. "Yes, it was quite the ride, but I'm okay. Just little stiff and sore." I introduce her to Doctor, explaining he's the Transformation Way director.

"I am honored by your visit, Dr. Hoffman." Her lavender eyes twinkle.

"And I am honored to meet you, Myrtle Mae." He smiles. "You can call me Andrew."

"I'd love to learn more about the rehabilitation program, Andrew. You haven't eaten lunch, have you?"

"No." He shakes his head. "I don't want to intrude—"

"Pshaw." She waves him into the room. "No intrusion at all. I'm always happy to meet new people and share a meal. Please have a seat."

The table is covered with a green-and-white checkered tablecloth. It has the ever-present tea basket on one end and a quart jar filled with fresh-smelling wildflowers in the middle. She brings us water and says she has hot water for tea on the stove and iced tea in the refrigerator.

I settle into a wooden chair, one bruised muscle at a time. "You weren't just hoping someone would drop by, you prepared for us."

"More often than not, if I prepare for visitors, they come knocking on my door."

Doctor says he's a coffee drinker and has never been fond of tea, but I tell him he should try Myrtle Mae's special blend. "It's like no tea you've ever tasted."

"Well, in that case, I'd better have a sample."

She pours hot water for us, sets the teapot on a trivet and hurries over to the counter.

I point out the cheesecloth bundles in the tea basket, so Doctor will know which tea to try.

"I've been experimenting with chicken salad," Myrtle Mae says, "hoping to duplicate the chicken salad a certain restaurant downtown serves." She winks at me. "You'll have to tell me if I've succeeded, Cassie."

Doctor's eyebrows twist. "Cassie?"

"My real name."

He cocks his chin and lowers his brow. "Real name, not a nickname?"

"Ruby Jade gives everyone new names. Our birthnames aren't good enough for FFOW. She changed my first name *and* my last name."

"I haven't had a chance to go over individual records, but I assume your name is correct there."

"The court documents, yes. And the liability release forms I signed. However, I don't know about any other paperwork Ruby Jade may have provided you."

Myrtle Mae sets plates in front of us. "My daughter has had a hang-up about names since she had hers legally changed several years ago."

"Your daughter?" Doctor stares from Myrtle Mae to me, his eyes wide and wary behind his aviator glasses.

"You guessed it." She arranges a napkin and silverware beside his plate. "Ruby Jade is my only child."

"But you're not at all…"

This is the first time I've seen him thrown off-balance, but it probably won't be the last. The FFOW world is full of surprises.

CHAPTER FOURTEEN

"You're right." I nod to assure Dr. Hoffman he hasn't lost his mind. "Myrtle Mae is not at all like her daughter. Somewhere along the line, Ruby Jade's wires got crossed."

Our gracious hostess places a basket of crackers on the table and stands beside me. "My husband thought the sun rose and set in Marilee's eyes. By the way, that's her real name." She pauses. "No, it's not. It's a nickname her father gave her. Her real name is Marilyn June. Whatever she wanted, Kenneth made sure she got it, whether we could afford it or not."

Folding her arms, she stares out the open window at the opposite end of the table. "My brother Norman is the only one who knows this…"

She turns to us again. "Norman brought me those wildflowers from the mountains."

"They're beautiful." I twist the jar to view the colorful assortment.

"Occasionally…" Myrtle Mae continues, "I'd see a look or a smile pass between Kenneth and Marilee that seemed to suggest something other than a father-daughter exchange. I questioned them about their relationship, separately and together, even said I'd go to counseling with them. They just laughed at me and told me I was jealous of their closeness."

Doctor nods as if encouraging her to continue but says nothing.

"By the time Marilyn left for California…" Myrtle Mae smooths a wrinkle in the tablecloth. "Her father had emptied our savings account and maxed out our credit cards. But he managed to pull together enough money to buy a plane ticket to go see her. That's when she told him, and I paraphrase, 'If you can't give me money, I don't need you in my life.'

"Kenneth moped around like a lost dog for weeks, barely able to drag himself out of bed to go to work. And then, without warning, he keeled over dead in the shower. I've always believed he lost his reason to live. Took me years of overtime to pay off the credit cards."

"I'm so sorry." I reach for her hand. "Must have been a lonely time for you, and then you were stuck with debt you didn't accumulate."

"Thank you. After a while, I realized I was happier on my own." She squeezes my hand and goes to the counter to get the chicken salad. "Marilee may have rejected her father, but she's still stuck on the 'daddy's little princess' pedestal." She pauses. "Except she's not so little now. I worry about the extra pounds she's put on in recent years."

"So, the weight is a new thing?" I ask.

"Yes, and it can't be healthy for her." She hands me the bowl.

I inhale the tantalizing aroma. "You did it, Myrtle Mae! It smells identical to the croissant sandwiches we ate."

"Can't smell any better than this tea." Doctor holds the cup under his nose. "If it tastes anything like it smells, I may become a tea drinker after all."

"Be nice, and she might share her secret recipe with you."

He laughs. "Secret means secret."

"Right, a secret is a secret." Myrtle Mae places a plate of cinnamon-spiced apple slices on the table and sits at the end. She takes our hands and bows her head. "Thank you, Jesus, for your daily gifts of good food, good friends and good times. You are a good, good God. Amen."

"Meow?"

I turn, laughing at the question in the kitten's plaintiff call. The tiny yellow-and-orange striped cat is in the opening between the kitchen and living room. Her tail stands straight up. She's grown since I last saw her but not much. "Citrus, did you just wake up?"

She yawns and stretches, as only a cat can, which makes me yawn, too.

Myrtle Mae jumps to her feet. "I'd better give her something to nibble on, or she'll be begging for our food."

Citrus follows her to two small rubber bowls in the corner and laps milk while her owner pours a handful of kitten food into the other bowl.

"Speaking of names," Doctor says. "Citrus is the perfect name for your cat."

"We thought so," Myrtle Mae says. "Cassie helped me name her."

His cell phone rings. He pulls it from his shirt pocket and glances at the readout. "I'd better take this." The phone continues to ring. He pushes back his chair. "Excuse me. I'll go outside, so I won't disturb you." Hurrying to the screen door, he opens it and puts the phone to his ear. "Dr. Hoffman speaking."

I add a scoop of chicken salad and a handful of crackers to my plate. "You're a good judge of character, Myrtle Mae. What do you think of Doctor?"

She sorts through the teabags. "I believe I'll try something different today." Picking up a purple packet, she squints at it then hands it to me. "Would you please read this for me? The print is too tiny for me to decipher."

The print on the backside is indeed small. "Says it's an aromatic fruity blend of green tea, rosehips, orange peel, ginger, strawberries, raspberries and blueberries. Sound good to you?"

"Yes, I haven't had that blend in a while."

I tear open the packet, drop the bag into her cup and add hot water.

"Thank you, dear." She spoons in a dollop of honey from her beehive jar. "About the good doctor, he seems to be a trustworthy man. I get the feeling he's torn between wanting to help those of you in the program and curiosity as to what goes on behind Follower doors."

She smiles. "I understand the curiosity part. After all, he's a psychologist or psychiatrist, one or the other. This place is a case study in craziness, if there ever was one. Bet he'd love to drill down deep."

"I believe he's a psychologist. However, if he's interested in FFOW, he's being very discreet about it."

"The man is in an awkward position, Cassie." She stirs her tea. "My guess is the only Followers he comes in contact with are program participants and Marilee and her cronies. He doesn't need a doctorate to know something is off-base. But he's paid to run the program, so he can't ask too many—"

Doctor opens the screen door. "My apologies for leaving the table."

"No apology needed." Myrtle Mae's eyes twinkle. "Your work doesn't stop because you're eating lunch with a little old lady."

He chuckles, pulls out his chair and resumes his seat. "I hadn't once thought of you as a little old lady. You're as lively and active as any teenager—and twice as lovely."

"Andrew, you're making me blush." She covers her cheeks with her hands. "But I have to say you've made my day." Beaming, she hands him the chicken salad. "Help yourself. I'll get saucers for your tea bundles."

Scooping up a cracker full of chicken salad, I take a bite. "Yum, Myrtle Mae. You did it. This is truly delicious."

She cocks her head. "You don't think it needs more salt?"

"The cracker adds some saltiness, so more in the chicken salad might be too much. Depends on one's taste buds."

After Doctor has had a chance to eat a couple bites, I ask, "You're not usually at TW on Fridays. What brought you here today?"

"Might have been more of a gut feeling than anything. I knew you were returning yesterday, and Vance Longpre was entering the program today. Because he's the pastor's son and she apparently initiated your recent arrest—" He looks at Myrtle Mae over the top of his glasses. "My apologies. I don't mean to—"

Her eyes flash. "My daughter has done some terrible things, but having Cassie stopped on her way to say goodbye to her grandmother was worse than appalling. She's reached a new low."

Myrtle Mae touches my arm, but her touch is so tender, I barely feel a twinge. "I am so sorry for what you had to endure, Cassie. Marilyn was furious you hadn't asked her permission to leave or to use my car. She doesn't appreciate Followers slipping out from under her thumb."

"Doctor okayed the trip, and so did Sebastian."

She shrugs. "I said as much, but she considers herself the ultimate authority."

"How did she know I had your car?"

"Her dogs got loose, and no one was around to help her catch them. Of course, they ran straight to my door. They hadn't had their kidney bean treats since before Sebastian left. She actually drove back here, so she didn't have to walk. And parked in the carport.

"Then she came roaring into the house—without knocking—ready to call the police to report the car as stolen. She assumed with my vision I hadn't noticed it missing."

Myrtle Mae rolls her lavender eyes. "Can't convince her I'm not blind as a bat."

"When I told her I loaned you my car to visit your dying grandmother, she turned all shades of red and purple. Even I could see that. She sputtered and stomped around, muttering nasty things about you and calling me a gullible old woman. The dogs hid under the table."

"I'm sorry." I shake my head. "I'm sorry you got dragged into my mess and had to face her wrath and endure her insults. What about your kitten?"

"I locked Citrus in the bedroom before I let the dogs inside. She didn't make a peep the entire time. Probably too scared."

Doctor's gaze flicks between the two of us, as if he doesn't want to miss a word of our exchange. Or maybe he's trying to grasp what he's hearing.

"Did the dogs get their beans?" I ask.

"What's this about beans?" Doctor looks confused.

I laugh. "Ruby Jade's shih tzus love kidney beans."

"I gave them the beans," Myrtle Mae says, "just before Marilee charged into the kitchen. Later, I got to thinking I could have told her Sebastian took my car to a repair shop and would pick it up when he returned. Would have saved you a lot of grief, Cassie."

"Too much lying goes on around here. I'm glad you told the truth. Despite my arrest and two nights in jail, I was eventually able to spend time with my grandma and other family members."

"What's this about lying?" Doctor asks.

"Seems everyone does it here," I tell him. "In a church, of all places. Followers will do about anything to protect themselves from Leadership wrath."

His eyebrows cluster, looking for all the world like tiny foxtails. "Huh."

Myrtle Mae adds more hot water to our cups. "On a more pleasant topic, what brought you to Montana, Andrew?"

"I'm only here part-time," he says. "I commute from Seattle, where my son and I operate a counseling center. He heard about the position here, and knowing I want to ease into retirement, he said this would be a good way to check out the Bozeman area. I'm an avid fisherman, and I want to move to a smaller community, so it might be a good fit."

"I think you'll like it," Myrtle Mae says.

"You will love it." I wave my fork at him. "Before my husband died, we kayaked or canoed most, if not all, the rivers and lakes in this area. We ran into loads of fishermen and fisherwomen, but there's plenty of room for more."

"I'm glad to hear it. Next trip, I'll have to buy a fishing license." He checks his watch. "Better get going so I can return the rental car before I catch my flight."

Myrtle Mae ushers him to the door with an invitation to come again.

"I'd enjoy a return visit," he says. "Very much."

I pick up Citrus and follow him outside. "Thank you for the ride, Doctor. I have a quick question before you leave."

He stops and waits.

"Marcus wasn't in the group today. Is he—?"

"When we announced you'd left to visit your grandmother before she passed, he told me his mother is seriously ill, but he hadn't been allowed to go see her. Or to have phone contact with his family or her doctors. I told him to go spend time with her. She's in North Dakota. He should return Wednesday."

"Uh-oh. I bet Ruby Jade had a fit when she found out."

He pushes his glasses up his nose and offers a wry smile but says nothing.

Back inside, I ask Myrtle Mae if I can nap on her couch before I begin work. My morning hasn't been strenuous, yet my energy is depleted and my entire body aches. Twenty or thirty minutes of sleep plus ibuprofen should revive me.

"Of course, you can nap here," she says. "But you'll rest better on my bed than on the sofa. Close the door, draw the curtains and take as long as you need."

"Thank you. Sounds wonderful." I push to my feet and stop by the bathroom on the way to the bedroom, Citrus at my heels. I let her follow me inside and shut the door.

I'm digging through Myrtle Mae's towels in search of Eric's picture when a doorbell clangs nearby, startling both me and the cat. I didn't know the house had a doorbell. Head back, Citrus is ogling the ceiling as if searching for the source of the noise.

Myrtle Mae's footsteps on the wood floor are hardly a scuff, but I can tell she's crossing the living room. A doorknob rattles, hinges squeak, and she says, "Well, well, my long-lost grandson. What brings you clear out to the north forty, Vance, dear?"

I suck in a gasp. What's he doing here?

"Funny, Grandmother, funny. I'm trying to find someone." His tone is less than endearing. How sad that Myrtle Mae's only child and only grandchild ignore her until they want something from her. And then they're disrespectful.

"As you know, I don't get much company. Who are you looking for?"

"Cassandra Turner."

What? I almost drop the towels on the kitten. My heart pounds. He harassed and insulted me this morning. Wasn't that enough?

"The young woman who assists Sebastian?" Myrtle Mae asks.

"Yeah. She's supposed to be doing yardwork, but I can't find her."

"I heard she was injured…" Myrtle Mae lets the thought unfurl.

"I talked with someone at the dorm. They said she was here."

"Maybe they were guessing."

"Yeah, maybe. I gotta make a bank deposit. Let me know if you see her."

"Bye, dear."

Peeking out the window, I watch Vance walk across the grass, away from the house. If he said goodbye to his grandmother, I didn't hear it. But I'm glad he's gone.

Myrtle Mae knocks on the bathroom door. I slip the towels onto the shelf and open the door. Citrus walks out.

"So that's where you two were hiding." She laughs.

"Timing was great." My heartrate begins to slow. "Thanks for covering for me, Myrtle Mae."

"Did you notice?" She tilts her head. "I did it without a single fib."

"Do you have any idea why he was looking for me?"

"No, but he has a reputation for chasing women. I figured if you didn't come to say "hi," you didn't want to see him."

I awaken from a deep dreamless sleep and maneuver from my stomach to my back. Yawning, I carefully stretch my arms and then my legs. The nap did me a lot of good. I feel much better. Catching sight of the clock on the nightstand, I blink my eyes wide and push upright. I slept for over three hours and haven't done a lick of work, as my grandpa would say.

Scooting to the edge of the bed, I let my feet dangle over the side. What yardwork can I do in an hour and a half that's out of Vance's view? *It's not fair, God. He can find me in his backyard and at Transformation Way and at church.* No place is safe from him, not even Myrtle Mae's house.

I slip from the bed and slowly bend to gather my shoes, one hand on the footboard for balance. Then I walk to the window to open the drapes. I can't believe I slept so long, but I have to admit it felt good.

Myrtle Mae isn't in the living room or the kitchen. I wander outside and find her seated in a lawn chair, watching her kitten play with a furry caterpillar curled into a self-protecting ball. Citrus pounces on it and bats it a whole five inches away.

I laugh. The cat's antics should keep Myrtle Mae entertained for years to come.

"Hello, sleepyhead." Myrtle Mae smiles at me. "Did you have a good nap?"

"It was wonderful, but you shouldn't have let me sleep so long. I won't get much work done today."

"With Andrew here earlier, I forgot to tell you I checked my phone messages this morning and found one from your mom—she wants you to call. And one from Sebastian. He said he heard about what happened to you. If you showed up for work today, I was to tell you to take his truck and go home to bed. Apparently, he's not worried about the yard, so you shouldn't be, either."

"Good to hear, but I'll find a little something to do before I leave."

"He also said he wants you to call him tomorrow, if you have a chance."

"Tomorrow?" I rub my eyes, no doubt smearing my makeup. "Tomorrow is Saturday, right? I've lost track of the days."

"Yes, tomorrow is Saturday. You're welcome to come here and stay all day, if you'd like."

"Thanks. I'll need to escape the dorm, for sure. I have an eight-thirty doctor's appointment and will come over afterward."

"On a Saturday?"

"The Salem doctor made the appointment for me. He wants my Bozeman doctor to check my wounds to make sure they don't become infected. I think I'm healing okay, but it'll be good to have her look over places I can't see."

"Your mom will appreciate knowing you have a follow-up exam."

"What did she say in her message?"

"She asked how you're feeling and said your brother arrived home safely."

"I'll call her and Sebastian after I see the doctor, if you don't mind me borrowing your phone again."

"Of course not, dear. Feel free to use it whenever you need."

Disturbed by the knowledge Vance was searching for me earlier, I decide to clear debris from the hidden path Corban and I walked together. Our first heart-to-heart conversation seems like ages ago. I slowly stoop to pick up a slender but sturdy pointed branch and even more slowly straighten. It'll be a good tool to knock pinecones to the side and stab scraps of paper, not that I expect to find any trash on the secluded pathway. But at least I can say I did some work today.

As I suspected, the trail is clean, but by the time I walk the path from end to end, my muscles have loosened and I'm moving better. I say goodbye to Myrtle Mae then traipse the distance from one house to the other. My senses are tuned to any sound or movement that could indicate Vance is on the prowl, although I'm not sure what I'd do if we met. Hit him with my pink purse?

I punch the code Sebastian gave me into the keypad and am turning the knob on the garage's backdoor when I hear one of the big doors begin to squeak and scrape. I gasp and jump away. Whether the door is going up or down, I can't tell, but I know better than to stick my head in there right now.

Before the door noise ends, I hear a car door slam and a motor roar to life. Vance's sportscar. I recognize the rumble. After a moment the rumble recedes and once again, I hear the big door. I wait several seconds before I crack the backdoor open to peer inside.

CHAPTER FIFTEEN

The heavy door rattles into place. Not until it's fully settled, do I enter the four-car garage and hurry over to Sebastian's truck on the opposite end. I don't see a camera, but in case the garage has one, I square my shoulders and try to walk with a self-assured stride.

My heart is pounding. I hate being inside Ruby Jade's house, though I'm not really *inside* her house. Yet, I need to appear confident, not like I'm sneaking in.

The key is still in the truck's ignition, thank God. I fasten the seatbelt, shove the clutch against the floorboard and twist the key. The engine turns over, and I breathe a sigh of relief. Tapping the button to open the garage door, I bite my lip, half expecting Ruby Jade or Vance to be framed by the rearview mirror when the door lifts. Neither one is behind me, thank God.

What I do see in the mirror is an unfamiliar black SUV. My heart, which hasn't quite recovered from the Vance scare, leaps into high gear again. The vehicle turns onto the long driveway and rolls slowly toward the house. My throat tightens. Something about the SUV shouts government. Did Ruby Jade set me up for another arrest? Will I be accused of stealing Sebastian's pickup?

Think, Cassie, think. I grip the steering wheel. *How will you prove you have Sebastian's permission to drive this truck? You don't have a note or a phone with a text from him or—*

I kill the motor and get out. Better to face whatever this is head-on than wait for the driver to come to the window. This is private property and I have my rights. What those rights may be for an ex-inmate, I have no idea. Hands at my sides where they can be seen, I force a smile onto my face.

The SUV stops behind the pickup, blocking my exit, and the driver's door opens. A tall African-American man gets out, shuts the door and walks toward me. He's wearing a short-sleeved blue Oxford shirt, no tie, and navy pants. His dark eyes never stop moving beneath his equally dark eyebrows and short-cropped hair. He glances at the house, the garage, me, the pickup, the road at the side of the garage, me.

A Caucasian woman steps from the passenger side. She's dressed in a similar fashion, and like the man, she quickly surveys the surroundings. Of average height, she has long red hair and wears glasses.

The man stops, pulls a two-sided card case from his shirt pocket and holds it out. One side has a photo ID and the other a badge. "Good afternoon. I'm Agent Milton Freese with the Federal Bureau of Investigation."

"And I'm Agent Helen Brewer." The woman displays her ID. "We'd like a moment of your time to ask a few questions."

FBI? Not what I expected. I nod. "Okay." The word croaks from my dry throat. I swallow. What do FBI agents want with me?

Agent Freese slips the case into his pocket and takes out a pen and a small notepad. "Please provide your full name."

My pulse hammers my eardrums so hard I strain to hear him. I give him my real name.

He clicks the pen and asks me to spell it for him, which I do.

"Thank you." Smiling, he lowers the pad. "We're looking for a Ruby Jade Paradise, formerly known as Marilyn June Fleming, alias Marilee Longpre. Are you acquainted with her?"

"Yes, she's the owner of this house." *You don't want me? You want Ruby Jade?*

"Do you know if she's home?"

I indicate the garage, which is empty, except for Sebastian's truck. "Her car is gone, which probably means she's not inside. But I can't tell you for sure. I've been doing yardwork in the back."

"Please wait here while I check."

Like I can go anywhere.

Agent Brewer and I watch the agent stride up the wide steps to the big purple doors. He hits the doorbell twice and pounds firmly on one of the doors. When no one answers, he repeats his actions. And when further knocking and bell ringing have no results, he returns to us. I wonder if the FFOW goons are watching from a porch camera.

My heartbeat slows to almost normal, and I take a breath.

"Just a couple more questions," Freese says. "I assume you're headed home for the evening."

"Yes."

"Two other names." He glances at his notepad. "Crystal Stargazer and Lacy Moonflower."

"What?" I give him an incredulous look. Who goes by sixties hippy names these days? "Are they sisters?"

He doesn't respond.

"Never heard of them."

"How about Araminta Davies?"

"Someone by that name might attend Ruby Jade's church. It's a big church and I don't know many people there."

"Arabella Davies."

I shake my head. Is that Araminta's alias? Such old-fashioned names.

Agent Brewer peers at me.

Did I not answer the question right? I have nothing else to tell them. I haven't met the flowerchildren they're looking for. Besides, women coming into FFOW with hippy names would surely be given new names right away.

"Your face is injured," she says. "What happened?"

No beating around the bush with these people.

"I fell down a mountain."

"Tell me more." Her expression is blank, but I get the feeling she doesn't believe me.

"I was hiking with my family in Oregon, and my cousin, who was climbing a boulder, lost her grip and knocked me over. We bumped and slid downhill and landed in a bush."

"Ouch." She winces. "It didn't happen here?"

"You mean in Montana?"

"Uh..." She lifts her chin. "Locally."

"Like I said, we were in Oregon." Are they investigating the cleanses? Those can leave bruises. But do members ever leave marks like what's on my face? I wouldn't be surprised.

"Any idea where Ms. Paradise might be?"

"The church office, maybe?" I shrug and consider telling them this is Ruby Jade's massage night. However, the possible presence of video cameras motivates me to hold my tongue. What was it my grandpa used to say? Loose lips sink ships? For sure, I'd be the torpedoed ship.

Agent Freese checks his watch. "I assume the office is closed by now."

"Could be. I don't know their hours."

Eyebrows furrowed, he stares down at me. "Do you attend Ms. Paradise's church?"

"Sometimes."

For a long moment, Freese studies me, and then he snaps the notepad shut. "I'm told the church's property is gated. Do you know the code to open the gate?"

Uh-oh. Here comes the torpedo. "I'm not allowed to share it, but you can push the button on the call box and talk with security or maybe the secretary. I'm not sure who answers the call box." Keeping my hand low, I motion them toward their vehicle.

One of Freese's eyebrows twitches. "I understand." He turns to Brewer. "We should go." Returning the notebook to his pocket, he starts for the SUV. She does the same.

I follow. When we're far enough away from the garage that I feel I can safely talk, I murmur, "Tailgate me in. Second building."

His voice low, Freese asks, "Why are you whispering?"

"Video cameras."

"Good call. I spotted two. Why the secrecy?"

"Maybe we can talk later."

He nods and speaks louder. "Thank you for your time, Ms. True."

"Yes, thank you," Agent Brewer echoes.

I walk to the truck and climb inside. Ruby Jade's front yard is not a good place to continue our conversation and I can't be late for dinner at the center. Besides, I'm ready for food and another round of ibuprofen.

The agents keep their distance on the highway. But when I take the turnoff to the church, Freese pulls close enough I'm careful to not stop without warning. With my record and the highway episode outside of Missoula, I don't need to be involved in an accident, especially in a borrowed vehicle. Besides, Penelope the Persnickety Pickup, as Sebastian calls his truck, wouldn't look good with a rumpled bumper.

At the FFOW entrance, I punch in the code. When the gate is high enough to allow the pickup access, I spurt onto Paradise Path, the black SUV right behind me. It sails through without a hitch and I lead the agents along the winding road. Now, they're a good two car-lengths behind me.

Near the church, I slow and switch on the right blinker. The SUV's turn signal activates, and Agent Freese pulls into the parking lot. I continue ahead. "Good luck, agents," I whisper. "You're walking into a hornet's nest."

After dinner, the other women leave for a work project, including Dana Marie. Evidently, she's not scheduled to massage Ruby Jade tonight. I wonder if our fearsome leader is avoiding the FBI agents. And I'd love to know what kind of reception he received at the church office, if anyone was there.

I'm tired but not yet ready for more sleep. Still wearing my FFOW work clothes, I wander to the pole fence that surrounds the cemetery and lean against the top rail. Lifting one sore leg over at a time, I check for cars but don't see any. Good. I don't have to sneak around. I make my way toward Inez's lover's burial plot to see if she's left any nasty notes for his wife. She blames the woman for his death and promised revenge. My pace is slow, but I have no need to hurry.

Something white is attached to Charles Allen's headstone. Before approaching it, I check to make sure I'm alone. Assured I'm not being observed, well, mostly assured—one never knows around here—I step close. Inside a plastic document sleeve affixed to the headstone with packing tape is a typewritten letter, a *lengthy* typewritten letter. I suspected I might find a note, but I didn't expect a novel.

Theresa Allen, it begins, *you are responsible for my lover's death! You killed Charles with your atrocious southern cooking. Only rednecks eat that greasy fried poison.*

I skim the rest of the letter. Inez rants about Theresa's lousy housekeeping, her frumpy appearance after birthing five children, how she burdened Charles with a houseful of brats he didn't want. How she was always begging for money, supposedly for food and clothes for the children, and on and on. When the accusations address intimate issues, I skip to the ending in search of a signature, which is also typed. *Charles Allen's Only True Love.*

"Ugh." I straighten and step back, feeling like I just showered in sewer water. What a horrible thing to do to a grieving widow. Once again, I check my surroundings. Seeing no one, I peel the plastic sleeve from the granite and hobble toward the greenhouse, trusting it has a garbage bin behind it.

I circle the greenhouse from a distance, searching for cameras. Finally, I approach and find a fenced dumpster in the back. I'm about to toss the letter into the trash receptacle when something tells me I should destroy it to ensure Theresa Allen and her children never see it. I've never met the woman, but I'll do whatever I can to protect her from Inez.

Slipping the paper from the plastic, I hold the vile thing between my forefinger and thumb, wishing my hands were gloved. I hate touching it. I lay the letter and the plastic sleeve on the dumpster lid and go over to the waist-high compost pile on the other side of the enclosure. Neither the dumpster nor the compost odor is pleasant, but I've got to finish what I started.

A shovel is propped in the decomposing vegetation. I pull it out and dig a cavity in the pile about two-feet deep. Then I set the shovel aside and shred the letter, dropping the pieces one by one into the reeking hole, a fitting receptacle for Inez's cruel words.

I find great satisfaction in flicking the final fragment into the cavity and covering the paper scraps with more compost. Even if a worker happens across a discernible word or two, he or she won't be able to comprehend the full picture. Unless, of course, they saw the letter when it was intact.

But I doubt a worker would have left it there. After all, this is a tattletale culture. Surely, they would have run straight to Ruby Jade with the obscene epistle. I stab the shovel into the compost pile. I can only trust I created a mystery, one that will never be solved.

I return to the dumpster, grab the document sleeve off the top and lift the lid. A horrible stench slaps me in the face. I drop the lid and step back, trying not to retch. Holding my breath, I peek inside again and see a dead raccoon draped over a cardboard box. No wonder it stinks.

The dumpster doesn't contain much, other than a few boxes and some tree branches plus a stack of plant-starter containers. And rotten fruit—apples, maybe. Could be the smell is what attracted the raccoon. But how did it get in the dumpster?

I've heard that raccoons make strange noises. Are those the odd sounds I hear now and then? Or maybe the cry comes from the animal that killed the raccoon.

I slide the plastic sleeve down the side of the bin. It disappears beneath a box and I drop the lid, confident Inez is not going to search for her letter in there. My objective accomplished, I hurry out of the enclosure and climb the small hill behind the greenhouse. Groaning, I lower to a rock to rest for a moment in the fresh evening air and glory in the fact I thwarted a villain.

Inez may think she has Theresa Allen tied to a railroad track and the cruel letter will soon destroy her. But it's not going to happen. Of course, I'll have to keep tabs on Charles Allen's grave, so I can destroy any other malicious missives evil Inez might leave there. One letter probably didn't relieve all the vitriol churning inside the angry woman.

I force my muscles to a standing position and brush off my pants. Too bad Corban isn't here to share the victory. This is one more secret I must keep to myself until we're on the other side of the FFOW river. When the big day comes, I'll throw a huge party. We'll eat Reuben sandwiches, sweet potato fries and any other food Ruby Jade has outlawed, like ham and devil's food cake.

In the waning light, a footpath captures my attention. Unlike the single-track gravel roads that crisscross the cemetery, the narrow trail meanders from the greenhouse into an aspen grove. I follow it and find nestled among the trees and grass what seems to be a mini graveyard. Strange.

The graves don't have headstones, only metal plaques set mere inches. Must be twenty or thirty of them. A couple small plots appear freshly dug.

One stiff knee at a time, I kneel to read the inscriptions, pushing aside tall grass as I crawl from plaque to plaque. Earthy aromas of newly turned soil and humus drift around me, laced by that of weatherworn metal. Above me, aspen leaves rattle in the breeze.

No dates or names are provided on the plaques. Only initials and genders hint at the deceased. *S's Son, B's Son, W's Daughter &Son, L's Daughter.* In the middle is a marble grave marker. It's square and has flowers engraved on each side of the words *Destiny's Child.*

What in the world? I sit on my heels and stare up at the trees. The gently quaking leaves reflect what's left of the day's sunlight. None of this makes sense.

Destiny's Child. Why are all the burial designations nameless except this one, and it's only a vague description? The close spacing suggests the deceased are children, maybe babies. I moan. What a sad thought. Or maybe their ashes were buried here, to save space. But the main cemetery has plenty of room. And children are interred there. I've seen their names and dates.

Is this a form of segregation? Ruby Jade made her feelings about skin color perfectly clear to me. Are dark-skinned children buried here and light-skinned children in the larger section? I shake my head to clear the confusion, which of course, doesn't help. Almost everything about FFOW has boggled my mind since my first day. Why would their cemetery be any less baffling?

I rest my hand on a tree trunk and push to my feet. Time to return to the dorm, change my bandages as best I can manage by myself, and go to bed. My afternoon nap got me this far, but I'm ready to crash.

I sleep hard all night and feel much stronger in the morning. At breakfast, the others bemoan their short night and the fact they have to return to the jobsite as soon as they finish eating. They're preparing a warehouse for an influx of cleaning products. One of the church businesses is expanding its office cleaning services to include product sales throughout the West.

Eunice asks about my plans for the day. I tell her my boss's brother died about the time my grandma died, so we've both been gone from work. "I hope to catch up with the weeding and trimming before the growth gets out of hand."

She frowns and I add, "After I visit my doctor." I spread cream cheese on the bagel half I just toasted. "I have an early morning appointment so she can check out my injuries."

"Very good." Eunice nods. "Just be careful not to get dirt in your wounds when you're working in the yard."

"Having a professional examine your injuries is wise." Dana Marie smiles. "I've seen your scrapes and cuts. You don't want infection to set in."

"If the rest of your body looks anything like your face…" Joleen laughs. "You must have some glorious bruises. Your doctor will be amazed."

CHAPTER SIXTEEN

Dr. Vasquez is seated behind the reception desk when I enter her office. I don't see any other employees. She stands. "Good morning, Cassie. I'll come around and get the door for you."

"Good morning." My doctor asked me to call her by her first name, but I still feel awkward using it, so I don't. Maybe later. I wait for her to open the door, and when she does, I tell her I'm sorry she had to come in on a Saturday.

"No problem. I'll do a quick exam, and we can both go about our day." She points me toward a room with an open door. "Sounds as though you had a bad fall," she says. "But I'm happy to see you again. I've been thinking about you and wondering how you're doing."

Inside the cold room, which smells like rubbing alcohol, I tell her I didn't change the bandages this morning because I figured she'd want to do it right. "Last night was the first time I changed them without help. It's definitely a hack job."

"I doubt it." She hands me a blue paper gown. "Take off everything. Your Oregon doc insisted I check you from head to toe."

"Waist down, all I have are bruises. My jeans and shoes protected me."

"I'll feel better if you'll let me do a thorough exam. It won't take long."

"Okay."

She steps out, apologizing for the cool temperature before she closes the door.

I undress, slip on a gown so thin it's barely more than tissue paper and shiver. I'm rubbing the goosebumps on my arms when Brianna knocks and walks in, her arms full. "I brought some extra gauze pads, ointment and tape, in case you're running low."

"Thank you. I can use them. But how much longer do I need to protect the scrapes?"

"That depends." She sets the supplies on a counter, pulls exam gloves from a dispenser on the wall and puts them on. "Turn around and I'll take a look."

She opens the gown.

I hold my breath, trying hard to suppress my shivers.

"Oh, Cassie," she says. "You are colorful." She peels the gauze from my back and shoulders. "You must ache all over. How are you feeling?"

"Exhausted. I had a long nap yesterday afternoon and slept nine hours last night, yet I feel as if I could fall asleep sitting here."

"Your body is asking you to give it the rest it needs to heal," she says. "Did the church people do this to you?"

"I was in Oregon, not here."

"I've heard so many horror stories about them following people who leave and harassing them, that I thought maybe..."

"Doesn't surprise me. However, I happened to be hiking with my cousins. Did the emergency room doctor tell you I fell down a mountain with a pregnant woman in my arms?"

"What?" She steps around in front of me. "His records indicated a fall and resulting abrasions, punctures and bruises, but no event details." With a shrug, she adds, "Emergency room docs encounter so much drama, they sometimes skip the circumstances and go directly to wound care."

Moving to my side, she slips the gown from my shoulder. "I want to hear all about your accident. But first, tell me how you ended up in Oregon. I've been told once a person gets into your group, they can't leave. I'm also curious to know why you returned."

While she tends my wounds, I tell her why I was in Oregon and how the accident with Natalie happened. I'm sure she knew recounting my adventure would distract me from the medication sting. It helps. I omit my arrest and jail time and don't tell her the leaders badgered my family, like she just mentioned.

"I'm so sorry you lost your grandmother, but I'm glad you were able to spend time with her before she passed away." She tapes gauze pads to my arms, shoulders and back and then checks the soles of my feet. "Both feet have healed nicely. How are your cousin and her baby faring since your fall down the mountain?"

"Last I heard, they were both doing surprisingly well. Natalie and John even named the baby after me. Cassie Anne."

"Perfect! An adorable name. How much did she weigh?"

"I don't remember any mention of weight, but she was incredibly tiny."

"What a miracle she survived the fall, that all of you survived without worse injuries." She steps back. "Your body definitely took a beating, but you're healing. I don't see any major concerns. However, I'd like to see you again in a week. If all is well, you'll be good to go."

"What about my job? I'm headed there right now."

"Part-time is okay, if you take it easy and wear long sleeves and gloves to prevent dirt from entering your wounds."

"Works for me." One more week to avoid volunteer projects. My dormmates will be envious and Leadership will be furious. I feel like a lazy sloth, but right now I don't have the energy to attend class plus work two jobs.

Do you need a prescription for a painkiller?"

"I have one, but I chose not to fill it because of my dependency issues and the fact I live with women with the same problem. So far, ibuprofen has kept me moving."

"Don't be afraid to use it before the pain becomes overwhelming."

"Thanks, I'll keep that in mind."

"You can dress now. I'll meet you out front." Brianna pulls a plastic bag from a drawer and drops the supplies in. "These aren't heavy, just awkward."

While I'm buttoning my blouse, I debate whether I should use Myrtle Mae's money to pay the bill or not. She told me to put gas in Sebastian's truck with it. However, I doubt she'd mind if I use it for medical needs.

My doctor is waiting at the reception desk.

I rest my pink purse on the counter.

She glances at it but doesn't say anything.

Opening the purse, I ask, "How much do I owe you?"

"You don't owe me anything."

"I don't?"

"I've been terribly concerned about you, Cassie, but I've had no way to contact you. Seeing you again, even in your present condition, calms my heart."

"Thank you. I appreciate your concern and your generosity."

"The more I research the church," she says, "the more convinced I am it's a cult."

"My brother has been researching it too, and he says the same thing."

"It has all the markings—a charismatic, narcissistic leader who demands a high level of commitment and rules with an iron fist. She insists on total control, right?"

"Right."

"A typical cult leader claims his or her organization is the only way to a better life, whether on earth or in heaven. Yet, in the end, it's all about the leader's ability to gain power, money and sex."

"The sex thing is interesting." I stare at the ceiling. "I guess you could say FFOW has a different twist. Members have to get permission, and then it's regimented." Thinking of Inez, I add, "Unless, of course, they're one of the leaders. The subject comes up all the time in weird ways. My guess is Ruby Jade has some kind of sex hang-up."

"I don't mean to scare you." Brianna tilts her head. "But last night I read cults are perfect places for rapists and pedophiles to hang out. Their crimes are never reported because they'd make the group look bad."

"How awful." I grimace. "I haven't heard of such a person in this bunch, but anything's possible."

"Can't hurt to keep your guard up." She hands me a brochure. "This lists city and county agencies and their phone numbers. I know making calls is difficult for you, but you may be in a position at some point to use one or more of these numbers."

I glance through the pamphlet. The format has been updated since my days on the streets when every policeman I encountered gave me a copy. I'll leave it in Sebastian's glovebox because I don't dare take it into the dorm.

After thanking her, I say, "I can give you a couple contact numbers. If you'd like."

"Yes, I'd appreciate numbers." She finds a notepad and sets it on the counter. "Ready."

"The first one reaches my supervisor, Sebastian Longpre."

"Is he, uh, trustworthy?"

"Yes, very. He's not a member of the church."

"Good."

I dictate the number and then say, "The second is for a sweet older woman named Myrtle Mae Fleming. She's associated with the church, but she doesn't participate in the craziness."

"Okay."

When she's done writing, I say, "One more."

She looks up. "You have an amazing memory."

"For whatever reason, booze didn't wipe out my numbers brain cells."

At first, I thought I'd give her Corban's number, but I hesitate for fear he or his family might somehow be exposed. Instead, I give her Dr. Hoffman's number. "He's the new director for the rehab program and an outsider who flies in from Seattle twice a week. Seems to be a nice guy and someone Ruby Jade can't tromp over. So far, at least, he's stood up to her and her sidekicks."

"Interesting." She tears the sheet from the pad. "I'll only use these if I haven't heard from you in a while."

"Thanks for watching my back. I have your number memorized and may be able to send a text now and then from one of those three phones."

"I'll appreciate whatever updates you can safely provide."

My doctor walks me out the door. She's been so kind to me, I feel like I'm leaving a good friend. "See you next week."

She must be feeling the same way, because she gives me a gentle hug. "I hate for you to return to an unsafe environment."

"If you're a praying person, I'd appreciate your prayers."

"I'll be on my knees for you, every day."

"Pray I can make it to graduation. I'm planning a huge party, and you're invited."

She grins. "I'll be there."

I'm almost to Ruby Jade's driveway, when an ambulance shoots from the side of the garage. The moment it hits the street, the siren blares and lights flash.

I stomp the truck brakes. Myrtle Mae? My heart skips a beat.

The siren screech blasts through the open pickup windows. Ears ringing, I try to catch a glimpse inside as it passes, but I can't see through the dark windows.

Heart pounding, I watch the departing ambulance in the rearview mirror. Maybe Myrtle Mae isn't the person they're transporting. Maybe the maid cut herself preparing food or fell down the stairs. Not that I want her to suffer any more than I want my dear friend to suffer.

I drive the narrow track from the garage to Myrtle Mae's house, searching for signs of life. The place feels deserted, but the huge property often feels uninhabited. I park the pickup in the carport and walk to the backdoor. The screen door is propped open, which is unusual.

I'm about to knock when I notice several weeds have infiltrated the pansies I planted by the stoop. Slowly and carefully, I bend to dig them out with my fingers. Tossing the weeds aside, I straighten, brush off my hands and lean in the kitchen. "Myrtle Mae, you home?"

I wait but hear no answer, so I step inside. Everything seems normal, other than the table and chairs, which are slightly askew, and a whiff of aftershave.

"No, she's not home."

I jump, startled by a male voice.

Vance saunters from the living room into the kitchen, a phone in his hand.

I should have recognized the aftershave smell I assumed emanated from a medic.

"Well, hello, Cas-*san*-dra Turner." His condescending smirk is as haughty as ever. "Paramedics took her to the hospital."

"What happened?" I inch backward toward the door.

"She tripped over a stupid cat and called my jerk uncle in California." His face clouds. I wonder if he's remembering Sebastian is not really his uncle. "He asked me to meet the ambulance and direct the driver back here."

I glance at the open doorway. Citrus could be halfway up a tree by now. If I don't find her, Myrtle Mae will be heartbroken. "How badly was she hurt?"

"How would I know?" He steps closer, flexing a bicep.

Am I supposed to be impressed?

"She could talk," he says, "if that's what you mean. They said she probably broke her hip."

"Oh, no! That's terrible! Are you going to the hospital to be with her?" He needs to leave, so I can search for the kitten. I'll check on Myrtle Mae later.

"What do you think I am, Cas-*san*-dra?" His dark eyebrows twist. "A mama's boy?"

Actually, a mama's boy is exactly what I think you are. "We're talking about your grandmother, Vance. She shouldn't be alone."

"Mom's on the way." He snorts. "She's going to give her what-for for sneaking in a cat when she wasn't supposed to have one."

Funny how the rules change to make Ruby Jade look good and to make everyone else, including her own mother look bad. I backstep over the threshold and onto the stoop.

"Just like you snuck a phone when you weren't supposed to have one."

I grasp the doorjamb. What's he talking about?

He brandishes the cell phone he's holding—Myrtle Mae's cell phone.

My heart thuds. What kind of incriminating trail did I leave behind?

"Yeah." He snickers. "My mother is finding these pictures of you and Dahlstrom quite interesting. I forwarded them all to her."

Oh, no! I forgot to show Myrtle Mae the pictures then delete them. The photos attached to Corban's texts disappeared with the texts, but not the one I took of him at the airport or those of my family. "He gave me a ride to the airport."

Vance's black eyes turn sinister. "You were alone without permission. Mom would've never allowed it."

"We were not alone. We were in the middle of a busy airport, surrounded by people." Thank God, none of the photos are of the two of us together.

"You don't have an assigned friendship and you didn't have a chaperone." He drops the phone into his shirt pocket and edges closer, invading my space with his arrogance and aftershave.

"I had a judge's permission, Sebastian's permission and the TW director's permission to fly to Oregon. But I didn't have a way to get to the airport. Corban offered to drive me there. I accepted." Why am I explaining my actions to this imbecile?

"Those dudes don't count." He scoffs. "The only one who hears from God is my mother."

"I'd better get busy." I start down the short ramp Sebastian built so Corban's mom could visit Myrtle Mae.

"Was the kid you left at the hospital Dahlstrom's baby?"

I stop.

"You snuck away to Oregon to have his baby, thinking we'd never know."

"What?" I squint at him. "I have no idea what you're talking about."

"I saw the picture."

"Of my cousin's baby."

Vance grabs my arm and yanks me into the house.

"Ouch!" His rough grasp is painful. "Vance, my arms are injured. Please don't."

"I checked out Grandmother's bed." His voice takes on a sickening seductive lilt. "It's soft, Goldilocks, just right for a good time, if you get my drift."

From beneath lowered lids, he surveys my body. "I've always wanted to bed a street tramp. Come with me, Cas-*san*-dra." His determined tone frightens me more than his greedy leer.

"I'm injured, Vance. Covered with bruises."

"I like bruises." He waggles his eyebrows. "They're sexy. The more bruises my wives had, the more they turned my crank." His face contorts. "Dahlstrom give you those bruises?"

I stare into his empty eyes, wondering what kind of lunacy lurks behind them. His breath reeks of alcohol, but he's not falling-down drunk, which is too bad. "You're hurting me." I hate that my voice quivers. My fear will only serve to fuel his quest for power and control.

"I like pain." He sneers. "On other people."

"Please let me go. I need to do my work."

"Your work today will be under my supervision." He drags me through the kitchen and into the living room, past the open front door. "I'll be sure to give Sebastian a good report."

My arm is on fire, but I resist his pull, screaming, "Stop, Vance, stop!" It's a long shot, but maybe a neighbor will hear my cry for help.

He swings around and slaps me, knocking me to my knees.

"Please," I beg, "don't—"

"Shut up!" He slides a wicked-looking blade from the sheath attached to his belt. "And get up."

I stagger to my feet. *Stop him, God. Don't let him—*

He pushes me ahead. "On the bed, now."

At the doorway, I turn to him. "Vance, you don't want this on your record. Let me go, and I'll pretend it never happened. No one will ever know."

"You haven't figured it out yet?" His fiendish laughter shoots a chill up my spine. "No one will ever know." He grabs my chin and jerks it so he's staring straight into my eyes. "Because what happens in FFOW, stays in FFOW."

Obviously, he's done this before, and he's convinced he can get away with it again. My fear turns to anger. I will fight him with every ounce of my strength, knife or no knife.

"Okay." I change my tactic. "I understand how things work here. But still, I'd appreciate it if you'd put the knife away." Fighting to keep my voice steady, I add, "It makes me nervous."

"That's the point." He brandishes the weapon. "Get it?" He snickers. "The point."

"I'll do whatever you want, but—"

"You will?" He sounds disappointed, as though he wants me to resist.

"But not with a knife in my face. I just came from the doctor. I've had enough pain today."

"You think I care?" He aims the blade at his grandmother's bed. "Over there."

Although everything within me pleads, *do what he says and get it over with*, I don't budge. I made a vow to remain celibate after Eric died, and I intend to keep it.

His eyes narrow, twitch and then brighten, like he's come up with a better idea. He unbuckles his belt. "First, you'll take off my clothes, Cas-*san*-dra. And then I'll watch you strip."

He runs the blade's flat side across my chest, his lips melded into a lascivious curve.

"You claim to be a musician. You can prove it by singing while you do a striptease for me." He snickers and slices a button from my shirt. "See what a nice guy I am? I'm helping you."

I don't move, fearing the slightest breath will trigger a stab in the heart.

He lowers the weapon, and I raise my hands, as if in surrender. "I'll do it, after you put the knife away."

Brow furrowed, eyes wary, he studies my face. "Promise?" A greasy black curl falls onto his forehead.

CHAPTER SEVENTEEN

"Like I said, Vance, it makes me nervous." I shrug. "I can't relax."

"You want to relax?"

"I'm thinkin' we could check your grandma's cupboards. See if she has a bottle of wine stashed away." I offer a demure smile. "Something to mellow us and make things even better."

"No!" His headshake is emphatic. "You're stalling. We'll have the wine afterward."

"Whatever you say." I try to sound pleasant.

He gives me a suspicious look.

"About the knife…" I let the word hang.

"Okay, but if you try any funny stuff, I'll have this blade out so fast your head'll spin."

"I understand." I wonder if he's thought far enough ahead to plan where he'll put the knife when he's nude. But I don't mention it, and I keep my hands high.

Slowly lowering the blade to his side, he keeps his focus on my face. The sneer never leaves his lips.

The moment he glances down to slip the tip into the sheath, I jab my fingernails into his eyes, raking outward from his nose in opposite directions.

He screams and unsheathes the knife, thrusting it upward.

I jump away.

Screeching like a banshee, he drops the weapon and clasps his hands over his eyes.

I kick the knife aside, pivot and knee his groin, followed by a neck whack with the blade of my hand.

He collapses on the carpet, yelping and swearing. One hand covers his eyes and the other grasps his groin. Thrashing about the floor, he cries, "stupid tramp" over and over and over. Tears drench his face.

I dart into the bathroom to grab a washcloth from the towel rack. Racing back into the bedroom, I snatch the knife from the floor with the cloth. No way do I want my fingerprints on Vance Longpre's knife.

"Call an ambulance!" Vance gasps. "You blinded me and smashed my—" His moan becomes a sob. "I'm dying!" He writhes beside the bed.

I hold the weapon away from my body. I need to hide it. But where?

Vance struggles onto his hands and knees. "Help me, Cassandra! You've got to help me!"

"Get out of Myrtle Mae's house, now."

"This is my house." He moans. "I own it."

I poke his rear.

He jerks and a spot of blood appears on his pants.

"Remember this knife, Vance? The one that'll make your head spin? Get out, while you're still in one piece."

"No, don't!" His voice trembles. "You have to help me. I can't see where I'm going."

I jab him again, this time a little closer to his area of concern. More blood.

He shrieks and scrambles toward the door but slams into the wall with a loud thump and falls backward. "I can't see." Sobs scramble his words. "…hurts."

"Did you get the point yet? The point you're the stupid one for messing with a street tramp?" So much more I want to say to the pathetic pansy, but I control myself.

Feeling along the wall for the doorway, he crawls through it and past the bathroom, blubbering and groaning. "I'll tell my mother and she—"

"I'll tell the cops."

"They won't believe you."

"I have the evidence."

He swears.

"Turn left and go out the front door."

Fumbling across the living room, he crawls to the threshold and inches forward.

I prick his backside one last time and kick him out the door, merely for the satisfaction of doing it.

He collapses on the porch, whimpering, "Stop, Cassandra, stop. I can't see, I'm—"

"Go home, Vance. Next time you think of assaulting someone, remember the street tramp you called Goldilocks."

I watch him roll off the porch, push to his feet and stagger toward his house. He stops and swings my direction, hands over his eyes. Calling me the "b" word, he mutters, "I'll get you for this. You'll pay."

I'd like to think this is the end of the matter, but I know better. If nothing else, I trust he'll be afraid to assault another person, male or female, young or old. Knife in hand, I slam the door shut, lock it and return to the bedroom to make sure no sign of our struggle remains.

Standing in the doorway, my heart pounds and my breath comes in gulps. I've got to dump the knife before someone sees me with it. Vance won't call the police, but his mother might. I survey the small room.

If I slipped the knife between Myrtle Mae's mattress and box springs, she might feel the lump. I could put it in a far corner of a closet shelf, but thinking of her poor eyesight, I'd hate for her to unknowingly encounter the sharp blade and be injured. The same goes for the kitchen cupboards.

Burying the weapon outside is an option. However, I'd have to get a shovel from the shed by the house, which would take time, as would digging a hole. Plus, I might be seen and questioned. For sure, I can't leave the knife in Sebastian's truck or take it to my dorm room.

I twist the knob on the spare bedroom, but it's locked. That leaves the bathroom. I study the narrow shelves near the door. The tallest shelf, which is way too high for Myrtle Mae, appears empty. I lay the knife on the counter, drag a chair in from the kitchen and stand on it. As I suspected, the shelf isn't in use. Leaving the nasty blade inside the folded washcloth, I place it against the back wall and step to the floor. The spot of blood on the knife's tip will dry soon.

I'm about to return the chair to the kitchen when I remember Eric's picture. Not once since Myrtle Mae put it in here have I had a chance to look at it. Now is as good a time as any. Who knows when I'll have another opportunity? Maybe it'll help me clear my head of Vance.

Pulling the framed photograph from behind the stack of towels, I sit on the chair to examine my handsome husband's face. If he had survived the cancer, his features would have matured a bit by now, but not much.

"Eric…" Without warning, my hands begin to shake, and I burst into tears. "I didn't, I would never—" Grabbing a towel, I bury my face in it. I stopped the rape before it happened. I didn't break my vow to remain faithful to my husband, yet I feel defiled, humiliated. Violated.

Sobs rack my sore body. I should feel relieved, triumphant even. But I inflicted serious damage on Ruby

Jade's son. If he tells her what happened—his version, that is—I'll suffer the consequences. And if he loses his sight, he'll blame me. I console myself with the knowledge he could see good enough to head in the general direction of his house.

Should I feel guilty? I don't. Not yet, anyway. I protected myself against Vance and the most horrific knife I've ever seen. I also avenged the assaults his previous victims suffered and, I hope, shocked and scared him to the extent he'll never attack another woman.

I set the picture on the chair, splash cold water on my face and dry my cheeks with a towel. Running my fingers through my hair, I give my reflection a glance. My eyes are red and puffy, and my bruised, scraped face is red and swollen where Vance slapped me. Oh, well. Not much I can do about it.

I return Eric's picture to its hideaway and am lifting the chair to carry it to the kitchen, when a woman's voice calls, "Knock, knock. Anyone home?"

I gasp. I should have closed the backdoor. But the voice doesn't belong to Vance or Ruby Jade. It's feminine and slightly familiar, yet I can't put a face with it. I call, "Just a minute," and shuffle the chair into the kitchen.

Corban's mom is parked on the stoop. "Cassie, what a nice surprise."

"Hi, Denise." I don't feel like talking right now and I'd rather she not see me looking even worse than the day we met. Yet, I'm glad it's her, not Ruby Jade.

Her expression turns serious. "You probably know Myrtle Mae was transported to the hospital less than an hour ago."

I nod.

"Sebastian asked me to get her kitten and keep it while she's hospitalized. I told him I wasn't sure I could catch it."

My knees threaten to buckle. I push the chair under the table and lean on the back.

She peers at me. "Are you okay?"

"I'm, uh, worried about Myrtle Mae. The EMTs said she might have a broken hip."

"Oh, the poor dear. How awful. I'd visit her, but if her daughter is at the hospital..." She shrugs. "Ruby Jade hates me, so I try to keep my distance. May I come in?"

"I'm sorry." I start toward her. "I should have offered to help you."

"No need." She waves me away. "This chair will go right over the threshold." She motors into the kitchen. "How are you feeling? Are you healing okay?"

"I saw the doctor this morning. She says I'm doing good." Of course, that was before the attack. Now I hurt everywhere, especially my arms, and I can barely stand.

I straighten the table and move a chair to make room for her wheelchair. Adjusting the flowered tablecloth, I ask Denise if she'd like some tea. "As you know, Myrtle Mae always has plenty on hand." I slide the tea basket in front of her.

"I'm glad to hear your doctor is pleased." She looks me over, one eyebrow raised, like she questions the doctor's judgement. "I'd appreciate some water, if you don't mind."

Her gaze returns to my chest.

I glance down. My blouse is gaping. "Oops." Embarrassed, I cover the gap with my hand, even though she's seen me shirtless. "I must have lost a button. I'll look for a safety pin in the bathroom." I stumble out of the kitchen, grateful for a reason to escape her scrutiny.

This is the first time I've opened the bathroom drawers, but I'm glad to find a plastic container of safety pins in the top drawer. Inserting the tiny pin with my trembling fingers is a struggle, but finally, I'm able to clasp it on the outside of the blouse. I'll have to be sure to change shirts before I join the others for dinner tonight.

I check my reflection again in the mirror. No wonder Denise is giving me funny glances. I look as traumatized as I feel. Wetting a washcloth with cold water, I spread it across my face and hold it there for several seconds. But as wonderful as it feels, I shouldn't tarry. I wring out the cloth, hang it on the rack and towel dry my cheeks.

On the way from the living room into the kitchen, I stare at my fingernails. "How did my nails get so dirty? Oh, I remember." Pressing my elbows against my ribs to control the shaking, I tell Denise I dug weeds out of Myrtle Mae's pansy patch before I came in. Microscopic chunks of Vance's skin are likely mixed with the dirt. Disgusted by the thought, I make a face.

"It's just dirt." Denise chuckles. "We all deal with it every day."

Dealing with dirt is one thing. Dealing with Vance is another. I take a toothpick from the porcelain toothpick holder on the counter and clean my nails before I wash my hands and pour us each a glass of water. I place a glass in front of Denise and sit across from her, clutching mine to control my quivering hands. "Where were we?"

She thanks me, takes a drink and sets the glass on the tablecloth. "I was telling you why you-know-who hates me. Reminds me—I saw Vance staggering between this house and the front house, probably drunk. His mother tries to keep his drinking under wraps, but it's no secret. I hope he didn't bother you."

My heart thumps my ribs. Now is my chance to tell her what happened. But I don't know her very well. Considering the way she stared at my blouse, she might assume I provoked the assault. Or maybe she'll think I was messing around with Vance. After all, I'm a street tramp and a jailbird, not a model Follower like her sons. And then she'd tell Corban, who'd be disgusted and never speak to me again.

I twist the glass from side to side. "Myrtle Mae called Sebastian when she fell, and he called...he called..." I can barely say the name. "Vance to direct the ambulance back here. I came as he was leaving. He had alcohol on his breath." Most of what I said is true.

She peers at me. "I don't mean to pry, but he's been known to—"

"He…" Tears well in my eyes. I want to tell her what happened, but I don't want to think about it right now. Maybe later I can tell her. It won't change anything. Vance made sure to inform me what happens in FFOW stays in FFOW. I clasp my hands in my lap and change the subject. "I haven't seen the kitten. Hope it didn't climb a tree." And I hope Denise can't hear the tremor in my voice.

Denise cocks her head. "I don't hear it crying, which is a good sign." She gives me an understanding smile. "Please know I'm available anytime you need a listening ear, Cassie."

"Thank you."

"Regarding Ruby Jade…"

I'm grateful she doesn't push me to talk about Vance. It's just not in me right now.

"She considers anyone in a wheelchair to be a useless sniveling weakling and demon-possessed," Denise says. "I make her look bad because she tried to heal me and failed. She'd kick me out of the church the same way she has others who didn't receive healing through her, but she knows Phil and the boys would go too. And she'd lose the tithes of four people."

"How awful. How can you stay, after everything she's done to your family?"

"We told you about, uh…" She glances at the open door and windows and lowers her voice. "Triple F, right?"

I nod.

"It's what motivates us and keeps us moving forward."

"I love the concept. I want to help."

"We'd be delighted to have you join us. But be aware my sons may act as if it's a breeze. However, truth be told…" She leans closer. "Insurrection is not easy and not without danger."

"I understand. Maybe after I graduate—"

Denise straightens, forearms on the table. "You do realize, Cassie, your graduation will be pushed out of reach every time you come close. Ruby Jade likes to keep the state money flowing."

"No, I didn't know that."

"We need to find a way for you to exit the program."

I slump in my chair. "I've put all my hopes and dreams into leaving in eleven months."

"I wish I could tell you it'll happen, but facts are facts." She pats my arm and then recoils. "I am so sorry. I know how sore your arms are."

"I'm okay." Right now, my heart hurts worse than my arms. I feel like I've just been sentenced to an eternity in hell. To never escape the program or FFOW or Vance is more than I can bear. "We should find the kitten. I hate to think how far she may have scampered with the door open."

"What's she look like?"

"Citrus is tiny, only a few weeks old, with yellow-and-orange stripes."

"Let's search inside first." Denise reverses away from the table and lifts the tablecloth. "Our cat disappears under furniture every time someone new comes around. A noisy ambulance and hyper EMTs bursting through the door could have scared the kitten into hiding." She peeks under the table and shakes her head.

I have my doubts about her theory, but Denise is the cat owner, not me. "If you'll check the living room," I tell her, "I'll check Myrtle Mae's bedroom and the bathroom." I'd rather she not get a whiff of lingering Vance odors. "The other bedroom door is always closed. This little house doesn't have many hiding places."

The moment I step into the bedroom, I smell him. His sweat, his booze-tinged breath, his overpowering aftershave. I tell myself I must focus on the task at hand, not the panic flooding my chest. I fight to calm my breathing. The odors could be my imagination, but whatever it is, I hate Vance's ability to do this to me.

One hand on the footboard, I carefully lower to my hands and knees before I lift the bed skirt. "Citrus, baby, where are you?"

From the far corner comes a soft meow.

"Over here, Citrus." I bend low. "It's safe now."

The kitten crawls near enough to reach. I scoop her into my hand and sit upright, holding her close. "I'm sorry you were scared, but you gave me a scare, too." Citrus responds by snuggling against my neck and purring.

With effort, I push to a standing position and walk into the living room, where Denise is checking behind an easy chair.

"Denise, meet Citrus Fleming." I laugh. "If I dare give a cat a last name."

She takes the kitten and lifts it so she can see its face. "What a sweet little thing you are." She lays it on her shoulder.

The cat sniffs Denise's neck and hair. Its purrs never falter.

"Citrus likes you." I hug my ribs to hide my hands. The trembling worsened when I walked into the bedroom.

"Either that…" Denise laughs. "Or the smell of my cat." She gives the kitten to me. "If you'll follow me to my van, you can help me put her in the carrier I brought."

Outside, she pushes a button on her fob and the van's side door opens. Another button activates a ramp that unfolds onto the ground. Denise steers her wheelchair inside. I check the surroundings for Vance, in case he has returned for revenge. Not seeing him, I climb into the van and deposit Citrus in the carrier.

I'm calmer now. The kitten does that for me. I'll miss both Myrtle Mae and her cat.

After I secure the latch, I tell Denise I'll get the kitten's things and return to the house, where I gather bowls, food and toys and stack them in the cardboard box Citrus sleeps in. I carry them to the van where Denise is fastening her seatbelt. She has already secured the wheelchair in front of the steering wheel. "Do you want the litterbox?"

"Let's wait. Maybe she'll use the one we have. I'd rather not clean two litterboxes, if I don't have to."

"I understand." I set the cardboard box beside the carrier. Maybe the familiar odors will keep the kitten from yowling all the way to the Dahlstroms' house. At the moment, Citrus is so busy sniffing the carrier, she doesn't notice the box.

I feel a stab of envy, which is crazy. My brother spent a night with the Dahlstroms, and now Citrus will be there indefinitely. I, on the other hand, have no idea where they live, but I know that like the kitten, I would be safe there.

"A question before you go." I slide into the passenger seat. "What do you think about me visiting Myrtle Mae at the hospital? Sebastian is letting me use his truck while he's gone."

Denise rubs her chin, a thoughtful expression in her eyes. "Ruby Jade is a jealous woman."

"Jealous of her mother?"

"Jealous of attention going to anyone but herself. She discourages close friendships, which you may have noticed, and I've heard she's unhappy you and her mother have a relationship. Knowing Myrtle Mae is close enough to you that she loaned you her car infuriates her."

"I have a feeling I haven't heard the end of it."

"And a judge dropping her case against you? That sticks in her craw like nothing else. I guarantee both you and the judge are now in her sights. She's run other judges out of town along with county commissioners, journalists and pastors who tell the truth about FFOW. I'm praying for you and for Judge Bock. If he's a good judge, unlike Snow, we need his presence in this valley."

She stops. "Now, where was I? Oh, yes, you asked about visiting Myrtle Mae."

"I'm getting the idea it might not be wise."

"I'm sorry."

CHAPTER EIGHTEEN

I sigh. "Guess I'll have to find other ways to support Myrtle Mae."

"Prayer, for sure," Denise says. "I'm concerned Ruby Jade will use this mishap to further limit her mother's world. More than once she's hinted at dementia, which you and I know is far from the truth. If Ruby Jade found a doctor willing to drown her mother in drugs, she could dump her in a nursing home and never have to bother with her again."

"That's scary." I wince. "I wish I knew how to help her."

"I'll give her brother a call. He's younger than Myrtle Mae and does his best to shield her from his nasty niece. Have you met Norman?"

"Not yet."

"I hope you get to meet him one of these days. He tries to fly under the radar yet keep tabs on his sister."

I climb out of the vehicle. The ramp folds into the van and the side door closes. Denise drives away slowly, maneuvering the wide curve that accesses the path leading to the street.

I wave goodbye, relieved Citrus is in good hands.

Mid-curve, Denise stops and lowers her window.

I walk over, wondering if I need to calm the kitten. But I don't hear any howls.

"Meant to tell you we thoroughly enjoyed your brother's stay with us." She smiles. "You'd have thought he and my boys had known each other for years."

"Kip is a great brother. Thank you for asking him to spend the night. I wish I could have been there with all of you."

"One of these days," she says. "Count on it."

Despite what she may think might have happened between me and Vance, I'm still welcome in her home. She has no idea how comforting her words are to me.

She reaches for her sunglasses on the dashboard. "My sons enjoy working with you."

"And I enjoy working with them. You raised two wonderful sons. They're—oh, no!" I cover my mouth with my hands. "I forgot to tell you."

"What is it, Cassie?" Denise hooks the sunglasses on the steering wheel.

"I got us both in trouble."

"Who?"

"Me." I lower my hands. "And Corban."

Her brow furrows. "How?"

"Myrtle Mae, Vance…"

Denise appears even more confused.

I take a long breath, frustrated with myself for doing something so entirely stupid when I knew better. "Remember when Kip and I were with your family and I asked Corban to not delete the pictures from Myrtle Mae's phone before I showed them to her?"

"Yes…"

"When she fell, she used her phone to call Sebastian who, like I said, called Vance to meet the ambulance and lead it back here. Vance was snooping around the house when I arrived, and evidently, he snooped in her phone, too."

"What, exactly…" Denise cringes. "Did he find?"

"Corban put an app on the phone that enabled us to talk and text privately." I give her the good news first. "Those texts disappeared into cyberspace. What didn't disappear were the pictures of relatives I asked Corban to save on his computer for me. I wanted to show them to Myrtle Mae, but I forgot. They might have been random shots of random people, except I posed for a couple pictures with my family and with my cousins."

I shake my head, trying to comprehend my latest predicament. "Vance forwarded all the photos to his mother. I don't know her reaction, but two pictures really got him going."

Her eyebrows cluster, and she squints like she's preparing for the worst.

"One was of Corban. I snapped it at the airport, so it was obvious Myrtle Mae didn't take the picture. Being alone with your son, even though we were surrounded by other travelers, was apparently a terrible transgression of FFOW rules."

"Oh. My. Stars." Her eyes grow wide. "That'll get the pot boiling."

"Yeah."

She asks, "What was the other picture? Was it worse? I mean, something Leadership can misconstrue."

"Remember the picture I showed you of my cousin's baby girl?"

"Uh-huh." Her curiosity is tinged with concern.

"Vance decided the baby was mine, fathered by Corban. I snuck away to Oregon to deliver her there."

"Oh, good grief." She rolls her eyes.

"Right."

"If they can't find dirt, they manufacture it." She shakes her head, a disgusted look on her face. "Phil says they should patent the process."

The kitten meows.

"I'd better go. But first, let's pray." She holds out her hand, and I take it. "Lord," she prays, "we have another ridiculous predicament, so ridiculous I hate to bother you with it. However, you and I both know Leadership can easily and readily make a mountain out of a molehill. If this little anthill mushrooms into something ugly, I plead for you to flatten it like a Montana prairie.

"I also humbly ask you to restore FFOW to the wonderful church it once was, to the glory of your name. Give Cassie strength, wisdom and confidence in you for the days ahead. You are a faithful, powerful, loving God, for which we thank you. Amen."

Denise squeezes my hand. "Sebastian, Myrtle Mae and the Dahlstrom clan are on your side, Cassie, along with your parents and your brother—and your all-powerful Creator. No doubt things will get worse before they get better. Yet one of these days, we'll look back in time and ask, 'How did we ever survive the craziness?' And then we'll tell each other how our Savior got us through."

She grins and drives away.

Before I leave the house, I straighten chairs, wash and dry the glasses we used and put them away. Staring out the window over the sink, I think about Denise. She's such a nice lady. I should have confided in her. But really, what's done is done. She can't stop the retaliation that's sure to come.

On my last walk-through to ensure the little house is pristine, I spy the missing button on the hall floor and pocket it. I'm about to shut the bedroom drapes, when I catch sight of a phone in the corner where the dresser meets the wall.

Myrtle Mae's cell phone! It has to be. I pick it up. Sure enough, it has big buttons. All I can figure is it fell out of

Vance's pocket and was kicked away during the confrontation.

I stare at the phone, debating with myself. Should I hide it with the knife to save as evidence? It has Vance's fingerprints on it. Yet, what do the prints prove? Nothing more than the fact he held the phone in his hands.

After only a moment's hesitation, I delete the photos. I'll put the phone in the pickup's glovebox for safekeeping and let Sebastian decide what to do with it after he returns.

I shut all the windows, keeping an eye out for Vance who might be on the prowl, and close the backdoor. But I don't lock it because I'll need access to water and a bathroom while working. I normally use the bathroom in Sebastian's hideout, but I'd rather not get that close to the main house. I know my sweet friend would understand.

Finally, I shut the screen door that's been propped open all this time. One hand resting on the sun-warmed doorframe, I bow my head and whisper, "Dear God..." About to pray for Myrtle Mae, I stop.

Ruby Jade was already hopping mad about the judge's decision and my trip to Oregon. And now, with the picture mess-up and what I did to Vance, she'll be out for blood. God is letting me stumble through the FFOW minefield alone—and I'm detonating one blast after another. He doesn't hear my prayers.

Cassie, I tell myself, head still bowed, *that's not true. Have you already forgotten how he got you out of jail in time to say goodbye to Grandma Hunt? Besides, this isn't about you. It's about Myrtle Mae. She needs God's comfort and healing—and protection.*

I also remind myself I've been down this road before. I can't abandon my faith. No matter how bleak my future, I've got to believe what Denise said. God is faithful, powerful and loving, even when believing is hard, so hard.

Climbing into Sebastian's truck saps what little energy I have left. I check the time. Not even noon yet and I'm totaled. I sit for a moment, mindlessly watching a squirrel hop from one tree branch to another. Then I catch myself and quickly scan my surroundings. I can't let Vance sneak up on me. If he has the slightest bit of vision, he'll attempt to even the score.

My heart pounds and I remain on high alert throughout the short drive from the back of the property to the front. Seeing no sign of Vance, I breathe a sigh of relief. *Please, Sebastian, come home. I hate to be a scaredy-cat, but I'm afraid Vance will attack again. He's strong, much stronger than I am.*

At the corner where the main road into Fellowship Neighborhood intersects with the highway, I turn toward town and the Sheriff's Department. I should report the attempted rape before Vance and his mother accuse me of assaulting him.

My body aches and my mind races with the summer breeze rushing through the open windows. Fresh, clean whiffs of new-mown alfalfa are almost enough to wipe Vance's stink from my sinuses. Almost.

I repeatedly check the mirror to make sure he's not following me. He probably isn't able to drive right now, but I can't count on that. Halfway to Bozeman, I remember the sheriff, like Judge Snow, is supposedly under Ruby Jade's thumb. What chance do I have to plead my case against her son? It's my word against his, and I'm the one still serving time. Sure, Vance recently spent a night in jail, but I've spent a whole lot of nights behind bars.

I have no proof, other than the knife. But they could say I stole it. After all, I'm the convicted thief. Would I be allowed to press charges? If I pressed charges, would the case go anywhere? Worse yet, would I be blamed for the attack?

As far as I know, Vance has never suffered consequences for his crimes. Someone needs to hold him accountable. But is that someone me? On the other hand, maybe what I did to Vance is a consequence the creep will never forget.

The closer I get to the Sheriff's Department, the more my hands shake. Clutching the steering wheel, I slow and almost stop. Yet, the futility of my situation and the sight of the jail where I was held for the last year keep me driving. They might want to do a rape test, even if I tell them it didn't happen. I don't want to endure the humiliation.

I'm tempted to head straight to Oregon and my parents' front door, even knowing I'd be arrested again. Instead, I aim for Fairy Lake about an hour from town, where Eric and I used to kayak. I haven't been there since before he got sick. The day is sunny and warm, and I want to avoid Ruby Jade's property and the FFOW campus as long as possible.

Leaving town again is risky. I know that. But Ruby Jade is busy monitoring her mother's care. I hope she is, anyway. And everyone else thinks I'm at work. Even so, the chances of getting caught are high.

I don't care. I have to get away.

Seated on a log, I sip bottled water and chew the energy bar I grabbed when I stopped for gas. I also purchased pepper spray at a sports store on the far side of Bozeman. Followers don't participate in sports, so I was fairly certain I wouldn't run into a church member.

I'll keep the pepper spray with me at all times. Unless I permanently blinded Vance, I'm confident he'll come after me again.

Lazy waves lap against Fairy Lake's shore. Birds sing in the trees and earthy aromas mingle with the fresh air. Across the emerald lake rimmed by evergreens, Sacajawea Peak and the Bridger Mountains rise into a cloudless blue sky.

Finished with my snack, I stuff the wrapper and bottle in the grocery bag. Elbows on my knees, I rest my chin on my clasped hands. This tranquil scene used to still my soul, but a tremor has invaded it. My heart jitters and my hands tremble. I despise the fear and humiliation that followed me to the special spot I once shared with my husband.

Hugging my ribs, I rock back and forth. Tears flood my cheeks. "Eric," I whimper, "I need you. Why did you leave me? I can't do this by myself any longer."

A scripture verse slips unbidden into my mind. *I can do all things through—*

"No!" I shout. "It's a lie. You could have stopped him, God. But you didn't. You deserted me. I was on my own against Vance."

Face in my hands, I cry nearly as hard as when Eric died. He deserted me. God deserted me. I have no one. My head tells me that's not true, but my heart says otherwise.

At dinner, I'm still too upset to say much. The only positive is the fact Vance is not sitting with the men. I'm sure we'd all agree his freedom to eat meals elsewhere isn't fair to the rest of us. However, I'm confident everyone is glad he's not here.

I'm worried about Corban. Will he be punished for driving me to the airport? He wanted to delete the pictures, but I wouldn't let him. If they punish him, we'll both know it was my fault.

The other women mirror my exhaustion.

"You girls okay?" Eunice asks.

"Long day." Shakyra flips her dreads behind her shoulders.

"Short night," Merikay adds.

I turn to Dana Marie. "You joining the work crew tonight?"

"Not sure." She sighs. "Last night's massage may be rescheduled to tonight."

"If they're going to work us this hard," Joleen says, "they ought to give us energy drinks or prednisone. My friend was on it once and it gave her all kinds of energy."

"Meth does the same thing," Shakira says, "but they're both illegal, so don't even go there."

"All we need is rest now and then." Liliana yawns.

I don't tell them I plan to go straight to bed.

Eunice nudges me. "Your boss called. Said to tell you your friend fractured her hip but she's out of surgery."

"Thank you." I hope Ruby Jade gets someone to help Myrtle Mae through her recovery. I'd volunteer, but like Denise, I'm not on Ruby Jade's favorite-people list.

The percussive strike of high heels on concrete resounds in the hallway. We lower our forks and sit tall, heads swiveling toward the wide doorway.

Our not-so-illustrious leadership team enters, chins high, eyes blazing. They're wearing pantsuits. Expensive pantsuits.

Joleen whispers, "Uh-oh."

I'm thinking Ruby Jade should be with her mother, not harassing underlings. Yet, I'm fully aware her priority is control. Whatever it takes, she'll keep a firm hand on the FFOW reins.

They march to our table and stop in a row, as if in formation. I almost expect them to salute, though I know they'd never show such respect to underlings. Inez steps forward. "Cassandra Turner!" She glowers at me. "Stand up."

Not the least bit startled I'm their target this evening, I send up a quick prayer and slowly rise. My dream of sleep dissipates like steam off the boiling pot Denise predicted. Thank God, I remembered to change my shirt before dinner. I hate to think what they'd make of a missing button. Ruby Jade would call me a liar if I blamed Vance.

"You hussy!" The word hisses from Inez's thin painted lips. "You lied, you stole, you seduced, you—"

An earsplitting screech silences her hypocritical diatribe. Hands on her ears, she whips around. Strobe lights flash in time with the deafening blasts. Everyone jumps up. Chairs crash to the floor. We cover our ears and swing this way and that, searching for the source of the horrendous noise.

Someone yells, "Fire in the kitchen!" Flames flare behind the serving window and the smell of burnt grease tinges the smoke now spilling into the dining area.

Ruby Jade points upward, screaming, "Sprinklers! They'll ruin our hair." The dining room sprinklers haven't activated, yet the Fearsome Threesome scurry out the way they came in, heads bowed and hands uselessly spread above their all-important hairdos.

"Side door!" Joseph shouts. "Everyone, hurry. Ronald, get out of the kitchen!"

The cook comes running and joins our mad dash. Skirting tables like horseless barrel racers, we bolt for the door. The distance isn't far, but we're huffing by the time we're safely outside the building. I haven't moved this fast in days.

Ronald rests his hands on his thighs, breathing hard. "Couldn't find a fire extinguisher." He blows out a breath. "I was going for baking soda, when the overhead sprinkler came on. I knew I had to hightail it out of there before I got covered with chemicals."

The fire alarm continues to blare, the noise so piercing I can hear it through the door.

"Did you call 911?" Joseph asks Ronald.

"Didn't have time."

"I'll do it right now," Joseph says, "in case Leadership hasn't called. They seemed a bit rattled. Or as my little son used to say in Spanish, 'their brains got loose.'" He winks and places the call before he walks away from us to talk to the dispatcher.

"Ronald," Joleen asks, "what happened?"

He straightens. "I was doing a little cleaning before I sat down to eat and…" Taking another breath, he continues. "Somehow, I managed to spill grease on the stove. Not sure what happened. Could be I didn't switch a burner completely off. Flames erupted like I'd poured gasoline on a campfire." He shakes his head. "What a mess, what a mess."

Opening the door, he peeks inside. Smoke rolls out, accompanied by the alarm blasts. The smell is worse now. Coughing, he closes the door and turns to us. "Hard to tell with all the smoke, but I didn't see a blaze."

Joseph rejoins the group. "Firetrucks on the way."

"Are they coming from town?" I ask. The place could burn to the ground before they arrive.

"They're with a rural fire department about three miles away. Should be here soon." He glances over the group. "Eunice, have you done a headcount? We need to make sure everyone is out."

"I checked when we left the building," Eunice says. "All the women are here."

"And all the men, except Marcus, of course." Joseph indicates Bentley and Samuel. "That includes our four-star cook." He clasps Ronald's shoulder. "Praise God you escaped the kitchen before it became an inferno."

The rest of us clap and cheer.

Joseph gives Ronald's shoulder an extra squeeze. "Don't worry, buddy. These things happen."

"Tell that to Ruby Jade." Ronald makes a wry face.

"Speaking of," Liliana says, "she'll have a fit if she sees us commingling."

Joseph gives her a funny look. "Commingling?"

"Yeah, you men hanging out with us women. We should separate before they find us."

He lifts an eyebrow. "I'm gonna drive over to the gate to meet the firetrucks. Anyone want to ride with me?"

"Let's all go," Bentley says, "the guys, I mean. A couple of us can ride in the back of your truck. It'll show we're not doing the mingle thing."

They start to walk away.

I catch up with Ronald. "Thanks for the interruption." I don't know where his allegiance lies, but he seems like a nice guy, so I take a chance. "Your kitchen will be a disaster, but you saved my hide, at least for the moment. I'll be glad to help with the cleanup."

"Ah," he whispers, "so the smoke cloud has a silver lining. Thanks for telling me. I'll remember what you said when you-know-who gives me heck." He grins and hurries ahead.

When I turn around, the van is waiting to deliver my dormmates to their appointed worksite. Dana Marie climbs in with the others, which I assume means she doesn't have to provide massage services tonight, thanks to the fire. So far, two of us have benefited from Ronald's accident.

CHAPTER NINETEEN

I'm almost to the dorm when sirens wail in the distance. The sound ricochets off the hillside. Soon, two big firetrucks pass the church and the FFOW dining hall. Led by a pickup with men in the front and back, the trucks rumble up Paradise Path and onto Transformation Way. From the outside, the TW building looks okay, but inside, it could be a hellhole—or at the least, a smoky, stinky mess. I hope they don't pause the program again.

Inside the quiet dorm, I say goodnight to Eunice and slowly climb the stairs to the second floor. I'm washing my face in the restroom when I hear another wail. An ambulance? Lowering the cloth, I listen, but the sound doesn't repeat. Maybe it was the animal scream I heard from my bedroom, or a bird cry.

Because my doctor changed the bandages this morning, I decide not to change them tonight. I squint at my reflection in the mirror. That was this morning, right? Seems so long ago. All I want is to crawl into bed.

I lock my bedroom door before I remove my shirt and pants and put on the t-shirt I've been sleeping in since I moved to the dorm. FFOW's flannel gowns are way too hot for summer. Plus, a t-shirt slides over my bandages easier than a long-sleeved flannel gown.

Clumsily kneeling before the window, I stare into the darkening sky, thinking how much I miss my husband's secure presence. And how much trouble I've made for Corban.

Someone knocks on my door. I jerk.

"Cassie, are you awake?" Eunice's voice.

"Yes, just a minute." I push to my feet and carefully slip on my robe before I unlock and open the door. "Hi, Eunice. I wasn't in bed yet."

"Good." She hands me her phone. "Your boss wants to speak with you."

"Thank you."

"You can give me the phone tomorrow." She lumbers toward the stairs. "I'm going to bed."

"Goodnight." I lift the phone to my ear, close the door and lock it. "Hi, Sebastian."

"Hey, Cat True. Good to hear your voice. R.J. called in a tizzy about a fire at the rehab center. I wanted to make sure you're okay."

"Everyone's fine, thank God, but I can't believe she's speaking to you after what happened in the California hospital."

"She's what I call predictably unpredictable. My theory is sometimes her sidekicks aren't enough. She needs a man in her life, something she'd never admit, of course. Today, with her mom being hospitalized and then the fire, I reckon she got discombobulated."

"How is Myrtle Mae? Have you heard anything more?"

"Talked with her a few minutes ago. A nurse helped her with the phone. She was out of recovery and groggy, but she knew who I was and wondered when I'm coming home. Said she misses me."

"We all miss you, even Ruby Jade, apparently."

"About returning to Montana…" He pauses, as if debating options. "I was gonna wait 'til I work through a couple more nuts and bolts for Quentin's estate and the family scatters his ashes next week. But now I'm thinking I should catch a plane to Bozeman."

"I'd love for you to return." Oh, how I long for his stabilizing presence. I grimace, sickened to know I have something in common with Ruby Jade. "But you can't do anything for Myrtle Mae while she's hospitalized, other than provide moral support."

I consider telling him what Vance did to me today. And what I did to Vance. But Sebastian has enough on his mind right now. And I have a feeling macho Vance is too humiliated by what I did to him to rat me out to his mother. Instead, he'll find another time when he thinks I'm alone and defenseless to retaliate. But I plan to always have pepper spray within reach.

"A couple charities are coming to haul off the stuff Quentin wanted donated," he says. "I need to figure out what's what. I also have meetings to wrap up details for the sale of his home and business and miscellaneous properties. As you might guess, I'm trying to do it under the radar, so certain people with a case of the gimmies don't get wind of it."

His tone changes. "You alone?"

"I'm in my dorm room with the door locked." I sit on the bed.

"We need to talk about a couple things."

"Okay."

"I had visitors a couple days ago. Two FBI agents."

"Was one a tall black man named Milton Freese and the other a woman named Helen Brewer?"

"Ah, they're a step ahead of me."

"I happened to be leaving work in your truck when they stopped by Ruby Jade's place. They were looking for her, but she wasn't home. Neither was Vance. They asked a lot of weird questions and then followed me to the church. I don't know if they were able to talk with Ruby Jade or not."

"Interesting."

"You have any idea why they wanted to talk with her?" I ask.

"I'm still putting the pieces together, but my guess is it has something to do with an illegal enterprise she had in California a few years back."

"She wasn't a pastor there?"

"Not unless you call shepherding prostitutes a pastoral duty."

"What?" My mouth drops. "You're kidding me."

"After several months at the nightclub, she got this half-baked idea to spin off from the place where she danced and start her own club. I told you she knows how to make a quick buck. Can't remember the name of the place, but she offered live music, pole dancing, booze and food in the front and strip dancing, drugs and prostitutes in the back. She was the featured singer on the live-music stage several evenings a week and had quite a following."

I remember the video the Pritchards showed me when I first arrived and how Ruby Jade's performance reminded me of a nightclub act. With such a beautiful voice, I'm not surprised to hear she had a fan club.

"Of course," he adds, "the authorities eventually got wind of the backroom activities, shuttered the club and tossed R.J. in prison."

I gasp. "Ruby Jade Paradise spent time behind bars?"

"Yep, a short time. She was pregnant when she went in and still pregnant when she got out, so it couldn't have been real long."

Yet, she has the gall to insinuate I'm a lowlife. She's as hypocritical as Inez who called me a hussy today.

I stand up and begin to pace the room. "If she paid her debt to society with jail time and a fine, why is she on the

FBI radar? I mean, I'm horrified she ran a strip club and a brothel, but she served her sentence."

"I had the same question for the agents. The response was vague, something about doing a fact check."

"Did they ask you about people with weird flower-children names?"

"They did." Sebastian laughs. "My guess is those are dancer or prostitute names."

"Oh, yeah. Makes sense now that I know more about Ruby Jade's history." Tree shadows flit back and forth on the ceiling. Ruby Jade's deference to Sebastian is also making sense now. Wouldn't take long for him to ruin her reputation around Bozeman in a big way. "What happened to those women?"

"God only knows. The reason I called is to put you on guard in case the agents decide to question Myrtle Mae. I'm fairly certain she has no idea what her daughter did in California. They had almost no communication. R.J. didn't even bother to return to Montana for her father's funeral."

"How sad." I moan. "Must have been painful for Myrtle Mae."

"I wasn't around then, but no doubt it was hard on her. When the partnership with my brother ended, R.J. returned to Montana, Vance in tow, and all of a sudden, she was a loving, doting daughter. Threw Myrtle Mae for a loop."

"I can only imagine. But how can I protect her from the agents? They can easily find her in the hospital."

"Got the hospital covered," he says. "But if you happen to run into them, don't tell them where she is."

"What do you mean, you have the hospital covered?"

"R.J. decided she's too busy to monitor her mother's care and named me the main contact for her. I'm now the doctor and hospital point person."

"What?"

"I know. Doesn't make an ounce of sense when she's there and I'm out of state. But I'm glad to do it. R.J. is too stuck on herself to stay on top of Myrtle Mae's needs. I told the nurses only R.J. and Vance, the Dahlstroms, Myrtle Mae's brother, myself and you are allowed to visit. Inez and Noreen are not on the list. I don't want those witches anywhere near her. When she's moved to a rehab facility, she may want some of her friends to drop by. But right now, she doesn't need a lineup of visitors."

"So, she's safe in the hospital. What about when she's released?"

"I'll bring her up to speed as soon as she's settled in the new facility. Better to find out from me than a couple strangers. By then, we should have a better idea why the FBI is rooting around Bozeman."

"Wish I knew if they were able to talk with Ruby Jade and get the answers they're looking for."

"She's a wily one, but my guess is any agent with half a brain can see through her baloney."

"It's all so confusing," I say. "But maybe it'll eventually make sense."

"Don't count on it." He grunts. "I'd better wrap this up and let you get some shut-eye. Almost forgot to ask. Heard you fell down an Oregon mountainside. You okay?"

"I saw the doctor this morning. She says I'm healing good and can work part-time. Reminds me, what do you want me to do?" I'm not anxious to return to the yard, but I'll keep the pepper spray handy.

"Glad to hear you're on the mend." He sounds genuinely pleased. "But I might get you a suit of armor, so you can't hurt yourself again. You seem to make a habit of it."

I laugh. "I would wear it. I'm tired of pain."

"About the property," he says, "you know what's what in the yard, Cat. Keep the weeds pulled and the bushes trimmed, so on the off-chance R.J. happens to glance out a window, she'll see a spic-and-span park. As you know, appearances are what's important to her. Are the rosebushes and flowers we planted in the front taking hold? Any wilting going on?"

"I haven't been in the front yard. Yesterday was my first day back and today was the Myrtle Mae scare. I'll check the rose garden tomorrow after church."

We say our goodbyes and I dial my mother's cell phone, fairly certain Eunice won't mind. Mom doesn't answer, which is no shock. My parents may still have relatives visiting who were in town for Grandma's funeral. Or they're at a neighborhood barbecue or an outdoor concert. They don't sit still for long.

I leave a message, telling them I feel better every day and I saw the doctor this morning. "She says I'm healing good." I pause. If I were there, I'd fall into my mother's arms and tell her all about the attack. She'd be furious, but she'd let me cry it out, and then she and Dad would help me decide what to do. But I can't explain what happened in a phone message.

"I may not have another chance to talk for a while." I try to still the quiver in my voice. It comes not only from the memory of the assault but knowing I might not hear my parents' voices for weeks or even months.

"Just so you know, this phone belongs to the dorm mom. Her name is Eunice Zaforris. We can't use her phone for regular communication—she could get into a lot of trouble, maybe even fired. None of the residents want her to leave because she's a really nice lady. But please hang onto her number for emergencies. If you can't get me on any of the other numbers I've given you, try this one."

I hang up then dial again. "Don't use Myrtle Mae's number. She tripped and broke her hip earlier today and is in the hospital. Please let Kip know and pray for my dear friend. She's a very special lady."

I'd love to talk to my brother while I have a phone, but he's hard to catch on a Saturday night, and I'm so sleepy I can barely keep my eyes open. I set the phone on the dresser and check the door to make sure it's locked before I crawl between the sheets. Blankets aren't needed on a night like this.

A coyote howls in the distance and something big flaps by my window. An owl, maybe?

Despite my exhaustion, sleep is a long time coming. I can't stop scrolling through the day's events. Over and over, my contemplations land on the assault, and my tears flow. Over and over, I'm tempted to dwell on the pain and humiliation and potential consequences of injuring Ruby Jade's son. But I refuse to allow Vance Longpre to consume my thoughts.

Instead, I dry my face with the sheet and focus on other incidents from today. I think about Myrtle Mae and her fall, helping Denise Dahlstrom with the kitten, and the curious way she looked at me when she asked about Vance. Then there was my afternoon at the lake and the TW kitchen fire. And Leadership scuttling out of the dining hall, hands spread over their heads. What a crazy day.

Hours later, I awaken from a dream about a kitten and an owl. They were staring at each other through the wire door on a pet carrier. Neither creature blinked or made a sound. Somehow, the kitten became a mountain lion, but the owl was still an owl. I couldn't tell which one was on the inside and which one was on the outside, which one was the predator, and which one was the prey.

Dawn's light seeps into the room accompanied by happy sound of birds greeting the new day. I push the remnants of the odd dream from my head and stretch. The ever-present ache is less this morning. I feel rested, like I can face another FFOW day—until a sharp pang in my arm reminds me of Vance's iron grip.

I sit on the edge of the bed. Today is Sunday—and church, where I'll be on the front row and Vance will be twenty feet away at his post. Unless he's blind. And that could bring a whole new set of problems in the form of his nasty mother. But if he's there, I'll be ready. The pepper spray is in my purse. In the meantime, I need to dress and apply the requisite FFOW makeup.

At breakfast, I return Eunice's phone and thank her for letting me talk with my supervisor. "He's out of town and had some stuff he needed to tell me." I don't want the others to get the impression I have special privileges.

She tells us the fire was contained to the center's kitchen, although the dining hall got a good dose of smoke. Only the stovetop and the exhaust fan suffered damage. "That's the good news," she says. "The not-so-good news is you girls get to clean the kitchen and wipe the dining hall walls this afternoon. I'll be glad to help you."

"So handy to have built-in slave labor." Joleen rolls her eyes.

"I, for one, am glad to do whatever it takes to keep the center open," Shakyra says. "Merikay and I have already been through one delay. I don't want to go through another." They share a knowing look.

"I want to put FFOW in my rearview mirror." Joleen shrugs. "Not that I won't miss you all."

"We hear you." Liliana's smile is warm, as always.

I don't have the heart to tell them what Denise Dahlstrom told me, that graduation may never happen for any of us. We are money in Ruby Jade's pocket. And if my experience is any indication, she doesn't want to lose control of even one participant for even one moment.

Discouragement knots my stomach. I need to talk to Myrtle Mae. She keeps me from getting bogged down in the daily grind of this place. Immediately, I regret the thought. My sweet, gracious friend just had a horrible accident followed by major surgery. I should be thinking of ways to help her, not how she can help me.

Before we can get started on the cleanup project, we have to go to church. I'd rather scrub walls than face Inez in

Sunday school or Vance in the church service. But I gotta do what I gotta do. I haven't yet recovered from the attack, and I'm uncertain as to how much God is involved in my life, yet I pray, *Help me, Jesus.*

Eunice drives me to the church building. I could walk, but it would take me a long time. My legs are sore, weak and shaky. Together, we wander into the single women's classroom and join our dormmates on the back row. Perfume and hairspray scent the air.

I sit between Eunice and Joleen, happy to have friends to sit with, for a change. Inez is not the teacher today, the best news I've heard since the judge told me I could go see my nanna. Two women I've never seen before, both sporting puffy highlighted hair and diamond-laden wedding sets, tell us they're filling in because Inez is traveling. Behind them is an easel with a huge flipchart, the first I've seen at FFOW. This should be interesting.

How telling that Noreen and Inez are free to travel, while the rest of us are only allowed to go to our jobs, church, work projects and Walmart. Something is definitely wrong with this picture.

The presenters smile at each other and then at us. Without introducing themselves, they jump into their subject. They must think everyone knows who they are. "This morning," says the shorter one, hands resting on the podium, "we're privileged to teach you procreation protocol."

CHAPTER TWENTY

Procreation protocol? Leave it to Ruby Jade to establish a protocol for an intimate act. I cringe. That's not something I care to think about, especially after I was assaulted yesterday. In any other church, I could leave the class, no questions asked. But not here.

The women around me glance at each other, eyebrows puckered. I know what they're thinking. *A lesson about procreation in a single women's Sunday school class?*

I take a long, tremulous breath. I've had to stuff my feelings before. I can do it again. Yet, forcing yesterday's degrading experience to the back of my brain requires all the willpower I can muster. The more I think about it, the more upset I get.

The ponytail on the teenager in front of me quivers and her ears flame bright red. I'm appalled she and I have to sit through this, but I'm also curious to know what these married women think we singles need to know. Or, more accurately, what Ruby Jade thinks we should know, no matter our age and whether or not we were previously married. I'm glad Myrtle Mae doesn't have to sit through this nonsense. Her whitehaired friends are not smiling.

"Yes, you heard right," the woman continues. "You may be single now, but you will eventually be matched with single men and need to know this information. Of course, you will only engage in procreation when our beloved leader deems it appropriate. In the meantime, pay close attention but do not take notes. No notetaking is allowed as you may become fixated on the diagrams and lustful thoughts would result, condemning you to hell."

I'm trying to digest the pile of hooey she just dumped on us, when the taller woman dramatically flips back the cover to reveal the first graphic. I look down. I don't want to see it. I can't see it, or I'll—

Joleen snickers and elbows me.

I glance at the chart. Stick figures. Smutty, lust-inducing, black marker-pen stick figures. Inside the round heads of the upright characters, an M indicates the male and an F the female. No anatomically correct stick figures for FFOW's single women.

Joleen smirks and I bite my lips to keep from crying or laughing out loud. I'm not sure which. This is beyond ridiculous.

And that's how the class goes. Silliness on top of silliness. Words like "fixtures" and "appendages" substituted for body parts. Embarrassing stick drawings of all the unacceptable methods. And, finally, ta-da! The only position permitted for the Followers, the missionary position. Whoever drew the two figures left a gap between M and F wide enough to prevent any unwanted pregnancies.

The woman flips the chart again. This time, two circles appear on the page with closed eyes and closed mouths. Followers are not to look at each other or open their mouths during "relations." The lust demon could be transmitted from one person to the other—and back again. Funny, I don't remember reading that in the Bible.

Relations must not be called "lovemaking" because God is the Creator. He makes love. People don't make love. The entire "transaction" is to last no longer than fifteen minutes. Any longer and the nasty lust demon might "take hold."

And then comes the birth-control discussion. Certain forms are accepted, but most are not. In the long-run, Ruby Jade is the ultimate birth control as she decides when birth control is mandated and what form, and whether or not a couple is ever allowed a procreation opportunity.

The class eventually comes to an end, but not before the "experts" ask for questions. Everyone stares straight ahead, barely breathing. The red-eared girl's ponytail hangs limp.

I consider asking what procreation positions the two women practice with their husbands and how often such activity is permitted, just to see their reactions. I'd also like to know if video cameras record their "interactions." But enough is enough. I'm sure the others are as anxious as I am to leave.

"Good," says the woman at the podium. "You are prepared for the marriage bed. Class dismissed."

Joleen murmurs, "I think I'm gonna barf."

"Yeah...me too."

I part from my dormmates and stumble down the sloped rosewater-scented aisle to my seat on the front row, my heart in my throat at the thought of seeing Vance. Hushed whispers follow my descent. Do the Followers view my beat-up face as confirmation of my bad-girl status? The urge to run out the side door grows stronger with every step.

To my great relief, Vance is not at his post. Yet, I know I won't be able to avoid him forever. If I did serious damage, he and his mother will be sure to retaliate. Will it be an eye for an eye or a return to jail?

Hands in my lap, I tell myself not to dwell on what-ifs and turn my attention to the platform, where the musicians are tuning their instruments. I haven't seen Corban for, what is it, three days? Feels like months. His gaze flicks my direction and then back to his music. He puts his trombone to his lips.

My heart sinks. He's either mad about the phone pics or his mother told him something is going on between me and Vance. I could be wrong, but—

The band starts playing and Ruby Jade shimmers onto the stage in the multihued, multilayered silk she wore my first night at FFOW. She raises her arms. Rings and bangles glitter.

The plexiglass pulpit silently drops to her level.

"Followers!" Her voice rings from the speakers.

The music ceases and the musicians lower their instruments.

"God gave me, your pastor, prophetess and psalmist, a new song this morning. It's a wonderful song with magnificent words and a beautiful melody straight from his heart to mine. I was so anxious to share it with you, I canceled the scheduled singing group."

The Followers jump to their feet and shout their acronym for "Praise God in heaven." "PGIH! PGIH!"

One sore muscle at a time, I rise to join the others. Sitting for an hour on a metal folding chair during Sunday school was hard on my battered body. I plaster a fake FFOW smile on my face, mouth PGIH and pretend to clap.

I study the musicians to see if they've been informed of this agenda change. By the way they're frantically leafing through their music, I would guess not.

Ruby Jade motions for us to sit and then turns to them. "Key of G. I'd like a short intro that goes like this." She hums a few notes.

They raise their instruments, but their troubled expressions remain. How many of them play by ear and how often does this happen?

The female violinist, a middle-aged woman, says something. The others nod and she solos the tune fragment.

Ruby Jade takes off from there, her rich contralto filling the room.

"I am the first, I am the last, there is no other God. I am the first, I am the last, there is no other God. Do not tremble, do not fear. Do not tremble, do not fear." She lifts a hand with its red-painted fingernails to the heavens. "There is no other Rock. There is no other Rock. I have made you, you are my servants. I have made you, you are my servants."

The instrumentalists straggle along behind her. I can tell they're searching for the timing as well as the tune.

"I am the Lord who made all things. I am the Lord who made all things. I am the Redeemer who formed you in the womb. I am the Redeemer who formed you in the womb."

The timing is getting sketchier by the note. And the words sound more and more familiar. I think Isaiah is where the song originated, a song that's supposedly straight from God's heart to hers.

"Sing for joy, you heavens. Shout aloud, depths of the earth. Sing mountains and forests. Remember these things, you Followers. You are my servants, you Followers. Remember these things. You are my servants, my servants, my servants…"

She holds the last note and lets it fade away.

The congregation rises around me, shouting, "Beautiful!" "Praise God!" "Sing it again!"

I join them, adding my fake enthusiasm, though I'm thoroughly disgusted. Not just because the music and the tempo are pathetic, but because Isaiah was writing to Israelites, not Followers. How self-serving for Ruby Jade to sing, "You are my servants" over and over. Nothing subtle about her blatant manipulation.

The musicians wait, poised to continue. But she motions them off the platform. "That will be all. We have a full agenda this morning and must move along." No "thank you," no "good job," no apology for throwing a song at them without written music or warning. Just "get off the stage."

Corban sets his trombone on the stand and walks to the edge of the platform. I'm wishing he'd come sit by me, when Ruby Jade says, "Corban Dahlstrom, join your brother on the front row." Her voice, which was congenial a moment ago, is now sharp.

Uh-oh. My heartbeat flattens like a pancake. She's going to skewer him, and it's all my fault.

Instead, she says a young member has asked to self-report and she has two announcements.

I glance around. Self-report?

"Cassandra Turner!" Ruby Jade shouts. "Face forward."

I despise myself for responding to a name that's as fake as everything else about this place, but I do as she ordered.

"While Jeremy is coming," she says, "I have unfortunate news. This week, Marjorie Boyer was diagnosed with advanced Alzheimer's."

A low murmur rustles through the crowd.

I repeat the name in my head, twice. Why is that name so familiar? And then I remember—Olivia's sweet aunt. She seemed totally cognizant and connected when I last saw her, which wasn't long ago.

"Such a travesty." Ruby Jade shakes her head. "She let go of Jesus, and now we have to put her away, I mean, put her in a memory care facility. If only she'd clung to him until the end."

Did Olivia get tired of Marjorie, or did the kindly woman not give enough money to Ruby Jade's jewelry fund? I'm so angry I want to scream, yet I have a feeling Marjorie will be happier removed from Olivia's domination and no longer sharing a room with Alice, Olivia's malicious mother. May God bless dear Aunt Marjorie.

A boy who looks to be nine or ten shuffles past me, dragging his feet.

Ruby Jade motions to him. "Grab that microphone, Jeremy, and come up here with me. I'll show you how to turn it on." She's using her nice voice again. I doubt it lasts.

"In addition to Marjorie's muddled mind…" She turns to the congregation. "Ignacio Garcia was diagnosed with stage-four brain cancer."

Someone near me whispers, "Oh, no."

"Obviously, he let go of Jesus long ago and was faking his commitment to us and to God. He never once asked me to pray over him." She breathes out a long sigh. "Will you people ever learn? Of course, I immediately excommunicated both individuals."

She stabs her finger at us. "From this moment on, they're reprehensible persons. Have nothing to do with either of them. No phone calls, no visits, no letters or text messages. We cannot allow their unbelief to spread in our midst."

What? At a time when people most need love and support, she's pulling the friends-and-family rug out from under them. As awful as the FFOW world is, it was their whole world, until now. But maybe the Dahlstroms can step in where others fear to tread. I hope so.

Standing beside Ruby Jade, Jeremy is almost as tall and pale as she is. His head is down, his shoulders are slumped and he's trembling, a sharp contrast to the usual bright demeanor the children display. Heads high and eyes wide, they plaster big smiles on their impassive faces. I've never heard a child cry or seen one act out during a service. They're perfect little zombies, perfect replicas of their robotic parents.

After our fearsome leader helps him switch on the microphone, she asks, "What is it you want to tell the congregation?"

Does he really want to tell us anything or has he been forced to do this?

"I…"

"Hold the microphone to your mouth."

He raises the mic. "I, uh, I…"

"Spit it out, Jeremy!" The mean voice, just as I expected.

"My dad said to tell you I, uh, I found a comic book and I, I read some of it."

A congregational gasp wheezes through the room.

Jeremy looks up. What does he expect to see? I doubt he'll find sympathy on anyone's face. I wonder what his mom is thinking. Did she agree with putting her child through this self-reporting torture?

"What was it about?"

"Spiderman."

Ruby Jade's lips curl. "Spiderman?" She drops her mouth open, acting like she's never heard of Spiderman, yet her eyes belie her fakery.

"Uh-huh." He nods.

"A man who's a spider, or a spider who's a man?"

"Actually…" Jeremy brightens. "Peter Parker was bitten—"

"Stop right there." She squeezes his shoulder, her long nails digging into his shirt.

He flinches and tries to pull away.

"I will *not* allow you to spew fiction filth on my congregation. Followers live in reality, not make-believe." Releasing her hold on the terrorized child, she orders, "Get on with your confession."

"That's all," he says, staring up at her. "I told you everything that happened." His voice shakes and his whole body is a plea for her to believe him. "I found the comic book and I read it. Well, some of it, before my dad took it away."

"Where did you find it?"

"In the Walmart parking lot."

"Not on a Walmart shelf?"

"No." Jeremy rears back. "That would be stealing."

"So, you think you know the difference."

He squints at her. "Uh-huh."

"Let your yea be yea and your no be no."

Jeremy looks like he doesn't have a clue what she's talking about. I understand his confusion.

She turns to the onlookers. "Travis Baker, Ryan Andrews and Anthony Helbaum. Come and explain to Jeremy Wilhelm what he knows."

Hearing the thump of running feet, I look over my shoulder. Three boys about Jeremy's age are rushing down the incline toward the platform, big smiles on their faces. I recognize Ryan, the bully from the third-grade class. To think Jeremy's parents instigated this farce makes me heartsick.

The boys clamber onto the stage. Ruby Jade nods and steps back, a self-satisfied smirk on her face. Hands clasped over her broad stomach, she twirls her thumbs one over the other.

Ryan is the first to attack. "You don't know nothin'." He shakes his fist in Jeremy's face. "You're stupid!"

Jeremy's lip juts.

One of the other boys steps close. "You're a stupid liar. You read the whole comic book, all of it."

Jeremy shakes his head. "No, I—"

"Yes, you did. God told me."

"But God doesn't lie."

"That's right. You're the liar."

Again, Jeremy appears perplexed.

The other boy says, "You're a stupid liar and a stupid stealer. You stole that comic book out of Walmart."

"No." Jeremy shakes his head. "No, I didn't. I found—"

"See?" Ruby Jade says. "You're lying again." Her thumbs switch direction.

Ryan jumps in, both fists raised, his stance wide, as if readying for a fistfight. "You're a stupid cheater. You cheated on the rules and read fic, fic..."

"Fiction filth." Ruby Jade kindly helps the boy.

He glares at Jeremy. "Fiction filth."

I bet Ryan has no idea what he's talking about. None of these Follower boys knows up from down.

"Spiderman helps people." Jeremy's innocent defense of a comic-book character draws more shocked huffs from the congregation.

"He's just a stinkin' nasty bug," Ryan says. "But Superman is good. He's the one who—"

The other boys lean in. "Batman," says one. "He's the best!"

Ah, maybe they do have an idea of what goes on in the rest of the world.

Not to be outdone, the fourth boy says, "My favorite is—"

"Shut! Up!" Ruby Jade's voice blasts across the sanctuary.

All four boys back away from her and huddle close.

Hands on my chair seat, I slide to the edge, ready to leap to the stage to break their fall.

"Get–off–this–platform!" Ruby Jade's face is as red as her fingernails. "You devil boys and your guardians will meet in my office immediately after the service. Every last one of you!" She blows an audible breath through her purple lips and shakes out her hands. Her silky layers tremble.

Jeremy drops the mic. The crackle reverberates like a thunderclap. Eyes wide, faces white, the boys jump off the stage and scurry back to their seats.

CHAPTER TWENTY-ONE

I press my lips to keep from laughing. Apparently, Jeremy's self-report didn't go as planned. While I hate that the boys will be punished for their transparency, it's gratifying to see one of the queen bee's carefully orchestrated humiliation ceremonies backfire.

Disregarding the embarrassing moment, Ruby Jade plunges ahead. "Ushers, stand by to pass the plates." No bless-this-offering prayer, no background music, no thanking God for his provision.

I hear the soft scuff of the ushers' shoes as the men fan out behind me.

"You may not be aware of the tragic news that has befallen our community." The red flush fades from Ruby Jade's face and is replaced by a mournful expression. She breathes a dramatic sigh. "A terrible, *terrible* fire destroyed the Transformation Way kitchen last night."

Moans and murmurs ripple through the auditorium.

"If we don't raise fifty-thousand dollars this morning to cover restoration expenses, we will have to close the center, which would be a travesty after we so very recently reopened it."

Fifty-thousand dollars for minimal damage? Most of which will be dealt with by free labor? What about insurance? And what about informing the congregation no one was injured in the blaze?

She motions to the men. "Start the plates after you add seed money."

Seed money? I turn my head. Not far from me, an usher is pulling a wallet from his back pocket. Yikes. Not a good day to be an usher.

"Remember, people." Ruby Jade tick-tocks her finger. "Give, and it shall be given unto you, good measure, pressed down, shaken together and running over. Only a fool would spurn such a marvelous opportunity for God's blessing."

The ushers go to work, and in no time at all, a dozen men are standing before her, each holding two offering plates piled high with cash and checks.

"Gentlemen," she says, "adjourn to the counting room. Tally God's tithes and offerings quickly but accurately and report back immediately."

They file out the side entrance.

Before the last man disappears from view, Ruby Jade roars, "Ronald Manford! Come forward and pick up the microphone."

Uh-oh, she's on a roll today. I take a long breath, count to ten and blow it out. Oh, to be in Oregon with my family, worshiping with them in a sane, loving, God-fearing—not tyrant-fearing—environment.

From the men's section, Ronald rises and walks to the front, a leery expression on his face. He gathers the mic and stops below Ruby Jade. Hands at his sides, he lifts his chin, awaiting his judgment. She loves his desserts, so I can't imagine she'd fire him over spilled grease. But as Sebastian said, she's predictably unpredictable.

One hand on the pulpit, she bends toward him. "Turn around and tell the congre-ga-shun…" She sways and slurs her words. "Wha-you…Transforma-shun…kit-chen."

When she says no more, Ronald raises the mic to his mouth. "It was an accident. I didn't start the fire on purpose."

She straightens, shaking her head as if to clear cobwebs from her brain. Her eyes flare and her face hardens. "Turn around, I said, and tell the Followers what you did to Transformation Way's beautiful kitchen."

Ever so slowly, one foot at a time, he shifts to face the congregation.

I give him an encouraging smile and pray God helps him through this irrational assault on his character.

"I spilled grease on a hot stove, and it caught fire."

"A fire that has caused a great deal of damage," Ruby Jade insists. "And because of you, this church has been fined one-thousand dollars!"

Ronald pivots. "What?"

"You heard me. Because you did not have a fire extinguisher in the kitchen, Faithful Followers of the Way, host of the rehabilitation program, suffered an expensive fine that tarnishes our reputation."

"When I became..." He faces the congregation, microphone at his mouth. "When I became the cook, I purchased two fire extinguishers with my own funds— because the kitchen had none." His eyes flash. "Noreen Nystrom took both of them last week. She said the school needed them for an inspection that afternoon and she'd return them right away, which, obviously, did not happen."

"Liar!" Ruby Jade screams from behind him.

He doesn't flinch, doesn't blink. "I swear I'm telling God's truth."

"Look—at—me!"

Slowly, ever so slowly, he twists her direction.

"Lies, lies, lies!" she rants. "All I'm hearing today. Don't you people get it? The Bible says liars will burn forever in the lake of fire." Her face is scarlet again.

"You…" One hand on the plexiglass pulpit, the other stabbing a sharp fingernail at Ronald, she declares, "You, Ronald Manford, will pay the fine. Every last penny of the one-thousand dollars will come out of your paycheck."

The pulpit wobbles. She lurches but regains her balance, shouting, "Maintenance, you said this was fixed!"

"From the back of the room, a man yells, "Like I told you, the manufacturer's rep fixed the podium, but he said the height-adjusting apparatus can't handle any more weight than a tablet or a notebook, maybe a small laptop."

Ruby Jade sucks in a loud breath through flaring nostrils and rises to her full height, all five feet of it. "More lies, more lies!" She waves her hands. "I can't take you devil people any longer. Church is dismissed. Go home, confess your sins and return tonight ready to receive truth."

With that, she staggers to the door at the side of the stage. I wonder if she's having a stroke or a heart attack. She grasps the doorknob just as Noreen pops in the other door. "Ruby Jade! The ushers are waiting to report."

Sure enough, the men are queued along the hallway, hands behind their backs—except for the two holding stacks of empty, I assume, collection plates.

"Tell them to meet me in my office." Ruby Jade opens the door.

"But what if we need to take a second offering?"

"We'll do it tonight."

The rehab center's doors are propped open, and huge fans are spaced throughout the building. In the dining room, the tables and chairs have been shoved to the center. Three tall ladders lean against one wall. None of the walls are as smoke-stained as I expected. The same goes for the ceiling. It's at least fifteen-feet high and made of acoustical tiles that can't be scrubbed. I hope they don't make us vacuum the tiles.

The air in the dining room is better now but still hard to breathe. A woman waiting at the serving window is wearing a breathing mask, the white disposable kind. When we get closer, I recognize Evelyn, the secretary for the church *and* the school *and* Transformation Way. Only her tired zombie eyes are visible. This Sunday afternoon responsibility, when she should be resting and enjoying her family, must come under "and other duties as required."

As always, my heart goes out to her. How long can she survive the pressure and the abuse? Maybe she's someone Triple F can help.

Ronald saunters in the side door with Joseph, Bentley and Samuel. Marcus won't return until Wednesday. Vance is also absent. I'm relieved he's not here, and I'm sure the others feel the same way. Yet, his privileged status is wrong and his supposed participation in the program a farce. I wonder if Judge Snow realizes how Ruby Jade manipulated him, again.

All the women from my dorm are present, including Eunice. Evelyn hands us rubber gloves and disposable breathing masks. We quickly don the masks. My eyes and nose are already burning. I'm surprised Leadership cares about our lungs and our hands. However, "care" may be too strong a word. They probably don't want respiratory issues to diminish the FFOW workforce.

Evelyn splits the eleven of us into two groups, which include both men and women. Evidently, commingling isn't an issue when it comes to dirty work. One crew will wipe the dining room walls and the other will clean the kitchen.

She leads us to plastic buckets stacked near the kitchen sink. Those who'll be wiping the dining room walls and furnishings are told to take two buckets and fill them with warm water.

A big bottle of Dawn and several jugs of white vinegar are on the counter. "Add a squirt of dish soap plus two cups of vinegar to one bucket," Evelyn says, her voice muffled.

"But don't add anything to the second bucket. It's for rinsing.

"Rags are in the first bin beneath the serving window. Take three. One to wash, one to rinse and one to dry. Toss the used ones in the empty bin."

I've been assigned to wipe the kitchen's blackened walls, cupboards and appliances along with Ronald, Merikay, Shakyra and Samuel. We're instructed to mix baking soda, ammonia and vinegar in our two-gallon buckets and fill them with the hottest water we can tolerate.

"Whoa." Ronald raises his eyebrows. "The vinegar-ammonia combination oughta overpower the smoke smell, if it doesn't knock us out first."

Evelyn gives him a look like, *Too bad. It is what it is.*

I could have begged out of this assignment, saying Dr. Vasquez told me to avoid anything that might compromise wound healing. But I can't abandon my friends, and the movement will do my muscles good. With any luck, Leadership won't venture into the building to sully their fancy clothes and we'll be able to talk freely as we work. Not that Followers know how to talk freely.

Finished with her instructions, Evelyn starts for the open doorway. Once she's outside, she pulls off her mask and hollers over her shoulder, "Call my cell phone if you have questions."

"What's your—?" Joseph asks.

But she's gone before he can finish his sentence.

"Oh, well." He grunts. "Guess we're on our own."

"Hey, it's not all bad." The breathing mask does little to dampen Joleen's loud voice. "We can—"

I elbow her and whisper, "Careful, the walls have ears."

Evelyn appears in the doorway again, phone in hand. "Message from Ruby Jade."

Joleen breathes a low, "Oops."

Standing just outside the kitchen, Evelyn reads, "To ensure you don't carry the smoke smell and residue into our sacred sanctuary, you must shower, wash your hair and change your clothes before the evening church service."

Heaven forbid we compete with the rosewater stench.

With those encouraging words, she disappears again.

"Seems to me," Eunice says, "we'll all want to shower when we're done here."

"Yeah, well." Dana Marie arches an eyebrow. "Consider the source."

"How about I rustle up some grub?" Ronald says. "I found enough untainted food in the fridge to throw together lunch." He surveys the blackened kitchen. "Not sure what I'll use for counterspace."

"We can wipe a couple tables and take them outside," Eunice suggests. "I'll help you fix the food out there."

He brightens. "Good idea."

I nod. "Nice day for a picnic." I've been missing outdoor lunches with my landscaping friends and Myrtle Mae.

We all get busy, helping Ronald and helping each other. Soon, we're seated under a shade tree, enjoying ham sandwiches, spinach salad, corn chips and mandarin oranges.

"Nice work, Ronald," Bentley says. "Good eats."

"Gotta get some food in our bellies, so we can make the kitchen usable again."

I'm working beside Ronald in the kitchen, scrubbing a counter clean, when he asks, "What do you think of the program so far, Cassandra?"

I stare at him. No one at FFOW has asked me for my thoughts about the program. I check our surroundings. Samuel is outside, washing the exhaust vent filter. Merikay is across the room, emptying a bucket at the sink. I don't know where Shakyra is—restroom, maybe.

Ronald raises an eyebrow, his eyes curious.

"I've been in other rehab programs." I keep my voice low. "But this one, well, I have to say it's one of a kind."

"You're telling me."

"Have you cooked for other treatment centers?"

"No, but I was a resident in a Nevada program a couple years ago." He slips off a glove and scratches his head.

"Oh, so you know."

Merikay begins refilling the bucket.

"Yeah, I know normal rehab." He lowers his voice. "And this ain't it."

"Sorry about this morning," I whisper. "And the thousand dollars. Insane."

He glances around the smoky kitchen. "I don't see five-thousand dollars' worth of damage here, let alone fifty-thousand." Pulling the glove back on, he adds, "Of course, if they actually paid people to do the smoke cleanup, it might cost a few pennies more."

I murmur behind my mask, "Surely, you've thought about leaving."

Ronald's eyes grow big and shift from side to side.

"I don't want you to go." I move closer. "But the fine is their problem, not yours. If you walk away, they can't stick you with it."

"I had a plan." His eyebrows crease. "The idea was to do a bang-up job here so Leadership would put in a good word for me when I apply for a loan to open my own restaurant. You know how bank officers think twice before doling out dough to ex-cons."

"Yeah." I give him a sympathetic nod. "But Ruby Jade does everything she can to keep people from leaving. Believe me, she will never give you a good referral. She not only hates to lose members, she loves your peach cobbler."

"That settles it." A bitter laugh bursts from behind his mask. "I'll never bake peach cobbler again."

"Doctor Hoffman is a kind man," I whisper. "He'll vouch for you. In fact, it makes sense for him to endorse you because he's the program director." I'm taking a chance, but I feel compelled to press Ronald to fight the abuse Ruby Jade is trying to heap on him. "What's keeping you from thumbing your nose at Leadership and taking off?"

"First off, I enjoy this job—or I enjoyed it, until this." He waves his hand, encompassing the kitchen from the serving window to the kitchen's back door. "I'm the one who caused this mess. I want to leave the kitchen the way I found it."

Merikay turns off the water as Shakyra walks into the room, carrying a water bottle.

I bend to wipe the tiled area between the counter and the upper cupboards. "Something to think about." I almost add, *I can connect you with people who'll help.* But I don't know Ronald and may have already pushed my luck by suggesting he disappear.

Later, I leave my weary but clean dormmates in the single women's section and continue my downward trek to the front row. Though I showered, I fear my sinuses may forever be tainted with the acrid smell of smoke. Oh, well. Smoke is the least of my concerns right now.

All hell is sure to break loose tonight for Corban and me. I'm tired enough to want to get the haranguing phase over with and move on to the punishment phase. It may last until graduation, if graduation ever comes, like the restriction against communicating with my family. One way or another, I'll get through this.

The instrumentalists begin to play and a dozen or so women in black pants and red jackets assemble on the steps leading to the platform. They attempt to sing the song Ruby Jade introduced this morning. Their version is more hacked than hers was, if that's possible, but the congregation struggles to sing along. I feel for Corban and Logan and the other musicians trying to make musical sense out of the song.

Finally, it ends, thank God, and the musicians join the congregation. Noreen steps onto the platform from a side door. As she strides to the podium, it silently rises to her height. I'm amazed it wasn't replaced this afternoon with something sturdier. But I've heard they're quite proud of their plexiglass wonder. "Wasn't that a beautiful song?" she asks.

The Followers cheer.

"Another treasure," she says, "to add to the melodies God gives our shepherd and psalmist specifically for this flock."

More cheers echo about the big room, but I'm thinking if I were God, I'd consider her comment an insult. And if I were a nonbeliever, I'd search for a divine being with an ear for music.

"Two announcements," she says. "I'm pleased to say the cleanup crew made good progress on the Transformation Way smoke removal this afternoon." She faces the single men's section. "Ronald Manford, you're the person responsible for the horrendous fire. Stand and tell us how soon the kitchen will be operational."

I look over at the men. No one stands. Corban and Logan, who are both seated on the front row, stare straight ahead.

"Ronald Manford, we're waiting for your report." Her voice is insistent. "This is the last time I'll ask and the only time I'll remind you to call the fire chief for an inspection after you install the new fire extinguishers.'

When he doesn't make an appearance, her eyebrows clump. "Well, of all the... Anyone know where Ronald Manford is?"

No one responds.

CHAPTER TWENTY-TWO

Stifling a smile, I study my hands in my lap. Ronald did it. He escaped. Good for him. I'm jealous but happy for him. He's a great cook and won't have trouble finding another job.

Noreen screams, "Devil man!"

I jerk my attention back to her.

"He turned on the Followers and rejected God." Noreen clasps the sides of the pulpit. "We will track him down and bring him back." Her face blanches. "I mean..." She falters then lifts her chin. "In my spirit, I sense he took TW equipment to use in the restaurant he wants to open. We must stop him. Now."

Hand shading her eyes, she peers into the congregation. "Evelyn, where are you? Does Ronald have one of our phones?"

From the sanctuary's middle section, the married section, Evelyn stutters, "I, I don't know. You, you're the one who gives out the phones."

Noreen frowns. "You should know."

"I'll go check your list in the office." Evelyn jumps to her feet.

"Never mind. Joseph, does Ronald have a FFOW phone?"

Joseph stands. "If I remember right, he came with his own phone. I sincerely doubt—"

She interrupts him. "Security, meet me at the center the moment I finish announcements. I'll call the sheriff and we'll proceed from there."

Pausing to gather more evil thoughts, I presume, she leans over the podium but then quickly backs away. Either it jiggled or she remembered Ruby Jade's experience. "This morning," she says, "you raised a mere twenty-one thousand, two-hundred and seventy-nine dollars for the restoration."

Someone claps but no one joins in. The clapping ceases.

"Less than half the amount needed." Lips pressed, she shakes her head. "Unless we receive the full fifty-thousand dollars, we'll have to shut the Transformation Way doors and leave the kitchen and dining room in shambles."

Noreen glowers at the congregation, sweeping her gaze from one side of the sanctuary to the other. "God told me someone held back a 401K this morning. Another person hoarded a college fund. Someone else kept their grandmother's diamond necklace hidden in a secret place." She shakes a finger at us. "How many times have we told you retaining family mementos is ancestor worship, evil to the core? Shame on you! Those trinkets will damn you to hell!"

With a flick of her hand, she orders the ushers forward to take the offering. "Remember," she exhorts, "God loves a generous giver."

What? I can't believe she twisted the "God loves a cheerful giver" Scripture to suit her agenda.

"Give from your heart," Noreen urges. "Give your all and God will bless you a hundred times over. Make sure your neighbor puts something in the plate." She steps away from the pulpit, arms folded, and watches the process.

Talk about peer pressure. Good thing I don't have a "neighbor" on the front row. The only money in my purse belongs to Myrtle Mae, and I know she wouldn't want me to donate it to a Leadership shopping spree. I pray no one contributes their retirement fund or college savings—or grandma's diamond necklace.

The silent collection completed, Noreen exits where she entered and Ruby Jade steps through the other door onto the stage.

I swallow. This is it. Judgment Day for me and Corban.

"I had a Spirit-inspired sermon prepared for this evening." She flips her dark hair behind her shoulders, first one side, then the other. "Of course, all my sermons are Spirit-inspired. However, this one is extra special. But I'll have to bring it to you another day. Tonight, we have family business to deal with of the most serious kind. It reeks of…" She pauses. "Fornication!"

Uh-oh. I clasp my hands in my lap. Here it comes.

She stops, tilts her head to the side and covers one ear with her palm. After a moment, she murmurs, "I see." And then, "Report to me as soon as you have a complete list."

Smiling, she lowers her hands to the podium, intertwines her fingers and begins to twirl her thumbs.

I attempt to interpret her grin. Is it a sadistic smile, a pleased one, or an "I know something you don't know" smirk? Hard to tell.

"We've had a change of plans," she says. "You will hear the sermon after all, and you will be blessed." She points over her shoulder at the wall behind her. "First slide, Frank."

A scripture verse appears above her head.

But the men put forth their hands, and pulled Lot into the house to them, and shut the door. And they smote the men that were at the door of the house with blindness, both small and great, so that they wearied themselves to find the door. Genesis 19:10-11 KJV

I fold my arms and sit back. Is she going to connect my supposed fornication with what went on in Sodom and Gomorrah? I cringe. Between Vance's assault and the

Sunday school stick figures, I have more than enough perversion to ponder for one weekend.

Too bad I don't have earplugs in my purse. If they were ever found, I could say I use them at work when lawn mowers are rumbling around me. *Yeah, Cassie.* I sigh. *Another lie.* Like Ruby Jade said this morning—lies, so many lies.

If she has me speak into a microphone... Even if she doesn't have me speak into a microphone, I'll shout the truth to the Followers. Corban and I did nothing wrong. However, I was assaulted by Ruby Jade's son, who threatened me with a knife and attempted to rape me.

She swivels, one hand extended toward the words on the wall. "I can sense the gears churning in your little brains, Followers." Chuckling, she turns back to us. "You're wondering who the men are inside the house and why they pulled Lot in with them."

"Right," a woman calls. "That's my question."

"And what's the deal with making them blind?" a man asks.

"I'm here to explain the truth of the matter." She clasps her hands, sets them on the bare acrylic podium and begins to twirl her thumbs. "As I was studying this passage," she says, "a revelation came to me."

"Hallelujah!" someone shouts.

"Yes, PGIH! Our Heavenly Father has revealed his truth to me." Her eyes sparkle. "And now I, your pastor, prophetess and psalmist, am about to reveal it to you."

"PGIH, PGIH!" The shouts vibrate my chair.

"The truth." She steps to the side of the pulpit and tilts toward us, hands on her thighs. "The truth is, we are the men and women inside God's house."

Murmurs of "Ahh, makes sense" and "I get it" undulate across the sanctuary.

"But men and women outside the house are blind," she says. "They've wearied themselves searching for the door into FFOW. Try as they might, they can't find it. We must reach out, not to join them, for that would risk a hellish eternity, but to pull them inside, where they'll be forever safe."

"Hallelujah, hallelujah!" The Followers leap to their feet, stomping, clapping and shouting. I stand and glance around. Some faces shine, like they've seen an angel. Others' eyes are closed or focused heavenward. Tears run down the cheeks of more than one person.

All this, after Ruby Jade told them a big fat lie in the name of God's truth. Surely, they know Lot's story. Surely, they know better than to believe such convoluted misuse of Scripture.

We sit, and she continues. "Ronald, our dear TW cook, is blindly searching for the FFOW door. But he can't find it. We love him dearly and must extend our hands to pull him inside the fold again."

You don't love Ronald. You love his cooking.

People clap and cheer.

"That's who we are." She lifts her hands high. "We're a welcoming committee for God's kingdom. With open arms—"

A loud bang at the rear of the auditorium stops her midsentence. I swivel in time to see Vance march into the sanctuary and a door bounce closed behind him. My insides twist. Where did he come from? How did he get involved? And why is he wearing sunglasses at night?

"I knew it," he shouts. "The dude stripped the joint clean!"

The door opens again and Pete steps into the room. He and Hank, plus the guy who guards the side doors with Vance and two other men, walk in and stand at the back.

Vance waves a sheet of paper. "This is only a partial list, Mom, but it's enough to put the idiot cook behind bars for life."

"Let me see," Ruby Jade orders. "And stop exaggerating."

Vance trots down the aisle and up the stairs leading to the stage. Tripping on the last step, he skids across the platform on his belly, arms outstretched, sunglasses spinning away.

The congregation gasps, but no one moves to help him.

Ruby Jade walks over to him. "Vance?"

He pushes to his knees. "My sunglasses! Where are my sunglasses?" Ugly welts line his temples. His eyelids are red and swollen. I don't know how he can see. He looks like something out of a horror movie.

"Over there, by the stage door on the right." Ruby Jade points but doesn't bother to get them for him. Instead, she picks up the paper he dropped.

He scrambles for the sunglasses, shoves them on his face and jerks the door open. Stumbling out the doorway, he slams the door behind him. I don't know where he's going, but I'm glad he's gone.

As if nothing unusual happened, Ruby Jade studies the paper, muttering as she reads. "Tragic, so tragic."

The other stage door opens.

I stifle a gasp. Is Vance back already?

But Noreen is the one who tromps onto the platform. "You've seen the list," she says. Her mic is on. She was prepared for this dramatic moment.

Ruby Jade nods, her expression serious.

"The authorities are already searching for him," Noreen informs us. "Ronald Manford will be apprehended soon."

For what? Leaving a church?

Noreen asks Ruby Jade, "Want me to read the incriminating list?"

Ruby Jade hands the paper to her.

"A cursory glance through the TW kitchen revealed these missing items." Noreen lifts the paper. "Each one of the highest commercial quality and value.

"Silverware, dishes, serving utensils, large mixer, large blender, forty-five-cup coffee urn, toaster oven, pots and pans, electric skillets and griddles, thirty-cup rice cooker, electric food slicer and at least a dozen extremely expensive chef knives."

Someone mutters, "How terrible." Others groan and grunt.

"You were right. He took everything." Ruby Jade shakes her head, her eyebrows knit. "I expected better of him."

I'd like to think she regrets this turn of events, but it's an obvious setup. Ronald couldn't have fit that much stuff into his car. And the security guys didn't have time to search the kitchen and compile the list. Plus, they wouldn't have known what was in the kitchen to begin with. Noreen might have had a checklist of original kitchen furnishings, but I doubt it.

Like my unwarranted arrest on the interstate, Ronald is being framed for something he didn't do. And it's my fault for encouraging him to leave. One way or another, Ruby Jade will manipulate Ronald's disappearance to her advantage. She'll finagle a deal with the sheriff or the highway patrol or the judge. The cook will be returned to the TW kitchen. And she'll get her peach cobbler.

Ruby Jade closes her eyes and lowers her head. Finally, she heaves a huge sigh, raises a hand and looks at her audience. "My heart is shattered. But as we discussed, we can extend a gracious welcome to Ronald and gently lead him like a lost lamb back into the fold where he belongs.

"He cannot exist outside our hallowed halls." Her voice grows louder. "He cannot be successful. He cannot be happy. Ours is the *only* righteous path, the *only* way to heaven!"

She drops her hand. "Goodnight, dear Followers." With that, she exits the platform. Surely, she didn't forget her plan to skewer me and Corban. I glance at Corban. His eyebrow twitches, and he turns away.

I step into the aisle, almost running into his mom, who has rolled down the aisle to the front. "Excuse me, Denise. I'll get out of your way."

"You're the one I want to talk with," she says.

"Okay." Is this about me and Vance? I'm ready to explain, to make sure she knows the truth.

"I've been eyeing that cute little purse of yours." She smiles. "Looks like a perfect size to hang from my chair."

I give her a mystified look and hold out the purse. "You think this is cute?"

"Yes." She takes the purse. "Please show me how the clasp works."

"It's easy, you just—"

"Please demonstrate."

I bend to show her how to open and close the clasp.

She murmurs in my ear, "Do you believe he took—?"

I shake my head. "Not for a moment."

"What I thought. We'll make some calls." She raises her head and her voice. "Pretty color. I wonder where I could find a similar one."

Noreen walks over to us. "What are you two—?"

"A little purse like this..." Denise lifts the pink purse. "Might be just right to hang on my chair. It's small—"

"But it has a long strap," I interject. "Could get caught in a wheel."

"Let's try it." She twists and starts to drop the strap over the headrest.

"Denise," Noreen snarls, "give it up."

Denise gives her a questioning glance.

"Forget the purse, forget the wheelchair. You've received the sympathy you craved. It's time for you to get up and walk." She points at the doors. "The service is over. Move along, both of you."

Denise hands me the purse, spins her chair around and motors up the aisle.

"Stay away from her." Noreen digs her claws into my shoulder. "She's a devil woman."

"Devil woman?" I give her a confused frown. "She seems nice enough."

"Fool." She inhales through flared nostrils. "But then, you're a devil woman, too. In a half-breed body. Your pagan people are voodoo worshippers."

She grabs the purse from me. "What were you showing Denise?"

"How the clasp works."

"That's dumb." She opens the purse and pulls out the spray canister. "What's this?"

"Pepper spray."

She scowls. "You can't have pepper spray. It's a weapon."

"It's for self-defense."

Noreen looks me up and down. "No one is going to waste their time attacking you." She pockets the spray and shoves the purse into my hands. "Get out of here."

I trip up the aisle, joining the stragglers wandering toward the double doors. Devil woman? Half-breed? Pagan voodoo worshippers? I'm glad my parents didn't hear the name-calling.

Eunice is waiting for me in the lobby, but we don't speak until we're in her menthol-scented car, exiting the parking lot.

"I saw Noreen talking to you," Eunice says. "Looked like she was giving you a hard time."

"She stole my pepper spray. Said it was a weapon." I blow out a long stream of air. "And called me nasty names."

"I hope you considered the source." She's driving slowly, only five or ten miles per hour.

"I did, but…"

"I know. That's how it was with my ex. After he beat me, he'd collapse on the couch, which was good. Meant I didn't have to sleep with him. But then I'd toss and turn, repeating his demeaning words in my head and trying to convince myself I wasn't ugly, stupid, irresponsible, a failure. And much worse."

"How terrible." I can't imagine Eric treating me so horribly.

She shrugs. "I'm over it, over him."

"How did you stop the words from playing in your head?"

"Time helps, of course. But first, I had to acknowledge those words came from a different man than the one I'd married. Before the alcohol took control, he was kind, loving, generous. A genuinely nice guy. But then, I guess you could say booze became his god." She sighs. "You know how it goes."

I nod. Sad to say, I know all too well how it goes.

"Took me years before I convinced myself to find a counselor. At first, I was ashamed to admit my husband abused me."

I think of my own shame, how I can't bring myself to talk about Vance's attack.

"Between binges," she says, "I'd catch glimpses of his nice side and start thinking he'd become his old self again. I also feared what he might do to me if he learned I'd sought counseling. But when I found myself hoping the next time he hit me would be the punch that ended my miserable life, I knew I had to get help. I began seeing a therapist. Eventually, she convinced me to leave him."

"Sounds like quite a process. Must have taken you years."

"It did."

"Noreen was the one who picked me up from jail," I tell Eunice. "At first, she seemed a little weird but nice enough. However, the more I see her in action..."

"The more she's like the other two?"

"Yeah."

"Nastiness is contagious."

I smile, thinking how I once feared Eunice might become like the FT. "Did the counselor give you any helpful suggestions?"

"Yes. She said to write the hurtful words on a piece of paper, tear the paper into tiny bits, drop them into a toilet and flush it, which serves a symbolic as well as a literal purpose."

"I'll do it tonight. What else did she say?"

"Write yourself a letter. Acknowledge the pain but declare her statements false." Slowing the car even more, she turns onto Transformation Way. "Then list good qualities about yourself based on what others have said and what you know to be true."

We drift past the men's dorm and then the rehab center. From the outside, one would never guess it suffered a "tragic" fire yesterday.

"You can start your list," she says, "by writing how I see you. You're a caring, courageous, smart woman, a tiger who's willing to buck the system, to fight for liberty and justice for all."

"Thank you, Eunice." Funny how she called me a tiger, like my grandma did just before she died. "But why do you think I'm a fighter?"

"I see it in your eyes. And so do those three women. That's why they're afraid of you."

"Leadership afraid of me?" I gape at Eunice. "You can't be serious."

"I've never been more serious." She parks in front of the women's dorm. "You're a threat to them."

"Then why did Ruby Jade try to keep me from going to Oregon and Noreen try to bring me back early?"

"Control." She switches off the engine. Behind her smeared glasses, her expression is thoughtful. "Ruby Jade likes a challenge. If they can bring you to your knees, tiger lady, they can bring anyone to their knees."

CHAPTER TWENTY-THREE

Before I fall asleep, I relive the ultra-satisfying moment I flushed Noreen's comments down the toilet, along with Olivia's, Ruby Jade's and Inez's hateful words. I haven't written any positive comments yet, but I will, including Grandma Hunt and Eunice telling me I'm a tiger. Right now, I'm too tired to think straight.

I don't know how long I've been sleeping when something awakens me. Thanks to street life and jail, my subconscious alerts me to the slightest noise. Someone is jiggling the doorknob.

Vance! My heart stops. I sit up and move to the edge of bed, trying not to groan out loud. I have to get the pepper spray from my purse. But then I remember Noreen took it from me.

Someone whispers. "It's locked."

"Should have known." A woman's voice. "She has a rebel spirit."

Noreen?

"Quick. Find the key."

It is Noreen. What is she doing?

Grabbing the robe from the foot of the bed, I slip it on over my t-shirt and bare legs.

Key's jangle.

Noreen hisses, "Quiet."

I'm tempted to crawl under the bed or slip into the closet, but I know hiding is futile. All I can do is wait and pray. Wrapping the robe about my legs, I stand, feet spread.

The latch clicks and the door cracks open. A narrow strip of hall light stripes the wall. The opening widens. Three silhouettes appear in the dim glow. One is obviously Noreen. Her backlit hairdo gives her away. I'm fairly certain the two bulky figures are male.

A flashlight beam leads them into the room and stops several feet from my bed, followed by a mishmash of perfume and sweat.

The keys clink again.

"Shh! The bed is over—"

"Noreen," I blurt as loudly as I can manage in my sleep-heavy voice. "What do you want?"

The men freeze. Her silhouette jumps back, jerking the flashlight. The beam darts about the room before landing on my face.

"You shouldn't be spying on us!" Despite her aggressive tone, Noreen's voice quavers.

One of the men shuts the door, blocking the hall light.

I shade my eyes from the flashlight beam. "You just broke into my room, yet you accuse me of spying on you?"

"Don't get sassy. You broke the rules by locking the door."

"What do you want?"

"I want you to shut up. Get her, men."

Before the scream in my throat can escape, a rough hand covers my mouth and an iron grip clasps my flailing legs. I claw at the hand, which releases only long enough to stuff a cloth into my mouth. I gag and try to spit it out.

"Hold her still," Noreen says. "I'll get her head."

I fight with every pain-racked muscle in my body, but the attackers are too much for me. They fetter my legs together and wind a coarse strap around my eyes and my mouth and then my body, binding my arms to my ribs. Noreen murmurs, "Take her away. After you deal with her, you'll return here to collect her belongings. I'll have them packed and ready and will let you know where to deposit them."

I can't see. I can't move. I can barely breathe. Why are they taking my things? Are they planning to kill me? What will they tell my parents who begged me not to return to Bozeman? I should have listened. My pulse throbs in my ears.

The men carry me under their arms like a carpet roll, one on each end. Breathing the only way I can, through my nose, I catch a huge whiff of unwashed underarm. Something tells me these men are hired thugs, not FFOW members. But I could be wrong. If Vance can be a member, why not these guys? They hurry through the silent hallway and joggle down the two sets of stairs. My head bounces, and I stiffen my neck to protect it.

Does anyone hear the men's footsteps or their heavy breathing? Does anyone see us? Maybe Eunice will awaken and call the sheriff. But that wouldn't help. He's a Leadership lackey, like Judge Snow.

Outside the dorm, the men slide me onto a hard surface. It's not a car trunk or a padded backseat, and it smells dusty. Could be a pickup bed, but I hear a door close with the slightest of clicks. Definitely not the sound of a truck tailgate being shoved into place.

Other doors open. The vehicle dips one way and then the other. My abductors are good-sized men, probably handpicked hoods to do Leadership's dirty work. How many other people have they abducted?

Again, they're careful to shut the doors quietly. This must be a van or a big SUV. Neither of them speaks, yet I can hear their breathing.

The engine starts, the vehicle reverses and then straightens. I can't panic. If I pay attention, I'll know my whereabouts if I have a chance to escape.

The driver turns left onto Transformation Way, the only direction the road goes, other than to the cemetery. After another left, this time onto Paradise Path, which is again the only option, the driver picks up speed.

When he slows, I'm fairly certain it's for the gate just before the highway, where he makes a third left turn. I've never been that direction. I'll need to memorize every turn, twist, valley and incline. The driver accelerates, negotiating the curves so fast I rock from one side of the vehicle to the other.

In a short while, he hits the brakes and takes yet another left. From the reduced speed and the sound of the tires, we've left the asphalt behind and are on a dirt road. My heart thrums my ribs. Are they going to dump my body in a ravine? I don't want to die.

I fight to slow my breathing. My arms are bound so tightly against my chest they're numb and I can't get a full breath. If I'm not careful, I'll hyperventilate and black out.

We bump along the rutted road. A headache mushrooms with each bounce. Fighting panic, I try to recall the twenty-third psalm to calm myself. At first, all I can remember is something about a dark valley. But then the words I need begin to come.

The Lord is my shepherd. Though I walk through the valley of the shadow of death, I will fear no evil, for you are with me. You prepare a table before me in the presence of my enemies.

My breathing gradually returns to normal. My pulse is not so quick to settle.

The vehicle jolts to a halt and I slam against the side. My heart leaps into my throat. Is this it? The place where they end my life?

Backing, the driver stops, pulls forward, turns and keeps turning. Is he making a U-turn or driving in circles? The tires crunch gravel. Forward, back, left, right. Round and round. This way then that way.

Is he trying to confuse me? If so, it's working. Crunch, turn. Crunch, turn. Crunch. I flip back and forth. Dust filters inside and breathing becomes even more difficult. I want to sneeze, but I can't.

He hits the gas and takes off on a dirt road. But this time I have no idea of the direction. We're on a dirt road and, eventually, a smooth road with twists and turns. Once again, he slows, and we leave the asphalt. Moments later, we roll to a complete stop—and he switches off the engine.

I start to shake. *Help me be brave, God. I'd love to be with you and Eric in heaven, but right now, I'm scared out of my mind.* I try not to visualize what they might be planning to do to me, yet I can't help but dread what's coming next.

Without speaking, they exit the vehicle. This time, they don't close the doors. The door or hatch at my feet opens and night air rushes in. I feel it brush my feet and then my knees, which must be poking from my robe. Again, I'm lifted and carried carpet-like, and again, my abductors' breathing sounds loud. My head hangs facedown this time.

The men's shoes don't scrape on cement or rasp on rocks. The sound is more of a swish. Are they walking in grass? I think I smell grass. Where are they taking me?

A door squeaks open. At least I assume it's a door. If they were going to kill me, they would have done it out in the country, away from civilization. In a place where they could bury me. Not in a house. But maybe this isn't a house. If it isn't, what is it?

Someone whispers, "Follow me."

They climb a couple steps. Dim light seeps at the bottom edge of the band that covers my eyes. I'm carried at least a dozen feet before they turn left, walk maybe another ten or twelve feet and stop. A door opens.

"In here." Noreen's voice. Of course, she'd be waiting to… To do what?

Knowing she's still involved is both disturbing and comforting. She didn't order her goons to push me off the side of the mountain. Apparently, she's not done with me, and maybe they aren't either.

Another quick left, and they dump me face-up on a hard surface, knocking the air from my chest and adding more bruises to my battered body. I groan.

Noreen says, "Cut her loose."

The word "cut" rockets a new wave of terror through my being.

Without a word of response other than their heavy breathing, the men flip me over. One long slice, and the strap around my face loosens. The next slash releases my arms. They leave my legs shackled.

"Sit her in the corner," Noreen orders. She's talking softly but no longer whispering.

Two hands, their grip like iron, grasp my shoulders and prop my back against a hard surface. The blindfold falls and the band around my mouth loosens. I blink and squint, peering through a massive headache.

A pair of pink Nike tennis shoes and two pairs of combat boots come into focus, followed by denim-clad legs. The no-Nikes and no-jeans rules must not apply to Noreen.

All three are wearing black t-shirts and the men have black masks on their faces similar to what we wore while wiping smoke residue. Only these masks look sturdier, which explains what I thought was heavy breathing. Their necks are cleanshaven, and stocking caps are pulled low over their eyebrows. Black fingerless gloves hide all but the tips of their fingers.

These guys have gone to great lengths to hide their identity. The only clues I could give a cop are that they're big muscular men and one man has darker skin than the other guy. And they sweat. Not exactly unique male characteristics. From where I sit, I can't tell eye color.

"You'll find two boxes..." Noreen glances down at me. "Cover your legs, Cassandra! Enough of your seduction." Motioning to the men, she points to the door. "We'll talk outside."

They step from the room, pulling the door shut behind them.

An agonizing rush of blood and feeling returns to my hands and arms. Ignoring the pain, I yank the gag out of my mouth, toss it aside and unwrap the black bands from around my body. Made of a tightly woven fabric, the pieces remind me of wide karate belts, only thicker. I wonder who came up with the idea—a rope, blindfold and gag, all in one handy strap.

The room is about the size of my dorm room, but it doesn't have a closet or a window or furnishings. The only objects are a metal bucket in one corner, a thin, gray, tattered blanket in another corner, and a television screen. A television? Followers only watch the weather station. It's encased in plexiglass and attached to a wall at about shoulder height.

I think of Zachary and what the deputies found in his cold basement cell—a bucket, a blanket, no food, no water. Gotta say the FT are consistent with their confinement strategies. The room smells like urine, which suggests I'm not the first person they've imprisoned here.

One hand on the wall to stabilize my wobbly legs and manacled ankles, I push to a crouch and then stand. I'm determined to face whatever comes. Shaking out my hands, I eye the tangled restraints at my fettered feet. How did I go from jail to this?

The door opens and Noreen the Nasty steps in. She studies me for a long moment before closing the door. "Well, well, Miss Sassy Mouth. What do you have to say for yourself now?"

I don't bother to reply.

"That's what I thought. Nothing." She snickers and moves closer, bringing her perfume cloud with her. "Consider this little hideaway a learning experience. You are an ignoramus, a stupid know-nothing. You have so much to learn from us, yet you've closed your mind to God's word. Your rebellion has been obvious from the day I rescued you from GCDC."

I clench my fists. Since when are the Fearsome Threesome and God's Holy Word synonymous?

"You're not leaving here until you've learned the lessons the Father has for you. We'll begin with the teachings you've missed." She pulls a set of keys from her pants pocket, walks over to the television and unlocks the clear case around it. Opening the front, she pushes a button on the TV. A moment later, Ruby Jade's face appears, declaring, "This is God's word for you today."

Noreen lowers the volume and turns to me. "Consider yourself blessed. This collection of sermons will run for twenty-four hours and repeat every day until your mind has been opened and God's gift revealed in you." Her expression suggests it's an unlikely possibility. "Then we'll assess your progress toward repentance and a proper attitude in order to determine your worthiness to serve Leadership."

What about serving God? And what about graduating from the program?

She adjusts the volume just above comfort level then locks the case. A sadistic sneer twists her flawless features. "Enjoy."

Through a migraine haze, I watch her leave. I'm not happy to be here, but I am pleased she's gone. Certain the room contains a camera—that's the FFOW way—I lean against the wall, fold my arms and survey my surroundings as best I can with my blurred vision. The ceiling corners are devoid of the usual video devices, which means only two places in the bare room could possibly conceal a camera—the ceiling light with its solitary bulb and the television.

Ruby Jade's loud voice is making my headache worse and her inane comments are already getting on my nerves. Maybe this is what hell is like, listening to bad preachers scream stupid stuff for eternity. I assume the purpose is to brainwash me, so I become a subservient doormat who bows to Leadership's every wish. Only God can protect my mind and heart from their evil intentions. I pray he does.

I begin to pace the room, shuffling my bare feet one at a time across a cement floor covered by a thin dirty carpet. I hope the brown spots aren't blood stains. Movement relieves my headache, to some degree. But my main objectives are to check the locks and find the camera without being observed, as impossible as that may be.

First, I touch my toes, and then I do a backbend, stretching my arms above my head. My sleeves slide down my arms and I see the scrapes are oozing blood here and there. I didn't have enough time after my pre-church shower to reapply the bandages, and I was too exhausted before bed to bother. I feel my face. It's sticky. The scabs must have rubbed off.

Brianna would have a fit if she knew I cleaned a fire-damaged kitchen this afternoon. And then tonight, I was manhandled by sweaty thugs, smashed around the back of a dusty vehicle and dumped on a filthy floor. The only thing dirtier would have been the shallow grave I feared.

I would clean the scrapes, but I have no water. Eric once told me prisoners of war sometimes douse their wounds with urine. I grimace. I'd have to become seriously infected before I could convince myself to do something so radical.

"You are filthy sinners!" Ruby Jade shouts from the television. "Unclean. Every last one of you. Admit your guilt and beg Leadership for a cleanse. Only when you confess and repent publicly will you be loosed from your demons." She lowers her voice. "This is what makes Followers unique. You confess your sin to one another and accept the consequences."

Funny how she doesn't mention her own need to confess and repent.

Stopping now and then, I shuffle slowly past the TV in order to study the acrylic box. The cover has openings on the sides and top, for ventilation as well as sound, I assume. But no hole is big enough I can reach in and turn off the noise. Oh, well. If I can tune out Ruby Jade in church, I can do it here.

I take a second look, this time to search for a video camera. Seeing no extra devices or a hole in the TV screen's plastic frame, I continue walking. At the door, I angle my body to surreptitiously test the unyielding knob and examine the two locks. The only way out is with a key or keys. The door is padded. Is that to prevent captives from pounding on it or to muffle the sound?

On the other side of the room, I do an awkward turnabout and trip toward the light. Once I find my balance, I extend my arms outward and rotate them, frontward and backward.

The movement feels good. I circle my wrists and roll my head from shoulder to shoulder. One arm over my head, I slide the opposite hand down the side of my leg and then switch arms to repeat the stretch on the other side. I do a chair pose, straighten, fold to touch my toes, and do it again.

Raising my hands above my head, I clasp them, forefingers pointed, and lean into a long backbend, eyeing the simple light fixture—one bulb shielded by an opaque glass cover. Hands high, I lean from side to side. My sore ribs rebel and I don't see anything that could be a camera. Where is it?

"What a marvelous experience it was," Ruby Jade is saying. "Coming up out of the Jordan River, I sensed the

Holy Spirit descend on me and God say, 'Well done, my good and faithful daughter.' Right then, I knew how Jesus felt."

Swallowing my disgust, I continue my snail shuffle to do another backbend, this time to view the light fixture from the other side. Who does she think she is? Mrs. God? What she said was out-and-out blasphemy.

Still not seeing a camera, I shuffle to the corner to peer behind the smelly bucket. Nothing's there, not that I expected it to be a prime location for a camera. Back and forth I go, convinced Leadership wouldn't miss a chance to video a captive.

Exhaustion, lack of sleep and the headache eventually overwhelm my determination. I fold the blanket and sit on it, my back against a corner. I doubt I can sleep with Ruby Jade's diatribes ringing in my ears, but I'm too tired and in too much pain to continue my quest. Ignoring her strident voice as best I can, I scrutinize every inch of the small room, floor to ceiling. What did I miss?

CHAPTER TWENTY-FOUR

And then I see it, an innocuous-looking beige outlet cover located halfway up the wall. I've heard of video cameras hidden in outlet covers, and this one is positioned to catch everything that goes on in the small room. Satisfied I solved the mystery, I slide down the wall to the floor and cover myself with the blanket, including my head. It doesn't do much to block out the light and doesn't muffle the sound, but it does prevent the perverts from seeing my face. I'll check the outlet cover tomorrow.

Finally, I fall asleep, but not for long. The hard cold floor, my bruised body and Ruby Jade's endless drivel wake me over and over. At some point, I must have fallen into a deep sleep because when I awaken and push the blanket aside, my surroundings confuse me. I don't understand why I hear talking and why the light is on.

I sit upright and glance around. And then Ruby Jade's so-called preaching brings it all back. I have no idea how long I slept, if this is the same night or the next day. The light is still on and the place doesn't have a window. But I suppose it doesn't matter. Leadership didn't provide a pen to mark the days on the wall. I shudder. Surely, they'll only keep me a day or two, just long enough to teach me those important FFOW lessons.

Movement across the room catches my eye. The door is opening. I might have heard the latch click, if the preaching volume wasn't so loud. I scoot into the corner, straighten my manacled legs and cover them with the blanket, wishing I'd had time to empty my bladder. Not that I'm anxious to balance above a bucket with chained ankles.

Ruby Jade and her rosewater essence clomp in, followed by Noreen. Two against one. Thank God, Inez is traveling. She wouldn't miss a chance to attack me when I'm down.

Noreen goes to the television, opens the case and pauses the video.

Oh, blessed silence. I try to act like this hiatus from the haranguing is no big deal, like I don't notice the heavenly hush. Like their mental torture hasn't gotten under my skin.

Ruby Jade comes over to my corner. Standing above me, hands in the pockets of her pantsuit jacket, she ever-so-sweetly says, "Cassandra, dear, what have you gotten yourself into?"

I stare at her. What have I gotten myself into? I have no idea how to respond.

Noreen moves to hover beside her, arms folded, her face a frozen smirk.

"You do realize," Ruby Jade says, "that your wicked family is responsible for your predicament."

Again, I can only gape at her.

"Your parents taught you terrible falsehoods and continue to do so. Only when you separate from them and turn to God can you be freed from their lies and be cleansed.

"Your father." Her eyes blaze. "The evil man not only treated me with disrespect, he encouraged you to wear worldly blue jeans. I saw the pictures. He's the devil incarnate, and your pagan mother is a voodoo woman entrenched in the occult."

Beneath the blanket, I dig my fingernails into my legs to keep from lunging at her. She'd have me arrested for assault and I'd go right back to jail. But it might be worth it. *God, you promised a table in the presence of my enemies. Where's the table?*

"You can't help it." Her eyes soften and a sympathetic smile crosses her face. "You can't help that you're a spawn of Satan, a half-breed born of the unclean. It's why you became a wretched alcoholic. It's in your blood, in your breeding. In your sordid upbringing. It's why you were jailed. And why you came to us for cleansing."

Her kind expression mutates into manic fury. Daggers flash from her purple eyes. Jabbing her red nails at me, she shouts, "Stand up, Cassandra Turner! Face God's wrath like a woman."

I'm shackled and injured, yet neither woman offers to help. Arms folded, eyebrows twisted, they glower and tap their toes, acting as if I'm trying their patience.

I pull my knees to my chest, use my hands to push to a crouched position and then, one hand on the wall, rise. The blanket falls to the floor. Now that I'm on my feet, I'm even more aware of my bladder.

"We can help you become God's child," Ruby Jade says. "But we'll need your cooperation and you'll need to meet our standards." She lifts her chin. "Any questions?"

"What are those standards?" I ask. "Do you have a list?"

Noreen juts her chin. "If you don't know by now—"

"Followers do not steal." Ruby Jade brandishes a fingernail in the air. "But you, you selfish pig, you duped my senile old mother and stole her car—and her phone." She shakes her head. "After all we've done for you."

"Your mother loaned her car and phone to me, out of the kindness of her sweet, generous heart." I fold my arms, matching her stance. "Ask her." Before she can respond, I ask, "How's she doing since her fall?"

Ruby Jade rears back, nostrils flaring. "None of your—" She stops.

I swear she was about to swear.

"None of your business. You stay away from her." She blinks several times, like she's trying to remember where her attack got sidetracked. "You left FFOW without my permission, Cassandra Turner."

"I had a judge's permission, Sebastian's permission, and Dr. Hoffman's permission."

"But you didn't have God's permission. His ways are higher, his judgments more righteous than man's."

You're not God.

"Besides, all three are men." As before, the way she says men makes the word sound nasty, yet I know how much she depends on Sebastian. "You seduced them all," she declares. "Judges respect and honor me, but you led them astray."

Ah, the humiliation still stings. "Believe whatever you want. I'm grateful I was able to see my grandmother before she died."

"She's a liar, same as the rest of your family. She didn't die, she faked it."

I squint at her. "We sat with her lifeless body for hours afterward."

"That explains it." Her purple eyes grow big. "Your evil Jamaican family duped you to draw you away from us. It was sorcery, pure, evil sorcery."

I clamp my jaw and clasp my hands behind my back. Arguing with the crazy woman is a waste of breath. And hazardous to my blood pressure. Pain pounds my temples.

"Jesus said…" She leans close. "'Let the dead bury the dead.'"

What? I scrunch my eyebrows, trying to grasp the connection. "His statement had to do with the Jewish tradition of private mourning for as long as a year and their wrong belief that decomposed flesh atoned for the person's sins. He was speaking about the priority of serving God and those who are alive, not the dead."

I learned that tidbit from a chapel speaker. It was the first time I faced the fact my husband's body, same as every other deceased body, had succumbed to decay. I still hate to think about it, but like my grandparents, Eric was a believer. The antidote is to picture them all happy and healthy in heaven.

Both women blink several times. Apparently, they didn't expect a theology lesson from me. "Well, there you go." Ruby Jade places her hands on her wide waist. "Trying to change the subject. Your rebellious spirit is raising its ugly head again. Unless we rid you of it, the beauty within will never be unveiled."

Noreen's eyebrow twitches, like she doubts they'll ever find beauty within my feeble frame.

God, I can't take any more of this insanity. Please make them leave. My brain and my bladder are at their limits.

"We're here," Noreen says, "to talk about your rebellion, not about forgotten Jewish traditions. For your information, the Followers are the new Jews. We have nothing to do with their ancient pagan ways."

I refrain from rolling my eyes. It's not easy.

"We assigned you to this timeout sanctuary," Ruby Jade says, "to teach you truth and give you an opportunity to repent of seducing Corban Dahlstrom and sneaking away to have his baby."

Sanctuary? My self-control shatters. "I did *not* seduce Corban Dahlstrom or have a baby." I aim a finger at her. "And you did *not* assign me. You chained me, kidnapped me and imprisoned me!"

"Liar, liar!" Ruby Jade screams. She digs her nails into my hair and yanks.

I fall onto my hands and knees.

Still screaming, "Liar, liar, liar!" she drags me across the room by my hair.

I grasp her wrists to keep her from pulling my hair out.

A phone rings near my head and keeps ringing.

"Ruby Jade," Noreen shouts, "Evelyn sent a text saying you'll be getting an important call. That's probably it."

Ruby Jade releases her hold on my hair. "Get your filthy hands off me, you half-breed."

I let go and sit back, breathing hard. I'm raking my hair from my eyes, when Noreen comes behind me and shoves the gag cloth between my teeth. She wraps her lotioned hands around my mouth and wedges my head against her chest.

I claw at her arms.

She swears under her breath and hisses, "Stupid slut, want a fingernail in your eyeball?"

I drop my hands. Does she know what I did to Vance?

Red-faced and wheezing, Ruby Jade reaches into her jacket pocket and extracts a phone. "Hello." Her chest heaves. "Oh, hello, Dr. Hoffman." She sucks in a breath. "I'm fine. Just finished a…" She wheezes another breath. "Strenuous workout." She winks at us.

Noreen chuckles.

If I could, I'd barf in her smelly hands.

"How can I help you, Doctor?" Ruby Jade asks. After a pause, she says, "I don't have time for a meeting. My schedule is full today. However, I've got a couple minutes right now to talk by phone."

Another pause, and then, "No, I don't know where Cassandra Turner is."

In my head, I scream, *Liar.*

"Did she skip class, again?" Phone balanced between her shoulder and her ear, she brushes her hands together, wiping my hair from her fingers.

He must have said something kind because she says, "I appreciate your concern and will have our secretary call her parents." Looking straight at me, she adds, "Cassandra is unreliable and irresponsible. She probably ran off again."

Lifting her eyebrows, she adds, "Now, wasn't that easy, Dr. Hoffman? No need at all for a meeting."

She listens, frowns and yells, "You can't do that!"

I feel Noreen tense.

"I don't care what he said or did, you cannot remove my son from the program without the judge's permission." Her red face contorts. "You're lying. Judge Snow would never allow—" She motions to Noreen and stomps toward the door. "You didn't ask my permission."

Noreen releases her hold on me, jumps up and scurries out of the room behind Ruby Jade.

Yanking the cloth from my mouth, I shout, "Doctor, it's me, Ca—"

The door slams.

I blow out a long breath. I may get my eyeballs scratched out for my desperate cry, but it was worth a try. Rubbing my temples and my traumatized scalp, I try to process what just happened in my so-called sanctuary. Did the perverts enjoy the show?

And then the facts coalesce in my head, as obvious as one, two, three. I hide my face in my hands, so the onlookers can't see my grin. *You did it, God. You prepared a table for me in the presence of my enemies. You kicked Vance out of the program, you sent the witches away, and you made them forget to restart the video.*

Why do I sometimes think God doesn't hear me, that he doesn't answer my prayers?

Assuming Ruby Jade and Noreen will be busy lambasting poor Doctor, I grab the blanket and head for the bucket. The blanket will provide a modicum of privacy—or at least give me a sense of seclusion in the presence of a video camera and the possibility of intruders. However, bladder relief will only happen if I can figure out how to balance with stiff muscles and shackled feet.

Sliding the bucket far enough out of the corner that I can step to the other side of it and face the corner, I draw the blanket around my shoulders and over my head. Beneath the flimsy shield, I tie the hem of my robe around my waist and drop my underwear to my ankles. Grasping the blanket edges, I rest my hands against the walls for balance and squat. It's an awkward position, but it works.

Later, I wander about the small room, sliding my fingers over the walls and catching whiffs of rosewater intermixed with urine. Not a pleasant combination. After several passes, I'm fairly certain the wall outlet serves as a camera host. The hole for the third prong on the bottom plug looks different. I'm not positive it's a camera lens, but it's as good a guess as any.

How odd the only outlet is located halfway up the wall and the room has an encased, wired television, yet it doesn't have a light switch. Was this room designed for imprisoning people or renovated for the purpose?

My headache moves to the back burner, but the restraints chafing my thin skin make my ankles red and sore. Before they become seriously enflamed, I stop, fold the blanket into a neat cushion and sit on it. Covering my bent knees with the robe, I rest my arms on them and bow my head to pray for my family and friends—and a way out of this prison cell.

I pray for my parents, who are grieving Grandma Hunt's death and who don't know I'm missing. Ruby Jade was lying when she told Doctor she'd have Evelyn call them. I saw it in her eyes. I pray for Kip. He'd kick the door in if he had any idea I was locked in this room.

"Whatever he's doing, God," I murmur, "whatever mountain he's climbing, please keep him safe and remind him to stay in touch with Mom and Dad."

The video camera may not have audio capability. What would be the point with Ruby Jade's continuous loud rants? Still, I'm not taking any chances. I keep my voice low.

I think of Sebastian. He's mourning his brother's passing and dealing with the sale of Quentin's home and business and who knows what else, other than fending off Ruby Jade and Vance. I pray he can come home soon to protect Myrtle Mae from her daughter. He has some kind of sway over R.J., as he calls her, that no one else seems to have.

"God," I whisper, "I miss Myrtle Mae. She's the sweetest lady in the world, and she's in pain. Please heal her hip and help her to be able to walk again, without a walker. Don't let Ruby Jade convince doctors she has dementia. Myrtle Mae loves her little house and her independence. And her kitten."

I pray for Zachary and his mother, Trina. "May their hearts be healed and their eyes opened to FFOW's lies. And may Deputy Lawrence Manning join their little family, if it's your will for them, Lord. He seems like a good guy."

I move on to another special couple, Marcela and Rodrigo. "Jesus, I'm so happy they escaped FFOW. Guide their future together and their recovery from what they endured here. Help them find a good college. And, somehow, someday, I want to renew my friendship with Marcela."

I pray for Candice and Scott to regain custody of Mylea and that Tristen won't be taken from them. Picturing the little guy reminds me of my namesake, Cassie Anne. "May her tiny body thrive, and may she never make the mistakes I've made."

The more I pray, the more people I remember to pray for—Eunice and my dormmates, Joseph and the male participants, Dr. Hoffman and Jenica. And Ronald, wherever he is. "Don't let Leadership get their claws into him," I plead. "And release Ruby Jade's hold on the sheriff and Judge Snow. Protect Judge Bock from her talons."

Forehead on my arms, I conclude by praying for Corban and his family. They've been through so much at FFOW, yet they're fighting for the freedom and welfare of others. I ask for wisdom and protection for each of them and for successful Triple F operations. If Ruby Jade doesn't release me soon, maybe they'll be the ones to rescue me.

I picture Corban walking in the door, hands in his pockets. His blue eyes sparkle, and he has a big grin on his face. The thought makes me smile, but only for a moment because I fear Ruby Jade will punish him for our "unauthorized" friendship, like she's punishing me. "Jesus," I plead, "bring us both through this accusation, no matter what happens to our relationship. Please be our shepherd warrior."

CHAPTER TWENTY-FIVE

Hunger and thirst soon become my constant companions. The hunger I can handle, but the never-ending parched feeling is hard. I swallow my spit, again and again, until my mouth is as dry as my hands. I long for a drink of water and a shower. By now, I can smell myself, same as when I was on the street. The headache is constant.

Without a clock or a sense of sunrises and sunsets, I lose track of time. Snoozing off and on and waking to a lighted room only serves to confuse my body's circadian rhythm. When I'm awake, I try to work on the unfinished songs in my head, but thanks to the headache, I can't focus or remember words. The "cradled in opulence" phrase comes to mind now and then, yet I don't recall the tune or the rest of the song. Unable to concentrate and without anything to do, I default to sleep beneath a light that never dims.

Resting on the hard floor is painful, but so are sitting and standing. I can't stay in one position for long. To exercise my mind, I imagine what kind of trap I might concoct with the partially full urine bucket, the blanket, the gag and the straps.

The age-old trick, balancing the bucket above the door so it dumps on the next person to enter, appeals to me. I'd love to watch Noreen splutter and squirm as my urine drenches her highlights, though I wouldn't stay around to enjoy the show. But try as I might, I don't see a way to do the bucket trick. What if I put it on the floor in front of the door to trip my jailer?

Oh, right. The perverts are watching. I have to come up with something that looks normal. Whatever "normal" is in a secret church prison.

I'm awakened by a howl, the first sound I've heard since my jailers left, other than my stomach gurgles and chains clanking when I move. I lift my head to listen. Maybe I dreamed the noise. Or I moaned in my sleep and woke myself. Real or imagined, the sound has my heart pounding.

The cry comes again, a deep, weird wail that sends a shiver up my spine. I didn't dream it. Am I in the woods? The howl came from somewhere nearby. I've heard wolves roam the mountains around Bozeman, but I've never seen one. I stand, willing my sore muscles into an upright position, and hobble around the room, alert to the slightest noise, one hand on the wall for support. My head throbs.

Two painful, dizzy treks about the small space and I haven't heard anything other than the clink of the chain between my ankles. Shivering, I settle into the corner and pull the blanket over my shoulders. The spooky sound was frightening, yet it suggests I'm not alone in the universe, which is a crazy thought. I wish I at least had a window to the outside world.

Street living taught me several things, one being the signs of dehydration. I have them all—bad breath, dizziness, coldness, an endless headache, muscle cramping, sleepiness. My wounds are red and rough, not healing like they should. I try not to scratch or rub my arms and irritate them further.

I promised Dad I'd call when FFOW life became intolerable. If I could, I'd call right now. Hearing his voice would be so comforting. A Hank Williams song comes to mind. After Eric died, before I put my guitar away, I sang *I'm so Lonesome I Could Cry* over and over. And now it's back.

It's true—I am so lonesome I could cry. And I would, but I'm too dry for tears. I miss my husband. I miss my family. I miss my friends. I miss Corban. I ache inside and out. My joints hurt, my muscles hurt. My soul hurts. The Bible says all things work together for good for those who love God. How can he possibly work this out for my good? How about Vance's attack? Nothing good came from that.

Words from an old hymn replace the Hank Williams lyrics in my head. *Whiter than snow Lord, wash me just now, as in Thy presence humbly I bow.* "That's all it takes?" I huff. "I bow and you wash? I don't think so. Vance made me feel like scum. The first chance he gets, he'll finish what he started, maybe in this very room."

Lines from the hymn keep coming. *Have thine own way Lord, have thine own way. Hold over my being absolute sway. Filled with thy Spirit, till all can see Christ only always, living in me. Christ only always, living in me.*

Elbows on my bent knees, my face in my hands, I close my eyes against the dizziness and the light that exacerbates my headache. And I remember why this agony feels so familiar. When Eric died, I decided God had turned a deaf ear to my prayers, so I turned a deaf ear to him. Alcohol enabled me to do that.

But then I returned to Jesus, and when I did, I sang, "Hold over my being absolute sway" with all my heart. I meant it.

This is different. My "being" was violated. Yet, I have to tell myself the truth. I am more than a body.

I am a multifaceted being. Vance may have assaulted me and emotionally traumatized me. However, his mother and her comrades have brutalized me in every possible way— spiritually, mentally, emotionally, physically. *And financially.* They've stolen my possessions and neglected to pay me for my labor.

Yet, their cruelty hasn't driven me away from the Lord. It's driven me closer to him. Why should I let Vance, of all people, define who I am and convince me to turn my back on God?

I tell myself a second truth, one I learned after Eric died. I can't live without Jesus.

A phrase from another old hymn comes to mind. *Though some may bear their load alone, yet I need Jesus.*

One after another, hour after hour, songs from my past flood my mind. For some strange reason, I can't access songs I wrote, maybe because they're more recent. But the Sunday school and church songs comfort and encourage me as I whisper-sing the words. *It Is Well with My Soul, Praise the Name of Jesus, Heavenly Sunshine, Jesus Loves Me, I've Got Peace Like a River, My God Is So Big...* On and on they come, as if God opened a playlist in my head.

Yes, Jesus loves me. And yes, he's bigger than FFOW and anything Leadership might throw at me. He's bigger and stronger than Vance, although I don't get why he allowed... I shut down my questions, saving them for another day.

Hearing a noise, I lift my head. Someone is unlocking the door. The metallic grind of a thick deadbolt resonates like a jackhammer in my silent cell. My heart races into high gear. *Lord, I'm weak and dizzy and chained. If it's Leadership, you know I can't stand against them. If it's Vance, you know I can't fight him off.*

I clasp my robe-covered knees to my chest and remind myself of the songs I just sang. I can either panic or trust God to protect me. I swallow then whisper, "You're bigger and stronger, Jesus. I choose trust." My voice may quaver, but I choose trust.

The latch clicks, sounding almost as loud as the deadbolt. The door squeaks open, but not far, and a black-clad arm reaches in, sets a six-pack of water bottles on the floor and closes the door. For a moment, all is quiet, and then the bolt slides noisily into place.

I shift my gaze from the door to the water bottles to the door. Who was that? Is the water safe to drink?

The water draws me like a magnet. I can't resist, yet I hesitate. Do I chance it? Or not? In the end, I whisper a verse from the fifteenth psalm, one I clung to on the streets. "My times are in your hands, Lord. Deliver me from my enemies."

Sometimes the enemy was addiction, other times a drug-crazed drifter. In this case, the enemy is FFOW Leadership. My time may be up. If so, the water will kill me, and I'll be with Eric in the presence of Living Water. If not, my dry tongue and parched throat will be relieved—and, I hope, my headache. Either way, it's a win-win.

Blanket over my shoulders, I crawl to the door and push to my knees, my back to the camera. A neatly typed note is taped on top of the plastic-wrapped six-pack.

Sip or you get sick. Leave trash by door.

The simple and short yet thoughtful communication touches me deep inside. If my eyes weren't so dry, I'm pretty sure I'd cry.

Pulling the bottles close, I tug at the heavy plastic that encases them, but I'm as weak and wimpy as Citrus when Myrtle Mae first brought her home. I take a breath to fight the panic building in my chest. *I need your power, God, or I'll be no different than someone with chest pain who can't open their nitroglycerin bottle.*

I rub my fingers over the top, sides and bottom. The plastic is impermeable, no matter where I poke at it. But then I feel an anomaly and turn the bundle to look more closely. A tiny slit near the bottom of one side is long enough for me to slip my thumbnail into it. With all the strength I can muster, I tear the plastic far enough to remove a bottle.

It's heavier than I expected. I read the label. Twenty ounces. *Thank you, Jesus.* Twenty whole ounces of water.

Now, to unscrew the top. I wrap the hem of my robe around the lid, squeeze and turn. Nothing. I try again. And again. Finally, the lid snaps from its anchor and twists off.

I've never heard a more satisfying sound in my entire life. Well, except maybe when Eric said, "I do."

I lift the bottle, take a big gulp—and remember the note. "Easy, Cassie," I whisper. "Take it easy." Savoring the moisture on my dry tongue, I wait a moment before sipping a bit more. I grasp the bottle with both hands and turn it round and round, admiring its sparkling clarity. It's beautiful and life-giving. Already, I feel better. My head is clearing. I can't imagine why I ever preferred alcohol over water.

Sip by sip, I finish the first bottle, and then I open the second. I'll keep at it, slowly but steadily, until my stomach stops growling and I feel a need to use the bucket.

I'm back in my corner, resting and recovering, four full twenty-ounce bottles at my side, when an idea comes. The bottles are heavy. I could use one as a weapon.

The lock rasps and clicks.

My heart jitters. If I had more energy, I'd jump up, knock the person over the head with a bottle and run away. But I'm not ready to take on anyone. Besides, my cuffed ankles could be a problem.

Like before, the door opens only a few inches and the slender arm deposits more water bottles on the floor. Is that to tell me I don't have to ration the water? The door quietly closes then opens again. This time, two tin buckets stacked together are left before the door is closed and the lock turned.

Every few hours or few days, I'm not sure which, my benefactor brings more water. I never see the person, but the size of the arm makes me think it's a woman. Now I drink when I'm thirsty and, using as little water as possible, I rinse my injuries, those I can reach. The sound of the locks no longer frightens me.

And then my angel—that's what I've started calling her—reaches in with a grocery sack. Food? Could that be food?

Before the door closes, I call out, "Thank you" with my raspy voice but receive no response.

I'm leery about what's in the bag, yet I have to look. Leaving my precious water bottles, I shuffle to the other side of the room, my leg chains clinking like toneless bells. Blocking the camera view, I kneel and open the sack. Inside is a box of crackers and a box of honey peanut butter squeeze packets.

I sit on my heels, feeling like I just won the lottery. The cracker box has a note taped to the top.

Eat slow. Leave trash by door.

I turn the boxes over and over in my hands. As far as I can tell, they're unopened. Sack in hand, I hobble to my corner, perch on the floor and open a third water bottle. I pour a tablespoon of the precious liquid in my palm and set the bottle on the floor. Rubbing my hands together to spread the water, I wipe them on my robe. I still feel dirty, but I trust my hands are cleaner than they were.

I open the crackers and squeeze a dollop of peanut butter onto one, my mouth watering in anticipation. The first bite is heavenly as is the next and the next. Despite my anxious stomach, I follow my angel's advice, whoever she is, and chew slowly and carefully, sipping water between bites. The peanut butter fills my senses, blocking the room's urine smell as well as my own body odor.

My hunger somewhat satiated, I lie on the floor beside my food and water. The headache and dizziness are gone and I'm not as cold as I was earlier. But I'm still weak and drowsy. Pulling the blanket over my head, I think how basic my life has become. Food, water, a blanket and a bucket.

CHAPTER TWENTY-SIX

In my dream, Eric and I are kayaking on a river. He's wearing sunglasses, yet I can tell he's worried. We're approaching a rocky section and discussing how to navigate it, when something awakens me. I blink, unwilling to leave my love behind. I long to return to the dream, but I can't. My senses are on high alert.

It comes again—a terrifying, heart-stopping wail. What animal is it and where is it? I flip back the blanket and stare at my surroundings. Where am I that it sounds so close? The otherworldly shriek rings through the room once more. And then all is quiet, thank God. My heart can't take much more.

Pushing to a seated position, I reach for a water bottle. After one sip, I put the cap back on. I could drink more, but I have no idea how long I'll be here or how much food and water they'll give me. They might threaten to take it all away to get me to confess to a pregnancy that never happened.

Slumped in the corner, I contemplate what to do with my time. Whether it's daytime or nighttime, I'm awake and will be for hours. The food and water suggest I may be stuck here for a while. I need to establish a routine, if for no other reason than to keep my sanity.

I'll begin each awake period with prayer, I decide, and any Scripture and praise songs that come to mind. Part of me questions God's goodness and the notion this captivity is supposedly working for my good, yet part of me desperately needs his presence. I'm grateful my injuries are healing and I'm gaining strength. I want to be sure to express my gratitude.

When I'm finished with prayer and praise, I'll eat, exercise and rest. I'm feeling stronger now, but I don't want to overdo. Afterward, I'll eat and drink some more, and brainstorm escape ideas.

Establishing a routine eases the hopeless feeling that nags at the edges of my brain and suggests I'll never leave this room. Lack of focus and purpose is depressing. I've been there in the past and don't want to go there again.

Before I start my prayer time, I sip a little more water. My emotions and concentration are less turbulent with hydration, it seems. Knees to my chest, I cross my arms on them and lower my head to pray.

"Jesus," I murmur, "I don't know why you let them put me here, but maybe someday I'll understand. Right now, please give me a scripture verse to contemplate and praise songs to sing."

Lifting my gaze to the ceiling, I wait. A moment later, a verse from John comes to mind. *Then you will know the truth, and the truth will set you free.*

How, I wonder, *will truth set me free?* But I asked for Scripture, and this is the verse I got. I will dwell on the fact that Jesus is the way, the truth and the life. The only Way. The only Truth. The only Life. Truth has the power to set me free. Jesus has the power to set me free—from myself, from addiction, from FFOW and from this prison cell.

"Amazing grace, how sweet the sound." I sing Grandpa Hunt's favorite hymn aloud. "That saved a wretch like me. I once was lost but now am found, was blind but now I see." Arms wrapped around my knees, I rock in time with the music, missing my guitar more than ever. "'Twas grace that taught my heart to fear and grace my fears relieved. How precious did that grace appear the hour I first believed."

For years, I thought the third verse fit my life, but now it's even more apropos. "Through many dangers, toils and snares I have already come. 'Twas grace that brought me safe thus far and grace will lead me home." Tears spring to my eyes and I sing that last phrase one more time. "And grace will lead me home."

"Lead me home, Jesus," I whisper, "lead me home. You're my hope, my only hope." I long for the peace and joy of home—and sharing it with others. I'm lonely. The next time my angel in black brings me food and water, I'll try to get her to talk with me.

I thank God for the food and tear open a peanut butter squeeze packet. Breathing in the nutty aroma, I promise myself that if I ever get out of here, I'll take time to let food aromas saturate my senses before I dig into a meal.

I squeeze the peanut butter onto a cracker and make a mental note to add peanut butter and crackers to the mountaintop picnic I'm planning for my graduation. My list is growing. Fajitas, Reuben sandwiches, Myrtle Mae's chicken salad, sweet potato fries, ham, devil's food cake, peanut butter and crackers. A strange combination, I admit, but I'll enjoy them all, even if no one else does. I think I'll add Mom's chocolate oatmeal nut cookies, just so my friends can have the pleasure of eating them.

Each item will have a special meaning for me and possibly Corban, if he hikes the Mount Killjoy trail with me. A pang resonates through my heart. I miss him. Does he miss me? Is he still living free, or did the goons get him too? I hope not.

After six crackers, I return the boxes to the grocery bag and place a hand on the wall to push to a standing position. It takes a couple deep breaths for my vision to clear, but then I begin my exercise phase by circling the opposite direction of my usual routine, burping peanut butter and sliding my hand along the smooth walls.

Later, I have no idea how many days or weeks later, I'm making the circuit again. Passing the door, I remember my benefactor's wish that I leave my trash within reach of the opening, but I have yet to do so. Every item from the outside is a potential aid to my escape. What I can do with used peanut butter packets and empty water bottles, I don't yet know, but I've pondered the possibilities for hours on end.

For now, the packets' foil edges are helpful for cleaning my teeth as well as my ragged fingernails. The empty water bottles make great pillows and drums for my praise time. I've even sat on them to give my bum relief from the hard floor. If I collect enough bottles, I'll try sleeping on them, but I hope I'm not in here that long.

That's it! I stop. *Peanut butter. I can use peanut butter.*

Shuffling to my food stash in the corner, I open another honey peanut butter packet and squeeze a little onto my tongue. Ignoring the painful chafing of metal against my raw ankles, I slowly circumvent the room again. All the while, I debate the best tactic to ensure a successful "operation," as the Dahlstroms would call it. Should I take a head-on approach or come along the side?

I decide the side maneuver will be the least obvious and slowly make my way to the adjoining wall, where I lean my shoulder on the outlet. Assured I've blocked the perverts' view, I press a peanut-butter blob the size of a pencil eraser onto my forefinger, move my shoulder and shove the brown paste into the lowest outlet hole.

I'm convinced that's where the camera lens lies, but I "butter" all six holes, just in case, plus the screw in the middle. The existence of a camera tiny enough to fit into a screw hole engendered many hours of conversation amongst GCDC women who wanted to keep an eye on their husbands and boyfriends. Every time I heard them contemplating ways to spy on their men, I thanked God Eric never gave me a reason to mistrust him.

Satisfied I've done a thorough job, I wipe the residue off the outlet with my sleeve and limp to my corner. I may be punished for my "rebellious" act, but right now, I'm pleased I did something to make my life a bit more tolerable. Amazing what a little food and water and a hint of victory can do for a person's psyche. However, I have to admit I'm beginning to feel like an Israelite who's eaten their fill of manna. I'm grateful for nourishment, but the thought of a salad or a steak, or even an apple makes my mouth water.

I'm opposite the door, dragging my clinking chain along, when a loud metal against metal sound from the door jolts me to a stop. What now? My pulse pounds my temples. I tell myself to calm down. My benefactor could be bringing me something extra, like toilet paper. That would be nice.

Another click. The door opens, and the Fearsome Threesome march in, consuming all the oxygen in the small space with their overpowering perfume. I thought I was lonely, but I could have lived an eternity without seeing or smelling any of these women again. My heart hammers my ribs.

Inez slams the door and the three of them look me over. I can only guess how pathetic I look. My greasy uncombed hair hangs in stringy clumps.

"This room stinks!" Ruby Jade announces, not wasting a moment of their precious time before stating the obvious. She glances about the room. "It's filthy, and so are you."

Help me, Jesus. I turn to face them head-on. *One is bad enough, but all three?*

"We are here to cleanse your soul," Ruby Jade says.

Uh-oh, another cleanse.

She turns to Noreen. "Why isn't the television on?"

Noreen ogles the TV like she's never seen one before. "I, uh, Cassandra must have jinxed it with her voodoo witchcraft."

Inez gives her a disbelieving eyebrow lift, and Ruby Jade says, "Well, unjinx it after we're done here."

"Have you heard from Jesus about your sin?" Inez asks. When I don't answer, she demands, "Well, did you?"

I lift my chin. "The Bible says if we confess our sins, Jesus is faithful to forgive them."

"Did you confess your sin of fornication?"

"No." I shake my head. "I have not committed that sin."

Like hungry fish, their mouths open in unison. Eyes wide, they do their best to appear horrified.

Inez steps forward and slaps me, knocking me against the wall.

My head bounces off the drywall and my knees wobble. Only by sheer determination do I remain standing.

"Liar!" She glares at me. "You are a hell-bound liar."

"Noreen!" Ruby Jade orders, "grab the water and the grocery bag and take them away."

Please, not my food and water.

Noreen scowls.

"Then you and Inez go deal with the Dahlstrom boy. I'll take care of this one."

So, they do have Corban—or maybe Logan. My heart sinks. It's not a huge surprise, but I'm sorry. Whoever it is, I pray God will help him endure their abuse.

Ruby Jade whips around. "Sit, Cassandra!"

Sliding down the wall, I squat and wrap my arms around my knees.

Noreen gathers the bottles and the grocery sack and gives me a dirty look, as if I'm the one who sent her away, not Ruby Jade. Watching my food and water—and weapons—disappear through the doorway nearly brings me to tears. But knowing a Dahlstrom brother may be close by makes me feel less isolated. I wish I could warn him the FT are out to get him, although I'm sure he's alert to every door click, same as I am.

The door opens again, and Black Sleeve leans a folding chair on the wall. The arm retracts, and the door closes.

Ruby Jade gets the chair, positions it in front of me, unfolds it and sits. The chair squeaks and groans.

"Cassandra, dear." Her lavender eyes with their small pupils—despite the dim lighting—are kind. "I don't normally have time to counsel our friends here in the sanctuary, but tonight I'm all yours. What's on your heart? What can I help you with?"

Does this mean Corban and I aren't the only ones in this so-called sanctuary? How big is this place? How many others are here? Maybe the creepy shrieks come from someone who's been imprisoned here long enough to go crazy. I shudder, reach for the blanket and pull it over my knees.

"You can tell me anything." Her smile is warm.

"Anything?"

"Of course, dear."

What's with the sweet act? Is she trying to trick me into a confession?

When I hesitate, she says, "Are you with child?"

What?

My expression must mirror my thought, because she says, "Pregnant. Did you entice Corban Dahlstrom to impregnate you?"

"I am not pregnant."

"Then it's true—you left the child in Oregon."

"I've never had a child. The baby in the picture is my cousin's, born while I was in Oregon." I pause. "But there is something you ought to know." She hasn't mentioned Vance's assault or injuries, so maybe she hasn't heard his version of the encounter.

She lifts her eyebrows in obvious anticipation and twirls her thumbs on her lap. "Yes, Cassandra?"

I stare straight into her purple eyes. "Your son tried to rape me."

She rears back, hands in the air. "That's a lie!" The chair teeters but doesn't tip.

"He assaulted me the day your mother broke her hip. Didn't you wonder what happened to his eyes?"

Bending, she comes almost nose to nose with me, her eyes dark. "Corban Dahlstrom got you pregnant and you're trying to make Vance the fall guy, so you can claim him as the father and get your hands on our money. I know how you jailbirds are."

And I know how you charlatans are. That money isn't yours. I consider slipping a strap beneath her feet and yanking so that she lands on her back. But Inez and Noreen are nearby, and I won't get far in these chains. I also don't want to be accused of assault.

"You don't seem all that surprised," I say. "How many other women and girls has Vance accosted?"

She slaps me.

I blink. But I don't flinch, and I don't back down.

"I'm not surprised you'd make a false accusation, but I am shocked you fabricated such a ludicrous story." She narrows her eyes. "My son would never—" She stops. "What about his eyes?"

"When Vance attacked me, I defended myself. And because you know about the attack, you're obligated to report him to the authorities."

"Report my own son? You're dumber than I thought. As a pastor, all I'm obligated to is clergy confidentiality. My parishioners' confidences are safe with me. I never report any of the—" She stops, then stammers, "I, I mean…"

I haven't seen her so flustered since the pulpit wobbled beneath her weight. "In the State of Montana," I tell her, "if the victim waives the confidentiality privilege and consents to disclosure, then the pastor or priest reports to the authorities." My college friend waived her right to privacy, her pastor talked with the police and testified in court, and the perpetrator was convicted.

"You don't know what you're talking about."

I stare at her.

"You can take Corban Dahlstrom to court for rape, if you want, but not my Vance." She stands and begins to pace the room. "You got him arrested once. I won't allow it again. In fact, I'll report you for attacking my son."

"Corban did not rape me, but Vance—"

"Quiet!" She pulls her phone from a pocket, taps it and lifts it to her ear. "Inez, we need to schedule a D and C to terminate Cassandra's illicit pregnancy."

I can hear Inez's loud voice repeat, "You say Cassandra Turner is pregnant? Did you get that, Corban Dahstrom?"

I groan, sorry to learn Corban is their captive and sorry for what he just heard. The announcement will be further confirmation to him that I hooked up with Vance.

"Yes, call the doctor. We must end the pregnancy immediately. We don't need any more half-breeds around here." She stuffs the phone in her pocket.

My brain swirls. The nuthouse just got nuttier. "You told Marcela and Rodrigo they'd make beautiful babies. She's a white American. He's from Argentina. Wouldn't you call their children half-breeds?"

I'm fully aware I'm pushing her don't-contradict-me button, but I have nothing to lose.

She swivels and kicks my shin with her pointed shoe. It hurts, a lot. I may not have anything to lose, but I have something to gain—pain.

"Don't talk to me about those wicked ingrates. They've chosen to walk the unrighteous road straight to hell. They're trash. White trash. Brown trash. Trash like you." She lifts her chin. "Vance and I, with our light skin, are of a superior race. I won't have you sneaking a dark-skinned devil child into our bloodline."

Before I can remind her she just implied Vance raped me, she says, "I never approved those two for childbearing. I kept them separated for a reason. And then you came along with your lies and incited their rebellion." She kicks me again.

I cry out.

Shrill laughter bursts from her twisted purple lips. "And I did not approve you for childbearing, you filthy pig. I ought to let you rot in here."

"I am not pregnant!"

"Shut! Up!" Her face reddens, her eyes bulge, her hands tremble. She wobbles about the room goose-like. And like an angry goose, she stretches her neck and snakes her quivering double chin my direction.

I push upward against the corner until I can stand. She's gone mad. I have to get away from her.

Dropping her jaw so far I swear it's come unhinged, she sucks air into her cavernous mouth. Her chest rises and keeps rising. An image of a superhero about to burst his seams enters my mind. I cringe. Not something I want to see.

I sidestep, but she follows, a predator stalking its prey, and lets loose the most inhuman, ghastly screech I've ever heard, one which surely came from the pit of hell. I fall to my knees, curl into a ball and cover my ears.

She screams again, penetrating the core of my being with a fiendish malevolence unlike anything I've ever experienced. Quaking so hard I fear I'll fall over, I steel myself for more screams and kicks. Instead, I hear groans and mutters followed by faltering footsteps and then a door click.

I look up. She's leaving the room, mumbling to herself.

I take a shaky breath and straighten, hands on my thighs, weight on my weak knees. My heart skitters, my insides quake. My brain is jelly, yet comprehension seeps through my horrorstruck haze. Now, I know the source of the hellish shrieks. It wasn't an animal or a crazed captive. It was Ruby Jade.

The door…

I gasp. It's open. She left the door open. Is this how the truth sets me free? I tell Ruby Jade the truth, and she goes nuts? Do I dare walk out? Maybe it's a trap. Maybe she's bringing reinforcements. Still, I have to check. I work up the wall to balance on unsteady legs and start for the door, dragging the chain.

I stop. The perverts—they can see me leave the room. No, they can't. I give myself and God a mental pat on the back. Thanks to the power of peanut butter, their eyes are blinded, at least in this cell.

I glance around the room. Should I take anything with me? Noreen left my precious garbage behind, but I can't think of a use for any of it right now. I grab a long length of strapping, wrap it around the chain between my feet and straighten, pulling the ends to my chest. Kept taut, it'll quiet the clanking.

Another breath to settle the dizziness, and I hobble to the door as fast as the chain allows. Escape is impossible, but I have to try. At the doorway, I lean out only far enough to survey my surroundings. One ceiling fixture lights a shadowed hallway that reminds me of the dimly lit dormitory hall.

Though a rosewater scent lingers, the airless space is silent and empty. Which way did she go? To my left is a long hall with a door at the end. To the right is what appears to be the juncture of two hallways.

I can't dawdle. The FT could appear at any moment. I have to make a decision.

I choose the direction I came in. The kidnappers turned left twice, so I'll turn right twice. From what I remember, the distance to the door we entered from the outside is fairly short. I don't know what's behind the door at the opposite end of the long hall.

Holding the strap with one hand, I quietly close the door and secure the deadbolt. Cringing at the noise it makes, I check both ways. Nothing happens. In the event Leadership returns soon, they won't realize I'm gone until they unlock and walk inside. That'll give me a few more seconds to elude them.

The vinyl-covered floor's cool surface is a refreshing change from the rough carpet. I pass a door similar to the one for "my" room and go to the end of the hall, where it joins another hallway with only one light. A door with a red exit sign is a short distance away. Good. That's how I remember the layout. Even so, my manacled trek from the corner to the door seems to take forever.

When I get close, I see the door has a keypad. Of course, the FT would have one more barrier to escape. But then, this may be the first of many. I was thoroughly confused by the time the goons delivered me here.

Remembering how Noreen walked into the Pritchards' kitchen without knocking, I punch in their house code and hear a click. That was way too easy. Hand on the crash bar, I hesitate to open it, fearing it'll set off an alarm. Yet, it's my only option.

I send up a quick prayer and shove hard. The door opens to a dark sky and cricket song. No alarms, no strobe lights. *Thank you, Jesus.* Once again, I think, *That was way too easy.* I have a feeling every household has the same code, so Leadership can have access anytime they please. Creepy.

CHAPTER TWENTY-SEVEN

Holding the door open, I breathe in the night air. For the first time in days, maybe in weeks or months, I feel like I'm among the living again. But what do I do now? I have no idea where I am or where to go for help. Or how to get there with bare feet and shackled ankles.

Something about the scene before me is familiar. Beyond a grassy expanse, tall trees sway in the moonlight. And below them... Headstones?

My mind takes a second to reorient, and then everything begins to click into place, including the twists and turns that confused my sense of direction when the kidnappers brought me here. Everything, that is, except the person with the black sleeve who brought food and water. Who was that?

Now that I know I'm standing at a back entrance to the first floor of the women's dorm, I can make a plan. I have no idea what time it is, but the moon is high in the sky over the cemetery. That means it's probably late enough the front doors are locked.

I'll make my way to Eunice's bedroom window, looking for rocks along the way to throw at it. If I wake her, and I pray I do, she can let me in the front door and, I hope, into her apartment. Unless Leadership has told her lies about me, I know she'll help me figure out what to do.

But maybe I don't have to throw rocks at her window. The Pritchards' code probably works for the front door, too. I'm about to step from the building, when I remember the camera above the front door. If the perverts catch sight of me, I'm done for. My heart sinks. I'm free, but not really, if I can't go for help.

I could hide in the cemetery and trust the groundskeeper I never met is as kindly as Corban said. But it's a big risk. The way I look, he might assume I'm an indigent and call the sheriff, who'd hand me over to Ruby Jade. Actually, I am an indigent. I release a frustrated sigh. I'm right back where I started.

The men's dorm is nearby, probably where they're keeping Corban. Joseph would help me. He's a good guy. But... I rub my eyes. The entrance to the men's dorm must have a camera, like the women's dorm. I look up, struck by the fear this entrance is also being watched. A light fixture hangs above the door, but it doesn't have a bulb, and I don't see a camera.

I'll have to return the way I came. Eunice's apartment is at the opposite end of the other hallway. It's a long trek for my sore ankles, and I could easily run into the Fearsome Threesome. Yet, it's the only way I know of to get to the dorm mom without being seen by a camera.

Turning away from the fresh night air into the stale hallway, I quietly close the door and retrace my steps. Needlelike pain shoots from my ankles up my legs, but I keep moving. At the corner, I lean forward just far enough to peek around it. Seeing no one, I tiptoe onward, past closed door after closed door, holding the chain taut, barely breathing.

Maybe Corban isn't in the men's dorm. Maybe he's imprisoned in one of these rooms and Inez and Noreen are still with him. But what happened to Ruby Jade? And who else is behind those doors?

Midway along the hallway, a muffled sound stops me. Is it Corban? I place my ear against the door and think I hear Ruby Jade. My heart seizes. It's probably her recorded preaching, but I have to get out of here, now. I shuffle away as fast as I can.

Finally, I reach the exit door, exhausted by the long walk. It's locked, but it has a keypad. Again, I try the only code I know. And again, the door clicks. I open it just wide enough to peer into the lobby. It's dark and quiet—and empty, thank God.

Hobbling to Eunice's door, I knock and wait, then knock another time. When she doesn't answer, I knock harder. Hands around my mouth, I press into the space where the door meets the frame. "Eunice! I need help."

Resting my head against the doorframe, I plead, *Please, God, wake her.*

Her lock clicks, and I straighten.

She opens the door as far as the chain allows. Backlit by an overhead light, she whispers, "Can I help you?"

I catch a menthol whiff. "It's me, Eunice. Cassandra."

She grunts and disappears.

I push my face into the opening. "Eunice, please. I need help."

Hearing footsteps, I pull away.

She returns, this time wearing her glasses. "Who is it?"

"Cassandra. Please let me in."

She unhooks the chain and opens the door.

I stumble in.

"Oh, dear God," she murmurs. "What happened to you?" She's wearing pajamas and looks very sleepy. It must be late.

"Quick!" I wave my hand. "Close the door."

She does as I ask.

I check for windows. Her living room drapes are shut. "Are all your curtains closed?"

"Yes. Is someone after you?"

"Leadership will be searching for me soon. Can you please turn off your overhead light, so they don't know you're awake?"

"Okay." She switches it off and turns on a small lamp that barely lights the room. "They said you ran away with a man."

"They kidnapped me." I lower the strap. "And chained me."

One look at my feet and she gasps, "That's terrible!"

"Shh." I put my fingers to my lips. "I've got to hide, but I'm desperate to get these leg cuffs off. They hurt so much. And I'm desperate for a shower. Do you happen to have a screwdriver?"

She's still staring at my feet.

"I know I stink," I tell her, "and I look like something the cat dragged in, but if you'd please help me—"

"Of course, I'll help you. I have something better than a screwdriver. If you can walk a bit farther, we'll have more privacy in the bedroom."

I follow her into the room, holding the strap taut to quiet the clink.

She has me sit in a padded chair beside the dresser. I sink into it. "You don't know how good it feels to sit on a chair."

She pulls a toolbox from beneath the bed. "Did they put you in a jail cell?"

"They locked me in a room at the other end of the hall, behind that door with the keypad. The only furnishings, if you could call them that, were buckets to pee in."

"That's inhumane." Her eyes narrow behind her thick glasses. "We need to report them to the police."

"Remember, Ruby Jade has the authorities wrapped around her pinky. Have you ever seen or heard anything in that hallway?"

"Once in a while, one of the leaders goes through the door, but they don't say why." She rifles through her tools. "I don't know the code, so I've never been in there."

"Have you seen a woman in black come from there or heard a weird wail?"

"I've never seen anyone but the leaders." She lifts her head. "Occasionally, I hear an eerie howl. I assumed it was a wolf."

"It's Ruby Jade, almost as if she turns into a beast or a demon." I shudder. "Most horrifying thing I ever experienced."

Eunice grimaces. "I won't even try to imagine."

"What's in the toolbox?" I ask.

She slips a headlamp over her messy hair and turns it on. "I haven't told anyone I have a side business. When I came, I was informed all ventures must be approved by Ruby Jade. She likes the money to go through her."

"Figures."

"This is something I've done for years. I don't intend to stop, and I don't intend to relinquish it to her."

"What's your business?" Sitting in a chair, having a normal conversation feels foreign yet normal—and dangerous, like I'm teetering between two worlds.

"I make wind chimes from glass, porcelain, ceramic and metal, which is why I have glass and wire cutters." She lifts a tool from her box that's at least a foot long.

Eunice doesn't strike me as the creative type, but I've pegged her wrong from the beginning.

"This is my heavy-duty pair," she says. "I'm pretty sure I can cut through the chain, but I'm not so sure about the cuffs." She kneels before me, headlamp aimed at my feet. "Oh, Cassandra, your ankles…"

"I know. They're filthy."

"They're rubbed raw. I'll apply ointment after you shower."

I pull my robe's blackened hem out of her way. The hairs on my unshaven legs glow in the headlamp light. "This is so embarrassing. I'm dirty and I stink. I'm sorry you have to do this."

She lifts her head. "I don't *have* to do this." The headlamp glares in my eyes. I blink and she lowers her head again. "I'm doing this because I *want* to help you, so stop apologizing."

"Yes, ma'am!" I smile and lean my head on the chair back. "I'd love to see some of your creations."

"They're in the trunk of my car. I supply a couple nurseries and several tourist shops. Summertime keeps me hopping."

"How do you get them to your car without being seen?"

"I take out small parts, several at a time. When I get to town, one of the nurseries lets me use a workbench to assemble everything."

"Nice."

"Keeps me from watching soap operas all afternoon."

"Like you could do that on a FFOW television."

"Right." She laughs as she positions the cutter. "I'll try not to hurt you."

Before I can respond, she throws her weight into the tool, jolting my ankle and sending shards of pain all the way to my knee. The metallic snap is followed by the muffled clatter of the chain falling on the carpet. She quickly snips the other end, which also rattles to the floor. "Got it!" The pain in the second leg isn't as bad as the first.

I spread my feet wide. Though still encircled by leg irons, my aching ankles are finally separated. "Thank you, Eunice. You can't imagine how good it feels to be free of that chain."

"Sorry I'm not a locksmith. Wish I knew how to get the cuffs off."

Not too many minutes later, I'm soaking in Eunice's bathtub beneath a cloud of coconut-scented bubbles. Once the ankle sting lessens, I relax and savor the blissful joy of being submerged in warm water. A big glass of cold water sits on one corner of the tub and a small plate of apple slices on the other. I've eaten half of them already.

My rescuer is seated on the toilet lid on the other side of the curtain, so we can plan the next step.

"Eunice." I moan. "This is wonderful. I'm in heaven." My ankles still throb, but the pain and the fact they're wrapped with steel doesn't diminish my pleasure.

"Good. Let me know if you need anything."

"I haven't asked you the most important question."

"What's that?"

"How long have I been gone?"

"Let me think." She's quiet for a short time. "Has to be a good three weeks or more."

"Three weeks? No wonder it felt like forever. I didn't have windows or any way to judge the passing of time."

"What do you want me to do with your clothes?" she asks.

"Burn the dirty things. I never want to see them again."

"I understand, but…"

"Hang onto that thought. I'm gonna dunk my head." Tilting my head back, I submerge my hair and float, eyes closed. I've dreamed of this moment for days. It's more satisfying than I imagined. Reminds me of my first shower in jail after I'd been living on the street. I raise my head and reach for the shampoo. "That was double heavenly."

"Now that I think about it," she says, "we should save your clothing—in their present condition—for evidence."

I groan. "That's disgusting, but you're right."

"And the chain and that strap you were using."

Oh, no!" I sit up. Bubbles slosh along the sides of the bathtub.

"What's wrong?"

"I don't have any clean clothes to wear." I slide down again and squeeze shampoo onto my palm.

"You can sleep in one of my gowns tonight, and tomorrow I'll get clothing from your room upstairs."

"They emptied the room."

"Oh, right. I forgot Noreen told me you'd stripped it of everything, even the sheets—"

"That's a lie!"

"I found it hard to believe, so I checked. The closet and drawers were empty, but the bed was made with sheets, a blanket, a bedspread and a pillow."

"You remember Ruby Jade's tirade from the pulpit about lies?"

"I remember."

"FFOW lies originate with Leadership."

"Any idea where they put your things?"

"Noreen told the thugs who kidnapped me she'd tell them later where to put my boxes."

"I can buy you clothing when I'm in town tomorrow."

"I thought you did childcare every day."

"I do, but the mom works mornings, so I have afternoons off, which makes my side business possible." She pauses. "I have an idea. Be right back."

I'm lathering the shampoo into my hair, relishing the luxurious feel, when I hear a jingling sound and peek around the curtain.

Eunice is slipping her key lanyard over her head. "Every now and then, I walk around this building, searching for the locks that go with these keys. I discovered a big storage area beside the bathroom on this floor. It has several locked cupboards, and I happen to have a key for each of them. I'll check right now. What should I look for?"

"Do you think it's safe?"

"If I encounter anyone, I'll say I couldn't sleep and decided to walk the halls."

One more lie. "Well…"

She frowns. "What?"

"We all keep lying to protect ourselves from Leadership. If everyone told the truth, we'd end the madness."

"It's God's truth. No way can I go back to sleep now."

I laugh. "Two big cardboard boxes. I doubt Noreen put my name on them, but you never know."

"Any identifying factors, like red shoes, or something that'll catch my eye?"

"You remember my shiny pink purse?"

"Yes, I remember that little thing." She opens the bathroom door. "I'll get my headlamp."

"Eunice." I push the curtain aside. "Please lock me in when you go." I may never feel safe again.

"I'll be sure to do that."

I hear her digging through a drawer. "I put a towel on the toilet seat for you," she says. "And a comb, fingernail scissors, toenail clippers and lotion on the counter. Let me know if you need anything else."

"Thank you. I can't wait to cut my nails."

After she leaves, I rinse my hair and apply shampoo a second time, massaging it into my itchy scalp. Once that's rinsed, I rub in conditioner and drain the tub. The brown-black residue left behind is appalling. I'll have to ask Eunice where she keeps her cleanser.

Standing, I pump a liberal dose of body wash into a washcloth, soap my body from my forehead to my toes and turn on the shower to rinse away the soap and the conditioner. Whoever said cleanliness is next to godliness had it right. I feel better inside as well as out. Though scars remain and my shins are bruised and swollen where Ruby Jade kicked me, my injuries appear to have mostly healed.

Stepping from the bathtub, I switch on the fan and grab the towel. By the time I'm dry, the mirror is cleared of moisture. I haven't seen myself in three weeks, and the sight of my skeletal ribcage startles me. Apparently, the peanut butter kept me going but didn't pad my bones. I hope they fed Corban better than they fed me.

I finger-comb my hair away from my thin face, pleased my eyes are clear and the fight is still there. Leadership's goal was to break my spirit, but that didn't happen, though I had moments when I saw no future other than to submit to their will. Thank God they didn't walk in on me during those down times.

Apparently, their technique has worked on others, which makes me sad. I don't know how many FFOW members have a relationship with Jesus, but he's the one who gave me hope time and time again. My experience with hitting bottom after Eric died and learning I can't live without Jesus prepared me to cling to him and trust him to bring me through the trauma. Others may not have had that advantage. I also had the benefit of not having to listen to Ruby Jade scream twenty-four-seven.

I sit on the toilet to trim my fingernails and toenails. One thing I know for sure, I will be more sympathetic to Followers and their mindless acquiescence from this point forward. God only knows what methods the evil women used to destroy their reason and resistance.

Eunice knocks on the door.

"Yes?"

"I found the boxes. They had your initials on them. Small print, but they were there."

"Amazing. Thank you. I'm excited to wear real clothes." Even FFOW clothes.

"I think she stuffed your laundry in one of the boxes because it smells smoky, like my clothes did after we wiped the dining room walls. You'll want to wash your things first."

Once again seated in the bedroom chair, I fold Eunice's roomy nightgown around my thin frame and stare at the ceiling while she tends my ankle wounds. "I have so many questions, Eunice, I don't know where to start."

"I'll be glad to answer what I can, but daylight is coming, and we need to make a plan." Her touch is gentle. Even so, the ointment stings and my foot twitches. "Won't be long before they discover you escaped. This'll be the first place they check."

"Okay, one question, and I'll save the others for later. Did Ronald return to the rehab kitchen?"

"Seems the whole episode was a setup. He never came back."

"Good for him." I clap. *And good for the Dahlstroms and their Triple F friends who thwarted Leadership's plan to capture him.*

She wraps my ankles with gauze, working it underneath the fetters. "Right after the stove and hood were replaced, the silverware, dishes, pots, pans and appliances that were supposedly stolen suddenly reappeared in the kitchen. Whoever took the stuff didn't bother to clean it. It all stunk and some items were covered with soot. We cleaned everything and have been using the kitchen. Until they hire a new cook, we're on our own to fix sandwiches or whatever we can find. Not sure who stocks the kitchen."

"Evelyn." I purse my lips. "I bet it's Evelyn."

"You're probably right. They work that poor woman to death, but it's been a good experience for the rest of us. The girls help me cook tacos once a week here in my apartment, and we've fixed other meals together. You don't know how many times they've said they miss you and can't believe you ran away."

I smile. "They're so sweet."

Eunice applies a final piece of medical tape and looks up at me. "I miss Ronald's cooking, but working alongside each other has brought the group closer together, men and women."

"Does Ruby Jade know? She doesn't want Followers to be buddies, especially those who aren't the same gender."

"I'm fairly certain she never steps foot into the rehab center. This whole affair has been embarrassing for her, not that she'd say so."

"But if Ronald were here and happened to make peach cobbler..."

"You're right." She chuckles. "A little embarrassment wouldn't keep her away from his cobbler." She slips white cotton socks onto my feet, over the gauze and under the metal cuffs.

I help her pull the sock tops through the leg irons. "Feels a world better, Eunice."

"I'm glad to hear that." She smiles. "One household evening, we got permission to make popcorn and watch the spring video in my living room. Joleen suggested we turn the volume down low and have a gabfest, a detail I neglected to include in my report to Leadership. We had a wonderful relaxing evening together. I plan to do it again."

"Oh, good. Then I can be there." I hesitate. "Depending on how this current predicament turns out."

Eunice stands and places the medical supplies on the dresser. "You're exhausted, Cassandra. You can sleep in my bed, and I'll sleep on the couch, where I can guard the door. But first, we need to talk through tomorrow."

She's right. Her bed has been tempting me. If it's as soft as it appears...

"First off..." She kneels by the bed, lifts the bedspread and begins pulling things out from under the side and the end, an amazing amount of stuff. Turning to me, she says, "I'm going to leave these things right here. If you hear someone knock, roll under the bed as far as you can go. I'll push all this in to hide you before I answer the door."

"Great idea."

"It'll be a tight squeeze."

"That's okay." I laugh. "I've lost weight."

"I noticed." She frowns. "I'll have to see what I can do to fatten you up."

CHAPTER TWENTY-EIGHT

"You're right, Eunice. We need to plan the next step." I'd love to crawl into her bed, but this is no time to sleep. I sit taller in the chair. "I should call people, but no one is awake at this hour. Can I wash my clothes while I wait to make calls?" I have to move to stay awake.

She sits on the end of the bed. "Who do you want to call?"

I contemplate her question. "My first thought is my family. But if they don't know I went missing..." I fight to focus my muddled brain, which is still adjusting to my new reality. "Then there's a deputy I met. However, he works for the sheriff, who might tell Ruby Jade. You've probably heard she pours money into his campaigns, so he'll do her bidding."

Eunice grimaces. "They're both corrupt."

"There's the Dahlstrom family, but the only phone number I know for any of them belongs to the guy who supposedly ran away with me. I just learned Leadership imprisoned him too. I'm certain they have his phone." I send up a quick prayer, asking God to free Corban like he freed me.

I yawn and rub my eyes. "My boss, Sebastian. He's probably the best person to talk to. He'll help us decide what to do." I hope he's back from California.

"He called a couple times to ask about you," Eunice says. "I was careful with my answers because he works for Ruby Jade. Do you think he's safe?"

"Yes, definitely. I call him Uncle Seb. He'd do anything for me." I love that she wants to protect me. "What time is it?"

She takes a phone from the dresser top and waits for it to power on. It buzzes, and she says, "One-thirty-seven."

"Sebastian is an early riser, but not this early."

"If you're going to ask for his help, you've got to talk with him now."

"What if his phone is off—or he's in Ruby Jade's house, for some strange reason?"

"I'll make the call, and I'll be cautious. If I have to leave a message, I'll word it carefully."

"I hate for you to get involved in my drama. If Leadership ever finds out..."

"What can they do to me?"

"Same thing they did to me."

"Maybe, but they don't have the hold over me they have over you. I heard you girls talking about how court orders bring in money to the church." She peers at me. "I'm going to call now. Okay, Cassandra?"

I nod. I don't know why I'm stalling. Maybe it's because I've had this peaceful interlude, a brief return to normalcy, and I don't want it to end. Without a doubt, all hell is about to break loose. I hate for Eunice and Sebastian to jump into the fire with me. But I have to admit I need their help.

In the small, quiet room, I can hear Sebastian's groggy voice and the question in it. "Hello?"

I smile. Hearing his muffled voice again makes me feel lighter, as if a weight has begun to lift from my soul.

"Do you recognize this number?" Eunice asks.

He responds, "Yes, I do."

"Good. Are you alone?"

"Yes, ma'am."

"I have someone who'd like to speak with you."

"Put 'em on."

She hands me the phone.

I press it against my ear and talk softly. "Hey, Uncle Seb. It's me, Cassie."

"Cat True! I've been hoping to hear from you. That's why I left my phone on. How are you?"

"I'm okay. How are you?"

"Fine and dandy, now that I've heard your voice. I was afraid R.J. might've done something drastic. I knew you and Corban hadn't run away together."

"She imprisoned me."

"She what?!"

"Ruby Jade, with Noreen's help, had a couple thugs kidnap me, shackle my feet and lock me in solitary confinement."

"Argh! If I were a swearing man..." He growls. "That's the last straw. Time to shut 'er down. Did they give you food and water?"

"Eventually."

"Not much," Eunice interjects loudly, "by the looks of her."

I put the phone on speaker and get up to close the bedroom door in case someone is standing outside Eunice's apartment. "Ruby Jade is losing it, Sebastian." I cringe at the memory of her scream. "She did this loud, weird, howl thing, like a wolf was right next to me."

"Huh." He's quiet a moment. "We've all got clumps of crazy in us. Some have bigger clumps than others."

"Hers is mushrooming, like those movies of nuclear bombs exploding."

"The FBI agents unsettle her."

"They're still snooping around?"

"They come and go. Where are you?"

"In Eunice's apartment in the women's dorm. I just escaped. The nasties don't know I'm gone, but they'll figure it out in the morning, if not sooner. What do I do? If I go to either the sheriff or Judge Snow, they'll return me to Ruby Jade or to jail. If I run away or hide, I'll be violating the judge's order to participate in the program. I may have already missed too many days."

"We need to stew on this a bit."

"Not too long," Eunice says.

"Do you know anything about Corban?" I ask. "I just learned they kidnapped him, too."

"I was going to ask you the same question. I have it on good authority he's not in the men's dorm."

"I was held on the first floor of the women's dorm. Just before I escaped, I heard Ruby Jade tell the other two to go to Corban. Maybe he's down the hall from here."

"If he's there, we gotta get him out fast."

"Right. When Leadership discovers I'm gone, they might move him." Or worse. I wouldn't put it past them to punish him for my escape.

He grunts. "Good point."

"I know the code to get into the wing, but as far as we know, Eunice doesn't have keys for the individual rooms."

"I have friends in low places," he says. "We'll see what we can do."

"Remember the cameras."

"Those blasted things are everywhere."

"But not over the backdoor, from what I could see."

"Great. Hang tight. I'll call you in a minute." And he's gone.

Eunice and I stare at each other. Now, I'm as awake as she is. A moment later the phone rings. I glance at the readout. "Hi, Sebastian."

"On the way," he says. "Where's this door?"

"First floor, the door closest to the cemetery. It's a single door, probably meant to be an emergency exit. I'll open it for you."

"We'll have to take a backroad and hike through the graveyard. Give us forty-five minutes."

"Okay."

The call ends, and Eunice says, "I'm glad he came up with a way to help your friend, if he's here. But what about you? We still don't know what your next step is."

"Throwing my clothes in your washer, that's my next step, if you don't mind." I can't sit still for forty-five minutes. I've done enough sitting lately to last a lifetime. And I'm anxious to wear something other than nightclothes. "We can talk about options with Sebastian. And Corban, if we find him."

Eunice doesn't seem pleased with the delay, but she nods and says, "I'll go change out of my nightclothes."

She's concerned about my future, but I can't think that far ahead right now. I dig a wrinkled shirt and pants out of the box that smells the least smoky. The clothes hang on me, like they're a size or two too big, but at least my pants don't fall off. My tiger-striped slippers are also in the box. I'm surprised Noreen didn't toss them. Maybe she doesn't know how much Ruby Jade hates my "sleazy" footwear.

I slip them on. They're a good reminder to be a tiger like Grandma Hunt and Eunice said. And the padding beneath my feet feels wonderful. Working fast, I separate my clothes by color and start a load.

Several minutes later, Eunice comes out of the bedroom wearing a stained t-shirt, sweatpants and sneakers. The headlamp is still on her head, but it's switched off. She has the wire cutters in one hand and a wrench in the other. "Here, take this." She hands me the wire cutters. "Not much protection, but better than nothing."

Afraid the sound of my slippers scuffing across the floor might alert the black-shirted angel, I leave them in the living room and tiptoe sock-footed into the lobby behind Eunice. The place is deathly quiet, which for some reason, makes me even more nervous. My dormmates are asleep upstairs, and I'm sneaking around like a thief downstairs.

I hope we don't wake them. If they got involved in our rescue attempt, they too could become objects of Leadership wrath. I wouldn't want that to happen to any of them.

I tell Eunice the code, suggesting it probably works for the front doors, too. She punches it in, and we enter the long murky hall. I ignore the déjà vu seeping into my psyche and thank God I no longer drag a chain. She closes the door behind us, silently releasing the latch. At first, I take baby steps, but then I remember my feet are free and take bigger steps. I have to be careful to keep my ankles apart and not clank the cuffs together.

In the far corner, where the two hallways meet, she whispers, "I'll stay here and watch the door to the lobby. You get the door."

Heart thumping, I hurry to the exit, punch in the code, and open the door just far enough to inspect the surroundings. Seeing no one, I widen the gap so Sebastian will see light from the hallway. A faded stripe from the solitary dim bulb spills onto the lawn. I'm scanning the cemetery, when movement catches my eye. Is he here already?

Moonlight silvers a furry tail. A fox is wandering between the headstones. Maybe it's the one I saw weeks ago. Seems like years since I last visited the graveyard—and since I last saw Sebastian. I hope he gets here soon.

I glance at Eunice, grateful she's guarding the other hall. An FT could be on the prowl, or my angel. As much as I appreciated the food, water and buckets she provided, she's one of them. I know better than to trust her.

Crickets chirp all around me. The one in the bush by the door is loud in my ears. Even that sound would have been good to hear during my solitary confinement. Maybe it would have made me crazy, but not as crazy as Ruby Jade's sermons. Thank God I was relieved of her annoying voice.

Eunice is right. I have to plan now for tomorrow and the next day and the next. I take a long breath to still my jittery nerves. Do I go through Officer Manning to present evidence against Leadership to Judge Bock, somehow bypassing the sheriff and Judge Snow? The possibility is slim without a good lawyer. Most likely, I'd end up in jail.

I could hide, but where? Eunice's tiny apartment is too risky. I peek at her again. Weapon at the ready, she's poised in a wide stance. I have a feeling she'd give her life to protect me, one of her girls, as she calls us.

But I can't ask her to house me. My problem is not a life-or-death matter. Not yet, anyway.

The dorm has lots of empty rooms. If I moved into the last one in the other wing upstairs, no one would know I was there. Problem is, I'd need to use the restroom now and then. Someone would see me, no matter how sneaky I was. And how would I get food? Steal it from the rehab kitchen? That wouldn't just be wrong, it would be stupid, and I couldn't live in the dorm forever.

Worse yet, I'd return to living the way I was a couple hours ago—in solitary confinement. I shudder. Not something I care to experience again.

I grip the wire cutters, lean out the doorway and look right and left and then around the corner. Relieved to not see anyone and that no one has spotted me, as far as I know, I retreat and return to contemplating my future. The most crucial issue is that the authorities would consider me a fugitive from the law, which could already be the case. Eventually, I'd be caught and sent to jail, or more likely, to prison. All in all, hiding is a dumb idea. I'd better call Officer Manning.

Bird chatter breaks through the cricket song. I peer at the dark cemetery, surprised to hear birds at this hour. And then I see a figure dart from one tree to another. Sebastian. I recognize his tall form. A second later, I catch sight of another person doing the same thing. Seb's friend from low places is following close behind.

I open the door wider, and they slink silent as ghosts from the shadows and across the grass. The instant they're inside, I close the door.

They're both wearing black, including thin gloves, lightweight beanies and thin waist packs. Their features are obscured with camouflage paint. Even Sebastian's mustache is covered. Seems like overkill to me, especially at night, but if Ruby Jade happens to show up, she won't recognize her "butler."

Sebastian whispers, "Where we headed?"

I lead them to Eunice's corner. She moves farther along the hallway, where she will intercept and stall Leadership to give us time to escape, if needed.

"Be aware," I whisper to the men, "someone who works for Leadership may live on this floor—a woman, I think. I only saw her arm. She brought me water and peanut butter and crackers and always wore black."

Sebastian nods. "Got it."

The other man dips his head.

At the first door, Sebastian whispers, "What do you know, a peephole."

What? I don't see one.

He pushes aside a barely visible tiny cover the same brown color as the door and peers inside. "Light's on, but I don't see much."

So that's how my angel knew I was on the other side of the room before she opened the door. I wondered. The peephole is so small, I thought it was another of the grommet-like fasteners that held the padding on the door. I frown. Somehow, a peephole feels more invasive than a camera. My only consolation is they couldn't watch me use the bucket, unless it's a special wide angle—

I shut down the thought. I can't go there. But I wish I'd known about the peephole. I would have peanut-buttered it too. And found great pleasure in blocking the view to my private world.

Sebastian places his ear on the door, listens for a moment, and then gives his friend the go-ahead. In less than thirty seconds, the man has the door unlocked. Sebastian reaches for the doorknob.

"Wait!" I whisper. "Video camera. In the power outlet."

He nods, pulls a cell phone from a case attached to his belt and drops to one knee.

The other man scans the hallway.

Silently turning the knob, Sebastian opens the door far enough to slip his arm in at floor level. A moment later, he straightens and shows me the picture. The room looks identical to "mine," complete with an acrylic-encased television and an outlet halfway up the wall. I don't see anyone, and I haven't caught a whiff of urine, which means the bucket hasn't been used lately.

Sebastian closes the door and nudges his friend. "Can you jimmy the lock, so their keys don't work?"

The guy winks, sticks a tool in each lock, does his magic and motions to the next room.

I whisper, "That's where they kept me." My stomach roils at the thought of returning so soon.

Sebastian must have read my mind because he wraps a steadying arm around my shoulder and walks me to the door, where we go through the same routine. I know the room is empty, but I want to be sure.

The humiliating urine odor can't be missed, and water bottles and strap pieces are piled in the corner with the blanket, as though I was a crazy hoarder. And maybe I was. But no one is in the room, and the TV is still paused. The peanut-buttered outlet makes me smile.

Our locksmith, whom I decide to call Magic, renders the locks useless and then motions to the other side of the long hallway, a question in his eyes. It only has one door, not a lineup of doors. Eunice's apartment accounts for the square footage just off the lobby. But what's behind that solitary door? My angel's living quarters?

Sebastian mutters, "We'll check it out after we finish this side." His ear against the next door, he whispers, "I hear someone talking in this room." He peers through the peephole. "But I don't see anyone."

Magic goes to work on the locks. Less than a minute later, he steps back, and Sebastian cautiously turns the knob. Cracking the door just wide enough to slip in his arm, we're hit with Ruby Jade's loud ranting underpinned by a strong stench. How fitting.

Sebastian yanks his arm back and gives me a wide-eyed stare.

I whisper, "It's a preaching video."

He reaches in to take a picture. I hold my breath. Is this where they've hidden Corban? The three of us study the photo. A crumpled blanket, a pile of water bottles, black bands. But no person is in view. My heart sinks. Did they sneak him away already?

Sebastian whispers, "Shall I snap another shot?"

I nod.

Sebastian pushes the door wider and takes two more pictures. But the room is empty. Five buckets occupy one corner. Someone was held here for a while. I hope they escaped, but I fear that may not be the case.

Sebastian mutters, "Why in tarnation don't they empty the slop buckets?"

"My guess," I whisper, "is it's one more way to humiliate captives."

Magic swears, the first word I've heard from him.

We leave the room, wait for Magic to tinker with the locks, and then tiptoe to the next door. Again, Sebastian hears something, probably Ruby Jade's endless nonsense. He peers through the peephole. "It's either a person or a pile of blankets in the corner."

CHAPTER TWENTY-NINE

My heart leaps to my throat. Whether it's Corban or someone else, I should go first. Sebastian and Magic with their blackened faces could scare them, and the person might scream. We don't dare awaken my angel, if she's nearby. I touch Sebastian's shoulder.

He glances at me.

I tap my chest, and he nods.

Finished with the locks, Magic quietly turns the doorknob and steps away. Ruby Jade's preaching blares through the opening. This room smells as disgusting as the previous one, which is to be expected.

I push the door far enough to peek inside. Someone is curled under a blanket in the corner. I say, "Hello" in my loudest whisper. The person doesn't stir. Probably can't hear me above Ruby Jade chastising the Followers for not doing enough cleanses. "You're dirty," she screams, "every one of you, from the youngest to the oldest."

I tell the guys I'm going inside. Magic indicates he'll guard the door, but Sebastian seems determined to stay with me. About to enter the room, I whisper, "The video camera is in the outlet. They'll see us."

His forehead furrows. "Better us than you. We're disguised." He rubs his blackened mustache with his gloved knuckle. "Tell you what. I'll back in and block the camera. Then you go in. We have to move fast."

As soon as Seb is situated, I hand Magic the wire cutters and step into a familiar scene. Ruby Jade's animated face on the television, urine buckets, water bottles, strap lengths, a grocery sack. Even the dirty gray blanket is the same. I greet the person again, louder this time, hoping to be heard above the strident preaching. "Hello. We've come to help."

Again, no response. Now, I'm concerned whoever it is might not be alive. I cringe and glance at Sebastian, who mimes poking the body.

I step close, lean over and pat what I think is a shoulder. "Excuse me—"

The blanket flips in my face and a person with peanut-butter breath comes nose-to-nose with me, screaming, "What?!"

I jump backward, hands raised, heart in my throat. I thought the individual beneath the blanket might be Corban, yet I barely recognize the gaunt, wild-eyed, hairy caveman before me.

Wrinkles radiate from his weary blue eyes. His cheekbones are bruised and swollen. A mustache conceals his upper lip and a straggly black beard covers his jaw. His disheveled hair is longer than I've ever seen it. No one would mistake him for a Follower, or even for himself.

"Who are...?" Rising to his knees, he stares at me, at Sebastian—and then the open doorway. Peering at me again, he stutters my name. "C-c-cassie?"

Hand on my heaving chest, I whisper, "It's me, Corban, and that's Seb, in disguise. We came to get you."

He pulls something from his ears and stuffs it in his shirt pocket. "What did you say?"

"We're taking you out of here." I lean down so he can hear me above Ruby Jade's loud harangue. "That's Seb in the camo getup. He's blocking the video camera."

"You know about the camera?"

"Yes."

"Don't worry." He pushes hair out of his eyes. "I put it out of commission."

I grin. "Peanut butter?"

Corban cocks an eyebrow. "How did—?"

"Been there, done that." I motion Sebastian over and tell him the camera is disabled.

He grunts. "I'd like to disable that stinkin' television." Taking Corban's arm, he lifts him to his feet.

Corban lurches, and I grasp his other arm. His legs are fettered, like mine were. However, the leg irons are around his pantlegs, not bare skin. And he's wearing socks. I'm glad his ankles weren't rubbed raw like mine. By the bruises on his cheeks, he endured beatings and God only knows what else.

"We'll cut the chain," I whisper. "Hang on." Darting out the door, I retrieve the wire cutters from Magic and rush the tool to Sebastian. "This is what Eunice used on my chain. Works great."

"Steady him." Sebastian kneels at Corban's feet.

I grip Corban's arm. He's wearing his work clothes, including worn jeans. After all this time, he still smells like grass, along with other less pleasant odors.

Two snips and he's free.

Corban gawks at his feet like he can't believe what he's seeing.

I spy his grass-stained boots in the corner and dart over to grab them.

"Let's get you out of here," Sebastian says. "Pronto." He clutches Corban's arm and directs him toward the door.

But Corban pulls away. Eyeing the few items in the room, he says, "I should take something."

I recognize the jarring struggle to instantly switch realities after weeks of solitary confinement. "Here you go." I pick up the chain and a section of strapping and give them to him. "Evidence and a weapon, if needed."

Still a bit befuddled, he lets Sebastian lead him from the room. But when he catches sight of Magic, he jerks free and raises the chain, ready to swing.

Sebastian steps between them. "It's okay, buddy." He hands me the wire cutters. "Take him to the backdoor, Cat, and wait there."

I reach for Corban's hand, but he continues to eye Magic, his muscles tense. "Seb's friend," I whisper. "He's good with locks. Come on." I tug him toward the backdoor. "Hurry."

He stumbles after me, stops and looks down. "Forgot I can walk now." He lengthens his stride, although he's still a bit unsteady.

We reach the corner, turn and don't stop until we're at the door. After I key in the code and open the door, he sucks in the night air as if quenching a desperate thirst. "The smell of freedom, finally." He looks around, his gaze darting this way and that. "Any idea where we are?"

"You'll never believe it, Corban. First floor of the women's dorm."

"What?" He turns to me, eyebrows scrunched. "I had no idea."

"Yeah." I hand him his boots. "Surprised me, too."

"I'm sorry they got you." One hand on the doorpost, he steps into the boots then bends to adjust the leg irons.

"And I'm sorry they got you." I keep my voice low. "A couple goons kidnapped me from my dorm room. Did the same guys grab you?"

"Logan and I were mowing Ruby Jade's yard." Corban peers down the hallway and then out the door. "He was in the back and I was in the front. Someone came up from behind and pulled me off the mower. I not only had the mower noise, I had earplugs in my ears. Never heard 'em coming. One minute I was on the mower, and the next, I was here. Must have drugged me."

"Earplugs? Was that what you pulled out of your ears just now?"

"Yep."

"I thought you might have used peanut butter and wondered why I didn't think of that."

"Might have worked." He gives me a wry smile. "But..."

"But it'd be gross."

"The earplugs didn't completely block out Ruby Jade's preaching, but if I put my hands over my ears, I could hum and block her out, for a while." He shudders. "I may never get rid of her voice in my head."

"Listen to a few Beatles songs or country-western. Get some new ear worms going."

He chuckles. "Did you have earplugs?"

I'm glad to hear him laugh. I was afraid of what the trauma might have done to him. "I only had to listen to her for a few hours," I murmur, "because Noreen forgot to take the TV off pause. But if I wasn't careful, I'd look at the screen and see Ruby Jade's frozen face with her mouth wide open."

"Ugh. You have any idea what day it is? Or the time?"

"It's early morning, and Eunice says we were missing for about three weeks."

He considers his long, dirty nails. "No wonder."

Sebastian and Eunice come running around the corner. She has the cutters in one hand and the big wrench in the other. Magic is behind them, but he stops at the corner, turns and faces the other hallway. Arms folded, legs wide, he's apparently standing sentinel for us.

"The next two rooms were vacant," Sebastian says.

I'm happy to know Corban and I were the only two captives but saddened to think we weren't the first and probably won't be the last.

"We disabled all the locks on this side." He aims his chin down the hall. "And the peephole covers. They'll never budge. The door on the other side has a more complicated lock. We'll have to come back."

I lean close. "What should we do now?"

He adjusts the beanie on his head. "We can either fight fire with fire or with dirt."

"Meaning?" Corban narrows his eyes.

"Meaning, we can do to the nasties what they did to you—kidnap, shackle, incarcerate and starve them." Circled by camo paint, Sebastian's fierce eyes flash in the muted light. "That's fighting fire with fire, which is mighty tempting—or we can heap on the dirt."

I cock my chin. "I thought you stayed out of FFOW business."

"I can't ignore the coldblooded abuse you two endured." Hostility radiates from him.

Eunice puts her finger to her lips.

He lowers his voice. "Others will suffer if we don't put a stop to the cruelty."

"I'm done with FFOW." Corban dips his chin as if to emphasize his statement. "Whether my parents are ready to go or not, I'm outta here. If you want, Cassie, I'll drive you to your parents' house or to Kip's. Anywhere you'd like."

"I appreciate the offer, but if I left with you, we'd both be arrested." I turn to Sebastian. "How do we fight fire with dirt?"

"It'll only work if you both do it. Interested, Corban?"

"Interested, maybe, but that doesn't mean—"

"I hear you." Sebastian lifts his palm. "What does dirt do to a campfire?"

Eunice is quick with a soft reply. "Smothers it."

"Right." He scratches his mustache. "Cuts off the oxygen and the fire dies. In a similar fashion, my plan will take the wind out of my boss's sails."

"I like it," I murmur, "but I can't imagine how—"

"You two return to your usual activities. Act like nothing happened."

"What?" Corban glares at him. "I can't show up at work after being gone three weeks and expect my supervisor to understand. She's probably already fired me."

Again, Eunice quiets them with a finger on her mouth.

"We'll talk about your job on the way outta here," Sebastian mutters. "Right now, we need to figure out what Cat's gonna do."

"I'll move your things into your room tomorrow while you're at class." Eunice seems onboard with the crazy idea. "And help you explain your absence to the other girls."

"Wait a second." Still propping the door open with my back, I put my hands on my hips. "Easy for you two to get excited about the idea, but we'll be walking right back into the devil's lair."

"What other choice do you have?" Sebastian asks.

"You could go with me to the courthouse to convince the judge—"

"What if he's not there or not convinced? Or determined to do Ruby Jade's bidding, no matter?"

I blow out a breath. "Okay. I'll do it, but Noreen and her goons broke into my room once. What's to keep them from doing it again?"

"We'll change the locks. Add more, if needed."

"You're going to march into the dorm in broad daylight and change locks?"

"I'll have a work order in hand, signed by the head honcho herself."

"Oh, really? And then I just show up as if I never left?" I give him an incredulous look. "That's craziness."

"Yep. Show up in the dorm, at class, at church, at work."

"How do I answer the questions, which are sure to come?"

"Eunice will help you figure it out."

I glance at her.

She nods, apparently eager to help.

"Work makes me nervous," I whisper. "I can buy pepper spray to ward off Vance, who's always on the prowl." I turn to Corban. This may be my only chance to defend myself. "What Inez told you about me? It was a lie."

He looks into my eyes. "I did not for one second doubt you or believe her."

"Thank you." Something settles in my soul. To be assured Corban trusts me is an anchor Ruby Jade's lies can't dislodge.

I turn to Sebastian again. "Ruby Jade is another problem. After what she did a couple hours ago... I don't know how to explain it, but she was like a wild animal or a demon. Terrifying."

Corban groans. "She must have done the howl thing."

"Yeah." I shudder. "Bloodcurdling." Half in, half out of the building, I stare into the darkness. To think I thought the unnerving sound came from a wolf...

"New rule," Sebastian says. "Ruby Jade's kingdom is destined for ruin, but in the meantime, none of you works on the property unless I'm there. And you will stay in sight of at least one other person at all times."

Corban and I nod. Maybe I'll ask Kip to buy me a Taser.

"Corban," Sebastian says, "get your family in on the playacting." He seems sure Corban will buy into his plan. "Cat and Eunice, what about the other women in your dorm? Can you trust them?"

Eunice and I eye at each other. "Yes," I say. "Eunice confirming my story will give it credibility. But what about

Dr. Hoffman and Jenica? What if they already kicked me out of the program?"

"Dr. Hoffman stopped by the other day, asking about you and Myrtle Mae." Sebastian looks at Magic, whose stance hasn't changed. "I told him she broke her hip and I had my suspicions about your disappearance. He said he was convinced Leadership's story was bogus." Sebastian focuses on me again. "I'm fairly certain he'll welcome you back with open arms."

"How is Myrtle Mae?"

"She's still in the rehab facility, about to be released."

Eunice checks her watch and murmurs, "Getting late."

"What day is it?" Corban asks. "If I'm going to—"

"Oh!" Eunice's mouth is wide. "This is Saturday night, or more accurately, Sunday morning. That means—"

"You're right." Sebastian purses his lips. "I'm way off base. Sunday morning and a church service where the Followers are all together puts a whole 'nother spin on things."

I'm getting the vision. "This might work better than returning to class and work."

"Yeah," Corban nods. "If they didn't know we escaped, and we walked in after the service started…"

Sebastian grins. "It'd knock their socks off."

"No Sunday school," Corban says. The light returns to his eyes.

"I'm all for that." Inez's class is something I haven't missed. "But…"

"But what?" Eunice asks.

"I've spent too much time alone at the mercy of Leadership. I'd rather not sit by myself on the front row."

"How about this?" Sebastian says. "Corban, you walk in with your family and the agents who've been investigating Ruby Jade. They need to see this."

"I've heard visitors need permission to attend services." I look from him to Corban. "Is that true?"

"It is." Corban nods. "Mom and Dad will say they're bringing friends. Anyone who helps us stop the abuse is our good buddy."

"Cat." Sebastian points at me. "I'll sit with you."

"I thought you never attend FFOW."

"I don't. Ruby Jade will be leg-slappin' happy."

"She's no dummy. She'll get suspicious and fire you."

"I doubt it, but it's no skin off my back if she does."

Eunice volunteers, "I'll join you."

"That's really sweet." I touch her arm. "But she might fire you, too."

"I'll get to watch the fireworks from a front-row seat." She grins.

Corban snickers. "It'll be spectacular."

"I've got a couple other people in mind." Sebastian rubs his chin. "Maybe I'll tell Ruby Jade I'm headed to church this morning and might bring a friend or two. She'll be in seventh heaven."

Eunice aims her watch at him.

"Gotcha." He claps Corban on the shoulder. "This guy's mom needs to see him walk in the front door, and I need to wash this gunk off my face." Turning, he makes a chirping sound and motions to his friend, who comes running.

Sebastian starts for the door, but Magic whispers, "Wait," and pulls out his tool pouch. He starts sorting through the tiny tools.

We all stare at him like he's lost his mind.

He finds what he was looking for and drops to a knee beside me. Two clicks, and he hands me the ankle cuffs.

I barely have time to thank him before he's removed the cuffs from Corban's legs. He gives them to him, whispering, "Evidence."

"Take me with you."

At the sound of a soft voice coming from the other end of the hall, we jerk our heads up and Magic whips around, still crouched but ready to spring.

A petite, dark-haired woman dressed in black is holding out her hands, a desperate, pleading expression on her pale face. "Please," she whispers. "They keep me here. They never let me leave."

I gasp. "Our food angel."

"Yes," Corban whispers, "our angel."

I look at Sebastian. "She was good to us. We've got to help her."

He has a strange light in his eyes and doesn't seem to hear me. Stepping toward her, one foot at a time, he asks, "Are you? Are you one of the twins?"

She backs away.

I hiss, "Sebastian!" and take a step their direction, letting the door close behind me. "You're scary in that camo paint. Let me talk to her."

The woman tilts her head. "Mr. Sebastian?"

He nods.

"Mr. Quentin's brother?"

"Right."

"I am Araminta. Please, I want to go with you."

Her name doesn't match her Asian features, but it's a name the FBI agents asked me about. Is this another Ruby Jade name change?

"I've looked for you for a long, long time." He angles a thumb at the other hallway. "Is Arabella back there?"

"No. She's gone." The woman's gaze darts to the other hall and back again. "Please take me with you. I want to find my sister."

"Come." He waves her over. "We're leaving now."

With one last fearful look at the adjoining hallway, she runs to us. When she gets closer, I decide she's about my age, possibly older. She's wearing a necklace that's half a heart and etched with the word "Sisters." She and her twin must have been close.

Magic stands and slips the tool pouch into his pack.

"We need to think of a safe place for this young lady," Sebastian says.

"I'd offer my apartment," Eunice says, "but it's too close to the church and doesn't have any hiding places."

"My parents are good at finding safe houses for people," Corban offers. "She can go with us." He turns to Araminta. "If you're okay being with a bunch of guys you don't know."

"I know him." She points at Sebastian. "He was kind to me when I was young, and you have also been kind. You always say thank you."

"And you." She smiles at me. "You say thank you, too."

"I'm grateful for all you did for us, Araminta. And I'm glad we can help you."

"Time to skedaddle." Sebastian eyes her tennis shoes. "Good thing you're wearing shoes. We've got some running to do."

I give him and Magic quick hugs, whispering my thanks to each of them. They act surprised.

Magic salutes, Corban winks, Sebastian clasps Araminta's hand, and the four of them take off across the grass, disappearing into the cemetery as quiet as a family of foxes.

I close the door. "And thank you, Eunice. You've been amazing." I'll think about Corban's wink later.

Wire cutters and wrench in hand, we glide noiselessly from the first hallway into the second. Seeing no one, we scurry past our angel's door, through the lobby door and into her apartment.

I'm still shaking when I transfer my wet laundry to the dryer. I'll wash more clothes later, but this'll get me by for a couple days. By the time the load is dry, maybe I'll be calm enough to go to bed. A couple hours sleep will be better than none. After all, I've mostly slept the last few weeks.

Eunice and I pace the living room and kitchen, trying to second-guess what Leadership might say or do tomorrow. And how I should respond. Finally, I plop into a chair. "My brain is fried, Eunice. I'm going to have to wing it and trust God to give me the words to say."

"Trust God?" She sits across from me. "After everything the church's pastors have done to you?"

"I've had three weeks to think about FFOW and God, and I've come to some conclusions."

She lifts an eyebrow. "I bet you have."

CHAPTER THIRTY

"To start with," I tell Eunice, "this isn't a church. It's a cult with a corrupt, perverted view of God and the people he created. In the leaders' minds, both are entities to exploit, not honor. They call themselves pastors, yet they're heartless sadistic manipulators. Wild animals are probably more civilized than they are. I've been in real churches, where the members love and worship God and love and care for each other.

"I admit…" I fold my arms. "For years, I was furious at God for allowing my husband to die. And I'm not happy I landed in this weird rehab program. The last few weeks have been over-the-top crazy. But I survived, and God actually gave me miracles in that smelly room down the hall."

She looks dubious. "Like what?"

"I prayed the twenty-third psalm, the part where it says the Lord prepares a table for us in the presence of our enemies. At first, things seemed to go from bad to worse. But then, I learned Ruby Jade's son, Vance, was kicked out of the rehab program. He's a lecher and a terror to all the women."

"I believe that."

"And then Noreen forgot to turn Ruby Jade's preaching tapes on after she paused them. The sermons run twenty-four-seven and cycle every twenty-four hours. All of a sudden, I had wonderful quietness. Also, right when Ruby Jade grabbed my hair and started dragging me around the room—"

"She what?!"

"She dug her claws into my hair and was yanking me across the floor, when her phone rang. She was expecting an important call, so she released her hold and answered the call. Let me tell you, three miracles in a matter of minutes did a lot for my spirit that day."

"Huh."

"Tonight, when Ruby Jade left my cell door open? That was the biggest miracle of all. She probably has no memory of exiting the room. Just went bonkers and then staggered out, mumbling to herself."

Eunice shakes her head. "Must have been something to see."

"You'd better believe I was praying you'd wake up when I knocked on your door. Took a few tries, but you answered. And the fact you had a tool to cut off our chains—and then Sebastian having a friend who could help Corban escape? Those are all miracles in my book. I'm overwhelmed by God's love and care—and friends like you who take risks for me."

She doesn't say anything. Just looks thoughtful. Finally, she pushes to her feet and goes to the hall closet. "If you don't mind, now that the adrenalin has dissipated, I think I'll try to get some sleep." She pulls sheets and a blanket from the closet.

The dryer buzzes, and I stand. "I plan to do the same thing, after I fold my clothes. Thanks for letting me use your washer and dryer." The machines are in a little room off the kitchen. I'm headed that direction when I stop and say, "Eunice, if you don't mind, I need to make another call."

"Make as many calls as you like."

Sebastian sounds wide awake. "I just dropped Araminta and Corban off at his house and am headed to my place," he says. "What can I do for you?"

I tell him about Officer Manning—not the details of my aborted run to town, but that he was Zachary's mom's fiancé and thoroughly disgusted with Zachary's imprisonment.

"He left the church right after the Pritchards' arrest and might be willing to help with crowd control during the service," I say. "But he works for the sheriff, so I'm not sure it's safe to let him in on our plan. What do you think?"

"What's his first name?"

"Lawrence."

"I know the guy."

"You do? Is there anyone you don't know around here?"

"I should say I know of him." Sebastian clears his throat. "R.J. fumed for weeks about a deputy named Lawrence who stopped going to her church and doesn't answer her phone calls. Not more 'n a couple days ago, I heard her on the phone, pestering the sheriff to fire him."

"Oh, great. He goes from being a bad guy to a good guy and gets fired for doing the right thing."

"It could happen," Sebastian says. "But I'm convinced R.J.'s power games are about to come to a screeching halt. How about you get some shuteye and call the deputy first thing in the morning?"

I mumble, "I'll do that," and fall into Eunice's soft bed.

I've barely closed my eyes when someone says, "Cassandra," and touches my back. I cry, "Leave me alone!" and flip away. But I get caught in the covers, which are heavier than the flimsy gray blanket.

A light clicks on, and I see Eunice pushing her stuff back under the bed. "It's okay, Cassandra," she whispers. "Just me."

I gasp for breath. "I thought…"

"Sorry I scared you. Just wanted to tell you I'm going across the hall to make coffee. The ladies will be down for breakfast soon."

Early morning events scroll through my head in fast motion. I'd take a moment to catch up with my thoughts, but she looks so worried in the lamplight that I smile and thank her for waking me. And for letting me sleep in her bed. "Felt like I was sleeping on a cloud."

"Wonderful." She turns to go. "I can see the apartment door from the breakfast room, but I'll lock it for you, just in case."

"Thank you." I untangle myself from the bedding. "I'll be right there. But first, I need to borrow your phone again."

Minutes later, I'm dressed and sitting with Eunice in the breakfast room, a half a banana and a toasted bagel slice on my plate and a cup of coffee in my hands. I'm hungry, yet I haven't taken one bite of food or one sip of coffee. Instead, I let the wonderful aromas seep into my senses. With each whiff, I will away the stench of the past three weeks.

I purposely sat in a chair that faces the window. I don't remember the Fearsome Threesome ever entering the dorm on a Sunday, but there's always a first. Today, of all days, I want to be ready for them. We're on equal ground now.

Sunshine is pouring in the window, the first sunlight I've seen in weeks. I welcome the sight of blue skies, green grass, flowers, bushes and birds flying from tree to tree, but the light hurts my eyes. I get up, adjust the blinds to shade the view and sit back down.

Footsteps sound on the stairs, and Eunice, who's at the end of the table, facing the doorway, whispers, "Joleen is coming."

Of course, the loudest, bubbliest, most curious resident would be the first to arrive. I'll be glad to see her, but I'm not sure I'm ready for her animated chatter. Every little sound makes me jump.

Joleen stops in the doorway. "Cassandra! Is that you?"

I smile. "In living color."

"But you're so…"

"Thin?" Eunice says.

"I didn't want to say it."

"That's okay." I shrug. "I'm fine. Haven't had much to eat lately, but I'll catch up soon."

"They said you ran away with some guy from church."

"They lied."

"I wondered." She puts her hands on her hips. "I mean, one day you were here, and the next day you were gone. And you never said anything about a boyfriend. You only mentioned your husband, the one who died."

I chuckle. "I've only had one husband, Joleen."

"Better get your breakfast," Eunice says. "When the others are all here, Cassandra will update everyone at once."

Joleen looks me over. "I'll fix you another bagel slice. You are seriously underweight."

"Thank you."

"Is that black coffee you're drinking?"

I nod.

She takes the cup from me. "I'm adding cream and sugar, whether you want it or not."

I laugh. "Didn't know you could be such a mom."

"Cassandra!" Dana Marie walks in. "Welcome back."

She's followed by Liliana, Shakyra and Merikay. They all look as though they'd like to say something, but they're not sure they should.

"Cassandra has been through hell," Eunice says, "to put it bluntly. She could use some hugs."

Wide-eyed, they gawk at her and then at me.

Liliana hurries over, wraps her arms around me and kisses the top of my head. "We missed you, sweet girl."

"I missed you all, a lot."

The others hug me and murmur their welcome, despite the guarded confusion in their eyes. Their squeaky-clean, fresh-from-the-shower aromas nearly bring me to tears.

Joleen returns my coffee.

"Please prepare your breakfast and join us as quickly as possible." Eunice motions them to the food counter. "She'll tell you about her, uh, adventure after our Bible reading and prayer."

Familiar early morning scents of coffee, toast, waffles and fresh-peeled oranges saturate my senses and awaken my spirit. The day has begun in a normal fashion. May it end normal, however God might define normal today.

As always, the Scripture and prayer are short. I keep my gaze on the coffee cup in my hands during the reading and close my eyes during the prayer. Still, I feel my dormmates' furtive glances. I'd be curious, too, about someone who supposedly ran away and then appears at breakfast without warning.

Eunice raises her head and gives me a nod.

I set the cup on the table and smile. Looking from face to face, I say, "I'm so happy to see you, my lovely friends. At times, I wondered if this day would ever come."

Curious expressions flit across their faces.

"I'm about to tell you a wild story, one you may find hard to believe. However, Eunice can attest to everything I say."

"Yes." Eunice pushes her glasses higher on her nose. "I've seen the proof and participated in the rescue of a second individual."

Their foreheads furrow.

Shakyra cocks her head, dreads swinging. "Rescue?"

"Yes." I smile. "But please don't repeat a word I say to anyone outside this room. You'll understand why in a minute." The toaster oven dings, and I jerk, sloshing my coffee.

"Sorry." Joleen jumps to her feet. "I was toasting you another bagel slice." She grabs a handful of napkins and hands them to me.

"Thank you." I wipe the spill with the napkins. "Long story short. Leadership had a couple thugs kidnap me and—"

"Kidnap?" They repeat in unison.

"Yes. And then they locked me up. Until I escaped, I didn't realize I was being held in this very building."

"I saw the room," Eunice says. She points out the breakfast room doorway. "Behind that locked door on the other side of the lobby."

The women stare at the door, gasping and crying, "Oh, no!"

Merikay says, "That's terrible."

Shakyra adds, "We had no idea."

"All this time, you were in there..." Liliana has tears in her eyes.

Eunice lifts her coffee cup. "I peeked in the room where they kept her. Let me tell you, it was barebones solitary confinement, not a five-star hotel."

"Made GCDC look good." I smile. "But here I am, thanks to God and Eunice. After she helped me last night, she stood guard while we rescued Corban."

"Whoa, whoa, whoa!" Dana Marie raises her hand. "Kidnap, escape, rescue, solitary confinement, Corban. Who's Corban?"

"He's the guy she ran away with, remember?" Merikay says. "The good-looking guy Ruby Jade made sit on the front row with his good-looking brother a while back."

"Except I didn't run away with him."

"Then..." She squints at me. "What happened?"

"Ruby Jade was mad because Corban Dahlstrom drove me to the airport after the judge told me I could go see my dying grandmother in Oregon. Actually, she was furious because the judge threw out her case against me. To punish us, she had both of us kidnapped.

"Just to make things clear…" Palms at shoulder level, I emphasize my words. "I had no idea they kidnapped Corban, and he had no idea I'd been kidnapped. Neither of us knew we were imprisoned in this dorm or that we were two rooms apart."

"Wow, that's crazy." Joleen shakes her head.

"I don't know how long I went without water. When they finally gave me food, it was peanut butter packets and crackers. That's all. But you can imagine how glad I was to have food and water."

Their curious stares are replaced by angry scowls.

"No wonder you're so thin." Dana Marie shakes her head. "When did you escape?"

"Early this morning, just a few hours ago."

"Did you and Corban escape together?"

"Like I said, I was completely isolated. Didn't even have a window. I knew nothing about my whereabouts or his. My only outside contact came through occasional visits from Leadership. You can imagine how wonderful and welcome those were."

Their eyes narrow. And then, of course, they want to know how I escaped.

"God gets the credit," I tell them. "Ruby Jade was in my cell, accusing me of stupid stuff, and then she started acting odd and had this weird howling fit. Really strange and eerie." I shudder. "Terrifying! And then she stumbled out without shutting the door. I was still in leg cuffs, but I followed her."

"Leg cuffs? That's criminal!" Joleen voices what the others must be thinking, judging by their horrified expressions.

I tell them about my escape and how Eunice helped me. And that others helped the two of us find and rescue Corban.

Liliana smiles. "You're the best, Eunice."

"Because you girls are the best," Eunice says. "I would do the same for any of you. We're asking you to keep this conversation secret because we're fairly certain Leadership has no idea yet that Cassandra and Corban escaped. During the service today, the two of them are going to make a surprise appearance. We want you to be forewarned anything could happen and to ask you to pray."

I tilt my head. "You want them to pray?"

"Yes." Her mismatched eyes are solemn behind her big lenses. "You are living proof God answers prayer, and you're going to need his help today. Leadership won't take your allegations lying down."

"It's time to get ready for Sunday school," Merikay says. "Let's hold hands and pray before we go." She takes the hands of those beside her and bows her head. "Dear God, Cassandra is walking into the lions' den, but you made those lions and you can shut their mouths."

Others add their petitions, and though Eunice doesn't pray, she finalizes the prayer time with a resolute "amen."

Their prayers for me are so touching, all I can do is whisper, "Thank you, sweet friends."

The others go upstairs to get ready, and Eunice and I return to her apartment, careful to lock the door behind us. I'm brushing my teeth in the bathroom, when she brings me her phone. "Sebastian wants to speak with you."

I rinse my mouth and take the phone. "Good morning, Uncle Seb."

"Hey, Cat True, you ready for fireworks?"

I roll my eyes. "You're enjoying this, aren't you? At my expense."

"You'll be fine. I've waited a long time to rattle the nasties from their fancy hairdos down to the soles of their high-falutin' shoes."

"Oh, yeah?" I'm not sure what he means about his wait, but I'm glad he's confident I'll make it through the morning. Mostly, I'm glad he and God are with me.

"Yeah, but that's not why I called. I'm calling to finalize plans."

"Is Araminta in a safe place?"

"Yes, she's going to be fine. It'll take time, but I think she'll be okay."

"Good. I'd like to get to know her. She's my personal angel, you know. Now, what about this morning's plan?"

"You, Eunice and I are going to walk into the service with my three guests. I've already told Ruby Jade they're coming. We'll be polite and respectful. The Dahlstroms will have two guests in addition to the four of them."

"What about the guys who patrol the parking lot and stand at the doors? And cameras? And Vance and the other sanctuary guards?"

"Cameras have already been addressed, and Vance is no threat. Something did a number on his eyes, but he won't talk about it, and he refuses to see an eye doctor. Supposedly because no such doctor attends the church.

"He sits in the basement, watching TV with his sunglasses on, drinking beer, popping pain pills, moaning and cursing some woman. Uses the "b" word liberally. I suspect he attacked a woman who fought back, and he doesn't want to tell an eye doctor what happened, 'cause the doctor might report him. You wouldn't know anything about that, would you?"

I smirk. One less monster to fend off. "I can't imagine why you think I'd know anything about Vance, but we can talk about it later. Right now, I need details."

"Gotcha. My buddies in low places are about to run radio-wave interference around the church campus. FFOW security men know the Dahlstroms and I are bringing guests, so they might not look too closely at us. But if they do happen to notice you and Corban on the loose, they won't be able to notify other guards or the nasties on their two-ways."

"Great. But what about cell phones?"

"The jammer will be activated the moment I drive my car through the gate. It'll block both radio and cell service, maybe even the church's wireless mics." He chuckles. "Wanted to warn you I'll be incommunicado for several minutes."

I bite my lip. What if a guard or Leadership sees me? Or people from the Pritchards' household? What will I do without Sebastian to protect me? I take a breath and blow it out. I wasn't able to communicate with him for weeks, and I survived. *Jesus, you're my hope and my strength, not Sebastian, although I thank you for him.*

"Is using a radio-wave jammer—?" I'm about to ask if it's legal, but he's a step ahead of me.

"Don't ask. Now, here's what I'm thinking. The two groups will gather at the back of the lot on opposite sides. The Dahlstrom bunch will approach the church's front doors first. We'll be close behind, but not too close. In the sanctuary, Corban's crew will walk the single men's aisle to the front row, and we'll walk the single women's aisle to the front row."

I breathe, "Okay," imagining how heads will twist from side to side. I'm scared, really scared, but grateful to have support from so many friends. Thank God, I won't be facing the lions alone this morning, and neither will Corban.

But I fully realize the situation could turn dangerous. Ruby Jade doesn't like to lose control. And she's getting crazier by the minute. God only knows what she might do.

Sebastian asks, "Did you get ahold of that deputy friend you mentioned?"

"Yes. He said he'll be there, in uniform, and he'll grab a buddy or two to join him. They'll station themselves near the rear of the sanctuary, where they can watch what's going on and will call for backup only if needed. The sheriff won't know about their participation unless something crazy happens."

"Perfect."

"Will their radios be jammed?" I ask. "If they need to call for backup, can they?"

For a long moment, he doesn't respond. "Hmm, I'll have to check."

CHAPTER THIRTY-ONE

Almost as soon as Sebastian and I end the call, the phone rings again. I hand it to Eunice, who answers and says, "She's right here," then returns the phone to me.

I give her a questioning look, but she just smiles.

After my tentative "hello," I hear, "Hey, Cassie Anita True, this is Corban James Dahlstrom. Remember me?"

I laugh. "Haven't seen much of you lately, but I'm glad to know you have a middle name, Corban James."

"That's about to change." Energy and enthusiasm have returned to his voice, thank God.

"Your name?"

"No." He laughs. "I'm talking about how much time you and I spend together. Just wanted to let you know we're on our way to the church. My family and I were brainstorming, and we came up with a name for this operation."

"Oh, right. You guys like to name your operations. What's this one?"

"Operation Lion of Judah. Revelation five says the Lion of Judah has overcome, triumphed and conquered. Jesus is our Victor."

"I like it. Gives me confidence."

"Yes! Confidence in Christ, not in ourselves."

"Thanks for the reminder." I think of my dad calling FFOW a lions' den and Merikay's prayer at breakfast. "We're walking into a lions' den, Corban. But the Lion of Judah can shut their mouths."

"Great thought. I'll hang onto it." He repeats what I just said to his family and then comes back on. "Before we get to the lions' lair, I wanted to ask how you're doing. You and I endured some tough stuff the last few weeks."

"I'm struggling to adjust to life on the outside, so to speak, but I'll be okay. How about you?"

"I feel like I'm in a fog. It's not as dense this morning as it was last night, but I know recovery will take time. Sebastian told me how you escaped, and I'm convinced the God who rescued us in such a miraculous way can heal the trauma. Our victory today will jumpstart our road to recovery."

"I hope so."

"I know so." Corban sounds way more confident than I feel.

"I'd better get ready for church," I tell him. "See you soon."

"Can't wait to see you again." I hear the smile in his voice. "Lead on, Lion of Judah!"

Eunice drives me to church. Neither of us has much to say. I pray no one gets hurt and I don't get kicked out of the rehab program. Without a doubt, it'll take another miracle. The Lion of Judah can handle it. I just wish the confrontation was over and done with.

The pink purse is in my lap and Myrtle Mae's hat is on my head. I found them in the boxes Eunice brought to me. I'm also wearing the sunglasses Sebastian gave me, partly because I'm still adjusting to light, and partly to hide my eyes until we get inside the sanctuary. Once I'm face to face with

Leadership, I'll want them to realize exactly who I am. Cassie Anita True. Not one of their puppets. Not one of their captives. Not Cassandra Turner.

We come upon a parking lot guard and I turn my head. Eunice tells me he glanced at us as we passed, but he didn't take a second look or lift his radio to talk. One down.

I blow out the breath I was holding and survey our surroundings. Followers are walking in pairs or clusters toward the church building, but they're near the front of the parking area and we're at the back.

I spy Sebastian's pickup at the far corner of the huge lot. Eunice drives that direction and parks beside it. He's already out and lifting a wheelchair from the truck bed.

After we exit her car, Eunice locks the doors, which strikes me funny. FFOW's high and holy place, peopled by Followers and guarded day and night, ought to be the safest spot on the planet. But we both know FFOW is neither high nor holy. And definitely not safe.

Sebastian opens his passenger door, sets his cowboy hat on the dash and leans in to gather Myrtle Mae into his arms. Pivoting, he gently places her in the wheelchair and holds it steady while she adjusts her position.

"Myrtle Mae!" I hurry over to hug her. "What a wonderful treat! I'm so happy to see you!" She smells like a hospital. "And I'm so happy you came today."

"My favorite flower girl." She grins her sweet beautiful grin. "I'm delighted to see you again and to be able to support you in person."

I straighten and ask, "Have you met Eunice, my dorm mom?"

"No." Myrtle Mae extends her hand. "But I've heard wonderful things about you, Eunice."

Eunice smiles. "Likewise. I'm delighted to meet you."

I tell Eunice that Myrtle Mae broke her hip and is temporarily in a wheelchair.

354 | Rebecca Carey Lyles

"I can walk," Myrtle Mae says, "and am about to be dismissed from the rehab facility. But Sebastian felt crossing this big parking lot might be a bit much for me."

"You're looking good," I tell her.

"You're looking scrawny." She frowns.

"I'm okay, really. I talked to Corban a few minutes ago, and he sounds like he's doing good. But I feel awful he was kidnapped. It was my fault, 'cause I left those pictures on your phone."

"Cassie." Her eyes flash. "You are not to blame for others' atrocious behavior."

A male voice says, "I'll second the motion."

I turn to see Dr. Hoffman and Jenica join the circle. He puts his hand on my shoulder. "I'm serious, Cassandra." Behind his aviator glasses, his gaze is solemn. "Don't take credit for evil done by others."

I smile. "Yes, sir."

Sebastian chimes in. "You're not on probation with God, you know."

"I like that." Jenica laughs and hugs me. "Good to have you back, Cassandra. I'm sorry for the horrific abuse you suffered the last few weeks and I want to help you however I can. My door is always open for you."

"Thank you. If Corban is interested, would you have time to talk with him?"

"Of course. Tell him a friend of Cassandra's is a friend of mine."

The newcomers greet Sebastian and Eunice, and then Doctor introduces Jenica to Myrtle Mae. "This is the sweet lady who made me that tasty tea and great chicken salad I told you about."

"Come see me anytime," Myrtle Mae says. "You, too, Jenica." She smiles at Eunice. "Please drop by for a bite whenever you can and bring Cassie with you. We've got to put some meat on her bones."

I laugh. "Eunice said the same thing."

"By the way…" Myrtle Mae cocks her head. "You look adorable in my hat."

"You think so?" I adjust the brim. "It was a lifesaver when I traveled, and I'm hoping it'll get me inside the church without detection. Then I'll give it back to you."

"Keep it. It's perfect on you."

"Listen up, folks," Sebastian says. "Time to rehash the plan and get on over to the sanctuary."

I look at him and then at the church building with all its arches—and my knees go weak. It's pretty on the outside but so very wicked on the inside. I don't want to do this.

Sebastian wraps his arm around my shoulders, steadying me. "Now and again," he says, "I put the cart before the horse. Myrtle Mae reminded me on the way here that we need to call on Almighty God before we enter the hellhole over there called a church. Let's pray, eyes open, like we're shootin' the breeze."

He indicates the parking lot. "The yellow-vested geezer guards are thick as fleas on a farm dog. Heaven forbid we have a prayer meeting without R.J.'s permission. Myrtle Mae, would you do us the honor?"

She takes my hand, her grip strong. I squeeze hers, happy she still has her strength.

"Lord," she begins, "How grateful we are to know we're not alone in this battle."

"Yes," I murmur, "yes, Lord."

"As Scripture says, the battle is not ours, it's yours. Cover us with your armor, surround us with your angels, empower us with your Holy Spirit. Disarm and destroy the enemy."

I peek at her. How can she pray those words when the battle is against her daughter?

A tear slides from her eye and down her cheek. "You are a good, good God," she says, "whose love knows no bounds." Her voice falters. "You can bring good from evil and give lasting peace and truth to this congregation." Her hand begins to tremble. "And you can save my daughter and her friends from Satan's grip. May they bow before you today."

"What's going on over there? Get your hands off that woman."

Turning my head, I see my buddy Hank coming our way, winding between cars.

I release Myrtle Mae's hand, pull the hat low and whisper, "I think he means you, Sebastian."

"Oh." He drops his arm.

Hank comes huffing over to us. He's wearing a yellow vest with the word "security" printed on it. "You know that's—"

"I'm new to this church." Sebastian raises his palms. "I didn't know putting my arm around my niece would be a problem here."

"Now you know," Hank says. "Service is about to begin. Better get inside, all of you." He peers beneath my hat brim. "You again."

I smile. What else can I do? "Hi, Hank."

He shakes his finger at me. "You're always causing trouble."

I lift my chin. "You're always looking for trouble."

"You're the one." He squints at me. "You're the one who took off."

"But I came back. And I brought all these guests with me. Ruby Jade is really excited to have them visit." For once, I'm telling the truth. Well, sort of.

"I'll see about that." He huffs and marches away, pulling his two-way radio from his belt.

"Sorry," I whisper. "He's the one guard around here who knows me." My heart beats double-time. "What should I do? Leave?"

"Nah." Sebastian doesn't seem concerned. "This is a good test of the communication blackout before the bombshell coming in a couple minutes."

Dr. Hoffman shades his glasses with his hand and stares across the parking lot. "He's tapping on his two-way and shaking it like it's not working."

Sebastian chuckles. "Exactly what we want to see. He'll get so caught up in figuring out what the tarnation is wrong with his radio, he'll forget all about you, Cat."

He aims his chin at the group assembling on the far side of the parking lot. "Looks like our friends are gettin' ready to move out." He goes through the plan again, reminding us to act like good Followers. Actually, it's not much of a plan. "Smiles on our faces," he says, "we'll march in behind our buddies over there, sit on the front row and wait for the nasties to react."

"That's it?" I'm sure my expression mirrors my skepticism.

"Don't think for a minute this is a passive approach," Doctor says. "Just the fact two people the church leaders had under lock and key are sitting on the front row, facing them without fear, will shake their confidence, unnerve them."

"But," I whisper, "I am afraid."

"Of course, you are." Jenica smiles. "So am I. Yet, your escape gives you a mysterious power they won't understand. It'll confuse and scare them. Returning to their territory instead of running away or going to the authorities is sure to rattle their cages. Shows tremendous courage.

"If they no longer have power over you two after what they put you through, what about the other members? They'll see how your surprise appearance stuns the nasties, as Sebastian calls them, and stabs fear in their hearts. Dozens if not hundreds of Followers just might walk out the door and never return."

"Also," Doctor adds, "seeing you two escapees are supported by several individuals with the power to upset their applecart will punch a big hole in their power balloon."

"Right." Sebastian nods and continues to give instructions. "When a response is required for something they say, we'll be polite. However..." He lifts a finger. "We won't bow to their demands, and we'll defend ourselves and each other, if needed." He pauses. "When possible, we'll leave the hard stuff to the deputies."

Hard stuff? *Oh, God.* I bite my lip. *I can't do this. I can't face Leadership. And Myrtle Mae? She's so frail. Ruby Jade will be furious when she sees her with me. Denise is paralyzed. What if—?*

Remember who I am?

I look up. *I do remember. You're Immanuel. God with me. I am not alone.*

The Lion of Judah is striding into the lions' den right beside me and Corban and our amazing friends. He's not a tiny, meek, helpless kitten like Citrus. He's huge, powerful, ferocious and invincible. Best of all, he's on our side.

Sebastian says, "Sorry I can't be more—"

Dr. Hoffman interrupts him. "Just a minute, please. What's this about deputies?"

"Several deputies will be seated near the back of the sanctuary," Sebastian says. "To help with crowd control, if that becomes an issue. Right, Cat?"

I nod. "I don't know how many, but my deputy friend was hoping to get two or three other officers to join him."

"Sorry I can't be more specific about the plan," Sebastian says. "Only God knows how this little visit is gonna go." He asks Myrtle Mae if she wants to finish her prayer.

"Your turn," she says, wiping her cheeks.

"Okay." Eyes open, he prays, "Almighty God, give all of us, especially Cat and Corban, the courage and strength to walk where few Followers dare to tread. May we do so with our shoulders back and our heads high.

"We humbly ask for your supernatural power, wisdom, protection and guidance. Shine your holy light to rout out the darkness that permeates this evil place." He lifts his hand. "Lead on, Lion of Judah! Amen."

I give him a quizzical look.

"Yep." He grins. "Operation Lion of Judah, off and running."

Corban and friends start for the building and we follow, maintaining the wide gap between the two groups. Like Sebastian prayed, I lift my head and square my shoulders. My insides may quiver, but I'm going to put on a good show and let God work.

I walk beside Sebastian, who's pushing Myrtle Mae's wheelchair. Eunice, Doctor and Jenica are behind us. My heart flipflops and the hat brim bounces with every step.

"Logan Dahlstrom was supposed to play in the band today,' Sebastian says. "He knows the song order and will tell us when they're singing the last song. That's when we'll enter the sanctuary."

Good thing Ruby Jade didn't hear him call the ensemble a band. But then I remind myself her tyranny is about to become a thing of the past. *Oh, God, I pray, let it be so. Please, let it be so.* I turn to Sebastian. "Where is Logan? I don't see him."

He chuckles. "The blonde with the big glasses."

Looking the guy over from the back, I believe it could be Logan. "Why the disguise?"

"No one is searching for Corban, that we know of." He lowers his voice. "Nevertheless, Logan figures people are less likely to recognize Corban and report his reappearance if he's not with his brother." He chuckles. "And then there's the fact those two get a big kick out of their clandestine operations. They're tickled silly they can both be incognito this morning."

The Dahlstrom brothers back in action. That's good. I'm happy for them, happy for the whole family.

Sebastian turns to the others. "Like I said, once we're inside the sanctuary, we'll form two lines. Cat and Corban first, and then the ladies in the wheelchairs. Dr. Hoffman, I'd like you to be the last person in our lineup, to keep an eye on things and protect the ladies."

"Glad to."

First? I swallow. Corban and I go in first. Heaven help us.

At the sound of heavy metal music, we all look that direction. A yellow-vested guard is standing between rows of cars, holding his radio as far as he can stretch his arm, a horrified expression on his face.

I nudge Sebastian. "You didn't."

He smirks. "It worked. Like I told you, friends in low places."

The noise stops but then starts and stops again. He must be switching the radio on and off. The man waves the two-way in the air like it's hot and turns his back. My guess is he's thinking if he doesn't see us, he doesn't have to report us. And he doesn't have to hear the devil music.

Two burly men in suit jackets are stationed at the church doors. They both appear to be in their forties. One guy is Hispanic, the other Caucasian. Their bald heads glisten in the sunshine. They look like bouncers, yet I'm fairly certain I've never seen either of them before, at a bar or at church. A niggling thought makes me take a second look. Could the pair be Noreen's goons?

Sebastian murmurs, "I overheard R.J. say she's tired of reporters and authorities snooping on her church services. Actually hired a couple outsiders, thugs by the looks of 'em. If you ask me, her paranoia is gettin' out of hand. Everyone who enters has to prove they have her name in their phone's contact list, unless they're preapproved guests."

"Interesting." I adjust my sunglasses and angle the hat to better hide my face. "What about the deputies? How will they get in?"

"They're already inside. Power of a uniform is my guess." He winks and turns to the others. "Open your phones' contact lists to Ruby Jade's number."

"Huh?" Doctor grunts. "What's that about?"

"It's what those two brutes at the door are gonna want to see."

"They were here for the first time two Sundays ago," Eunice tells us. "Feels like entering a federal facility."

"I agree," Jenica says. "What an odd thing for a church to do."

"You can say that again." Doctor sounds disgusted.

I stop in my tracks. "I don't have a phone. Leadership took it."

The others come to a halt around me. Sebastian looks thoughtful, and then he says, "You're my guest today. You don't need a phone." He scratches his jaw. "In fact, all of you are my guests. I didn't give R.J. names. Just told her I'm bringing five visitors. Keep your phones in your pockets."

We start for the church again. Eunice comes alongside me. "Nervous?"

"Yeah."

"Remember, they were afraid of you before. Now, they'll have even more reason to fear you. Be a tiger. Roar against oppression! The girls and I have your back. We'll be praying for you."

I smile. "Thank you, Eunice. You are a huge encouragement to me."

Corban and crew approach the guards. His parents show their cell phones, motion to their four "guests," and then make their way into the building. But when we approach, the Hispanic guy says, "No hats in the building."

He's wearing a nametag. It has two words—*George*, and below it, *Security*. The other guy's badge is similar. *Doyle. Security.*

I slow my steps. "Okay."

"I'm Ruby Jade's property manager." Sebastian shows them his phone screen. "These fine folks are my guests today. Ruby Jade said she'd tell you to expect visitors."

I remove the hat and fluff my hair, my panicked attempt to act natural.

Myrtle Mae grabs the wheels on her chair and heads for the door.

"Stop!" Doyle raises his palm. "Wait here while we confirm."

She spins the chair around like a pro. I picture her zipping through the rehab facility hallways, and I have to hide a grin.

George mumbles, "Hope this thing is working now," and switches on his radio. Distorted electric guitar twangs blare from it like a flock of geese all squawking at once.

"Oh, my!" Myrtle Mae covers her ears.

"What kind of church is this?" Doctor's voice is loud.

I glance at him, surprised by his outburst.

Jenica pats his arm and yells over the music. "Maybe we came to the wrong church."

"We're in the right place." Sebastian sounds irritated.

I turn to him.

He's frowning. "My boss would be terribly upset if she heard—"

"Hey!" Doyle jabs George's ribs with his elbow. "Turn the damn thing off."

George stares at the radio like it's a confusing foreign object. "Try yours."

"We already tried it, and that parking lot dude said he's having the same trouble."

"Try again."

Doyle eyes George for a moment but finally switches on his two-way, with the same results. Shaking his head, he stops the music. The guards look at each other and then at their radios.

Sebastian clears his throat.

George waves us inside.

I'm proud of Sebastian for keeping a straight face.

CHAPTER THIRTY-TWO

O nce we're standing in the expansive foyer, I spy more guards, including Pete and Hank, but none of them notice us. They're in the corner, waving their two-ways, chattering like agitated magpies. This is probably the most excitement they've experienced in months.

One of them says Satan has possessed their radios. He's playing devil music to scare them away from church. Another man says the devil got into the sound system, too, and the sound techs had to shut down the microphones. It's an attack straight from the pit of hell.

Now, I'm the one trying to keep a straight face.

But Sebastian looks worried. He whispers, "Won't take 'em long to put two and two together."

We meet the others just outside the closed sanctuary doors, and I catch a close-up glimpse of Corban. Even in a suit, his weight-loss is apparent, yet he looks energized and excited, and the spark has returned to his blue eyes. Makeup masks the bruises on his pale face, and his hair and beard have been trimmed since I last saw him. Tapping my chin, I indicate his beard.

He winks, and I manage a nervous smile in return. No matter how okay he and I may look, we need God's supernatural strength to survive the upcoming confrontation. And not just to survive but to defeat evil.

Logan stations himself beside the sanctuary doors. If Sebastian hadn't warned me, I wouldn't know the guy is Corban's brother. He's wearing big black-rimmed glasses, his now-blond hair is combed back, and he has a hint of five o'clock shadow. The effect is contemporary and un-Follower-like, one sure to raise Leadership hackles, except that they won't recognize him.

All I can do is whisper, "Wow."

He grins, reaches for a door handle and opens the door a couple inches. The rosewater stench and the sound of singing sift through the opening. He closes the door and lifts a finger, mouthing, "One more."

For the first time, I notice an instrument case at his feet. Strange. Is he planning to play a trumpet charge when we enter? Surely not.

Denise and Phil offer me encouraging smiles, and the FBI agents nod my direction. They're both wearing navy blazers, and they both look tense. The sight of them is a stark reminder this is a not a friendly reunion. Things could get ugly. Ruby Jade's unearthly howl rings in my ears, and my insides quake. I grab the back of Myrtle Mae's chair.

She looks up at me. "You all right, sweetie?" She's been quiet since we started this journey into the lion's lair, not her usual talkative self.

"Yeah." I blow out a breath. "Just had a *what in the world am I doing?* moment."

"Remember, God is in control. He will use you in a mighty way today." She takes my hand. "He's about to part the waters and send a crystal-clear message to the Followers. Soon, they'll have to face the fact their leaders are wolves, not shepherds."

"This has to be hard for you." I give her a sad smile. "I know you love your daughter."

"I do love her, but for years, I've asked the Lord to do whatever it takes to bring her to her senses. And to her knees."

A harsh voice demands, "What are you people doing?"

Myrtle Mae drops my hand.

Hank marches over to us, the usual scowl on his face. "The service has started." His wandering eye drifts outward and then focuses on us again. "Get on in there."

"We're waiting for the songs to end." Logan's voice is higher than normal. Is that intentional or a result of nerves? "Don't want to disrupt the singing."

"Better than interrupting the preaching," Hank insists. "Go on in and find a seat. Single men on the left, single women on the right. Married couples in the middle."

Even if he doesn't recognize Corban and Logan, you'd think Hank would remember Phil pushing Denise into the sanctuary in her wheelchair every service, year after year. But maybe he's providing the information for the visitors. He catches sight of me again, frowns and lifts his radio.

My stomach clenches. His radio may not work, but all he has to do is rush to wherever the FT hang out and tell them the runaway has returned.

Logan glances from him to Sebastian, who gives him a quick nod.

"Okay, folks." Logan opens the door wide and waves us in. Myrtle Mae and Denise are wheeled inside first. The rest of us follow. As each person passes, he whispers, "Commence Operation Lion of Judah."

By the time I reach him, I can barely squeak, "In his power" in response. Nerves on edge, I step into the sanctuary. *This is it, God. I'd sure like to hear you roar today.*

Someone bumps my shoulder.

I jerk away, but it's Corban.

He murmurs, "Sorry. Just wanted to say, 'Go get' em, tiger.'"

I smile into his kind, searching eyes. I can tell he's as concerned for me as I am for him. I whisper back, "Follow the Lion!"

He grins and winks, and my heart soars. No matter what happens this morning, I'm grateful to know my relationship with Corban is on solid ground.

The song ends, but the congregation remains standing and the instrumentalists start the intro for the next song. Without microphones, the sound isn't as full as normal, yet the mixed vocal ensemble at the front and the other Followers join in with their usual unison enthusiasm. I notice four men in dark shirts and khaki pants standing in the very last single men's row and breathe a sigh of relief. We shouldn't need the deputies, but I'm glad they're here.

Ushers approach us, curious expressions on their faces. Corban salutes them and trots to the head of his line. I move to the front of mine, my heart in my throat. *Here we go, God.* I watch Corban, so I can time my descent into hell to match his.

He thrusts both fists into the air, shouting, "For the Lion of Judah!" and takes off.

Startled by his outburst, I hesitate. But then, emboldened by his daring, I wave my hat, yell, "Follow the Lion!" and rush down the aisle.

I'm sure not everyone heard us over the loud singing. Yet, heads turn and those we pass have wide-open eyes and mouths. Good. A little shock and awe to kick things off. We jog by my dormmates in the women's section. They wave and clap. Joleen, who's on the end, high-fives me.

All these friends. All their prayers. The Lion of Judah before us, beside us and behind us. My trembling heart is full.

We reach the front. I sit in the end chair, as usual, remove my sunglasses and slip them in the purse before I deposit it and the hat beneath the seat. Sebastian parks Myrtle Mae beside me and sits on my other side. Jenica and Eunice are next, and then Doctor.

I glance at Corban. He's seated in the single men's front row between his mom, who's wheelchair is in the aisle, and his dad. Next to him are Agent Brewer, Agent Freese and Logan. None of us stand with the congregation or join the singing. I revel in the fact I'm sitting with friends on the front row, no longer alone, no longer obligated to act like a Follower. And... I check the doorway. No longer threatened by Vance, thank God.

The singers falter, one here, one there, eyebrows knit. They glance from me and my supporters to Corban and his, yet they keep singing. By the time the song is over, only one of them appears, by the look in his eyes, to have figured out we're the duo who supposedly ran away together.

On the way to their seats, the singers and instrumentalists straggle past. Their expressions suggest they can't decide if we're friend or foe, regulars or guests. I don't know about the others, but Myrtle Mae and I smile and nod as if we're old friends.

Just when I'm beginning to relax a bit, Noreen opens a side door and strides onto the stage.

My heart stops. I swear it does. And I stifle an involuntary gasp. I thought I was ready for this, but I'm not.

Myrtle Mae reaches over and takes my hand.

Sebastian puts his arm around my shoulders.

I blow out a long breath. I'm not alone.

Noreen is wearing red today, from the red clip in her blond hair and her bright-red lipstick to her shiny satin dress and patent-leather heels. Animated and smiling, she sets her papers on the pulpit, puts her hands to her mouth and calls, "Is the sound working yet?"

Someone from the sound booth yells, "We tested five minutes ago, and it's still not operational."

"Test again."

"If you say so."

A jarring heavy metal riff fills the sanctuary, shaking the chandeliers and vibrating my ribs. Noreen covers her ears, her face now almost as red as her dress. But the music doesn't end until she punches a forefinger at the back wall and, mouth wide, yells, "Stop! Stop! Stop!" I can't hear her, but her words are obvious.

Hands on the pulpit, she drops her head as if she's just survived a terrible ordeal. Finally, she looks up. "Forget the devil music and listen carefully to me, people. I'll talk loud, but it's up to you to hear what I have to say."

As always, responsibility is placed on Followers' shoulders, not on Leadership's. Drawing in a breath, I lift my chin, determined to do my part to end the oppression.

Sebastian pats my shoulder and removes his arm.

"I hear we have visitors today." Noreen puts on her happy face again.

Myrtle Mae squeezes my hand before releasing it.

"We want to welcome you," Noreen says. "Oh, I see some of you are in the front row. We're so glad—" She looks at Corban and then at me and gasps. "No, no, no!" Clutching the pulpit, she leans against it, all color gone from her face. "It can't be, can't be..."

The pulpit wobbles.

She jumps back, hands in the air and lurches over to the musicians' chairs. Falling onto one, she bends, elbows on her knees, head in her hands. Swaying back and forth, she moans, "No, no, no..."

Other than her groans, the big room is utterly silent. No one rushes to ask what's wrong, not even her husband.

The door on the other side of the platform opens and Ruby Jade peeks in. "Noreen Nystrom, what in the world is going on?" She looks at the pulpit and then at Noreen and steps into the room. She's wearing a blue satin outfit with matching accessories. "I asked you, what's going on?"

Noreen aims a drooping, wavering finger at the congregation. "It's, they—" She shrieks, "We're undone, Ruby Jade, we're undone!"

"That's enough. Be quiet!" Ruby Jade marches across the platform. "What have you people done to your assistant pastor?"

Noreen straightens and glares at the congregation. By her expression, I can tell she's thinking, *Of course. Why didn't I think to blame them?*

Again, silence prevails. I'm pretty sure the Followers have stopped breathing.

Hands clasped, forefingers steepled, Ruby Jade narrows her eyes and aims her purple nails at us. "I will find the culprit or culprits and get to the bottom of this if it takes all day." She starts on my side of the room, at the far end of my row, pointing at Doctor and then Eunice and Jenica.

She looks astounded but pleased. When she comes to Sebastian, she smiles. He told her he was coming and bringing guests, but evidently, she didn't expect to see TW staff with him.

And then her focus finds me. My heart drums my ribs, but I hold my head high and look directly into her lavender eyes. They widen and her head twitches. She blinks like she can't believe what she just saw. Her hands begin to shake. What little color she had drains from her face. She grabs the pulpit.

"You," she whispers. "You don't belong here. Leave. Now."

"Marilyn June!" Myrtle Mae declares. "You're the one who should go."

Ruby Jade jerks. Either she somehow didn't notice her mother before, or she ignored her presence. "Mother, go sit where you belong. You shouldn't be with, with that voodoo woman."

"Time for *you* to leave this church, dear." Myrtle Mae's voice is gentle yet firm. "Your charade is over."

"You're wrong, Mother. This is *my* church. These are *my* people." She lifts her gaze and spreads her arms. "Right? You Followers are my people, right?"

Noreen says, "Of course," but the troops don't rise to repeat her words.

"No!" As if catapulted, Corban leaps from his chair. "For the record, I am *not* one of your so-called people. I am *not* a Follower!"

Noreen stares at him, eyes wide.

As one, the Followers gasp, the first sound I've heard from them since the singing stopped.

Seeing him for the first time, Ruby Jade whimpers, "You, too? How did...?" I think it's the sight of the FBI agents that sends spasms through her body, shivering the satin.

"This woman," Corban shouts to the crowd, "imprisoned me and Cassie True, known to you as Cassandra Turner. For three long weeks, she kept us in chains, beat us, deprived us of food and water."

"That's not true!" Ruby Jade yells. "Noreen and Inez did it."

Noreen jumps to her feet. "I don't know what she's talking about." She eyes the stage door like she's about to run.

Corban swivels, his focus on Ruby Jade. "Noreen and Inez and those thugs you hired, the men guarding the front doors at this very moment—they did your dirty work for you." He points at her. "But you, Ruby Jade Paradise! You came into the room where you held me captive. You hit me, you kicked me, you threatened me with death."

"She did it," Noreen cries. "She's the one!"

I turn and am gratified to see two deputies heading for the doors at the rear of the sanctuary. The other two deputies move to the side exits. I also note that people are leaving their seats in the back and creeping forward, to better hear, I assume. The aisles are full.

"Because I love you," Ruby Jade insists, her voice unsteady, "and I don't want you to go to hell, I set you aside to purge you, to save you from your sins. It's better to bruise than to burn. You know that because I've taught it since you were a boy."

I cringe. I hadn't heard the "better to bruise than to burn" line before. What a sick woman.

Myrtle Mae whispers, "Oh, Marilee."

Now, it's my turn to take her hand.

"Jesus is the One who saves us from our sins," Corban says. "Not you. All you do is unleash the evil that saturates your sick soul."

Again, the Followers suck in a collective breath.

Ruby Jade rears back. "How dare you speak to me with such disrespect!"

Corban walks to the foot of the platform. "Like your mother said, Ruby Jade, it's over." His voice is loud and clear. "You're through. Time to turn in your keys and give yourself up to the authorities."

"I will do no such thing! I've done nothing wrong." She looks indignant, and I have a feeling she believes what she says. She's so into herself, she thinks whatever she does or says is above reproach.

Agents Brewer and Freese come alongside Corban. Freese holds out his badge. "Marilyn June Fleming, alias Marilee Fleming, Marilee Longpre and Ruby Jade Paradise, you are under arrest for the abduction and murder of Arabella Davies, also known as Arabella Longpre and Lacy Moonflower."

What?

Myrtle Mae clenches my hand. Apparently, this is news to her, too.

"I did not kill her!" Ruby Jade grabs the podium. "It was an accident. Vance didn't—" She leans toward him. "You have to believe me, you have to." Now, she's pleading, almost in tears.

"You're also under arrest," the agent continues, "for the abduction and illegal detention of Cassie True, Corban Dahlstrom and Araminta Davies, aka Araminta Longpre and Crystal Stargazer. Related charges may be forthcoming."

My mind whirls, trying to integrate the allegations with what Sebastian has told me about Ruby Jade.

"Araminta?" Ruby Jade's mouth drops open. "Can't be." Her eyes narrow. "Did the little vixen sneak away and tell you a bunch of lies?"

Agent Brewer pulls handcuffs from her blazer pocket. "Ms. Paradise, you can walk down those steps—"

"No, no, no!" Ruby Jade swings her head back and forth "You can't arrest me." She grips the podium's acrylic edges. "This church needs me. I'm their pastor, their prophetess, their—"

The plexiglass pulpit screeches, separates from the base with a loud crack and topples, throwing Ruby Jade onto the steps. She lands face up, her chunky body straddling the two bottom stairs.

For a moment, everyone sits in motionless, stunned silence. Corban looks at the agents, and the agents look at each other.

"Help me," Ruby Jade wails, "someone help me!" She flaps her arms.

Myrtle Mae pushes up out of the wheelchair, walks to her daughter, and sits beside her on the lower step. She pats her shoulder. "Marilee, dear, stay calm. Help is on the way."

Still murmuring encouragement, she pulls Ruby Jade's long skirt past her knees to cover her legs and slides her sleeves over her arms. But not before I notice that Ruby Jade's legs, like her arms, are covered with an ugly red rash.

The woman who has spent years condemning the infirm yells, "I can't move! Help me! I can't move!"

Myrtle Mae smooths errant strands of hair from Ruby Jade's face. "I'm sure someone has already called for an ambulance to take you to the hospital."

CHAPTER THIRTY-THREE

Sebastian and I go over to stand by Myrtle Mae. Corban's family joins him. Agent Brewer pockets the handcuffs and she and Agent Freese step to the side.

"Pills!" Ruby Jade cries, waving her hands. "I need my pills."

"I'll get them." Noreen scurries to the nearest platform door and opens it.

Inez is standing there, arm outstretched like she was about to turn the knob. She steps onto the platform, surveys the crowd and asks, "What's going on? Why haven't the ushers brought me the offering money?"

Noreen points to where Ruby Jade has fallen.

Inez strides across the platform. The shiny green blouse beneath her black pantsuit shimmers in the chandelier light. She peers down at Ruby Jade and then at those of us standing at the base of the stage. Her cold gaze returns again and again to me and Corban. But instead of acknowledging our escape, she narrows her eyes, and a cunning expression overtakes her impassive features.

"You thought you could trick us," she hisses, hands on her waist, "scare us, stop us. But I'll have you know, you are wrong!" She looks from us to the congregation and extends her arms. Her voice rises like a crescendo. "These wicked false Followers may have brought our beloved leader to her knees, but they have not destroyed this church. Faithful Followers of the Way will prevail, PGIH!" She clasps her hands together, waving them above her head in victory.

But no one joins her, no one responds.

"Inez, please," Ruby Jade begs, "my pills, I need my pain pills."

Ah, pain pills. Now I get it. Now it all makes sense. The rash, her constricted pupils and slurred speech, falling asleep at weird times. Maybe even her mood swings and excessive weight. She's an opioid addict, much like a heroin addict. I've been told in substance-abuse classes that opioid pain relievers and heroin are chemically similar and produce similar effects.

Vance stumbles through the open doorway. "I just heard my mom fell. Where is she?" He takes off his sunglasses and peers from one end of the platform to the other. Red scars flare across his swollen eyelids and temples. His eyes are mere slits with a yellowish discharge. My guess is they're infected, possibly due to the dirt beneath my fingernails, or maybe his own negligence. Whatever the cause, I can't say I feel sorry for him.

"Over here." Inez points, and he comes close, shuffling his feet to the edge of the stage.

He stares at his mother. "What're you doing down there?"

"Vance, honey, please." By now, tears are running down Ruby Jade's temples and into her hair. "My pills. I've got to have my pills. My purse is in my office."

He glances at those of us standing nearby, as if he's noticing us for the first time. "What're you lookin' at?"

"Like I was saying..." Inez raises her hands in triumph again. "With Noreen's assistance—and Vance's." She grabs his arm and pulls him close. "I will keep the church doors open. We won't miss a single meeting, and that includes tonight's service!"

She reaches for Noreen, but Noreen moves away, eyes flashing. "Who put you in charge?"

Inez lifts her chin. "I did."

Noreen shoves her. "I'm next in line. I was on staff first."

Inez shoves her back.

"I am the heir," Vance roars. "I am the new leader." He puts on his sunglasses and turns to the crowd, hands outspread. "I will lead you to new heights, to—"

From below them, Ruby Jade bellows, "Stop!" And then she lets loose the same spine-chilling howl she screamed at me hours earlier. "Bring me my pills!"

A shiver shoots up my spine, and we all pull back. But Myrtle Mae lurches away from her daughter, knocking into Sebastian, who steadies her. Over and over she whispers, "What in the world? What in the world?"

Confused, frightened murmurs ripple through the congregation, followed by the rustle of clothing.

I turn.

People are on their feet, shoving into the already full aisles. "I want out of here!" someone screams. "Let me out of here." And then everyone is shouting and pushing and crying.

Sebastian mutters, "People are gonna get hurt."

I don't see any deputies, but what can they do to slow the panic?

The sound system blasts on, saturating the room with dueling distorted electric guitar riffs. The Followers stop where they're at and cover their ears.

I elbow Sebastian and mouth, "Brilliant." I don't know who thought of using the "possessed" sound system, but it's incredibly effective.

The loud noise abruptly ends, and in the silence comes the wail of a siren.

"Clear the aisles!" Inez yells. "Sit down! Make way for the paramedics!"

"Sit, sit!" Noreen motions for everyone to sit.

The Followers resume their seats.

Vance looks around like, *What just happened?*

Ruby Jade sobs and turns her head toward the congregation. "After all I've done for you people, you can't do one little thing for me. I'm your beloved leader, your pastor, prophetess and psalmist. Your princess."

She reaches for Myrtle Mae. "I'm still a princess...right, Mama? Daddy told me if I danced for him, I'd always be his princess, and he'd give me whatever I wanted."

"Yes, he called you his princess." Myrtle Mae settles beside her daughter again. "But, Marilee..." She takes her hand. "When did you dance for him?"

"You know, Mama. When you went to your book club and to choir practice. He took me into the bedroom and—"

Myrtle Mae whispers, "Every time I asked, you denied anything was going on between you two."

"It was our special secret." Ruby Jade smiles.

My heart twists, aching for both of them. For Marilyn June, the little girl manipulated, used and abused by her father. And Myrtle Mae, who's suspicion about her husband and daughter has finally been confirmed, something I'm sure she wishes wasn't true.

Vance returns to the edge of the platform. "What are you talking about, Mom?"

Sebastian murmurs, "They're here."

I look toward the back of the church. Two medics are trotting down the aisle, rolling a gurney between them. I move away, along with the others, to give them room. Sebastian helps Myrtle Mae into a front-row chair. I sit beside her and hold her hand, wishing I could do more to ease her pain. She says nothing. Just stares straight ahead.

The EMTs work fast, evaluating Ruby Jade and discussing how to stabilize her spine. The entire time, she sobs and begs for her pills. Finally, one of the medics glances around. "Anyone know where her pills are? We'll take them with us."

Inez says, "Noreen, go get her pills."

Noreen folds her arms. "You get them."

Pivoting toward Vance, Inez orders him to go for the pills.

He scowls. "Don't tell me what to do. Do it yourself."

The man stares at them like, *What's wrong with you people?*

"I'll get the blasted pills," Sebastian says. "Just tell me where to find 'em."

Inez huffs, gives him a dirty look and marches across the platform to the stage door.

Behind us, I catch snatches of hushed Follower conversations. They mutter about the devil music, whisper that Ruby Jade could be paralyzed for life, and cautiously voice their concerns regarding the leadership power struggle. I check for deputies again and see two standing at the sanctuary's side doors and two at the main doors.

Maneuvering the stabilizing backboard beneath Ruby Jade is a challenge. And sliding her from her awkward position on the stairs to the gurney is no small accomplishment, one that requires the assistance of the two nearby deputies. Sebastian, Doctor, Phil, Corban and Logan all offer to help, but the EMTs prefer the assistance of the professionals.

Ruby Jade reaches her hand to Vance who, along with Noreen, is still hovering above her. "Vance, honey…"

Instead of responding to his mother, he takes off his sunglasses again and squints at me through his swollen lids as if he just realized who I am.

Something is definitely wrong with his eyes, yet I'm fairly certain he sees and recognizes me. I feel vulnerable sitting with his elderly grandmother, but then I remember she's a prayer warrior and the Lion of Judah is with us. I refuse to let Vance Longpre intimidate me.

Inez stomps onto the platform and over to the medics, eyes blazing. I wouldn't be surprised if she threw the pill bottle, but she gives it to them and straightens. Hands on her hips, breathing hard, she eyes the congregation.

Myrtle Mae's focus never leaves Ruby Jade. Right now, she's not aware of anything or anyone other than her daughter and those caring for her.

I release her hand and step over to the FBI agents who are standing together at the side of the platform, arms folded. Freese is the closest one, so I ask him, "What happens now that you've arrested her?" I keep my voice low. Everyone's focus is on the EMTs, so I figure we can have a private conversation.

"I've made some crazy arrests." He shakes his head, a bemused expression on his face. "But this one takes the cake. In fact, it didn't really happen. We couldn't complete the arrest. Guess we'll be visiting the hospital later."

"Murder?" I ask. "Really?"

"We have all the proof we need," he whispers, "except the ashes."

"Ashes? How do you know the body was—?"

"Can't say. Just wish we could find what happened to the remains. Might have been scattered, for all I know."

As clear as if I'm on my knees in the secret cemetery, I see aspen-leaf shadows dancing over a marble square. It has flowers engraved along the sides and the words *Destiny's Child* in a fancy font. Of course! I'm stunned by the realization. Of course, Ruby Jade would blame destiny for the terrible crime.

The men around Ruby Jade get to their feet and back away. The medics adjust the gurney to full height and turn it the direction they came. But the uphill push is a struggle. The deputies and Logan and Corban rush to help. I'm proud of my friends and grateful God has given us the strength needed for this traumatic day.

All eyes follow their progress up the aisle, but no one speaks, until a little voice says, "Bye-bye, Ruby Jade." Others join in, softly calling their goodbyes. Watching them watch her departure feels like a funeral, yet I see no tears.

I turn to Freese and grab arm.

He gives me a surprised glance.

I crook my finger.

Eyebrows creased, he bends near.

"Adjacent to the church cemetery," I whisper in his ear, "hidden within an aspen grove, is what appears to be a burial ground for children. I may be wrong, but the slab in the middle just might be what you're looking for."

His eyes widen. "Right under our noses?"

"Right under your noses."

Agent Brewer gives us a curious glance.

Freese thanks me and turns to her. "Our work's done here. We need to go." They leave through the side entrance. The deputy nods as they pass.

I walk back over to Myrtle Mae. She's dabbing her cheeks with a tissue and looks incredibly sad. This has been a heartrending morning for her. God only knows what she'll be facing next, but I should be with her.

I'm about to sit when I'm grasped from behind and hauled onto the stage. It only takes a moment and a whiff of aftershave to realize what's happening. I knew Vance had spotted me. Why did I let down my guard?

Someone screams, and Followers jump to their feet, shouting, "No, Vance! Don't!"

His cheek against mine, he mutters, "You came back, like all the other fools who return to this church. But it's too late to give me my knife. I got another one, a better one." He raises an ugly blade before my eyes and twists it back and forth. Chandelier light flashes from its polished surface.

I hold perfectly still, barely breathing, my heart in my throat.

"She trashed my eyes," Vance yells. "I'm about to trash hers!" He waves the knife.

Inez and Noreen scurry off the platform, but Sebastian, who's near the stairs, raises a palm. "Listen to me, son. You're upset about your mom. Drop the knife on the—"

"Don't call me son!" Vance' voice is loud in my ear. "You're not even my real uncle."

Myrtle Mae comes to Sebastian's side. "But I'm your real grandmother," she insists. "We can talk about this, Vance. I'm sure something can be done for your eyes."

"You don't know nothin'. You're just a crippled old woman."

I cringe. Hasn't Myrtle Mae endured enough heartache today? I'm sorry she came with us. Eunice leads Myrtle Mae to a chair.

Doctor, Phil and the four deputies join Sebastian at the foot of the platform.

Vance's grip on me tightens. "Payback time, tramp. I'm gonna—"

Loud shouts reverberate from the back of the sanctuary. "Operation Lion of Judah!" "For the Lion and for the Kingdom!" Corban and Logan come pounding down separate aisles, arms high.

"Who is it?" Vance demands, his face near mine.

"The Army," I tell him, wrapping my fingers around his musclebound forearm.

"No, it's not. You're lying!" He jerks the weapon upward, and I hold on the best I can.

"Yes, it is. The Army of God." I knock the side of my head against his, hoping to hit a sensitive spot by his eye.

He swears and rears, taking me with him. My feet leave the ground, and the blade comes dangerously close to my cheek. I try to twist his arm away, but he's stronger than I am, much stronger. I kick at his shins and head-bang him again. The top of my head catches his chin.

Cursing and calling me nasty names, he backs away from the men at our feet. And then we're in the stage doorway. I'm not sure whose heart is pounding faster, mine or Vance's. But one thing I know for sure, his muscles are hard as steel.

Corban and Logan bound onto the platform. The others follow.

"Stay back!" Vance stabs the knife at them.

Everyone retreats a couple steps, except an older deputy, who says, "Easy now, son."

Vance grinds his teeth. "Do—not—call—me—son."

"Okay, okay." The officer pats the air with his palms. "We just want to talk."

"Go away!" Vance waves the blade in the air. "Leave us alone!"

Inch by inch, Logan moves to the far left of the men. Corban slips to the right, near where the musicians usually sit. I glance from one to the other to let them know I know they have a plan. I tighten my grip on Vance's arm. Whatever happens, I've got to keep the blade away from my face.

"Hey, dude," Logan calls. "That the only way you can get a woman? Hold her at knifepoint?"

I freeze. What is he doing?

Vance yells, "Shut up!"

The deputies jerk their attention to Logan, and Manning shouts, "That's enough!"

Corban disappears from my line of sight.

"With a face like that," Logan jeers, "even a baboon would turn its back on you."

"Who is it?" Vance barks. "Who's talking? Is it one of those damn Dahlstroms?"

I'm trying to decide how to answer him when a loud noise sends shockwaves from Vance's body into mine and he goes limp. Still entangled, we fall backward through the stage doorway and bounce down steps. We twist to the side and he starts to fall on top of me. The strength has left his arm, yet he's still grasping the knife. I bend his wrist and push against the floor with my knees, but Vance is heavy, so heavy.

And then we shift the other direction. I shove his arm away. Corban yanks me from Vance's grasp and kicks the knife out of his hand.

Deputies pour through the opening, one after another. Though Vance is out cold, they flip him over and cuff his hands behind his back.

A big grin on his face, Deputy Manning steps over Vance to shake Corban's hand. "Nice work, dude. About time someone knocked some sense into Longpre's head."

"We can only hope." Corban returns the handshake.

Manning winks at me. "Another day, another adventure, Ms. True. You okay?"

"I think so."

"Knife didn't get you?"

I look at my hands, glance over my body. I'm not bleeding, and my clothing is intact. "Guess not. Don't know how, but I'm grateful. And I'm happy no one else got hurt."

When Manning walks away, Corban gives me a curious look. "What was that about?"

I take a long breath and blow it out. "I'll tell you over those fajitas you promised." I am so ready to leave this place.

"It's a deal." He takes me by my shoulders. "You sure you're okay?"

"I'll probably start shaking in a minute, but right now I feel great, thanks to you. What did you do to him?"

"Snuck out the other door and hit him over the head with a music stand. See it over there?"

"Oh, wow. It's the heavy black kind."

He smirks. "The heavy black kind."

I eye Vance's prone body. "It worked."

"Until he started to fall on top of you, and I had to kick him the other direction."

Logan leans around the stage doorway. He's holding his trumpet. "Hey, you two, you gotta see this."

When we step through the doorway onto the platform, onlookers jump to their feet, clapping and cheering. My dormmates run down the aisle, shouting, "Cassandra, Cassandra, Cassandra!"

I frown at Corban. "What's the deal?"

"They're happy you're safe."

"Oh, right. They don't know what happened back there." I wave and blow kisses to my friends.

Hearing a noise behind me, I flip around, fearing Vance is after me again. But it's only Logan. He closes the stage door we entered and walks to the other one to close it.

People are still cheering.

I turn and wave again. This time I notice Sebastian and Doctor Hoffman are positioned with Deputy Manning on one side of the platform, and Phil and two deputies on the other. The arrangement looks too balanced to be random. The missing deputy must be guarding Vance.

Inez and Noreen, who are now standing by the overturned pulpit glare at me. Some things never change. They spin to face the audience, motioning for the crowd to sit and shouting, "Quiet! "Sit down!" Being good Followers, the people return to their seats, except for our Lion of Judah friends at the front, which now include my dormmates.

Inez extends her arms to the congregation. "We're so sorry for the debacle you just observed." Her syrupy voice oozes compassion. "Noreen and I have been aware for some time that Ruby Jade and Vance are unstable individuals. However, we knew you revered your leader and her son."

"Yeah." Logan comes up beside me. "Like the Jews revered Hitler."

"We didn't want to disappoint you," Noreen says, "but now that they've shown their true colors, we must move on. Inez and I have agreed—"

Deputy Manning trots up the platform steps. "You hit the nail on the head, Ms. Nystrom."

The women twist toward him. Even from behind, I can tell, they're scowling at him. How dare he interrupt them?

"Time for you and Ms. Curtis to move on. You're both under arrest for abduction and false imprisonment."

The other men spread around the base of the platform.

"You can't arrest us," Noreen declares. "We have a church to lead. Besides, it was Ruby Jade's doing. All of it. Go arrest her in the hospital."

He nods to another deputy. "Read 'em their rights."

"Stop it!" Inez stomps her foot. "This is ridiculous. You're doing this 'cause of that tramp over there." She swings her long fingernail my direction. "The witch seduced you, every one of you men. You should be ashamed for falling under her spell."

Manning shakes his head, one eyebrow raised as if he can't believe what he's hearing.

I'm thinking, *So, now I'm a witch who casts spells*, when Corban whispers in my ear, "I've fallen under your spell."

I roll my eyes and turn my attention back to Deputy Manning. But I can't stop the grin that spreads across my face.

"Keep it up, ladies," Manning says, "and you'll be charged with disturbing the peace and resisting arrest."

Like a mirror image, the two remaining members of the unholy trinity swivel and start for opposite stage exits. Corban and Logan jump in front of the doors, blocking them.

Inez screeches, "Get out of my way!"

Left standing between the two guys with my back to the wall, I ready for an attack. Yet, in their panic, the frantic women don't seem to see me. They whirl and dart from one side of the platform to the other, high heels hammering the wooden platform like frenetic woodpeckers.

Jaws set, eyes blazing, the men close in, step by step until they're on the stage.

Noreen and Inez scuttle about, screaming, swearing and flapping their arms. A sweaty perfume haze follows their frenzy. Finally, they lower their heads and allow the officers to lead them through the sanctuary's side door and out of sight. Logan closes the door behind them. I'm almost disappointed they didn't go flailing and kicking, but it wouldn't have been pretty.

Corban and I look at each other and then at our Operation Lion of Judah friends, who erupt in a cheer along with my dormmates who clap and shout, "Hallelujah!" The shocked congregation is less enthusiastic, but many of them join the celebration.

Phil Dahlstrom steps behind the fallen podium and waits for the room to quiet. "Please, everyone, have a seat." He motions to those of us still on the platform. "I won't be long, but I want everyone to be comfortable."

Sebastian, Doctor, Corban, Logan and I find seats on the front row with the others. I love sitting with friends, surrounded by love. No longer ostracized, no longer chastised, no longer dreading what might happen next.

Well, maybe when my heart quits pounding and my frazzled brain adjusts to all the changes of the last few hours, then maybe I'll no longer dread what happens next.

For the first time, I take a good look at the downed pulpit that will never rise again. I'd like to think Ruby Jade and her cronies will never rise again, but she has charismatic, maybe even demonic powers, and I fear people will be drawn to rally around her.

"Friends, this has been quite a morning," Phil says. "We'll all be processing the events in our minds for weeks to come." He motions to his sons. "Guys, I know you just sat down, but would you please lift your mom onto the platform?"

Logan and Corban hurry to Denise's side, grab her wheelchair and carry her up the steps. They settle her beside Phil and return to sit by me again. Corban takes my hand, and I smile at him. I'm liking this guy better every day.

Phil places his hand on Denise's shoulder. "In case you don't know us, my name is Phil Dahlstrom, and this is my beautiful wife, Denise. We're longtime members of this church. In the early days, it was a wonderful loving church." He turns to Denise. "Is that fair to say?"

"Oh, yes." She beams. "We cared for each other's needs, had sweet worship times, played and laughed and served together."

"But then," he says, "leaders came along who forgot they were supposed to shepherd the flock, not hound and fleece the flock." He raises his palm. "Those days are over, folks, so I'm not going there. But after the dust settles, my hope and prayers are for this congregation to dig into Scripture, discover what a true Bible-based church is all about and rebuild from there."

Denise smiles. "I'm excited to return to a community focused on faith, hope and love." She raises her hand high. "And the deep-down joy of Jesus."

The Lion of Judah tribe claps and cheers. Other Followers join us, but from the scattered applause, I can tell it's not everyone. Like me, they've had a lot of changes to deal with this morning.

Phil calls me and Corban to his side. "As Corban told you, these two were imprisoned by our former leaders for several weeks. Be sure to ask them about their escape early this morning. It was nothing short of miraculous. Let's give them a hand for having the courage to face their captors and expose their crimes."

Not all, but most of the Followers leap from their seats, smiling, cheering and shouting, "PGIH!"

Hearing Ruby Jade's favorite phrase jolts my spirit, and not in a good way. But, yes, praise God in heaven. He has done amazing things.

Phil asks if either of us would like to speak.

Corban defers to me. "Ladies first."

I hesitate only a moment. "As Phil said, God performed a miracle for us. I am forever grateful to him. I'm also grateful for the friends he used to help us escape and those who supported us today, these dear people on the front row. I love you all."

When the applause ceases, I say, "Ruby Jade changed my name from Cassie True to Cassandra Turner and informed me that in Greek mythology, Cassandra was an unheeded prophetess. Although I had no intention of prophesying, Ruby Jade was careful to warn me she was the church's prophetess and any prophecy I uttered would go unheeded.

"Since coming to FFOW, I've missed my family and I've missed freedom. Most of all, I've missed God's grace. He gives it freely, yet grace hasn't been freely shared among the Followers. You can heed me or ignore me, but I'm confident God's amazing grace can and will flow through this church once again."

Most people are smiling and nodding, but several, including Olivia and her mother, leave the sanctuary.

Corban lifts his hands. "Amazing Grace! That's exactly the song Logan came prepared to play this morning. Come on up, bro."

Trumpet in hand, Logan takes the steps two at a time.

Someone calls, "That's Logan?"

Logan grins and waves. "It's me."

"Cool hair!"

"Thanks!" Raising his trumpet to his lips, he begins to play.

Corban motions for the people to stand. "Let's sing about God's amazing grace."

Logan finishes his intro, Corban does an upswing, and together, we sing John Newton's most famous song.

> *Amazing grace, how sweet the sound*
> *That saved a wretch like me!*
> *I once was lost, but now am found;*
> *Was blind but now I see.*
>
> *'Twas grace that taught my heart to fear,*
> *And grace, my fears relieved.*
> *How precious did that grace appear*
> *The hour I first believed!*
>
> *Through many dangers, toils and snares*
> *I have already come.*
> *'Tis grace hath brought me safe thus far,*
> *And grace will lead me home.*

We sing the last line again. *And grace will lead me home.*

Corban smiles and takes my hand. I know what he's thinking. We've come through many dangers, toils and snares. God's grace has led us home.

Epilogue

Following the graduation ceremony and luncheon, my cousin Natalie and I ride with my family to the Mount Killjoy trailhead. We're both excited. This is our first hike together since our tandem tumble down the Oregon mountainside.

We have a lot to celebrate—being together again, healed bodies, a happy, healthy, adorable baby girl, my graduation from the rehab program this morning, and freedom for all. Today is the Fourth of July. We're planning to party 'til the last fireworks fizzle.

Now that Judge Snow's benefactress is incapacitated and the Judicial Standards Commission is scrutinizing his relationship with Transformation Way, he's become quite cooperative. He agreed with Doctor's plan to extend the class time from half days to full days and condense the yearlong program into weeks rather than months.

We've been allowed to finish the program in the Transformation Way facilities, although authorities have temporarily closed the church and school buildings. They're dissecting the finances and searching the premises, including files and computers. I wish I could have seen the investigators' faces when they found the surveillance equipment.

The participants worked hard, and we met our goals, all nine of us. Vance doesn't count. He was only in the program long enough to get kicked out. Although we've officially graduated, Jenica and Doctor recommended to the court that some seek further treatment and have weekly urinalysis tests. But I'm free to put my past behind me and forge ahead, thank God.

Kip wanted to walk from the Transformation Way campus to the trailhead. It's not super far, but the distance would extend the hike by ten or fifteen minutes. The rest of us said we preferred to save our energy for the mountain, and he acquiesced.

We pass through the church gate, which sits open today to give visitors easy access to the campus, and turn left onto the highway. The turnoff for the Forest Service road, another left turn, is a surprising distance from Paradise Path, though both roads lead to the FFOW campus on one side or another. All I can figure is the Forest Service's trailhead access must skirt church property, which is apparently more expansive than I realized.

Seated in the backseat between Mom and Nat, I'm certain I've never been on this rutted two-track before, yet the longer we're on it, the more it feels familiar. My vision darkens, my breath comes in shallow bursts, and I fight a dread that doesn't make sense.

This is the happiest day of my life, other than my wedding day. No cars are ahead of us, yet I smell dust. Suffocating dust. Eyes closed, I try to tear the seatbelt off my chest.

Mom touches my arm. "Cassie, are you all right?"

"Oh." I blink and stare at her. "This must be…"

Dad pulls the car into the trailhead parking lot, and the sound of tires rolling over gravel reinforces my suspicion.

"This is where…" I shake my head to clear the panic. "This is where I thought I was going to die." I unbuckle my seatbelt. "But I didn't."

"Oh, sweetie." She takes my hand. "I'm so sorry you had that awful experience. Thank God they only…" She shudders. "I mean, kidnapping you was terrible, but…"

"Right." I blow out a long breath.

Nat squeezes my other hand.

Dad parks the car and turns off the ignition.

"Before we get out," Mom says, "let's pray for Cassie."

And that's what my family does for me. They thank God for rescuing me and Corban and giving us the courage to expose Ruby Jade and her cronies. They praise him for turning evil into good and using Operation Lion of Judah to trigger an early graduation. They ask God to lift the dark cloud, fill me with peace and enable me to have a wonderful celebration with my friends.

"We love Cassie, Lord," Dad prays, "and we love you. You are a mighty God. The last few weeks have given us a hint of your amazing resurrection power. Thank you for the privilege of sharing Cassie's freedom, victory and joy on her special day. In your Son's precious name, amen."

Everyone says "amen," and I whisper a tearful "thank you."

The first person I see when I exit the car is Zachary. He comes running, and I kneel to give him a big hug. "Thank you for hiking with me today, Zach. It's great to see you again." His bright eyes, wide smile and upturned freckled nose dispel any shadows lingering over my soul.

"I'm sorry, Miss Cassandra…"

I take his hands. "Sorry for what?"

"Sorry they locked you in a room, like they did me."

I give him a sad smile. "Thank you. I thought of you often when I was in there. But now all those mean women are in jail. They can't hurt you or me or anyone else."

"That's right." Deputy Manning comes up behind Zachary and puts his hand on his shoulder. "I've seen them there. Won't be long before they're sent off to prison."

Trina is close behind. "Congratulations, Cassandra. You did it, against all odds."

"And crazy odds they were." I stand to hug her. I'd rather not be called Cassandra, yet it's how a lot of people know me. In time, we'll return to our real names.

"I got new hiking boots." Zachary proudly shows me his boots. "Same as yours."

"Mine are old and don't have cool colors like yours," I tell him. "But I love them. They're super comfortable." I'm wearing the boots Eric gave me, my favorite pair of jeans, the "I am the Cat's Meow" t-shirt Sebastian bought for me, the kiwi necklace from Kip, and the hat from Myrtle Mae. Head-to-toe love.

Sebastian and Araminta walk over with Fenwick and Francis on leashes. After I've properly greeted the enthusiastic dogs, I hug Araminta and thank her for coming. Reentering society has been difficult for her after so many years of isolation, but she loves to feel wind in her hair and sunshine on her face. I understand.

Helen Brewer and Milton Freese, the FBI agents, enlisted Sebastian and Denise's support when they had to inform Araminta her sister was no longer living. Araminta was saddened but not surprised. Following the accident that took her sister's life, every time she asked Ruby Jade about Arabella, she was told she was still hospitalized and couldn't have visitors. But then one day Ruby Jade said Arabella had run away from the hospital and Araminta was to stop asking about her.

Araminta, who knew Ruby Jade's tendency to twist truth, feared the worst, yet she never stopped hoping she'd see her sister again. Her account and a rusted necklace confirmed the findings that had originally led the agents to Ruby Jade. Wired to the small box of ashes the agents discovered beneath the "Destiny's Child" stone, the half-a-heart necklace engraved with the word "Twin" matched the "Sisters" half-a-heart necklace Araminta had worn for years.

From what the FBI pieced together over time, Vance shoved Arabella and knocked her down a flight of stairs. The impact broke her neck. Ruby Jade, realizing the girl was dead, told Araminta and Vance she was taking Arabella to a hospital.

Instead, she delivered the girl's body and a handful of cash to a mortician who frequented her brothel. He cremated Arabella's corpse and recorded her death in a private notebook. But he did not report it to the State of California. Eventually, the undertaker's shady dealings were discovered, along with the notebook, the contents of which were of interest to many people.

Araminta no longer remembers her parents' names or her real name. Or how she and Arabella connected with Ruby Jade after they ran away from home. But she does recall working in her home and in her nightclub's backroom, where they were known as Crystal Stargazer and Lacy Moonflower. A handful of people, including Sebastian and Quentin, knew the twins as Araminta and Arabella Davies, Ruby Jade's nieces. Others thought they were Ruby Jade's adopted daughters, with Longpre as their last name.

None of it was true. They were slaves who received no love, no education and little outside contact with others, except at the brothel, where socializing was not the patrons' intent. Sebastian and Quentin met the girls but rarely saw them or spoke with them.

When Ruby Jade moved to Montana, Sebastian noticed the girls' absence and asked about them. Ruby Jade told him they ran away. Before he could ask if she'd contacted the authorities, she told him they were of age and could make their own decisions.

Because he and Quentin doubted her story, Quentin informed the FBI of the girls' California appearance and disappearance, and Sebastian searched Ruby Jade's Montana home and property, to no avail.

Though Araminta's story is terribly sad, I'm excited for her future. She has lots of support, and Denise is planning a memorial service to help her say goodbye to her beloved sister. I hope Araminta and I will become good friends.

More and more people gather in the parking lot. Their happy smiles—real smiles not fake FFOW smiles—warm my heart. We'll be quite a group heading up the hill.

Logan, Corban and Phil Dahlstrom join me and my family. Logan's dark roots are beginning to show, but so far, he hasn't cut off his blond hair. Corban, who now sports a goatee, gives me a long hug and whispers in my ear. "You were the smartest, sweetest, nicest, bravest, beautifulest, strongest woman in the graduation lineup this morning, Cassie Anita True. Congratulations on your accomplishment! Now, you're free to marry me."

"What?" I pull back. Ever since FFOW imploded, we've gotten together whenever possible. I've been to his house and jammed with him and Logan in their basement studio. I'm beyond happy to play my guitar again, even while going through the agony of rebuilding the calluses on my fingertips.

Corban has seen my dorm room and wheedled Grandma Hunt's "Kitten" nickname out of me. I've shown him the apartment where Eric and I lived. He's shown me Shelby's grave. We've picnicked at Fairy Lake and walked its perimeter hand in hand. But he's never mentioned marriage.

He winks and walks away.

I grin. Sneaky guy.

I turn to look for Denise and then remember she's driving Myrtle Mae, Eunice, Natalie's husband, John, little Cassie Anne, and the food up Mount Killjoy's backside. They'll wait for us at a picnic area near the top. Natalie was willing to strap on her daughter and take her up the hill. But John, who's still traumatized by nearly losing both of them on the Oregon mountain, opted to keep Cassie Anne with him and help carry picnic supplies to and from the van.

These days, Eunice goes where Myrtle Mae goes. She appears to have taken her under her wing, almost as if she's become the caring daughter Ruby Jade never was. Myrtle Mae can get around fine, but Eunice is determined to keep an eye on her. My sweet violet-eyed friend doesn't seem to mind the attention. She needs it. Her daughter's incest confession "knocked her for a loop," as Sebastian said, and she's been seeing a mental health therapist to help her work through the guilt and the grief.

Doctor also makes a point to drop in for lunch or tea now and then. And Norman, Myrtle Mae's brother, is now free to visit anytime he pleases. I met him right after the church implosion. Like my brother, he keeps a loving eye on his sister.

Because Eunice has to vacate the dorm along with the rest of us, Myrtle Mae invited her to move into her spare bedroom, a room I hadn't seen until recently. The door was always closed. Myrtle Mae said Ruby Jade locked it to protect the "valuables" she stored in the closet.

When the FBI asked to search the room, Myrtle Mae didn't have a key for it. They picked the lock and discovered hundreds of CDs and DVDs. The CDs featured Ruby Jade vocals, and the DVDs included videoed vocal performances, pole dancing and strip dancing. They also found boxes of eight-by-ten autographed pictures and dance costumes of every color, size and style.

I happened to be lunching with Myrtle Mae when she was asked to identify a couple of the pictures and album covers. Ruby Jade was slender and stunning, yet her smile didn't reach her eyes. When I said I was sorry she searched for happiness in all the wrong places, her mother said, "Our God is a God of hope. He's not finished with my daughter."

Other boxes contained DVDs of two identical Asian girls pole dancing and performing acrobatics in skimpy outfits, plus photographs of them in sensual poses. I'm glad

I didn't see the pictures. Araminta had to identify them, which must have been humiliating and likely triggered bad memories. But maybe it was good to see her sister again.

Uh-oh…the knife! I suck in a breath. I forgot about the knife. If the FBI found it in Myrtle Mae's bathroom, they've got to be wondering how it got there. I'll call one of the agents first thing in the morning.

Phil elbows me. "Penny for your thoughts."

"Sorry." I blink and refocus. "Watching family and friends gather for this hike with me is a dream come true."

He smiles. "Everyone here?"

I hop on top of a flat boulder to survey the group. My dormmates wave and shout my name. They all have a friend or family member or two with them—everyone, that is, except Joleen, who's already asking Kip about mountain climbing. Smart woman.

José and the male TW participants opted to return home with their families after the graduation ceremony and reception. I don't blame them. But Doctor is here with his son and grandson, and Jenica has brought her family. I recently learned both of them were hired by the Department of Corrections to investigate Transformation Way after the previous director reported improprieties. I'm glad to know they continued to receive paychecks, despite the church closure.

Ronald, who's hiking with us, returned for the program's final few weeks, as happy to be back in the kitchen as we were to have him. He also prepared the graduation luncheon but won't be staying in Bozeman. An anonymous source has provided the funds for him to open the restaurant of his dreams in a nearby town. I have a sneaking suspicion the source is Sebastian Longpre, who told me his brother left money to help people harmed by Ruby Jade's tactics.

I catch sight of Marcela and Rodrigo. Arms around each other, they are one happy couple. Her parents and brother and sister are with them. I'm so glad the family has been reunited. At the reception, I learned Marcela and Rodrigo have narrowed their university choices and hope to finalize soon. I also learned from Marcela that illegal "foster" parents within the church have been quick to return children to their rightful parents.

When I asked about Mylea, she said she ran into Candice and Scott at a grocery store. They had both children with them and said they'd moved out of the Pritchards' house. I cheered when I heard that.

My sweet doctor, Brianna, and her husband are here. They attended the graduation ceremony and the luncheon, where she gave me a beautifully cross-stitched perfect-for-me wall hanging.

Dear Past, Thank you for all the lessons. Dear Future, I am ready.

After I missed my follow-up appointment with her, Brianna called Sebastian and learned I'd disappeared. As she stitched the wall hanging, she kept praying that one day she'd be able to give it to me. I was brought to tears by her thoughtfulness and her faithful prayers. I'm gratified she and her husband decided to hike with us.

From my vantage point, I can see the now-vacant FFOW buildings in all their impeccable glory. They remind me of the time Jesus called hypocritical religious teachers "whitewashed tombs" and said they were attractive on the outside but full of dead men's bones on the inside. If I didn't "get" his words in the past, I certainly get them now.

Denise and Phil have high hopes of returning the church to the loving, caring community it once was. In the meantime, they're working with a court-appointed auditor to figure out the finances and all the related businesses. Several local pastors have volunteered to take turns leading services when the church doors reopen. Doctor and Jenica have expressed a willingness to counsel interested FFOW members through the transition.

I look down at Phil. "Gang's all here."

He climbs onto the rock, puts his arm around my shoulders and raises a hand. "Hey, everybody…" When the group quiets, he says, "Knowing this young woman and her cousin rolled down a mountain not long ago, I asked Cassie if I could pray before we take off. But first, she wants to say a few words."

I laugh. "Just so you know, we don't plan to do a replay for you." My friends cheer, and I thank them for joining me.

"This is a celebration hike, one I've been anticipating for a long time. I appreciate that you're willing to celebrate with me and the other graduates by hiking a challenging trail. It'll be worth it, I promise. Lots of good food and a mountainside seat for tonight's fireworks show are waiting at the top."

"And Mom's cookies!" Kip shouts.

Everyone claps.

I smile at Phil. "Thank you for offering to pray for us."

He thanks the Lord for a gorgeous day to honor the graduates and to celebrate freedom. "Freedom," he says, "is something almost every person here understands better than the average American, which is good. You've blessed this nation. Now, we ask your blessing on the restoration of the church family that united us and on our hike up Mount Killjoy. Despite the difficulties ahead, may we find joy in the journey. Amen."

A chorus of amens follows, and we're off. The first part of the wide trail isn't bad. It runs along a creek and is shaded by tall trees. The creek gurgles, birds sing and my friends chatter. The air is sweet and fresh. Francis and Fenwick, who are now off-leash, yip and run back and forth, sniffing plants and rocks and licking bare legs.

I stash Myrtle Mae's hat in my backpack and take advantage of the easy section. According to what Hank the security guard told me months ago, the path turns into a series of switchbacks at the top. Working my way to the back of the line, I speak with each person along the way. When I get to Zachary, Trina and Lawrence, who tells me to call him

Larry, I say, "You can call me Cassie. I have a question for you."

"Shoot."

"At that final FFOW service, when Corban said the kidnappers were guarding the church's front doors, I saw two deputies leave the sanctuary, but they weren't gone long. Were they able to arrest the guys?"

The stocky man grins and helps Trina, Zachary and me over a log. "At first, the suspects acted as if they were going to fight, but then they started edging away, about to run. All our men had to do was pull their Tasers and the suspects cowered like puppy dogs with their tails between their legs. Evidently, they'd been zapped before."

I laugh. "Did the deputies lock them in the department SUVs and go back inside the church?"

"Even better. They handcuffed them with their arms around trees. The jail officers have had fun calling them tree huggers. Gets 'em every time." He snorts. "No doubt they're headed for prison, so maybe they can put the humiliation behind them."

He stops in the middle of the trail. "You know you're gonna have to testify. Right?"

"That's what my attorney says." I don't want to relive the experience, but the kidnappers need to suffer the consequences for their part in the Fearsome Threesome's cruelty. I've been told I'll also testify in Olivia and Owen's kidnapping trials as well as those for Ruby Jade, Inez and Noreen. Unless, of course, they plea bargain and rat each other out, which would be fine with me.

From what I've heard, the abduction, false imprisonment and neglect charges filed by the attorney representing me and Corban are only the beginning of the accusations the FT will face. The newspaper has hinted at about every crime known to mankind. Theft, fraud, embezzlement, money laundering, rape coverups, illegal surveillance, and physical, mental and emotional abuse of men, women and children. Financial abuse is under consideration as is election fraud.

Ruby Jade faces separate charges related to harboring and pimping the runaway twins, Arabella's death and concealing that death. She's also been charged with illegal possession of prescription drugs. There are probably more charges, but the allegations I know about are enough put her away for a long, long time, if she's convicted.

"I hear they're closing the dorm," Trina says. "Where are you going to live?"

"Sebastian Longpre has become like an uncle to me. I'll live with him until I move onto the MSU campus in the fall."

"So, you're going back to school," Larry says.

"I hope to finish the music degree I started years ago, except now it'll be music therapy." The moment Jenica suggested that occupation, I knew it was right for me. I may do a concert now and then, but music therapy will enable me to help others, like others have helped me.

"I'm glad to hear you're staying in the Bozeman area," Trina says. "You'll be able to come to our wedding."

"Oh, wow, that's wonderful. Congratulations!" I hug them both. "I always thought you two were a great couple."

Zachary beams. "Larry's going be my daddy."

I hug him, too, just because I'm so happy for him.

Hank was right. The steep switchbacks and the narrow, rocky trail at the top are grueling. Our legs burn and we stop to rest at almost every turn. But finally, Logan, Natalie, Corban and I are standing at the summit, enjoying the fresh breeze and cheering the others onward and upward. Below me, trailing behind the pack, are my parents, Joleen and Kip. Kip? My mountaineer always-the-leader brother at the tail end? He helps Mom over a rough area and then Joleen. What a guy.

From there, we take a short path that winds around the rocky wildflower-strewn mountaintop to a picnic area shaded by ponderosa pines and tamaracks. It overlooks the wide valley between Mount Killjoy and Bozeman. We reserved all seven picnic tables to make sure we had enough. One by one, the hikers plop onto the benches or sit with their backs against trees, basking in the coolness. Everyone, that is, except Nat. She goes straight to John, who's bouncing Cassie Anne on his shoulder.

Eunice and Myrtle Mae hand each of us a watermelon slice and a paper towel. Denise offers drinks, honey peanut butter squeeze packets and congratulations on our achievement. "You did it. You conquered the mountain!"

Oh, how good it feels to sit. And, oh, how wonderful the watermelon tastes. When everyone is settled and quiet, I stand. "Thank you for celebrating with me and for not turning back. That was a tough hike."

"Tough?" Logan snorts. "An understatement, if I ever heard one."

The others either laugh or groan.

I smile. "I'm really glad it's over and we all made it to the top, which is how I feel about those of us who graduated this morning. Liliana, Merikay, Dana Marie, Shakyra and Joleen, we conquered the TW mountain! I'm very proud of each of you and grateful we were able to climb together."

Everyone cheers and claps. Kip, who's seated with Joleen at a picnic table, gives her a thumbs-up.

"From the moment I discovered the Mount Killjoy trail," I continue, "I was determined to climb it when I finished Transformation Way. As you know, oftentimes that seemed like an impossible dream. But here we all are, including our wonderful dorm mom, Eunice Zaforris, who never stopped encouraging us and who helped me and Corban escape. Wave your hand, Eunice."

She grins and waves. I love how happy she is these days.

"And about the big meal I told you to expect? It's still coming. The watermelon is only an appetizer."

"It's delicious," Brianna says. "One of the best hydrating foods a person can eat."

"Very yummy and very juicy," Zachary declares.

"You're living proof, son." Trina laughs and wipes his chin with a napkin.

I smile. "Just so you know, each food item we'll eat later has gained special significance for me since coming to the church and the rehab program. For instance…" I motion to Corban. "Want to tell them about the honey peanut butter packets?"

He stands, takes a packet from his mom and lifts it for everyone to see. "This saved my life and Cassie's life, along with water, thanks to Araminta over there."

She ducks her head. "I did what I was told."

"But you did it. The day you set the water inside my door, I'd never before seen or tasted anything so pure, so wonderful, so…" He stops, overcome with emotion.

Instantly, I'm there, seeing the door open, her arm, the water. Tears spring to my eyes and I step close to wrap an arm about his waist.

He puts his arm around my shoulders and finishes his sentence. "So life-giving."

I wipe my cheeks and whisper, "I'll always remember that moment, Araminta."

"And then you brought these…" Corban brandishes the packet. "Manna from heaven. It may be a while before I can eat peanut butter and crackers again. The memories are too raw right now."

He pauses and I nod. I understand exactly how he feels.

"But I will never forget that first bite of sustenance," he says. "And how grateful I was to God and to an angel dressed in black. Thank you, Araminta."

Everyone claps. Some wipe their eyes.

Corban tosses the packet on the table and we both sit at the base of the tree trunk we're sharing.

For a long moment, the only sounds are sniffs and bird trills in the trees. And then Marcela's dad says, "We left the church some time ago and haven't heard what happened to the leadership team and to Vance. I know Ruby Jade ended up in the hospital, but what happened to the others?"

Sebastian unwinds his lanky frame from a picnic table. "In case you don't know me, I'm Ruby Jade's property manager." He motions to Myrtle Mae. "And this is her mother, Vance's grandmother. Inez and Noreen are in jail, awaiting trial. R.J. would be with them, but she's still in the hospital. She's not paralyzed, as some feared. However, she has to use a wheelchair to get around. Surgery may help. But before that can happen, the docs want to get the drugs out of her system. She's been an opioid addict for years, so it's no easy task."

Several people's eyes widen. I know what they're thinking. *Ruby Jade? A drug addict?*

"They're also looking into other options for post-surgery relief. In the meantime, as you might imagine, she's up in arms, mad as a cornered rattler."

Most of us nod, and some share knowing looks.

"They're giving her low doses of painkillers," Sebastian says, "but not at the levels she craves. Top it off with law enforcement interrogations and her attorney telling her she may spend the rest of her life in the slammer, and she slipped over the edge. Went bonkers and was admitted to the psych ward, where no visitors are allowed, at least right now."

Corban and I look at each other. I whisper, "The howl?" He grimaces. "Must have terrified staff and patients alike."

"She was a temperamental child," Myrtle Mae says, "who preferred to have her way, no matter the situation. But maybe she'll settle down once she goes through withdrawal and surgery and accepts the changes in her life."

Liliana, gentle as always, asks, "Is this conversation difficult for you?"

"No, it's not." Myrtle Mae's voice is firm. "I've asked God for years to bring my daughter to her knees, whatever it takes. This is the way he answered. I hurt for her and my grandson, but I know my Savior is drawing them to himself and to repentance."

"What about Vance?" Logan asks. "I figured he'd bail out of jail by now, but I haven't seen him around."

I shudder at the thought of Vance on the loose again.

"He's still behind bars," Sebastian says. "Early on, it looked like he might be able to bail out, even though Judge Bock set bail at several hundred thousand dollars. But then a rash of assault charges came flooding in. Evidently, seeing Vance attack Cassie at church triggered other victims to file reports."

I'm not shocked by the revelation, but I'm saddened so many suffered in silence. I remember the relief I felt when I finally told my friends and family what Vance did to me in Myrtle Mae's house and what I did to him. Shortly after that, I told the police. I hope those who filed charges feel the same relief and that they seek counseling. Jenica has been a huge help to me.

"I heard a rumor about a secret cemetery," Marcela says. "And some girl's ashes."

Sebastian points at Araminta. "Her sister."

"I am so sorry." Marcela puts her hand to her mouth. "I didn't know."

"That's okay." Araminta offers a shy smile. "Nobody knew. But she wasn't alone. Many babies were there with her."

"What?"

"The caretaker is a good guy," Phil says. "Friend of the family. When Ruby Jade forced girls and women who got pregnant without her permission to have abortions, they'd ask for the remains and take them to him. Out of his own funds, he made sure each child had a proper burial and a nameplate. He also kept a list of the women and their babies and how the babies died. Some were miscarried, one of them by Vance's wife after he beat her. Another resulted from a whipping Inez gave a teenage girl."

Brianna gasps. "That's horrible."

"Yes," Denise says, "but those days are past, and a new day is dawning."

"Hey, thanks, Mom!" Logan jumps to his feet. "That's a great lead-in to a song Cassie and Corban and I wrote about God breaking through clouds of lies to shine his truth on our hearts."

"Your guitars are in the back of the van," she says. "I parked in the shadiest spot I could find."

Corban and Logan go to the car to get our instruments and I take a drink of water. After so many years without my guitar, to think I can play it anytime I want still amazes me.

Everyone seems relieved to move past the sadness and hear a happy song. We sing it a couple times and then teach it to them, so they can sing along. Soon, Denise announces it's time to eat.

Some people help carry food from the van to a table and others arrange the food. Dad and Phil fire up two camp stoves, one to heat the foil-wrapped sandwiches, fajitas and fries on a metal tray, and the other to fry hamburgers.

I point out my special foods, explaining that Logan, Corban, Myrtle Mae and I had a good time eating fajitas in Ruby Jade's backyard, and Corban and I ate Reuben sandwiches and sweet potato fries on our first date. "It was unauthorized, but we're calling it a date. The chicken salad comes from the afternoon Myrtle Mae and I paraded around downtown Bozeman dressed in muumuus."

"Muumuus?" Mom raises her eyebrows.

"You'll have to ask Myrtle Mae about it."

Myrtle Mae winks at Mom. "We'll take you along next time. You'll be stunning in a muumuu."

I giggle at Mom's startled expression and finish the food list. "The ham and devil's food cake are included because Ruby Jade disapproves of them."

Everyone claps.

I thank those who indulged me and my cravings by providing the foods I requested. "Sebastian made the fries, the Dahlstrom men assembled the Reuben sandwiches, and Denise fixed her wonderful coleslaw and potato salad. My dormmates and I helped Eunice make the fajitas, Myrtle Mae whipped up her delicious chicken salad plus baked a huge batch of blueberry muffins, and my mom brought her wonderful chocolate oatmeal nut cookies all the way from Oregon.

"And last but not least…" I point at Dad. "My father is the one flipping burgers."

"That's a lot of food." Joleen laughs. "Are you trying to make us sick?"

"I intend to sample everything, but you can eat what you like."

"I'm with Cassie." Corban comes up beside me. "Everything on this table means something to me too. Let's hold hands and thank God for this special day, this special time and this special food."

After we've eaten our fill and then some, two vans Sebastian hired to drive us down the mountain arrive with camp chairs. The men help the drivers set them up along the ridge, so we can watch the fireworks display at the fairgrounds outside Bozeman. We may not hear the booms from this far away, but the view should be great, and the dogs won't be traumatized.

Though it's not yet dark, we settle into the chairs. I'm seated between Corban and Mom. Dad and Sebastian are beside her. Francis and Fenwick curl at Sebastian's feet, exhausted by all the running around they've done today.

Corban takes my hand, and I smile, still marveling at our freedom to enjoy each other's company.

Sebastian covers a burp with his hand then leans over to address Mom. "Pardon me, ma'am. I'm full as a tick."

Mom grins and nods.

"Sebastian," Dad says. "Cassie explained it to me, but if you don't mind, tell me again. How is it you have the same last name as the guy in jail and the church leader who was hospitalized? Or maybe that was just one of her aliases."

"It's complicated." Sebastian adjusts his chair to face us. "Goes back to before she changed her name to Ruby Jade Paradise. Truth is, we never had the same name. Marilee Fleming, the name she went by in California, and my brother made a deal that her illegitimate son could have his last name, but he never said *she* could have it. Didn't stop her from pretending to be married to Quentin—and then pretending to be divorced from him.

"When she moved here, she and I made a deal, or so she thought. I would let people assume she'd once been married to my brother and wouldn't mention her strip dancing, or her illegal nightclub with the brothel and drug-dealing in the backroom, or her prison time. She wouldn't tell people I'd been in the slammer again and again due to a drinking problem and related issues. Or that she took a percentage of my paycheck to pay off the bail money she'd floated me.

"Truth is, I'm okay with people knowing my past. Jesus Christ covered my sins on the cross—past, present and future. The real reason I hired on with her was to search for the twins."

Sebastian frowns and pounds his leg with his fist. "Fries my gizzard. The evidence was all around me in the back house, in the women's dormitory and in the cemetery. But I missed it all."

"You helped rescue Araminta," I say. "That's what matters. I'm surprised you're still Ruby Jade's property manager. You did what you came to do. Your work is done."

"Yes and no." He looks thoughtful. "I hate for Myrtle Mae and Eunice to be alone on that big property. Working on-site gives me a chance to check in with them every day, help them if they have car trouble or need repairs of some sort. And in the event some judge decides Ruby Jade should sell her possessions and return the money to the church, I want the buildings and grounds to be in shipshape."

"Besides…" Sebastian's eyes twinkle. "Someone has to be there to collect the guns the Followers leave on the doorstep."

"Guns?" Dad's eyes widen.

"You know the people Cat used to live with were arrested for locking up a kid, right?"

"Right."

"When the authorities went back in to look for other captives, they found a big ole safe, which is common in Follower households. I don't know if they got the combination from the Pritchards or brought in a locksmith, but when they opened it, they found gold, silver and guns, lots of 'em."

I whisper to Corban, "Did you know that?"

He shakes his head. "No, but I'm not surprised."

"The day after the big blow-up at the church," Sebastian says, "I found a stack of firearms behind the garage, including several machine guns. Now, every few mornings or so, I find another pile. Followers must be scared spitless they'll get caught with 'em on their property."

"But…" Dad frowns. "I've heard Montana's gun laws are some of the most liberal in the nation. Why are the church members afraid? Is there a registration issue?"

"Montanans don't have to register guns, not even machine guns, which can only be used for ornamental or scientific purposes, whatever that means, not as weapons. Defeats the purpose of a machine gun, as I see it." Sebastian grunts. "But they didn't ask me."

He arches an eyebrow. "A number of silencers and modified guns have also been left, including sawed-off rifles and shotguns. Last I knew, the modifieds were illegal and silencers have to be registered with the feds. My take is people are dumping everything, legal and illegal, to avoid the appearance of evil, as the Bible says. Big firearm collections could suggest they're plotting to overthrow the government."

"Do you think they were preparing for an attack or possibly planning one?" Dad asks.

"Both," Corban says. "Any kind of media or government criticism was considered a mini attack leading to the big one. More than once, Ruby Jade suggested we strike first. She wanted us to stockpile food, water and toilet paper in case of a standoff. But only certain households were trusted with the gold, silver and guns."

"Oh, so there was an anti-government plot of sorts." Mom leans over to hug me. "Thank God that never happened."

I ask Sebastian, "What do you do with the guns?"

"I call the acting sheriff, and he sends a couple deputies over to collect 'em."

"Acting sheriff?" I squint at him. "What happened?"

"The other dude is on administrative leave while the Division of Criminal Investigation looks into his dealings with R.J. and the church."

"Wow, I'm sure behind on the news."

"You had your nose to the grindstone the last few weeks."

"It was worth it." I smile. "As of today, I'm a free woman."

"That's right." Corban squeezes my hand. "You're a free woman."

Grinning, I look into his blue eyes. I know what he's thinking.

He winks and my heart does a cartwheel.

Someone calls, "How about some more music?"

"Good idea," Corban says. "Enough Follower talk."

He and Logan get our guitars. After we tune them, we scoot our chairs close and begin with "America the Beautiful." From there, we sing every patriotic song we can think of. My family and others add alto, tenor and bass to the melody line. The choir-like effect does my harmony-hungry heart good.

A soft breeze drifts across the ridge, bringing rich, earthy scents of humus and pine—and a pair of hawks riding the current. They circle round and round, as if to get a closer look at the noisy creatures perched on the mountainside. One of the birds screeches a cry so loud it can be heard above the singing, and they take off, presumably for a quieter hunting ground.

My parents smile at us from time to time, and my mom wipes tears from her cheeks—happy tears, I can tell. She and Dad never gave up on me. Today is an answer to their prayers as much as it's an answer to mine. I am blessed.

Just when my sore fingers are about to reach their limit, Corban suggests we conclude with "The Battle Hymn of the Republic."

The last hint of sunlight fades in the west and the first fireworks explode over Bozeman. Together, we sing, "Glory, glory, hallelu-jah, glory, glory, hallelu-jah..." I can't imagine any better words to send out beyond the mountain and over the FFOW campus tonight.

"Glory, glory, hallelu-jah!" The three of us strum hard. "His truth is marching on!"

Corban calls, "One more time!"

Again, we sing, "Glory, glory, hallelu-jah...his truth is marching on!"

Yes, God's truth is marching on, as it has throughout eternity.

DISCUSSION QUESTIONS

1.Cassie struggles with the Follower persona she's adopted for survival inside the cult. She asks herself, "Does my individuality shine through the façade the church forces on us?" Are you in a situation where you feel you must pretend to be someone you are not in order to survive or succeed? Discuss the long-term effects of maintaining a facade. Who knows the real you?

2. Because of FFOW rules to sever ties with family members who are not in the cult, Corban has few memories of his grandparents, while Cassie is blessed with many fun and loving memories. Reflect on memories of your grandparents. Are your memories good, bad or non-existent like Corban's? How have those memories impacted your life? How have your grandparents influenced your grandparenting or your plans to grandparent when it's your turn?

3. Cassie's dad explains what a "faith-plus" church is and suggests that whether positive or negative, "pluses" are non-Biblical. Do you agree or disagree with his statement that "faith in Jesus is no longer a priority"? Have you ever attended a faith-plus church? Did you feel led to leave or to stay and work for change, as did the Dahlstroms? How were you able to identify the faith-plus theology?

4. After Vance's attack, Cassie reminds herself, "God is faithful, powerful and loving, even when believing is hard, so hard." Describe a time when believing God was there for you was hard. How did you make it through? How did God encourage you or provide a way of escape?

5. While deliberating whether to report the attack, Cassie thinks about how Ruby Jade conceals her son's unlawful behavior. "As far as I know, Vance has never suffered consequences for his crimes." How does lack of consequences affect Vance's actions? If accountability is a

good thing, what does accountability look like? Who holds you accountable or has done so in the past?

6. Consider the author's use of birds in this story. Review how and where birds were used. What did the different types of birds signify? What did the birds' actions imply? How did the author affect your understanding of the story by including the birds?

[Bonus question: What kinds of cats are used in the story, and how are they used?]

7. Like Ruby Jade, Noreen is a master at twisting and misquoting Scripture. She subtly changes "God loves a cheerful giver" into "God loves a generous giver" to wring more money out of the Followers. Do you know the Bible well enough to catch erroneous teaching? If not, draft an action plan to become well-versed in Scripture and able to compare what you are taught with biblical truths. (In Acts 17, the Berean believers examined the Scriptures daily to see if what Paul said was true.) What should you do if you encounter misuse of a Bible verse, passage or concept?

8. Cassie is struck by how the church building is "pretty on the outside but so very wicked on the inside." The same might be said of the FFOW leaders. Share a time when you were fooled by someone or something that looked good on the outside compared with the reality on the inside. Did the discrepancy cause you harm? How long did it take you to realize the disparity? What did you learn from this experience?

9. Cassie selected special foods to celebrate completion of her program and freedom from FFOW. What did each food represent? Share special foods that you associate with significant events in your life. Why do you think food creates lasting memories for us?

10. The Dahlstroms name the final confrontation with FFOW leadership "Operation Lion of Judah" because the Lion of Judah has "overcome, triumphed and conquered." Are you facing a battle in which you need the Lion of Judah

to walk alongside you? Do you believe, as Cassie did, that He brings victory? What would help you remember He's with you always?

Questions crafted by Pat Watkins

RELIGIOUS CULTS

"Legalism is the pursuit of good works abstracted from faith in an effort to garner God's favor and blessing. Moralism is the attempt to obey or impose the ethical commands of the Bible abstracted from the gospel of Jesus Christ. Much preaching in Christian churches is simply a collection of legalistic moralisms. ...Hearers are trained to seek identity in performance—not Christ, and the result is a graceless community."
Dr. David E. Prince, pastor and seminary professor

"Spiritual abuse occurs when someone in a position of spiritual authority, the purpose of which is to 'come underneath' and serve, build, equip and make God's people MORE free, misuses that authority, placing themselves over God's people to control, coerce or manipulate them for seemingly godly purposes, which are really their own."
Jeff VanVonderen, author, motivational speaker and interventionist

"Cult members and people trapped in abusive groups and relationships can indeed escape and build new lives. We can also offer valuable insights to people who are or have been in toxic groups and relationships. The pain and struggles...are real—yet, so is resilience. And so is post-traumatic growth."
"Escaping Utopia: Growing Up in a Cult, Getting Out, and Starting Over" by Janja Lalich and Karla McLaren

"Nobody else has been in your shoes. Nobody else knows what you've had to do to cope or survive. It might not be pretty, and you might not be proud, but there is hope. And nobody else can claim it but you. When my friend (who was also in jail at the time) turned to Jesus, she was able to say, 'I feel innocent again.' Let's claim hope and change the world with our innocence."
Angela Ruth Strong, author, speaker and fitness instructor
(https://www.angelaruthstrong.com/)

"In my distress I prayed to the Lord,
and the Lord answered me and set me free."
Psalm 118:5 (NLT)

CULT AWARENESS

Advocates for Awareness of Watchtower Abuses: http://aawa.co/

Cult Education Network: https://culteducation.com/

Cult Research: http://cultresearch.org/

Cults in America Article: https://bit.ly/32Yro6q

Ex Mormon Christians United for Jesus: http://www.unveilingmormonism.com/

Ex Mormon Files: https://www.exmormonfiles.com/

Facts about JWs: https://www.jwfacts.com/

Families Against Cult Teachings: https://familiesagainstcultteachings.org/

Freedom of Mind: https://freedomofmind.com/

Holding Out Help: https://holdingouthelp.org/

International Cultic Studies Association (ICSA): https://www.icsahome.com/

MeadowHaven: http://www.meadowhaven.org/

Open Minds Foundation: https://www.openmindsfoundation.org/

Religious Cults Info: Resources, Answers and Hope: http://religiouscultsinfo.com/

Safe Passage Foundation: https://safepassagefoundation.org/

Spiritual Abuse Characteristics: http://thewartburgwatch.com/2013/07/18/spiritual-abuse-and-common-characteristics/

Watchman Fellowship: https://www.watchman.org/

Wellspring Retreat: https://wellspringretreat.org/

TANGLED TRUTH
ACKNOWLEDGEMENTS

A kind and generous group of beta readers and proofreaders enabled me to write "The End" to *Hidden Path* and the PRISONERS OF HOPE SERIES. Laurie Bower, Lori Charlier, Pat Cory, Val Gray, Gail Harmon, Norma Hubka, Alissa Ketterling, Jim Ketterling, Steve Lyles, Mary McGuire, Michelle Netten, Linda Newport, Kathy Schuknecht, Shawna Thackrah and Pat Watkins all offered excellent corrections, suggestions, reactions and much-needed encouragement.

Thank you, *all* of you, for sharing your time, thoughts and expertise with me. *Hidden Path* is now a vastly better book than what I originally wrote, thanks to your input.

Several educators also assisted me with this novel. Retired NICU nurse trainer, Shirley Moon, suggested the birth scene (we happened to be hiking at the time!) and offered invaluable advice regarding an emergency preemie delivery on an isolated mountainside. I met Sheila Swartz when I attended her C.S. Lewis class. She also teaches Greek, is learning watercolor painting and drives a hand-controlled wheelchair van. Her explanation and photographs helped me describe the van in the story.

Brian Phillips, retired fire chief, taught me about overhead sprinkler systems in commercial kitchens. Pastor/teacher/counselor Bob Thompson shared information regarding religious trauma syndrome plus thoughts about shepherds who fleece their flocks. In addition, he provided a humorous explanation of Portland airport intricacies just when I needed a laugh.

I'm grateful for sweet friends who come to my aid when online searches don't tell me everything I need to know. Any errors in the book are mine, not theirs.

May God richly bless each of you for your kindness to me.

WINDS
of
HOPE

REBECCA CAREY LYLES

THE PRISON GATE CLANGED SHUT behind Kate Neilson, the sound as loud and harsh in her ears as coupling train cars. She'd heard that clatter of metal against metal hundreds of times during her five years of incarceration. Yet with each slam, her stomach lurched and her shoulders jerked. Try as she might to steel herself against the jarring crash, she couldn't help but react like a startled bird.

For the first time, Kate stood on the visitor side of the barred gate that separated the reception area from the wide fluorescent-lit hallway leading to the cellblocks. She still had to walk out the front door of the building and through a gate in the fence that surrounded Patterson State Penitentiary. But she'd crossed the final interior barrier.

The female correctional officer who escorted her, Officer Arledge, paused and spoke into the radio clipped to her gray shirt, notifying the control desk of their location. Kate clutched the plastic sack that held the meager possessions she'd accumulated during her time at Patterson and took a steadying breath. The room smelled vaguely familiar.

Floor wax. That's what it was. The smooth surface at her feet was so highly polished it reflected the ceiling lights. On the other side of the bars, the gray concrete floors were mopped by inmates but never waxed.

She could have turned for one last glimpse through the gate. After all, the building housed the culture that had transformed her from a lost-and-lonely Pittsburgh street tramp into a college graduate with a marketing degree. Instead, she focused on the double glass doors at the other end of the room, doors that led to freedom and to her future.

Unlike the muted light that filtered from the glass blocks imbedded in her cell wall, sunshine streamed through the doors, illuminating columns of dust motes. But as much as she itched to dart across the room and charge outside, she had one more hurdle to clear. Between her and liberty stood a reception desk staffed by two male COs seated before computer monitors.

She had a side view of the men. Like the female officer, they wore light gray shirts, dark gray pants and black duty belts. Loops and pouches attached to the belts held flashlights, pepper spray, eye protection, handcuffs, handcuff keys and more—but no guns. Kate couldn't see their feet, but she'd never seen COs wear anything but black work boots identical to what the officer beside her had on her feet.

Arledge motioned her toward the desk. "The last phase of your checkout is here."

Earlier that morning, just before she left her unit, Kate had been strip-searched. She'd endured the humiliating contraband hunt on more occasions than she cared to remember, and she hoped to never again hear, "Strip, Neilson." But right now, she would comply with everything the COs asked of her—whatever it took to walk out those doors today.

At the desk, Arledge stated Kate's last name and inmate number. One of the men said, "I already have your file pulled up, Ms. Neilson."

Kate smiled for the first time since she'd started the nerve-racking trek from the far side of the massive compound. Whether intentional or not, he'd called her Ms. Neilson, not just Neilson or her number.

The printer behind the man whirred to life and spit out two sheets of paper, one after the other. He pulled them from the tray. "We have two final forms for you to sign." Sliding one of the papers onto the counter, he said, "This one says we returned all the items you had with you when you were admitted."

Kate pressed her lips together. Admitted suggested she'd been checked into a hospital for short-term care, not into a prison for five mind-numbing years of incarceration. She kept her thoughts to herself and placed the bag she'd carried across the complex on the counter.

The other officer produced a sealed plastic pouch from beneath the desk. The clear pocket on the front had also been sealed. Inside was the card Kate filled out when she first entered the facility. He pulled scissors from a drawer, cut the bag and the pocket open, and shook out the contents.

A lacy red thong landed on top of the pile. The corner of his mouth twitched and he glanced at the other male officer before giving her instructions. "Check the contents against the card. If everything is there, sign the form." He handed her a pen.

Kate ignored his smirk and pushed aside the underwear, along with the skimpy tank top and threadbare cutoff shorts she'd been wearing when she was arrested. The clothing still held a hint of the perfume she favored back then. She checked off the items. No bra was listed because she hadn't worn one that night—she never wore one when she worked the streets.

The collection was small. She was glad to see her watch, a birthday gift from her Great-Aunt Mary, but the screen was blank. Probably needed a new battery. She picked up her driver's license, saw that it had expired, and made a mental note to stop by the DMV to pick up a manual.

She would have to take the driver's test again to get a valid license so she could drive to Wyoming. Her stomach jumped again, but this was a happy jolt because she'd been accepted for a marketing internship at a guest ranch. Her girlhood dream of visiting a Wyoming ranch was about to come true.

Worn black sandals, a comb, lip gloss, two condoms and a mascara tube were the only other items on the counter. The money she'd had in her pocket had been deposited into her commissary account. Kate checked the final box. "Everything's here." She took a moment to read the form before she signed it.

"Place your possessions in the bag," Arledge said, "and take it to the restroom over there. After you change into street clothes, return the bag, shoes, socks and uniform here. You may keep the underwear."

Kate started to go, but Arledge stopped her. "Leave your ID."

Kate pulled the lanyard over her head and around her long hair. The ID tag dangling from the end weighed no more than a credit card, yet she felt as though a boulder lifted from her shoulders. To rid herself of prison ID meant she really was on her way out of Patterson.

Winds of Hope and the other novels in the KATE NEILSON SERIES are available where books are sold online. For more information, check out my website
http://beckylyles.com

ABOUT THE AUTHOR

Rebecca Carey Lyles grew up in Wyoming, the setting for her award-winning *Kate Neilson Novels*. She and her husband, Steve, currently live in Idaho, the beautiful state that borders Wyoming and Montana, the setting for this series. Together, they host a podcast called *Let Me Tell You a Story* (beckylyles.com/podcast). In addition to writing fiction and nonfiction, she serves as an editor and a mentor for aspiring authors. *Hidden Path* is the third and final novel in the *PRISONERS OF HOPE SERIES*.

Email: beckylyles@beckylyles.com
Facebook author page: Rebecca Carey Lyles
Website: http://beckylyles.com/
Twitter: @beckylyles

NOTE FROM THE AUTHOR

Thank you for reading this story and caring about those ensnared by religious cults. I hope you enjoyed *Hidden Path* and will consider leaving a review or rating online wherever you share your thoughts about books. If you'd like to learn about future releases, I invite you to go to my website – beckylyles.com – to register for my rare-and-random newsletter. You'll receive a free eStory as my "thank you."

http://beckylyles.com/newsletter---freebies.html